CARVED OBSESSION

A DARK MAFIA ROMANCE

BY LILITH ROMAN

Lilith Roman Books

Carved Obsession
First Edition | February 2025

This is a work of fiction. References to real people, places, organizations, events, and products are intended to provide a sense of authenticity and are used fictitiously. All characters, incidents, and dialogue are drawn from the author's imagination and not to be construed as real.

Editing by Sugar Free Editing
Proofreading by Michele Ficht
Photos licensed from depositphotos.com

ISBN 978 1 0683390 2 8 (eBook Edition)
ISBN 978 1 0683390 3 5 (Paperback Edition)
ISBN 978 1 0683390 4 2 (Alternate Paperback Edition)

To find out more about the author please visit lilithromanauthor.com

AUTHOR'S NOTE

They're feared. Powerful. Ruthless.
And they don't just love... they worship.

Welcome to The Sanctum Syndicate series of interconnected standalones. Carved Obsession is book 4, a dark mafia romance that took a completely different turn than I planned. Carter made me wait, and Scarlet is an absolute firecracker. Happy Reading!

Love,
Lilith

Start the Series in Kindle Unlimited:
Book 1 – Dangerous Strokes, a Dark Mafia Romance
Book 2 – Reckless Covenant, a Second Chance Mafia Romance
Book 3 – Manacled Hearts, an Age Gap Mafia Romance

CONTENT WARNING

This is a work of fiction and should be taken as such. It contains dark themes and sensitive content that could be triggering for some, including graphic language, sexual content, and violence. Due to recent publishing guidelines, the list couldn't be included here, but can be found on the website: https://lilithromanauthor.com/lilith/books/warnings/

CARVED OBSESSION

THE SANCTUM SYNDICATE BOOK 4

LILITH ROMAN

PLAYLIST

The Four Seasons: Concerto No.2 in G Minor - Antonio Vivaldi, Adrian Chandler, La Serenissima

Der Erlkonig - Grand Caprice, Op.26 - Heinrich Wilhelm Ernst, Franz Schubert, Ning Feng

Sonata for Violin Solo No.1 in G Minor - Johann Sebastian Back, Hilary Hahn

Moonlight Sonata 1st Movement - Ludwig van Beethoven, Marioverehrer

Nocturne No.20 in C-Sharp Minor - Emile Pessard, Frederic Chopin

The Red Violin Caprices: Theme - John Corigliano, Philippe Quint

Tzigane, M.76 - Maurice Ravel, Maxim Vengerov, Irina Vinogradova

Middle of the Night (violin) - Joel Sunny, Dramatic Violin

Shut Up and Listen - Nicholas Bonnin, Angelicca

Nothing Else Matters - Vitamin String Quartet

Where Did You Sleep Last Night? - Ramsey

Je te laisserai es mots - Patric Watson

I Wish A Bitch Would - Delilah Bon

Paint It Black - Wednesday Addams

WITCH - Delilah Bon, ALT BLK ERA

Parasite - AWAY, Roniit, Crywolf

Me and the Devil - Soap&Skin

Hearing Damage - Thom Torke

I'm yours - Isabel LaRosa

Babel - Gustavo Bravetti

Slow - Amanati, Roniit

Forsaken - Adam Hurst

Hotel - Montell Fish

Fitzpleasure - alt-J

Blue Lotus - Solv

PROLOGUE
Scarlet

Six months earlier

Salt bites my tongue, sharp and briny in the humid air. The churning waves don't come from the nearby ocean; they're inside me, a storm brewing deep in my chest. Frustration swells, feeding the unrelenting rage clawing its way to the surface. It seeps from my pores with every aimless step I take through Queenscove's quiet streets under the moonlight's faint glow.

I thought the hour-and-a-half drive to seek comfort from my parents might calm me, but I reached the city far too quickly, and along the way, embarrassment joined my fury. I couldn't face them. I drove past their house, parked on a random street, and stomped my way between the old period buildings. Past the dark alleys. Through shaded parks.

I walked. I even ran. None of it cleared my head.

It hurts.

It *fucking* hurts knowing how goddamn naïve I was.

She is—*was*—my best friend. Ariana's betrayal cut as deeply as his. We were teenagers when we first bonded, two vastly different girls. Unlikely friends. And then Bernard came along. I thought she stayed for me, for our friendship.

The memories are tainted now. I think she actually stayed for him—my husband. *Her fucking lover.*

My soles smack against the asphalt. Punishing, determined strides carry me on an unknown path. Searching. Craving. Adrenaline isn't kicking in. Need burns in the slithering fibers of my muscles. The darkness of the backstreets, the eerie quiet, the lurking unknown—none of it shadows my anger. The calm I crave never comes. Neither does the destruction.

It has to. Otherwise, things get . . . complicated. Destructive. Murderous.

After the first few times, Dad and I found ways to focus my reckless energy. But I can't do that now. Killing my husband and my best friend to rid myself of this madness bubbling beneath my flesh isn't an option.

I take yet another random turn between the tall stone buildings, hands clenching, sharp nails digging into my palms. I'm one step away from ripping the skin off my chest so I can get some relieving air into my lungs.

A pain-stricken grunt disturbs the silence, and I stop dead in my tracks.

Sweet adrenaline threads beneath my skin, satisfying cool infiltrating the heat, and I finally take a decent breath in.

I'm about to take another step when my heart jitters in time with the three thuds resonating in the distance. Another pained grunt follows.

My legs rationalize with my rage, not my brain, and they move down the street, toward the disturbance.

This is such a fucking bad idea.

The thought tugs at the corner of my lips. Mistakes were going to be made tonight, regardless. I already committed one when I showed far too much weakness by leaving my own goddamn house instead of kicking *them* out.

"You thought you could escape us? Escape *me*?"

The next beat of my heart falters as the smooth, smoky voice slips through the darkness. It's enticing. Enthralling. Its low, calm, and calculated rumble catches my attention by the throat, vibrations snaking deep in my belly as the sound waves call to me. I can't help but answer. I follow its echo through the shadows.

A grunt follows what I can only describe as a deep yelp, but that enticing voice cuts off the sounds. "It was a rhetorical question. Your boss's stupidity is evident. Did you think you could simply swoop into Queenscove and establish your business here?" His eerily calm, cold tone echoes through the empty street. "In our city?"

My feet lock in place, soul shaking at the rage in those last three words. They sounded like a crack in a mask. Too loud, too passionate. I begin walking again, passing another dark alley.

A faint, gurgling chuckle echoes. *I'm close.*

"Because we can, asshole. You'll never bring us down!" The second man sounds croaky, almost tired.

Silence stretches.

"Vassalo has fallen and risen once before," he continues, a sleazy quality to his tone, "and he came back stronger. Nothing can take him, or his organization, down. We are a hydra—cut one head and two more will come. And they will come for you. Your *Sanctum* will fall."

Holy shit. The man with the enticing voice is part of The Sanctum.

The name of their organization is spoken in hushed tones well beyond Queenscove. Whispers of illicit affairs flow through the salty, humid breeze. Talks of unfathomable wealth and untouchable violence. An organization that exists in the shadows. Always watching. Common folks are happy believing they're just rumors in the wind, but people who belong to the same world, or on its outskirts, know they're powerful enough to take full political control of Queenscove if they want to. So powerful that Dad told me to make sure I stay off their radar.

I'm about to break that promise.

A sharp yelp follows a loud snap and a deep thud.

"Your *hydra* is losing heads faster than you can grow them. Your first mistake was crossing the threshold into our world and thinking you could use our city to traffic people. Children!"

Venom drips from his voice, urging me to squeeze my thighs together and ease the ache it brings.

"We didn't take them from your fucking territory!" the other man rages.

"Your second mistake is thinking that we care where they came from. Don't waste my time with lies. We already shut down one of your attempts."

Oh god . . . human trafficking in Queenscove?

If there was ever a time to side with a criminal enterprise, this is it. Shivers run down my spine, anxiety mixing with the excitement, as the voices are now close enough that I can hear someone panting.

One more step and I stop. A heated, staggered breath makes its way into my lungs as I turn my head toward the darkness, facing the lurking danger. I should turn away, run in the other direction, but that thought brings back the unstable rage that drove me down this path in the first place.

I can't. I won't go back.

I need this.

I need to feel something other than the murderous sting of betrayal.

As my eyes adjust to the darkness, the scene falls into place. A tall, well-dressed man stands facing away from me. His waistcoat hugs his wide back, perfectly fitted over a light shirt wrapped around imposing shoulders and strong arms. And his ass. Damn, his ass threatens to pull my attention from the matter at hand as he looms over a figure kneeling on the ground.

I can't discern any more details, so I do another stupid thing and take a step inside the alley.

"Fuck you!" The kneeler spits. "You can't break us! We're too big for you." He doesn't sound as confident as he thinks.

One thing's for sure—he is not the owner of the enticing voice. The man who stands impossibly proud with his back to me is. Then I notice his extended arm. A gun shines in his hand, the barrel ending in a silencer aimed at the man on the ground.

"Nothing is too big for us. And I already have everything I need from you." Ice rolls off his tongue as he shakes the phone he holds in his other hand.

"But I gave you nothing!"

"Your phone, password, history, and all the trackable information I require." He slips the device into his back pocket and cocks his gun, driving an excited shudder through my muscles. "And we also have Adam Young. Your brother-in-arms apparently knows more than you. He's currently strapped to a metal chair deep in the underground, and I worry my partners won't wait for me to start what I can only hope will be a very satisfying interrogation."

The slight gasp coming from the ground elates me. It's hard to discern through these shadows, but I hope fear is etched on his features.

"He'll never talk! We'll carry on our operation over your dead fucking bodies, and we'll break every unwilling, tight little hole that falls into our laps. You'll die knowing that you failed!" He spits a mouthful at the standing man's feet, the color too dark to be something other than blood.

Where is all his confidence coming from? He's gonna fucking die in a minute, but his disgusting words fuel a bile-rising tightness that grows as this piece of shit talks.

An eerie silence cloaks the imposing man standing before him. He cracks his neck to the left, then to the right, his movements slow. Calculated. Bending time to his will as the man kneeling before him awaits his unavoidable execution.

"You insult us, and you dare think you're untouchable on the ground hallowed by us? You're not as good at your job as I thought, because you shouldn't have the balls to speak those words, considering how fast your numbers are dwindling. That's the problem with factions. You might not know how many of the others have fallen."

Every word he speaks draws me closer, like a hypnotic chant with a mesmerizing rhythm. The fury so calm, so collected, I welcome it as my steps falter barely ten feet away.

The man on the ground jerks, eyes widening, and the misplaced hope in his gaze lands on me. I'm slightly startled by my shift from secret observer to participant. He thinks I'm about to interrupt his execution. Or maybe that I'm the right distraction for his escape.

I'm not sorry to disappoint him; he will die tonight.

That familiar, bone-chilling pleasure spills through me, steeped in darkness and death, in screams and thrills. Finally.

The ecstatic shudder threads through my nerves and

heats my skin before I see it—the slight shift in the man standing with his back to me. The heat grows as I look away from the sack of meat kneeling on the ground, and tingles of fear join the heartbeat. The sheer force of the stranger's gaze hits me deep enough in my belly that my breath tears from my chest. We're connected by burning slivers of lightning searing through me until my hands tighten into fists to relieve the pressure. Pure need makes me squeeze my thighs together.

But him . . . He is unmoving. A marble statue with shadowed eyes. The gun remains aimed at the kneeling man, but the sparkle in the abyss of his gaze fixes on me. I wonder what color his eyes are.

I can feel him in my bones. The crushing force of this moment threatens to bring me to my knees. It's devastating, filled with cravings and potential desires.

Yet, there he is—unaffected.

With tightening fists I tear myself away from his heat. He has a job to do, and I'm invested in it now. The corner of my lip twitches in the grin that froze with his attention on me, and I break that treacherous gaze, looking down at the other man.

His gaze burns into my flesh like it wants to melt away each layer until he finds the answer to a question he will never ask. This feeling, this searing, is so new, so unfamiliar. It threatens to become addictive.

Fuck.

It will . . . it will become addictive.

My eyes widen when the man on the ground scrambles to rise, his gaze wild with fear, and the heat is gone abruptly; my skin turns cold. A split moment passes. A muffled pop pierces the silence just as the man's head whips back, and he hits the concrete with a thudding *crack.*

Before the bullet split his skull, the brief realization of the coming death tore through his gaze. The light left his eyes, and his consciousness with it. And right there, in that moment, I found it. That feeling I've been craving with my entire soul. It's raw. A heady mix of violence, fear, and unyielding satisfaction. But something new snakes through—pleasure. Shuddering, spine-tingling fervor. And it's utterly terrifying.

My cheeks ache with the wide tug of my grin. I can't help it. The sensation is electrifying. Even as the shooter's shadow moves toward me, I'm unfazed.

This vengeance wasn't mine, but for one sweet, violent moment, I felt it. It soothed my need for retribution. I'm energized. Alive.

I give myself one more heartbeat before I focus on the handsome stranger again. On his high, carved cheekbones, and the deep shadows in the hollows beneath them. On his short, perfectly straight nose and chiseled, square jaw. And on the defined lips, neither thin nor plump, but enticingly full, nonetheless.

Enticingly full . . . Oh my god. What is happening with me?

A stray strand of hair falls from the backswept mass atop his head and brushes against his thick, slightly curved eyebrows.

I don't dare follow my exploration lower than his tattooed neck—the distraction far too great now—but I don't need to see more to know that this six-foot-something hunk of a man is as gorgeous as he is dangerous.

He takes one more step, and the nerves around my spine pull me to straighten all at once. I should be scared, but anticipation and exhilaration prevail, and fear seems to be the last thing on my mind. At least, not the self-preserving kind of fear. There's a sizzle in the air, and I find it impossible to keep still as I shift my weight from one leg to the other. This man's eerie silence doesn't help.

"Did he really . . . traffic children?" I had to say something to cut this tension.

Plus, I have to stall. Judging from the chilling look he's gracing me with, escaping might be my only chance at survival.

"Yes."

His answer startles me.

I nod once, barely remembering the question. "Are there more?"

"More of . . . ?" His brow shifts slightly, and I feel like he's a teacher correcting my grammar.

"Children."

"Yes."

"He didn't suffer . . ." I sigh.

"No, he did not. It was quick." He speaks those words too abruptly, the sudden change in tone telling me he mistook my words for relief.

"Shame." I shrug. "You should have made him suffer. Shoot the knees first." I gesture toward the man on the ground. "Stomach after. I hear it hurts like hell. Dying from a stomach wound, that is. People like him don't deserve a quick death. Make the next ones suffer."

I look up in time to catch the slight twitch at the corner of his lips. No way was he about to smile. Somehow the expression would look foreign on his stern features.

"The next ones?" His low, slightly gravelly voice warms me as he bows his head, his gaze running up and down my body. He lingers on certain areas, sending a debilitating shiver through my flesh.

What the hell is wrong with you, Scarlet? This man is probably gonna kill you in the next two minutes!

"You spoke of an entire operation. So, there are more where he came from."

"And you would like me to make them suffer." His words are a question and a statement all at once.

I nod, regardless.

The silence settles once more. I don't peg him as a man of many words, yet this quietness is charged with tension I can't decipher. It coils around my bones and muscles, tightening and pulling me further into the belly of the beast, closer to him. Like some fucked-up calling toward some crazy-ass destiny.

I have to leave before I make yet another stupid decision.

"What now, *kitten?*" He takes a small step into my personal space and only a couple of feet separate us.

But that's not what startles me. The term of endearment does. Or is it a taunt?

"Now we mind our business. I'll be on my merry way, and you can carry on with *the culling,*" I say, laughing at my own words. "But seriously, it sounds like it's imperative for your *mission* to be brought to its natural conclusion."

I'm just about to take a shaky step back when the ground threatens to break open and swallow me whole. Because the stranger smiles. An earth-splitting smile tainted with malice and promises of bloodshed, yet so devastating that I struggle not to fall into that crevasse. If I do, he'll have me forever. And the last thing I need is another charming asshole to ruin my life—figuratively or not.

"You seem intelligent enough to know that I can't let you go. Not after you witnessed this." Menace vibrates through his voice and straight into my nerves as he closes the distance between us and touches the barrel of the gun to my stomach, dragging it slowly upward.

Before I can stop it, a slight whimper breaks between my lips.

Our eyes widen at the same time—mine with embarrassment, his in surprise. I bite my lip, laughing as I enjoy the confusion wrinkling his forehead.

"I wasn't expecting anything less than that," I say with an amused confidence, which is growing at an alarming, reckless rate.

For some reason, the prospect of this man killing me—or trying to, anyway—thrills me, further fueling that reprieve I sought when I found myself in this predicament.

A loud bang shatters the silence, and I whip around as he takes a step to the side to look past me.

"Don't. Fucking. Move." He punctuates each word with such dominance that I almost obey him as he rushes out of the alley in search of the disturbance's source.

But obeying him is the last thing I will do. For a smart man, it's pretty silly of him to think I'll simply stand here and await my execution.

With a sly grin on my face, I shake my head, watching his beautiful, tight ass move out of sight.

"Until we meet again," I whisper into the night, then slip away in the familiar shadows.

CHAPTER 1
Carter

One hundred ninety-eight days and nine hours.

One hundred and ninety-eight more than it should have taken me to find a simple woman.

One who caught me killing a man.

Caught isn't quite the right word, is it? She stood and waited. Urged me on, with wickedness shining in her dark eyes. It's imprinted on my retinas. Just like the recklessness pulling at the corner of her lips and that slight fear I could clearly see in her tensed body, not strong enough to hold her back.

Death was not new to her. Murder wasn't either.

Yet I wish it was. Her expression was bright, enthusiastic, pure in an unhinged kind of way, and I really want to know how it looked the first time she witnessed it.

I shake the thought away before it grows roots. It's not the only peculiar one to have sneaked through since I lost her that night. *Since she escaped me.*

It makes no sense. With my research and hacking skills that make criminal organizations fucking shake, I should have been able to find her by now.

It's unacceptable.

"You're lost in thought."

My vision refocuses on my surroundings, the quiet barroom of Midnight puzzling back together.

Maddox stands next to me, his imposing, brutal stature shadowing me. He's only a few inches taller than my six-foot-three frame, but he's definitely bulkier than my toned, lean-muscled body.

The rest of our speakeasy is empty right now, the lights a bit too bright. The two employees on shift are doing inventory prior to opening tonight, but they're in the back, and The Sanctum's fighter and I are alone.

He doesn't press for a response to his statement.

I don't feel the need to give him one.

He and I are a little different from the others. I'm quiet because it's just the way I am. I prefer to observe. Listen. Maddox uses the quietness as a shield. I don't blame him. Four of us lead our syndicate, yet I think I may be the only one who truly knows what happened in his life.

At least the bare bones of it, not his version of events. I'm not sure he ever shared that with anyone. Maybe Vincent, since they've always been brotherly close. The story would probably be too emotional for me, anyway.

On the other side, Vincent Sinclair and Finnigan Hennessey are more than comfortable talking. A lot. Too much, sometimes. Though Vincent, our resident Serpent, has such a talent with words, he can make a mute man talk. He doesn't need the pain I like to inflict to pull information out of people. But I've seen him enjoy it on several occasions, regardless.

Finnigan used to be our very own careless playboy. It all stopped with Evelyn Shaw. Little Maya too. He still talks and jokes too much, but he no longer uses that humor as armor. He was so transparent in his suffering, I'm surprised none of the others noticed just how much he hurt all alone, with nothing but one-night stands warming his bed.

Vincent, though, hid his longing very well over the years. All directed at one specific woman—Morrigan O'Rourke. Now she shares his last name. He's loved her for so many years, kept her there in his heart until the time finally came and he got her back. I have to admire her, because she hasn't changed him. Never demanded he tone down his ruthlessness. I appreciate that.

Though, I have trouble wrapping my head around this love that has taken over them. Finnigan and Evelyn too. Such a strange phenomenon, devoid of logic or reason.

"Things have been quiet." Maddox speaks again.

Have they?

Maybe I was wrong. He sounds like he wants to press without prying.

"Things are rarely quiet," I say.

"There hasn't been any stirring. Anything . . . revealed."

I turn to him, and he gives it one more second before he faces me too.

"None," I say.

He's fishing, and I know exactly what for.

He sighs, the sound too soft to come from exasperation. "Are you worried?"

"She has no proof. Only her word against ours. We both know which weighs heavier."

I catch him nod as I turn my attention back to the crystal glass I'm slowly swirling on the bar. He's slightly unsure of my words.

"Any leads?" Maddox asks.

I shake my head. I've kept them updated since I first told them about *her*, one month after it happened. I waited, thinking I would find her by then. Little did I know.

"Maybe she was a tourist, and she left shortly after."

Clutching the glass, I empty the contents down my throat before rising.

"Maybe."

"Carter."

I turn at the greeting. One of our security guys walks in from the short entrance corridor.

"James is coming through the back," he says.

I nod. "Otto is in the office, and there are two employees in the back doing inventory. We'll be back before opening tonight."

He nods and waves goodbye as Maddox and I head toward the exit.

Midnight, our speakeasy, is our only truly legitimate business—if you ignore The Fightclub, which Maddox manages in the expansive basement. Mainly because we use it for both legal fights, where he is the reigning champion, and the money laundering business Finnigan has become an expert at. So, we can't exactly call it *legal*.

This is the joy of ruling The Sanctum together—we're all specialized and focused on specific areas. The tech team and the speakeasy are my *babies*, as Finnigan calls them.

Vincent's specialty, on the other hand, is not all that palpable. He understands and sees how everything moves in this society, obtaining information out of thin air, weaving connections, and moving through the shadows that seem to speak to him. And he's the master of interrogation without violence. Not my personal preference, but still.

Midnight, though? It's my sanctuary away from home.

Our unofficial headquarters too. Comfortable. Moody. The entrance is concealed in a back alley, a secret we've tried to keep, though people in Queenscove talk. Rumors fly. But admission is by both membership and password, so rumors alone wouldn't gain them access.

Realistically, we have a year—at a stretch, two—before we have to close this location and re-open somewhere else. A speakeasy only works if kept secret. Private.

And considering our clientele, privacy is paramount. Politicians, criminals, good and bad, come here for neutral territory. They fear us—The Sanctum—but keeping us close is better than risking being on our bad side. And sometimes, we use them. Much less than we used to since we figured out we shouldn't break the hand that feeds us, but we still listen in, extracting relevant information when they're enjoying our complex cocktails. We just avoid using the gained knowledge on the person we got it from.

And that is our core business—information. Our power lies in our knowledge. Our fortune is built on it. Information may not be tangible, but it sure as hell generates a lot of income when traded or held against someone. Blackmail, exchanges, money, secrets, rights, swaying, trades, and deals . . . so much can be done with the right information. When they try to keep secrets from us, if Vincent can't make them talk, they rarely escape me. With network access, I can find any information about a person who has ever touched technology. Even the corners of the dark web aren't dark enough to blind me. I'm good. And it's not ego talking, just pure fact.

Yet, not good enough to find her.

Maybe Maddox is right. Maybe she was just a tourist.

That knowledge pleases and disappoints me all at once. Because the intrigued look in her eyes is still here, looming in the back of my mind.

We step into the shaded alley, the backs of the gray-stoned period buildings shielding it from the midday sun. They do nothing for the subtropical humidity of our coastline, though. We walk under the old stone archways on the winding alley toward one of Queenscove's main streets that should be bustling with both locals and tourists right about now.

"Is Finn coming, or is he hiding with Evie in their new beach house?" Maddox breaks the silence.

"You sound a little salty about that."

He grunts in response. Maybe he's feeling left out. Finnigan is the third one of us to have found who is likely to be his wife in a few years. Ronan, his brother, was the first, though he hasn't been officially part of the syndicate in many years. Even some of our employees seem to have found love within our organization. Maybe Maddox craves the same connection. I sure don't. I don't quite understand the appeal. Sure, I meet with women, we *play*—mostly in Morrigan and Loreley's club—but I've never felt the need to expand on it.

We walk onto the main street, the sun burning hot over the people filtering onto the shaded terraces of the restaurants and cafés lining the sidewalks.

I've traveled extensively due to our work. I even went to university up north from our southern coast, yet I never found a place I enjoyed more than Queenscove, with its stone-or-brick period buildings steeped in character, the green borders lining the streets filled with birches, palm trees, and colorful flowers, and the old wrought iron streetlamps that were restored years ago.

There's something about our city that appeals to me. Maybe it's the lack of skyscrapers, making it look so much less like a city than it should. Or maybe it's the fact that we actually had an influence on the way this city looks and operates. In the past, we used our influence to sway a couple of ordinances. One was about raising the allowed height of new structures, and the other was about limiting short-term rental permits and new hotels.

We had our own personal interests in this, since Queenscove is already a tourist spot and we didn't need it to become even more popular. More people mean more chances for people to discover just how rooted in the underworld this place is. Our port and rail connections make it very desirable for all sorts of illegal activities.

My phone vibrates in my pocket as we walk toward the restaurant, and I stop to pull it out.

"Finnigan's already at The Anchor with Vincent and Cillian," I say as I read the text.

"Cillian?" Maddox mirrors my thoughts.

I read the text again, but there's no explanation as to why Vincent's brother-in-law is joining us for lunch. The redhead got thrown into the deep end of heading his old man's family business, and even if it's been just over a year, he sometimes comes to us for advice. He may be family to Vincent now, but the man seems to know how to keep The Sanctum close. The right way. Even if his businesses are mostly legal.

The tips of my fingers fly over the touchscreen as I send a response to Vincent, though I glance before me as I begin walking again. The restaurant is barely five minutes away from here and I could find out the answer soon enough, but I have an inherent distaste about walking into a situation unprepared.

A familiar ghost of a current coils in my stomach.

"One of these days, you're going to trip and fall on your face."

I cock an eyebrow, throwing a glance his way in response, before going to check for a reply.

Minutes pass without one, and the restaurant is only a few steps away now.

The current sizzles in my abdomen as my fingers tighten around the phone. Almost three decades of this and I haven't gotten used to the ridiculous sensation.

I stop a few feet in front of the door but turn my back to it. As if on cue, the phone vibrates with a new text. Just like that, the current dissipates.

"Cillian's there to chat about the docks," I say.

"Yeah, I kind of assumed."

Well, I needed to be sure.

I slide the phone into my front pocket and look up, seeking Maddox, but what slams into my line of sight instead, doused in lively pastel clothes that make everyone else look monochrome, is . . . *her.*

The current is back. Goosebumps nettle over my skin, and the noise of the street traffic separating us fades away.

One hundred and ninety-eight days and there she is.

Across the street, carrying two cups of coffee, a brown paper bag hanging on her wrist, she opens the door to her shiny, dark-green sports car.

As if she feels the touch of my gaze, she looks up. Straight into my goddamn eyes. And I curse every single car passing by, interrupting my line of sight, because she looks gloriously surprised. A slight tinge of shock, or maybe fear, rounds her eyes.

My feet move before I can stop them, but a hand pulls me back just as a car honks as it speeds past me.

"What the hell are you doing, Carter?" Maddox growls.

The woman I've failed to find is now smirking at me. She's fucking smirking. It's both condescending and innocent, and embers catch fire deep inside me in response. My fists clench as she raises the coffee cups to me in salute, then dips down to climb into her car.

No!

She's not getting away this time.

I won't allow it.

I look left, ready to step onto the busy street and rush to her, but two tourist buses drive by, blocking both my sight and my way. A deep groan vibrates through my throat.

"Goddamn it, come on," I whisper to myself, urging the damn buses to move faster.

But when they clear, the parking spot is empty and the dark-green car is nowhere in sight. A heated tightness clutches my lungs, holding my breath hostage within them.

She's gone.

CHAPTER 2
Scarlet

"Well, fuck me sideways!" I exclaim.

A wide, cheek-straining smile possesses my face. I can't help it. I can't control it. Adrenaline rushes through my nerves, and fear and anticipation tighten my fists around the steering wheel as my foot presses harder against the gas pedal.

It's been months since I *met* him in that alley. The chances of us running into each other were close to zero since I didn't live in Queenscove, but since I moved here, I kept waiting for the unavoidable moment when he would find me.

Every single time I was out, I couldn't relax. Always looking over my shoulder. At night, I kept checking out the window, tensed constantly.

I decided to find him instead. I've seen him several times during this time, but I've been confident he's never seen me once.

If I wasn't convinced before, I am now, because there's no way I would have misunderstood this feeling. I felt him like a brewing storm silencing the world. Sizzles of current rushed over my skin as he yanked the air from my lungs. He was everywhere around me, and I was stuck in his violent vortex.

And there was so much violence in his eyes. Even from across the street, there was no missing it. Too many shadows looked back at me. Too dark. Threatening.

He tried to come for me, though I doubt he would have done anything in the middle of the day with all those people around.

The thought bears logic, yet . . . vengeance was so deeply etched in his frown that I don't trust he wouldn't have found a way. Right there. In the middle of Queenscove. I only got away because of pure dumb luck, and he doesn't appear to be chasing after me.

This is the second time pure luck was the reason I escaped him. The first was when he turned his back on me in that alley, and I ran, hiding in the shadows. I'm dangerously lucky when it comes to evading anything nefarious, but I can't help wondering if this is a sign that my luck is running out.

I slow the car and take the first left, then pull into the small parking lot behind a three-story building. I barely acknowledge parking the car as that night from six months ago filters through my memories.

Time has flown by and stood still all at once. I'm not quite the same person I was then. Pain and anger left wounds, and the aftermath ruined any leftover good memories. My soon-to-be ex-husband and best friend might not be dead, yet I had to mourn their losses either way.

And that's why it feels like no time has passed at all . . . because he's not fucking letting me go. Bernard has an agenda, and delaying this divorce is how he plans to get what he wants from me. For his sake, I hope he's not holding his breath.

After what I witnessed in that alley, I couldn't go home. I went to my parents' house, trembling with rage once the adrenaline dissipated. I thought witnessing the chilling nature of murder would keep me satisfied for a while, but it only lasted the ten-minute drive. Regardless of the manic laughter that overcame me, the thrill of it all, I managed to keep it together all through that night and the following morning. But the moment I went back to *our* house, I fucking lost it.

Our bedroom was unrecognizable when I was done with it. The expensive mattress was burned and ripped to shreds, the furniture was broken into jagged pieces, and every single thing of his was destroyed. I wanted to decimate every last trace of us, of *them*—my best friend and husband. The fucking assholes.

That night, I slept in the spare bedroom. He had the decency to leave me alone and not return home. At least that first time.

Thoughts of the dangerous man from the alley kept me sane. Kept me alert. Kept me alive.

And he finally found me. In all his tall, dark, and vicious glory. Sweet Jesus, he's broken out of both dreams and nightmares. And my dreams of him have been . . . entertaining, to say the least. Intense. But the vision of him in real life doesn't compare with my fantasies.

He's more.

So much more.

Tall, lean, and strong. Sinewy forearms showing under the rolled-up sleeves of his white shirt. Harsh yet beautifully sculpted features, and that kind of firm posture that exudes so much confidence—it's intimidating without even trying.

So many nights I silently willed him to find me, even through the shivers of fear infused with the pleasure I was giving myself at the thought of it. But now that it's real, the fear seems to beat the pleasure.

What will he do? Will he really kill me because of what I know?

I jump out of my skin when a knock sounds against my window.

"Willow! Jesus Christ." The blonde-haired woman smiles as she takes a step back so I can get out.

"Sorry, sorry. I didn't mean to scare you." She puts her hands up and shrugs.

"You didn't. You just startled me."

"You did seem quite lost in thought. All good?"

No.

"Yes, all good, Willow. What are you still doing here? I thought you couldn't work this afternoon," I ask, changing the subject. With her, I have to do it fast. The woman is such an empath, she doesn't take long at all to read you.

"I was just on my lunch break. Carmen asked me to stay while you two have lunch. I'm off after."

"Oh shit." I whip around and rush back to the car, pulling a bag of pastries from the passenger seat, along with my coffee. "Almost forgot these."

Willow narrows her gaze on me. "Are you sure you're okay?"

Rolling my eyes in response, I set to walk past her when my phone vibrates, the chirping ringtone following. I fumble to readjust everything in my hands and look at the screen—unknown number.

Fuck. Third call today.

"Go in, Willow. I'll be right in."

She nods and complies. Albeit reluctantly, as she's taking

in my barely suppressed exasperation.

Swiping at the screen, I answer and prop the phone against my ear. I don't speak a word, though.

"Afternoon, *wife.*" Venom laces his tone. He doesn't want to be tied to me any more than I want him tied to me. Yet here we are.

"Talk to my lawyer, Bernard. I have nothing to say to you."

"I don't care about what you have to say. I'm calling about what you need to do." The venom carries further.

I burst out laughing. "You may have a different definition of *need* than the rest of the world, sugar. Leave me the fuck alone."

"You never used to be so petty. So vengeful and . . . disobedient. Not with me. Does it hurt your ego so much to give me what I need?"

"Disobedient?" Red-hot rage colors my vision at his gall. "Are you under the delusion that I was nice to you because I was *obedient*? You pathetic little man. I gave you fucking respect as a human, as my partner, while I thought you were giving it to me too. Now, all of that—"

"You dare call me—"

"All of that," I rage at his interruption, "*dear husband,* was burned to fucking ashes the moment I found you in bed with my best friend. Those ashes flew in the goddamn wind when I discovered it was going on for so long behind my back. And no, it doesn't hurt my ego to give you what you want. I simply don't fucking want to, because you dare fucking blackmail me with the divorce."

"Listen to me, you little bitch. I will get what I am owed!" he seethes. "If our divorce is not enough incentive, I will hit you where you hurt the most—your family. The Camoras do it for a living, as you well know, and I will not shy away from treating you like one of our customers who doesn't pay their debts."

"Owed? You truly are delusional. I gave you what I did out

of the goodness of my black little heart. There was no deal set in stone, no contract, not even a goddamn promise. A quid pro quo while it suited me. Give me the divorce and leave this marriage with your ego intact. And don't you fucking dare threaten my family."

The phone shatters into dozens of pieces when I hurl it at the ground. I don't even think I hung up, but fuck him! How dare he threaten my family!

I stomp over the scraps of glass and metal and slam my block heels over and over until the shards resemble gravel. When I step away, that smoldering flame inside me has calmed back down, but Bernard's words still linger. He doesn't have the guts to go after my family. Nothing but empty words.

Fuck, I hate that he gets to me like this. I've been trying really damn hard in the last six months to deny my instincts when it comes to him, but if he keeps this up, I will risk it all to get satisfaction. And it would be so damn sweet.

Getting divorced before I turned twenty-nine wasn't on my bucket list, but it sure fucking is now. There's shy of four months left until October. He better make me a free woman by then, or I might just start a war.

I take one slow, deep breath in, allowing it to fill me with an ounce of calm before I go into the store. I rescue my sim card, just in case it still works, and head inside through the back entrance of my stepmother's jewelry store. Well, technically it's the family's shop, but she's the master jeweler. She and dad have something going on this afternoon, and she asked me to look after the place until closing time at four.

I don't usually do this, so hopefully I still remember how to work the register and talk to strangers. Customer service isn't really my thing.

"Scarlet, is that you?" she calls out from down the corridor.

"Hey Carmen!" I greet her as I walk into the front of the store that shines with precious metals and stones locked behind wood-framed, tempered glass displays.

Willow is already busying herself by wiping down some jewelry cases.

"Hi honey! Thank God you're here. I'm starving!" Her eyes sparkle when she notices the paper bag in my hand.

"And here I was, thinking you're happy to see me," I say, chuckling.

"Of course I am!" The curly-haired woman wraps her arm around me, rubbing my shoulder as she guides me toward the office at the back. "Because you brought food."

"I'll remember that." I shake my head, smacking her hand.

"Before I forget . . ." I stop, turning back before the door closes. "Willow, before you leave, can you take a broom to the . . . slight mess at the back?"

The blonde woman raises an eyebrow. "Slight mess?"

"I dropped my phone."

That eyebrow stays perfectly raised, even as she nods silently.

"Everything okay?" Carmen asks as we walk down the corridor and into the office.

"Peachy."

"Scarlet . . ."

"Bernard called. I wish Dad would have never taught me to restrain myself. If logic doesn't touch Bernard, why should I be guided by it?" I roll my eyes, taking a seat in the padded chair behind the small dining table Carmen has in here, and drop our lunches onto it.

"Because, as your dad taught you, you have to protect yourself. Considering the man Bernard proved to be, he's definitely not worth going to jail for. Right?"

I roll my eyes, though more at myself than her words.

"He's not even worth this conversation."

"Exactly. Neither your dad nor I am opposed to some old-fashioned vengeance, as you know. But with a family like the Camoras—granted, it's a tad different now that their dad is gone—you have to be smart about it."

I frown as I take in her words. "So . . . what you're saying is that neither of you are truly opposed to me taking my sweet revenge on that idiot, but I just have to calculate my odds?"

"Well, Arias hasn't said anything. He'd probably prefer if it didn't get to that, but I think the last six months have proven that there are limited ways to resolve this." She sighs as she unwraps her lunch.

It's true. I'm pretty open with Carmen and Dad. They know almost everything that has happened, and though Dad isn't showing it to me, I know this frustrates him too. Especially since Bernard and I were kind of shipped together because of his relationship with his late father. But those genes didn't seem to have transferred, and though I know Dad would love to storm into their office and tell them to rein in their brother, we don't know how much the Camoras know of our operation. Their father was vaguely aware, and Bernard also is, since we've been together for six years, but we don't know if anything was shared further. We demanded secrecy, but who knows.

Carmen's right—I have to be smart about this.

My mother would have denied me this type of perspective. She doesn't even fucking compare to Carmen. She might not be my birth mother, but she is more of a mom to me than Emily Glass ever tried to be.

Dad truly is lucky. He didn't intend to find a partner after Mother, but Carmen came out of nowhere. There was no way either of us would have let her go. She's sweet, cunning, talented, and head over heels in love with him, even after all these years. I was seventeen when they met, eighteen when they got married on a whim, and she's been in our lives for eleven years now.

"I got you a Serrano-ham and cheese pastry, and a brownie for dessert." I dodge that conversation. I don't want to waste any more words on that asshole.

"Music to my ears." She complies without arguing and brings us two glasses of water, two empty glasses, and a bottle of wine from the wine fridge she keeps religiously stocked here. "Anything else bugging you?"

She can read me like a book sometimes, because regardless of my ex, I can't stop thinking of the man who looked at me like I shattered the earth beneath his feet.

"Nothing. Just hungry," I lie.

She cocks her head, the three permanent wrinkles between her brows deepening. "Okay."

"Did you move any of the new pieces today?" I change the subject again.

"A few, yes. Another twelve online, and I have one left."

"That's fucking fantastic. Well done!"

"Like you ever doubted me," she says with a smug look on her pretty, olive-skinned face.

"I didn't, but I'm just glad we're getting rid of the Erickson stones. I was getting antsy about carrying them. There's been some heat about them, even if the police can't be called, since they were stolen in the first place. But there's talk going around."

"But the job you and your dad pulled was clean. Erickson hasn't discovered who pulled the heist and stole his jewelry. Right?" Carmen looks a little bit worried now.

"No, he hasn't. As always, we left no trace."

But I never get overconfident about these jobs. Even after all these years. Because overconfidence leads to complacency, and that turns into error. So, we are meticulous, careful, and extremely calculated. I also monitor the situation for months, and even years after, to make sure no one catches wind of us.

Though, calculated is not how I feel right now. No . . . I feel positively reckless.

There's fire burning through my veins, even as I put on this calm mask with Carmen, and that need to look over my shoulder has returned with a vengeance.

As I slowly chew on my pastry and smile sweetly at her, fear, excitement, and a sliver of doom run wild through my soul.

My time is up.

My days are numbered.

The Carver is coming for me.

Carter

"WHAT THE HELL ARE YOU going to do, Carter? You can't chase her through town in the middle of the damn day!" Maddox plants his wide frame in my path, stopping me from rushing back to Midnight, where my car's parked.

"Get out of my way, Severin," I seethe.

"Not until you tell me your plan. Because whatever you're about to do concerns us all. Not just you."

The next inhale lands heavy in my chest. He's right, but that doesn't mean he's entirely correct. Yes, my actions bear consequences on all of us, but this only concerns me. *She* was my fuckup.

"Don't talk like I've done anything to put our Sanctum in danger. Ever. Between us, I think I'm the only one who hasn't. So, again, Maddox, get out of my way."

The impact of my words reflects in his eyes. An emotion I can't quite place shines through the amber, but I don't have time to dissect it and figure out what it is.

He sighs, shaking his head, but steps aside. I walk away with determined steps, but a giggling woman and her child cross my path without looking, cutting me off and stopping me.

This singular pause triggers something within my brain.

On a loud exhale, I clench my fists, then take a deep, centering breath inward.

What the fuck am I doing?

This is illogical.

First of all, the woman is already gone. I can't possibly predict where to find her.

Second of all, there are much better ways of finding her now. I can use Queenscove's CCTV system. Her license plate. Even criminal records or images of her for reverse searches. I have something to go by, finally.

One more breath in, and calm settles.

It's okay. It was just a momentary lapse in judgment.

Understandable, since I've been trying to find her for so long.

My memories of that night are vivid, and even though I stared at the same person today, she looked . . . different. She exhibited a feral confidence, when the night we met she was just feral. A need I couldn't quite place had overshadowed her. And she'd seemed awfully excited about the murder I was committing. But today, with all that brimming confidence, she looked . . . radiant.

Radiant?

"So? Are you coming?"

I clench my fists tighter to keep from jumping as Maddox pulls me out of my irrational daze.

Radiant?

Turning, I walk past him and straight into the restaurant.

I have no intention of recounting the events to Vincent and Finnigan. Especially not with Cillian there. I already feel a certain way because Maddox witnessed what I can only describe as a brief moment of madness.

Normally, I would be quite interested in listening to the type of situation Cillian has been describing to us. He's taken over his father's business and some people have been breathing down his neck. This is the type of information I take interest in. Usually. But I cannot bring myself to care now.

Somewhere in the back of my mind, I've been assimilating the information he's throwing at us, yet the importance of it hasn't registered. Dark eyes are all I see. Thick, wispy lashes, and wavy hair falling in neat, dark waves. The image of her isn't soundless, because words from the night we met echo along with it in a soft, delicate voice—*you should have made him suffer.* There was no remorse, no fear, no tremble in those syllables. Utterly fascinating.

My hunger is gone before my order arrives. I manage a glass of spiced rum and three bites of food, then excuse myself before the others are even midway through their lunch. I tell Vincent and Finnigan that I'll fill them in later, say my goodbyes, and head straight for Midnight.

I know what he'll think, so I text Maddox to let him know I'm leaving to do my research on her, not go after her. It will ease his mind, and for some reason, I care about that.

Caring. What an unusual concept. Somewhere in our timeline, I've attached myself so tightly to these people that I would do unspeakable things to protect them. I actually have. I know how they look at me sometimes. Like my lack of empathy and emotions pertains to them too. They wonder how easy it would be for me to drop them. To simply turn my back and choose a completely different path.

It wouldn't be easy. And it's never going to happen.

But they never asked me personally, so I never told them.

The five-minute walk back to Midnight takes me barely two. I rush in, passing quickly through the barroom and startling the staff and security. I don't offer an explanation as I head straight to the office, grab my laptop, and hurry to my car. I'll be better off at home with my entire tech setup.

No resources will be spared for her.

This kitten is out of lives.

She's mine.

CHAPTER 3
Scarlet

oth Willow and Carmen are gone. The back door is locked, blocked, and alarmed. It's just me at the front of the store, along with two customers who talk and laugh as they point at various pieces in one of the vertical display cases.

"May we see the baguette-sapphire set, please?" the gentleman asks.

"Of course," I say with a polite smile.

I'm certain it's not their first time here. I recognize her earrings. Carmen made them about a year ago. She was applying the finishing touches when I visited her workshop.

I walk over, open the case, and pull out the stand with the earrings, necklace, and bracelet. I lock the display and I'm about to head back to the main counter when the front doorbell chimes.

A fiery chill nettles up my spine, stopping at the nape of my neck, the grip tight, forcing my head to turn. But I resist. I push back because it can only be one person, and I will make him work for my attention. Though a slight, uncontrollable tremble in my shoulders betrays my composure.

"I'll be right with you," I call over my shoulder, glancing just long enough to catch a glimpse of his intense gaze burning into me. Enough to let him know I'm aware *he* is here, but he has none of my attention.

That should go down well.

"Please, follow me." I address the customers as we walk to the counter.

Stepping around it, I place the jewelry pieces on the velvet-lined tray. All the while, I'm vividly aware of each and every one of his slow, determined steps as he moves through the store. Watching. Stalking.

"I really love the cut and the filigree of the setting," the woman says as she picks up the earrings and holds them up to the light.

"Mrs. Brasa's craftsmanship is as exquisite as always," her partner states as he inspects the ring. "It's all yours if you want it, my love."

She turns to look up at him, warmth and adoration brimming in her eyes. "Are you sure? I already have so—"

"I'm sure." He cuts her off, plucking the earrings out of her fingers and returning the jewelry to the tray. "Would you wrap these up for us, please?"

"Of course," I say with a nod, and then I transfer the jewelry to the wrapping station.

I hear *him* pacing through the store, and I take my time packing the large velvet box. Then I move to the cash register, bending the seconds to my calm nerves.

I may be teasing him, but I'm also putting it off for my

own sake. Now that the reality is here, the thrill might taste sweet, but the dread is here too, floating in the air with its bitter notes.

"Thank you," I say to the woman. "I hope you enjoy wearing them."

"I will. Thank you very much," the woman says with a blinding smile before they both turn and head for the exit.

This is it. The moment I've been expecting for months.

I flinch when the gentle sound of the closing door feels more like a deafening boom. It has a finality to it, punctuating the life I have led so far and what awaits after. *If* anything awaits after.

With reluctance, I turn my attention to the man himself. He's no longer watching me but looking into one of the large display cases that covers the walls. If he's looking at what I think he is, it's a watch that costs more than half the other watches we have in stock. A man of expensive taste.

Not that I'm surprised, considering how he's dressed. He's broken out of the golden age, wearing Oxfords, fitted suit pants, and a tailored tweed waistcoat over a shirt that hugs him a bit too well. There's already a shiny watch on his wrist, and surprisingly, a few rings on his fingers. His hair is pristinely swiped back at the top of his head, the sides and back shaved close, and there's a shade of stubble on his chiseled jaw.

As he slides his hands into his pockets, the confidence pours out of him in waves. Forearms tense beneath rolled-up sleeves as he pulls his shoulders back like he's preparing for a fight.

Meanwhile, a drop of sweat tickles its way between my shoulder blades, down beneath the waistband of my lavender A-line skirt. One deep breath later, I move toward him and stop, shoulder to shoulder, keeping a foot of distance between us. My gaze stays forward, though.

"Mrs. Brasa-Glass." He rolls my name off his tongue, stroking every single letter with that smoky voice. It sounds new. Like he's still testing to see how it feels to say it. He must have just found it out.

"Miss," I correct him. "Welcome." I motion to the ungodly expensive watch. "Are you interested?"

I don't miss the sharp rise of his chest and the longer than necessary pause before he answers.

"It's surprising what treasures an inconspicuous store can hold." He shifts his attention to me, his gaze molten lava against my cheek, but I stay put. "And a secret, too," he adds.

His breath brushes against my ear, and goosebumps feather beneath the warmth, running viciously down my neck and wrapping around my throat. I think I dreamed of this sensation licking my skin. Or maybe I wished it.

"Just because something has yet to be found, it doesn't make it a secret. Regardless, precious pieces are the specialty here. But not many as expensive as this watch." I've never been so damn polite in my entire life.

I risk a quick side-glance his way, catching the fevered intensity of his gaze.

A second is enough.

Two would be a trap.

Three would be my undoing.

He looks like a walking wet dream in tailored clothes, with a face carved by Renaissance masters.

"If not a secret, then what?"

I shrug. "It's not up to me to give it a name. I'm not the one who's been seeking it."

He exhales slowly, the sound of the air reverberating from deep in his chest, like a dragon breathing fire just before he's about to truly attack.

"You're a bold kitten."

I can't suppress the sharp inhale filling my lungs with fire. That term of endearment is too close to the edge of condescension to hit the right spot, but it does anyway. This man has a maddening, hypnotic effect on me, and I find myself leaning into the unspoken, yet promised, violence.

It's suicide. Yet I seem to be keen on tying the noose myself.

"You must not be used to people speaking their mind around you." I peer over my shoulder, and the clashing of our eyes feels like an explosive volcanic eruption.

A magnificent destruction that threatens to decimate, burn, and melt me until I'm part of its cataclysmic soul. I wouldn't look away, even if I knew better. A part of my soul burns for that havoc, begs to be part of it. To finally find its perfectly fitted half.

His eyes are mesmerizing. I thought they were blue, but they're not just that. They're also gold and green. Dark and bright. And every other shade humanly possible fitted into those saturated blues seeping into a spellbinding hazel. Only, the colors would be nothing without the cruel intensity of this man's soul, an eerie emptiness staring into me like it's absorbing my very essence.

There is a depth in there, devoid of life. Of feeling. Of caring. A bitter, contrasting abyss. And it's looking right back at me.

Maybe, just maybe, I'm not the only one affected here.

Too many seconds pass without an answer from him. Without any word at all. And being caught in his bone-chilling stare, as he decides if this is the moment to strike, makes me jittery.

Yet, I can't look away.

"Interesting setup you have here."

Finally, he speaks!

Though the man seems to have found a formula for how to convey his point by using the fewest words possible.

"The setup isn't quite mine, sir, but I trust you already know this."

His right eyebrow springs up, the curve giving his already cool demeanor an even icier edge. I'm unsure what triggered it, though.

I force my composure, no matter how difficult it proves. Something about this man's energy threatens to bring me to my knees. And I refuse to bend.

"You only work at your stepmother's shop."

I grin, albeit politely, enjoying the incorrect information he offers, then shake my head. "No."

"You are now." His tone shifts a sliver of an octave, bringing forth shielded frustration. Even when he only uses three words. Again, efficient.

"I'm helping out. It's a rare occurrence since I'm usually quite busy," I tease.

He hums in response, though a slight growl vibrates through and lands straight in my belly, filling it with unwelcomed warmth.

"You didn't answer me. Are you interested in the Vacheron Constantin watch? The Tourbillon model in green truly is a masterpiece."

He cocks an eyebrow as he gently tilts his head. The scrutiny as he holds my gaze is unsettling. Exhilarating. And downright terrifying.

How fucking thrilling!

I bite the inside of my lip to keep from grinning like the madwoman I know I am, a rumbling of excitement threatening to burst behind my ribs.

"So?" I push.

"Attempting to sell me a watch won't stall me." The

words darken, deepening with a slight growl. Just as it does in my fantasies, when I stroke between my thighs. The same voice guiding my recent orgasms.

"Stalling? Sir, I've been here all along." I turn to face him fully, though I take half a step back, his proximity overwhelming me. "Truthfully, I thought you would have found me by now."

I don't enjoy his accusations—first he thinks my family kept me tucked away, and then he thinks I've been hiding for all this time.

"Careful now, kitten. You may have claws, but I bite." He turns to face me as well, only a couple of feet separating us. And I swear those are the most words he's spoken to me in one go.

Something reckless shifts within me, and I roll my eyes at him. The response comes from his gaze alone, a darkness descending upon it as he tilts his head down.

"Shall we cut to the chase?" I question.

"Why didn't you call the police?"

So that's a yes. "Why would I?"

He cocks his head, studying me. "Most people's healthy response to murder."

"Most people consider what you've done to be a bad thing."

His answer is the infinitesimal narrowing of his eyes and slight tilt of his head.

I shake my head slowly, rolling my eyes. "I didn't lie that night just to make a good impression. It sounded like you had an important job to do, and I wasn't about to be in your way. I still won't. If you think I give a crap about the death of some piece of shit child trafficker, then your research on me is incomplete, sir."

There it is again, that tiny twitch in his eyes, widening ever so slightly at my choice of words. It's a tinge of surprise, maybe.

Or maybe I'm just seeing what I want.

What my fantasies have conjured up in the last few months

"Why should I believe you?" He takes a step forward into my space.

My spine snaps tight. The proximity is electrifying. Every hair on my body rises, and every nerve ending urges me to run the fuck away.

I take half a step back. Not because of the fear. At least, not only that, but the sizzling static between us.

"Have I given you any reason to mistrust me? Have the police knocked at your door? Have the papers written about you?"

"The absence of proof is not proof, Miss Brasa-Glass. Maybe the police are building a case as we speak."

"You're an intelligent man. Do you truly believe that?"

"I wouldn't be an intelligent man if I didn't consider it." He steps closer, once again reducing the distance separating us.

Is he really planning to kill me? No way. I didn't give him away. Didn't interfere. I'll be fucking *offended* if he actually tries.

"Fine. Consider it. Look into it. Put me under a lie detector test if it will make you feel better."

A second is all it takes. He grabs me and pushes me into the little alcove away from the shop's front window. My back slams against the wall as his body lines up with mine, trapping my wrists in one hand above my head. His free hand presses something smooth against my throat.

Quick, staggered breaths push my heaving chest against his, and our lips part in stunned silence. The temperature in the space soars.

His only answer is a grueling shake of his head, his peculiar hazel gaze fixed on my utterly boring eyes.

I frown when the smooth object shifts against my throat, bringing a slight pressure.

Oh, hell no! That's a fucking knife.

Is this bastard actually planning on murdering me in the middle of the day? In my family's jewelry shop? There are freaking cameras everywhere.

A fleeting snag pulls at my skin, as if the air itself caught on it, and I frown.

"Did you just nick me?"

He cocks his head and looks at my throat. Then the bastard smiles. "You thought you got away."

"I wasn't hiding. You simply didn't find me," I reply, ignoring my nerves running rampant on the inside.

His brows knit together, and I know I hit a sensitive spot. I insulted his abilities.

"This is not a game. In the real world, bad men win every time, and I can't leave any loose ends."

I could fight back. I have enough training to hold my own, and in the last few months, while working to get my divorce finalized, I've been focusing all my rage on even more workouts. But at this moment, I don't want to be in control. I want to see how it plays out. The adrenaline junkie inside me yearns to see how close to death he can lead me.

"Go on, then. Fucking kill me. But I promise you this, I'll crawl out of my shallow grave and haunt you. Your sanity will be my fucking prize." I'm clearly done with politeness. It's not my style anyway.

A shimmer brightens his gaze, the slight curve of one of his brows showing something far from anger. If only I had time to dwell and analyze. Instead, I jerk against him, itching to fight back.

But he presses harder against me, and when my right leg slips to the side, one of his slides right between mine.

My eyes bulge, and self-preservation kicks in at the pressure felt in the most inappropriate spot, considering the situation. I struggle against him, trying to shove him away, but that only increases the pressure from his taut body. From that strong thigh settled too high between mine.

Surely, he must know what he's doing.

I bite the inside of my lip, holding my breath as I fight an almost uncontrollable urge burning through my lungs. He squeezes my wrists tighter, the side of the blade bearing down on my throat, and my body thrums under his intense gaze, his intoxicating scent, his unbearable proximity, and I finally expel that breath I was forcing down.

And it comes out exactly as I hoped it wouldn't . . . like a lustful mewl.

A charged, breathy moan that for one split second made the unquenchable abyss of his eyes sparkle. Fucking sparkle.

Oh, sweet Jesus.

He needs to either kill me already or move the fuck away. His thigh against my core, the knife at my throat, my wrists in his tight hold . . . it may scream assassination to him, but fuck if it doesn't spell explosive orgasm to me.

No, Scarlet, I think it spells insanity.

I'm powerless to stop him when that powerful muscle twitches beneath me, adding a tiny bit more pressure. The moan might have betrayed me, but I really hope my pussy isn't drenching his thigh right now.

"Who's stalling now?" I challenge, like I actually have a death wish.

I don't. And I don't think he's going to kill me.

"Fine." Like a sudden summer storm, his gaze darkens with cold fury.

My eyes widen. The seconds stretch as his elbow rises higher. The blade against my throat shifts and turns. Slight, sweeping pressure trails across my throat, and like the fucking cry of angels themselves, the front doorbell tinkles.

He stiffens as two people cheerfully talk among themselves, walking into the shop. His full lips straighten, nostrils flaring as his arms drop. He allows one second longer before he steps away and to the side, tucking the blade away inside his waistcoat.

Saved by the bell.

I'm shocked I had to be saved. I thought that keeping quiet about his nightly affairs would earn me some brownie points. That we had a fucking connection.

I'm fucking hurt!

He speaks no words as he steps out of the alcove's shadows and back into the sunlight washing over the store. He takes one final look at me, then moves to leave.

I walk out as well, but I don't follow him. Watching him leave feels like the beginning of a story, not the end. And considering he just tried to kill me, I'm going to make this story entertaining as hell.

He pulls the door open, stops, then turns just enough for his gaze to snag on me. "See you soon, Miss Brasa-Glass."

I grin, embers of fury igniting in my soul at his nerve. "Goodbye . . . Mr. Pierce."

CHAPTER 4
Carter

r. Pierce.

Two little words that hold much more meaning than they should. They echo long after the jewelry store door shuts behind me. Long after I walk away.

All this time, she's known who I am. Months of her having the upper hand.

I was all too aware of my failure before, but this piece of knowledge hits my ego dead center.

I could have been in jail now.

Yet, I'm not. Why?

I don't understand this woman. Her drive comes from something unfamiliar. I can't make sense of her. She's a complex ribbon I can't find the ends of, and I'm fucking yearning to unravel her.

She's had my freedom in her delicate hands all this fucking time.

It's unsettling.

Dangerously riveting.

Her expression as I walked away nudged me further down this perilous path; she was seething. The fury shined brightly in her espresso-colored, round eyes. It first appeared when I took her up on her challenge, but it embedded deeper once I slightly cut the side of her delicate throat with my dagger. I was ready to slash it from ear to ear.

Fuck, I didn't even want to do it.

I should have, damn it. I still should. I'm convinced she has no proof. She probably can't send me to jail, but it's the fucking principle of it all. And after all her taunting, daring me to kill her, I craved to make her bleed.

It hasn't gone away. Something about the look in her eyes, lacking in fear but drowned in defiance, compels me to slice her open just so I can see how she ticks beyond those high cheekbones and perfectly bowed lips. What goes on in that reckless mind of hers?

I must squash this need. It's irrational. Pointless.

Utterly ridiculous.

Scarlet Brasa-Glass must die.

But first, I have to do more research on her. Her family. I need to see what impact her death would have on us. Or, at the very least, her sudden disappearance.

My phone vibrates, and I pull it out of my pocket to find a text from Maddox.

Any updates?

I ponder for a few seconds, but as I start the car and pop it into gear, I relent and admit to myself that I have to let The

Sanctum know. This concerns them as much as it concerns me. I swipe Maddox's name on the phone screen, and he answers in two rings.

"Are you good?" he asks on the other line.

"Yes."

"You found her, I presume. Is she . . . ?"

"No," I say before he finishes the question he can't ask over the phone.

"You sound frustrated."

Do I?

"I'm good. Are you all at Midnight?"

"For now. I'm heading to The Fightclub to train for tomorrow, Finn has some business to tend to, and Vin is heading home before going to Morrigan's club."

What a great fucking idea Vincent has. Metamorphosis is just the place to replace the incessant image of the woman with dark eyes and silky walnut-colored hair.

I just need a play partner who can actually do the job, because I have a feeling removing that particular vixen out of my mind will be damn near impossible.

"I'm coming over to give you all an update." I hang up before he can say anything else.

The drive goes by both too fast and too slow. Fifteen minutes didn't seem like enough time to formulate a plan that would make sense to my *brothers*. They'll expect results. Retribution. And all I have to offer is fascination blended with confusion, and neither will satisfy their—*our*—need as The Sanctum.

I feel selfish, and I'm not sure how to justify this.

I'm not even sure any of them will expect me to justify it, but they will be curious. That's why I'm standing in front of this back door, staring at the reinforced metal like it can give me an answer. I'm the heartless one of the group. I'm the one who gets the job done with no remorse or thought wasted. I hunt, I catch, and then I carve. No afterthought given when it's all for us and our safety.

Yet . . . they'll know something is different. That's the problem when you let people get close for so long. And I have no idea how to show them it's not different at all.

Because I don't believe it myself.

Before I push the door open, I pull my phone out and do what I've been itching to do since leaving the jewelry store—I text *Miss* Brasa-Glass.

Don't get too comfortable, kitten. I'm coming for you.

Her number was one of the few things I found of hers. The small size of her online footprint was surprising. Almost shocking. She's not even on social media. Any of them. I was close to checking her medical records in lieu of anything else, but that seemed unnecessary.

With a charged, deep breath in, I scan my watch, enter the code on the keypad, followed by my fingerprint, then walk inside the back corridor. It splits in a few directions; our office, storage rooms, down the steps to The Fightclub beneath, and finally, another short corridor leads to the main barroom of Midnight, which is where I'm headed.

The woodsy smell infused with leather and expensive cigar smoke soothes my previous spinning thoughts in an instant. Midnight is almost as comfortable to me as my home.

The guys wait for me, lounging on the mismatched sofa and comfortable armchairs around our usual table. Vincent, dressed in his usual all-black suit to match his eyes. Maddox, with his buzz-cut hair, wearing black cargos, heavy boots, and a gray T-shirt stretched hard over his stacked muscles. And preppy, pretty-boy Finnigan, with his blond curls, white shirt, and sky-blue chinos. The main lights are off, and they're bathed in the dim, moody glow of the many lamps dotted around the space.

"We heard you finally found your mystery woman." Finnigan breaks the ice.

She's not *my* mystery woman, but I only offer him a raised eyebrow in response.

"And she's still alive?" Vincent cocks his head. His question sounds more like stating the obvious.

I take a seat across from them, in a low-backed armchair upholstered in a decadent mustard velvet, and brace my right ankle over my left knee, settling in. Before I answer, I rub my hands against the armrests' soft, electrifying texture. Only once. Enough for that sensation to soothe its way through my veins.

"I was interrupted," I offer. "Her name is Scarlet Brasa-Glass. She moved to Queenscove about five months ago. Her father and stepmother already lived here, in an estate at the edge of town. They own a jewelry store, where I just came from. I haven't found anything else on them. They're . . . quiet."

Vincent narrows his eyes a fraction. I share the clear sentiment from those dark pits. I have not found one single thing wrong with this family in my research, though it was brief. I'm not saying there aren't good families out there, but this is Queenscove.

"She's going through a divorce that started six months ago," I add.

"Interesting timing," Finnigan interrupts. "I wonder what prompted it." No one misses the sly grin wrinkling his eyes.

That's not what I wonder at all. What I think about is why was she out, all alone that night? She was burning up with reckless energy and it was painted all over her soft face. Was this why? The divorce? What upset her? Was it her soon-to-be ex? Why is she divorcing him?

Stop.

So many questions run rampant in my brain, almost punishing me, since lacking explanations is not a state I'm used to. Or care to get accustomed to, either.

"The soon-to-be ex-husband is part of the Camora family, in Bonray. Where they used to live together," I continue.

Finnigan rubs the scruff on his chin. "The name rings a bell."

"Loan sharks. Small organization, but it's not the poor they deal with." Which makes me question the Brasa-Glass family's morality, regardless of what I have *not* found on them.

"Bonray is only an hour and a half away," Maddox acknowledges. "She could have gone straight back home after she saw you, and that's why you couldn't find her."

"Precisely. Her family seems to keep to themselves. She could have hidden with them, too. Regardless, she lives here now."

"Since a few months ago. Yet you never ran into her until today."

"She knows who I am." I shake my head once, drawing a deep breath through gritted teeth. "She's known this whole time."

Vincent leans back on the sofa, the firm look in his black eyes the exact one I was trying to avoid. "What I find interesting is that she lived far enough away to be off your radar, and yet . . . she chose to move here. Where you are. Where you can find her." He says that last sentence with a sigh. "Strange, don't you think?"

I don't answer, because I'm still trying to unravel that particular puzzle. From our brief conversation, I understood that she believed I had no reason to kill her.

"Is she a threat?" Finnigan's tone turns darker.

I ponder for a moment, remembering her words that were strangely charged with sincerity and a demure attitude toward murder.

"I don't believe so, but I could be wrong. Vincent could be a better judge of character. However, the idea of turning me in and stopping our previous mission seemed almost preposterous to her. And murder didn't faze her."

"Very interesting." Vincent narrows his eyes, pondering.

Exactly. And my initial background check on her and her family showed zero suspicious activity, no questionable past. Nothing to indicate that there's a reason why this strange woman is so utterly unmoved by the events of that night. It doesn't add up one bit.

"What do you want to do?" he asks.

Hunt her down. Tie her up. Question her. Kill her. Or . . . keep her. Play with her. Make her weep on my cock until she reveals all her secrets.

"I'm undecided."

"But you already attempted to eliminate her?" Finnigan asks.

"Dagger to the throat, yes."

"And how did she react to that?" he says.

I sigh, blowing out a slow, heavy breath. "Eerily calm with the blade to her throat, but pissed off when I started slicing."

Ravenous might be a better word for the look in her eyes. The main reason why I want to delay her death is because I have to know what it means. Does she act on it? Will she reveal her true colors?

Finnigan snorts. "Almost like someone else I know."

I glare at him because there's no way he's comparing that woman to me. No fucking way. But that stupid grin tells me that's exactly what he's doing.

"I'm happy to pay her a visit and get a read on her,"

Vincent states.

The idea of him and Scarlet in the same space, together, alone, makes me irrationally annoyed.

He continues when I don't weigh in. "If her lack of action so far says anything, it's that she's not a threat to you. Or us. No matter what, Carter, you know very well we will trust your decision. But make sure you make it for the right reasons."

I'm not entirely sure what "right reasons" he's referring to.

Pride is reason enough. The fierce look in her eyes is, too. What I usually need is a reason not to kill. But Miss Brasa-Glass confounds me and for the first time in a long time—*ever*—I'm stuck. Struggling to justifying.

Though, Vincent and all the other guys' attitudes and trust are . . . umm . . . I guess the right word for it would be *comforting*.

"I'm going to the club tonight," I say, getting up to leave.

"Metamorphosis?" Vincent asks.

I nod to him in response.

"I was expecting you to be thirsty for some . . . carving," he says, "not burning off that type of steam. Is this woman—?"

"See you later." I turn on my heels to head out of Midnight.

The guys protest, but I don't care for their silly lines of questioning.

Before I'm out the door I check my phone, just in case I missed its vibration.

My shoulders slump.

No new text flashes on the oscreen.

* * *

Venetian, steampunk, horror, and more . . . so many masks surround me as I walk into Metamorphosis.

Masks must be worn at all times. This is the main rule in the fetish club owned by Morrigan Sinclair, who is Vincent's wife, and Loreley Dietrich, her best friend. It doesn't matter what type of mask you bring as long as it isn't sheer or see-through.

One guy even came wearing a wolf head once. Considering it looked like it came from a mascot suit, most people seemed to struggle to contain their laughter around him. Until he ended up making one woman squirt and cry for half an hour straight, all while she was strapped to a St. Andrew's cross. Everyone saw that wolf mask a whole lot differently afterward.

Regardless of what people wear, the mask's purpose is to protect our identities and provide comfort to everyone. Most people don't want to know that it's their boss watching them get paddled while strapped over a leather horse.

I personally don't care much. Those who have come in contact with me will likely recognize my tattoos, anyway. Not the ones on my body, but my throat and neck, forearms, and one hand. The back of my neck holds a very vivid and, as I've been told, eerie eye, always visible above the collar of my shirt or jacket. An abstract, ornamental grayscale piece resembling splinters and shards explodes around my throat. There is no meaning. I simply wanted chaos, irregularity, madness in lines, and pain. I wanted pain.

The designs are recognizable to those who have been close enough to me, and if they see me here, I don't care. At least they know The Sanctum is everywhere. Even in their deepest, darkest fantasies.

Because this is what Metamorphosis is at its core—the place where you can feel safe in your own skin. The mask you wear either helps you morph into the person you wish to become someday, or . . . it's the real you that you cannot show to others.

For me, the mask is a mere accessory. I am exactly who I'm supposed to be. But I have to admit . . . there is a different thrill in the knowledge that I have no idea who's watching me.

I have control in every single aspect of my life. I make it my mission to gain as much knowledge as possible about all that surrounds our businesses, Queenscove, our associates, and beyond. And Metamorphosis is a contrast to it all.

I know who I'm looking for tonight—Margo. Though here, she goes by Magpie to protect her identity. She hasn't shared her real name with me, but I found it out anyway. Despite the rules, and considering who I am, my cock doesn't touch just anyone, regardless of the latex layer of protection.

Margo is one of two women I play with here from time to time. There were a couple more, but they had to be discarded. I don't care for attachments, and they refused to stay on the right side of the boundary. Margo seems to understand that this is an exchange, a tit for tat. She gets pain and pleasure, and I get the mental release that comes with inflicting it.

Perching on the last free barstool, I order a still water and turn to face the rumbling crowd. Almost all the round tables dotted around the center stage and in the shadows of the vast space are occupied, and all around them people are either dancing or simply caught in conversation.

It's what I like about this place—you can come to watch, play, talk, or educate yourself on the lifestyle. There is no pressure, no expectation. A bracelet system is in place, and patrons know how to engage with you depending on the color you wear.

However, the most interesting things don't happen on this stage, but down the wide corridor to the left of the bar, where six playrooms sit, three on each side. The wall is only hip-height, and the rest is all window, apart from the door, allowing anyone to watch what's happening beyond it. If the players want, the curtains can also be closed for private sessions. Or the window can be turned into a mirror, for those who like the thrill without seeing who or how many watch them.

"I wasn't expecting to see you today."

"Hello, Magpie." I turn to the left, where Margo appeared.

"I'm still getting used to your new mask. The top half with all its antique gold baroque elements is pretty, but the skull bottom half, weathered and grim, looks so . . . aggressive."

That was the point.

"Are you available tonight?" I cut off the small talk.

"Always for you. Shall I go secure a room?"

I nod.

"Room three?" she asks.

I nod again.

She smiles from underneath the pink-feathered mask covering her down to the tip of her nose, and turns on her heels.

I watch her walk away, waiting for that spark to show up in the tips of my fingers. The one that makes me itch for a paddle, for the feel of a pulse under my fingers as I ram my pierced cock into her, for the crack of the braided whip as it hits the skin. And so much more. My brows knit together as I keep waiting for that moment, yet even by the time Margo returns, it doesn't come.

"I wasn't hiding . . . you simply didn't find me."

Scarlet's daring words penetrate my mind, spoken in that soft voice that I can't rip out of my brain no matter how hard I fucking try.

That must be it—I'm distracted. Tense. And that's why my enthusiasm hasn't come yet.

It will. It must.

The whole point of tonight is to get the dark-eyed woman

out of my goddamn mind.

My pocket vibrates and I fumble to pull out my phone, rolling my eyes at my own impatience.

Bring it on, *killer-boy.*

Over and over, I read that challenge, along with that ridiculous nickname she gave me. With each re-read, I squeeze the device harder until I swear I feel it crack.

This kitten is playing with fucking fire.

CHAPTER 5
Scarlet

At some point in the last half an hour, the music has turned ethereally sultry. Lascivious notes thread through the dimly lit space as a woman performs a burlesque show on stage.

But my attention is somewhere else—the small crowd gathered in front of one particular window, down the wide corridor. I've been visiting this club for about three months now, and something interesting is always happening over there. I wonder what it is tonight.

I make my way between the people who all seem keen to look at my wrist to check where I stand, but I excuse myself every time someone attempts to stop me. I want to see what's there. The curiosity has been killing me since a woman gasped loudly enough that I heard her over the music.

Gently nudging the bodies standing before the window,

I finally make my way to the front. It takes me a moment to acknowledge the image before me, and a moment longer to understand it.

"It can't be . . ." I whisper to myself.

But it is—the motherfucking Carver himself stands before me, with only glass separating us. And he is not alone.

As much as I loathed my teenage years, always trapped inside the house by my darling mother, pouring my frustration into learning code and honing my tech skills has made me who I am today. And it allowed me to keep my eye on Carter Pierce over the last six months. From a safe distance, but close enough to observe patterns and find out more about the man.

I visited Metamorphosis for the first time after seeing him come here several times. There was always a steady flow of people going in. I got curious, so I did my research, and when I found out what it was, I had to snag a membership.

Little did I know that this fetish club would become a little obsession of mine.

Just like the man himself.

I never play, only people-watch and enjoy the delicious drinks. Twice we ended up here at the same time. Adrenaline might be my thing, but I wasn't about to chase death at his hands. So, once I noticed his pattern, I began avoiding the club on the days Carter usually comes. The man is quite strict about his schedule.

Or so I thought.

He's not supposed to be here today.

Yet, there he is, with a woman, breaking the pattern.

The blonde is ridiculously attractive, especially with her arms tied to a strap hanging from the ceiling, and a spreader bar keeping her legs wide open as she squirms and yelps. Because right between them, a thin metal pedestal stands with a large red dildo at the end of it, the tip spreading her pussy wide open. It looks to be completely soaked, and I bet none of that is lube. She's brightly flushed, hair clinging to damp skin as her head leans against her arm. She's facing the corner of the room, so I get a glimpse of her red ass and back, slightly purple in places from where Carter's braided whip makes contact. Repeatedly.

And he's still at it.

It has to be him . . . I've studied every inch of this man in photos and videos I found online while I was waiting for him to come for me. Granted, there wasn't as much media as I thought there would be, and most were from various philanthropic events in Queenscove.

The philanthropic part was both shocking and pleasantly surprising.

But those photos were enough for me to notice and now recognize that chaotic black-and-gray throat tattoo that resembles a splintering explosion.

He turns, and the creepy eye on the back of his neck stares straight into my soul. There's no denying it's Carter Pierce under that half-skull mask.

And he's touching . . . her.

I haven't spoken those words, yet their bitter taste still coats my tongue.

He runs his middle finger down the naked woman's spine, and when her muscles twitch, attempting to arch into his touch, my fists tighten.

Something about this image feels utterly wrong. It doesn't fit. Something is missing.

The woman moans as Carter slides that one digit around her waist, over her hip bone, around her navel, and down her belly. He whips her thigh right as that finger reaches her drenched pussy, and the scream she lets out as he slaps her clit is charged with a wanton moan I feel straight in my core.

My fists clench harder, teeth grinding together, yet my own center throbs and yearns.

Why is this bothering me so much?

What's wrong with this image?

God, the way he touches her, the way she tries to squirm, her moans and cries of pleasure and pain, they're . . . *exhilarating*. With each assault, she seems to disappear deeper into a state of mind-bending pleasure I cannot even fathom. She smiles maniacally and cries passionately over and over again as Carter works her unlike anything I've seen since coming to this fetish club.

But that's not the cherry on the cake. It's his unbending attention. He doesn't just watch her—he studies her. The effect of every touch, every strike, the way each of his words lands. He's completely in tune with her and her needs. He stops before she even gets a chance to use her safe word. He restarts when her breathing calms and her lips quirk on one side. He brings her to the edge of oblivion and drags her back down on breathless cries I feel in my soul, and I'm close to weeping myself at the sight.

This is beyond impressive.

This—*he*—is mesmerizing.

Metamorphosis holds a good pool of interesting customers, and I've seen my share of incredible people playing together, but Carter is something else. With pulled-back shoulders, stance straight and proud; sinewy, tattooed forearms beneath the rolled-up sleeves of his shirt; the dusting of hair peeking from his open collar, almost obscured by his tattoos; and the simple way he stalks . . . he's nothing like the men I've seen play here.

He's in a league of his own.

A masked god.

And the problem with this image finally dawns on me—

her. She is the wrong one. Because it's not me.

It's goddamn infuriating!

How dare he make me desire what he's offering to another woman!

How dare he awaken this starving need to find out if there's an ounce of possibility for me to feel what she feels!

How fucking dare he!

And after he tried to kill me, nonetheless.

The nerve of this man.

I thought we had a connection. Some form of mutual respect. I guess I'll have to teach him a little lesson.

But until I form that plan, I'm glued to this wretched window and this infuriating man, watching as he clamps her nipples, a chain connecting them, and holds them with a painful tension as he violently spanks her clit. Tears stream down her cheeks, a mad smile pulls at her lips, and ecstasy paints every feature. This goes on for minutes on end, until her legs begin to shake, and she looks up at the strap connecting her to the ceiling like she can will it loose with one gaze.

When her breaths come in rapid bursts and her eyes turn glassy, Carter stops spanking her and loosens that strap, immediately grabbing the whip. The moment is instant. She impales herself on the slickened dildo, bouncing on it as Carter holds the delicate chain connecting the clamps on her nipples, and whips her between each dip.

Her orgasm comes five blows later, and I'm convinced it rattled the fucking window. I'm both mesmerized and frustrated. Which is why I must step away. The last thing I need is to witness the aftercare part of this scene.

Is it brief? Is it intimate? Is it sweet?

I turn on my heels before I get the answers.

I don't know him, and he doesn't know me. Yet, this wild voice inside my head rages with unfounded jealousy. I could claim that it's because I'll never experience what she just has. That I'll never feel on my own skin that mad combination of pleasure and pain because my biology failed me.

Those are true as well, but they aren't the main reason for this jealousy.

I'm truly screwed.

* * *

I don't know how much time passed since I returned to the bar, but I already finished my first Necromancer cocktail and I'm halfway through the second when I notice Carter sitting at the bar. Three stools away from me.

I'm not sure he can see me here. There are quite a few people between us, both sitting and standing. Regardless, I doubt he'll recognize me behind the white full-face Pierrot mask I'm wearing.

He took his time with the aftercare, I guess. Yet, he's alone now.

Maybe I should have left, just as before, but I'm done avoiding him.

I sip more of my cocktail, reveling in the anise-flavored burn and wishing for more of it as I watch the man ordering his own drink. Is he a straight-up whiskey kind of guy? Vodka? Or beer?

No. Definitely not beer. Or maybe a Corona on an excessively warm summer day? Vodka seems too . . . simplistic. It must be whiskey, then.

Only, it's not at all.

A delicate pink flower floats in the drink the bartender slides in front of him.

What the . . . ?

He pulls the tumbler close, dips one finger in, and swirls

the flower through the drink exactly three times while I wipe actual drool from the corner of my mouth. He then slips that very finger beneath his mask, and deep in my core, a sizzle blooms. Oh, good god, what is this man doing to me?

The woman he was with is still nowhere in sight. Though, I can't help but notice the *vultures* circling. One chick has already walked by him three times, and he's been sitting down for only two minutes. Another one is sitting on the next stool over from him, and she seems to be leaning further and further in. Maybe, just maybe, he'll grace her with his attention.

And here I fucking am, judging these women when I'm doing the same thing—watching him.

I tell myself that my reasoning is completely different. The man wants to murder me, so of course I'll be watching to make sure I'm ready when he comes for me.

Actually . . .

I pluck my phone from the pocket of my black circle dress—a tame, knee-high number with a low neckline that squeezes the crap out of my boobs but gives generous cleavage—and go straight to my text messages, tapping enthusiastically.

And here I thought I would be dead by now. Busy, killer-boy?

He pops his drink down and spins on the stool until his back meets the bar, then reaches into his pocket. When he pulls his phone out, he throws his gaze around like he's making sure no one can see his screen.

I don't miss the flexing of his forearms or how hard they tense as he clutches the device and types.

Interesting.

So, I do have an effect.

My phone vibrates, and I turn away from him to read

and reply.

Eager, kitten?

Just bored. So many months have passed…

I can't help but tease, just to piss him off.

I hope you enjoyed them. You won't get to see the next one.

We'll see about that.

A wild grin strains my cheeks. Drinking the rest of my Necromancer, I drop from the barstool and head toward the stairs that lead up to the exit.

Just as I pass him, I pretend to lose my footing, bumping into the man himself. His large hand wraps around my waist, catching me before I make full contact.

"Oh gosh! My apologies," I exclaim as I lay my palm on his shoulder, giving it just one little squeeze, before I straighten.

So much lean, hard muscle . . .

His masked expression is unreadable, but I catch the slight tilt of his head as it moves down my body, then up again.

"No harm done." His smoky drawl is hard to hear over the music, but his palm still rests on my waist. Such a simple, innocent touch with so much potential.

"Enjoy the rest of your evening, sir," I say, my hand running down his bicep.

He nods, reluctantly letting go, and I turn, taking a centering breath in as I walk away with slow, determined steps.

I toss a little sway in my hips for good measure.

Throwing a glance over my shoulder, I catch him watching me, and a little pride blooms in my soul.

I open the rideshare app on my phone and order one. Then, as I walk up the stairs, I check to make sure he's not watching me anymore.

My fingers fly over the keyboard as I text him back.

Promises, promises. Sleep tight, killer-boy.

I know he has resources and skills since he had no trouble tracking my car, finding me at Carmen's store, and learning my phone number. I set up all my shields on this phone too, yet I wonder if he can crack them and trace me to find that we share a location?

Wouldn't that be fun? Him knowing I'm here, yet not being able to see behind the masks?

Christ almighty, I could have so much fun with that.

But I need to get my ass home, lock myself inside in case he decides to take me up on my challenge, and attempt to sleep through the night. From ear to ear, I grin as the adrenaline floods my veins and exhaustion sinks in. Because it happened. He came for me.

And it's nowhere near over.

While he may be on a mission to silence me—not that I ever intended to talk—I have my own agenda: sweet motherfucking revenge for my broken black heart.

I should have some common sense and at least try to be afraid of his attempt on my life, but all I feel is an exhilarating freedom I want to drown myself in. Just like that first night we met . . . I feel alive.

And I intend to stay that way.

Let the games begin, killer-boy.

CHAPTER 6
Carter

"This just won't do," I say to myself with a long sigh as I watch the city's CCTV cameras on two of the six thirty-inch monitors fixed on the wall above my desk. The others hold the brief information I managed to find on the wretched kitten.

Her largely undocumented life surrounds me on these screens.

They're fixed on flexible brackets I've adjusted so that the outside monitors are on a slight diagonal angle. They immerse me in whatever research or work I'm doing, but there's nothing useful to be immersed in now.

Scarlet lives on the same estate as her father, at the edge of Queenscove where CCTV is sparse or non-existent and the houses are pulled away from the road. In their case, according to satellite images, they own enough land that the buildings I can see might as well be in different neighborhoods, separated by hedges, fences, and thickets of trees. I can only guess which belongs to the woman I'm looking for. Probably the smaller cottage-like building on the northeast side, next to a large pond. I have no idea why that one seems most relevant out of the three houses, but it does.

This is what I've been doing, watching Scarlet's property, or trying to, since I woke up from the best sleep I've had in months, though that might not mean much, since I've been sleeping like shit.

Regardless, it seems pointless. I checked the two cameras that come close to the property boundary, but all they see are the roads leading to the estate. No house, no drive, no nothing. A distant, tall hedge and nothing else.

I need more. I need to see her house. Her windows. *Inside . . .*

I woke up with an itchy need scratching through my veins. A frustration that demanded satisfaction. It didn't get it last night. Not for lack of trying, but I just couldn't get myself in the mood at Metamorphosis. I still played, but I could not fuck. It felt wrong, somehow. I can't find a rational explanation for it, and that is simply unacceptable.

To make matters worse, Margo could tell something was off. It's one thing to be off my game, but it's another for it to show. I can't let any cracks reach the surface. They might embed, and I can't allow that.

This, though—the inability to have eyes on Scarlet— doesn't just frustrate me. It downright angers me.

For some reason, my brain finds it important to lay eyes on her. These days, it seems to be working on its own accord. Finnigan would call it intuition. I call it ridiculous distractions from the norm.

I lie back in my thickly padded computer chair, clutching

the mouse in one hand while rubbing the hem of my T-shirt between my index and middle finger.

A strange habit.

The feel of the hem between those digits pleasantly tickles a part of my brain that finds comfort in that particular texture. So, I carry on, as always, while I switch between different cameras, hoping that a new feed will magically appear. No such luck, of course.

I move to the only photos I found of her online. Nine in total. A shocking amount, considering the age we live in. It's almost suspicious.

Fuck, *it is* suspicious.

Two photos aren't even of her. They're of someone else at an event, and she appears in the background. Only, there's something about Scarlet. The way her walnut-colored waves flow down to the middle of her back. Her creamy skin against the dark-green dress. Her sweet smile, even as she looks away from the camera, hiding a wickedness the lens doesn't manage to capture. She may be in the background, but she stands out.

I wish I hadn't noticed that.

The third photo is from a sealed record. Black eye and burst lip, the same pixie grin shining in her gaze and the curve of her lips. She beat up someone in school when she was sixteen. Badly enough that they ended up in the hospital with three broken fingers, a fractured arm, and a broken nose. And there is no remorse whatsoever on her face.

I'm intrigued. Thoroughly.

The last six photos awaken a masochistic sense in me that I sometimes forget exists. I have no desire to see the pictures. They infuriate me for reasons I fail to understand, yet I keep fucking looking at them, regardless. They're from her wedding with Bernard Camora a few years back.

She looked happy.

Searing heat melts beneath my skin at the images that have wrongness to them. Unexplainable, infuriating wrongness. Mostly aimed at Camora.

Yet, I keep staring, allowing the images to burrow deeper into my nerves.

I have to get to her.

Scrape her out of my fucking mind once and for all.

Without a second thought, I lock my screens, rise, and head straight out of my office and toward the dressing room attached to my bedroom. I quickly change the sweatpants to a pair of dark-blue slacks, then pull on a shirt, roll the sleeves, and finish off with a light gray tweed waistcoat, socks, and brown leather shoes.

I pass by the mirror, forcing myself to leave the house without fixing my messy hair at the top of my head. But as I approach the bedroom door to leave, the compulsion makes my palms itch and my teeth clench. With a deep sigh, I turn on my heels and head to the en suite bathroom. I attempt to rush, but in the end, I still make sure my hair looks as it's supposed to—perfectly neat. Slicked back, as always.

With one final look in the mirror, I hurry to the garage, straight to the F-type Jag parked there. The mood calls for something agile. Then I'm out the door, waiting for my gates to open, rolling my fists around the leather steering wheel that threatens to bend beneath my hold.

My phone rings and almost makes me jump.

"Yes," I say more aggressively than I should.

"Good morning to you too."

Vincent.

"You left your Range Rover at the club last night, right?" he continues.

"I did."

"I think you should come here."

"I'm busy."

I make a right after the gates close behind me and drive toward Queenscove's outskirts.

"Carter, your driver's side door is cracked open. Only enough that you can see it if you're close, but it's clearly unlocked."

I almost slam on the brake at those words.

"Is mine the only one broken into?" I keep calm as I run through the list of what they could have taken from my car, but there's barely anything in there.

For security reasons, I refrain from keeping things in my cars. Especially if I plan on leaving them away from my home overnight. Which I usually do, either in Midnight's or Metamorphosis' parking lot if I'm drinking more than a couple. The difference is that the speakeasy has a gated, secured lot.

"I had a look. There are only five cars here, and yours seems to be the only one broken into."

Fuck.

I have something more important to deal with right now, and it grates me that this break-in sounds targeted.

"There's something else," he adds.

"What?"

"Did you leave anything on your driver's seat?"

I frown, squeezing the steering wheel a little too hard. "No."

"They left something for you."

"Don't touch anything." I rush through the words as I slam on the brake and turn the car around, heading back toward the club. "Check around and underneath for a—"

"Already done. No bombs. But I'm not sure about the inside."

"I think it's clean." I hear Morrigan, his wife, in the background.

"I'm on my way." I hit a button on my car and hang up.

Why the hell would someone break into *my* car?

* * *

"Is that what I think it is?" Vincent asks as I hold the offending object left on my driver's seat.

We checked the Range—no devices. Nothing stolen. Nothing moved.

"It's a puzzle box. A complex one, at that," I say, flipping the wooden contraption, similar in size to a Rubik's Cube, in my hand.

"Do you think it's a trap?"

I look at the symbols and shapes etched into the cube, the seams and divots serving a purpose I have yet to identify. "No, I don't. But whatever it is, I'm fucking pissed."

"You want to go inside and give it a go?" Morrigan asks. When I look up, she's nodding toward the club.

"I'd like to check your cameras." I have to wait for Otto to come pick up the car and drop it at my house anyway.

"Come, then." She turns and heads straight to the club without checking to see if we're following.

Ten minutes later, we're in the office, rewinding through the footage.

"There." I point at the screen when a hooded figure dressed in loose black clothes finally shows up. "Rewind until you find the moment they came to my car."

"There it is." Vincent stops her. "Play it."

Three seventeen in the morning. The club only closed an hour before.

We watch in silence as this person comes from the shadows, walking with a grating confidence straight to my car. There's no hesitation, no cowering. I notice something in their hand, and I tense as I wonder if I missed a device stuck somewhere.

"They had a key?" Morrigan exclaims as the person simply unlocks the door.

The lights start flashing and the alarm goes off as they climb in, and we lose sight of what they're doing. My shoulders relax when I realize they were holding one of those immobilizers that disable car alarms. Forty-two seconds pass, and then the lights go off and the sound stops. That's fast. Very fast.

"Did you hear it? The alarm?" I ask.

Loreley owns the four-story period building which houses the club in the basement, her apartment on the top floor, and Morrigan's on the third. She and Vincent slept here last night; they didn't go back to their house in the woods.

He nods, but Morrigan answers. "I did. From up there, you can't really localize the sound, though. I got up to go to the window, but it stopped by then. The thing is, we're in the center of Queenscove . . . Alarms aren't uncommon, especially on the weekend and with the tourists that we get."

As much as I want to be frustrated, it's illogical. This is not on them. And whoever did this was impressively quick.

"Can you download the footage, the whole thing, from just before I arrived?" I ask her.

"Yeah. I'll pop it on our server. You can access that, yes?"

"I can. Thank you."

Vincent cocks his head as he watches the end of the clip. "After they disabled the alarm, they spent a bit more time there. Only a minute or so, but longer than it would take to leave a puzzle box on the seat."

He's just pointing out the obvious as we watch the hooded figure climb out of the car and carefully push the door until it just catches the latch. Then they stroll away from sight.

I want to hope that a different camera angle would give me a view of their face, but I know I won't see a thing. They're wearing all black from head to toe—sweatpants, and a baggy hoodie pulled over their head so that it shades their face too. Though, that also appears to be covered with a ski mask or something.

"I think you're right," he continues. "I don't think the box is a trap, and it might tell you why they lingered in the car."

My phone vibrates, and I take it out to find the text I've been waiting for. "Otto is outside. I'll give him the key and head home."

For the first time in a long time, I'm uncomfortable. These last two days seem to have been dominated by states of mind I'm largely unfamiliar with. This one, I don't like. I've been given a task by a complete stranger who broke into my fucking car, and it seems I have no other choice but to do it. I'm being controlled, and it's awakening that simmering creature within me that demands satisfaction in pounds of flesh and spilled blood.

But things have been unseasonably quiet lately . . . I have no people on the roster to torture.

I squeeze the puzzle in my hand, feeding on the sharp pain from one of the corners as it digs deeper into my skin. *I guess the quiet times have officially ended.*

"One of us should be with you when you open the box," Vincent offers.

"I'll be fine. I'll let you know what I find. See you later."

I turn and walk away before they can stall me with further futile conversation. If this box is a trap—a bomb—I don't want anyone else to go down with me. I suspect it's not, but I'm not willing to risk any of them.

"Check your cars," I say loud enough for them to hear as the door shuts behind me.

I suspect I was the only one targeted, but better safe than sorry.

CHAPTER 7
Carter

I hacked into the city's CCTV system for the second time today, this time to find the cameras around Metamorphosis. Four currently occupy just as many of my computer screens. None show the face of the culprit.

Considering the situation, the confidence with which they carry themselves is irritating. It not only suggests experience, but preparation too.

Only, that would be impossible since I only decided to go to the club late in the afternoon. There wasn't even a plan to leave my car there, and it's not something I do every time I frequent the establishment.

No. This smells like seized opportunity after some degree of preparation. It also smells like surveillance—they've been watching me.

And I have no fucking distinguishing factors by which to locate and watch them. All I see is this hooded figure disappear down an alley between the backs of two old stone buildings. I switch to another camera angle that may catch the alley from the distance, but it's too dark and this person dissipates into the shadows. I check footage that captures the other side of the alley, but the angle only sees half of the entrance.

"Fuck!"

Pulling up more cameras in the area, I sit back and watch the monitors for any trace of this person. They have to show up on one of them. No matter what, they would have left the area.

Unless they live there.

Three hours and countless rewinds later, and I can practically feel the bulging vein in my throat throbbing with frustration. That's all I seem to feel these days—endless frustration. Because the hooded figure is nowhere to be seen. Just drunk people returning to their hotels and homes, and others leaving disheveled after getting exactly what they went there for. No one stands out.

Which means it could be any of these people. Or someone in a car. Or they could live here.

I have no more information than I had when I was staring at my car.

Only the puzzle.

With a deep sigh that feels more like breathing fire, I grab the damn thing and start powering down my system.

Wait.

There's something else I didn't check.

I didn't assume the gender of the person who did this. What if it was a woman? What if it was *her?* No cameras capture her property, but maybe I can see her car on the road. Or something . . . anything to indicate it was her.

Better yet, I'll hack into her phone and get her location data. Finding her number was easy. Hopefully, remotely accessing the device will be just as easy.

My phone vibrates on the desk, and I turn it over to find a text. Speak of the fucking devil.

I had more time to think about this, and I need to tell you something.

Do tell.

I'm truly hurt.

I may be mad, but I feel a tug at the corner of my lips.

It was only a small cut.

I mean emotionally.

This should be good. Surprising that the physical injury doesn't faze her. Or the potential scar.

I thought we had something... an unspoken, rational understanding. I don't hand you over to the cops, you don't kill me for no good reason. Then you go and slice my damn throat!

Understanding? Wishful thinking is more like it.

You're alive, aren't you?

Semantics, killer-boy.

Accuracy in accusation is important.

Noted. Now, what do you have to say for yourself?

> I already said what I needed to say.

> Blah, blah, you're coming for me, blah, blah. I'm talking about hurting my feelings. What are you gonna do about that?

I cock my head as I re-read that text. She's playing me, right? Or is she truly mad? Because it sounds like, once again, she's baiting me. Jesus, she's an odd woman.

Yet . . . there's a flame in my chest that seems to send sparks with each thought of her. Each text. Each interaction. She may be odd, but damn, is she intriguing.

> Considering what I'll do to you soon, your feelings won't matter anymore.

> Tsk, tsk, tsk... once again
> You can hide it, killer-boy, but I know you like me. Admit you don't actually want to get rid of me.

> Now, what gave you that idea?

> You.

My eyes go dry as I stare at that text for what seems like a small eternity. Either she's delusional or there truly is something happening to me.

I don't answer. I can't. I turn my system back on and, starting with the cameras, I work my way through the only two in Scarlet's area. Nothing stands out. A couple of taxis, a few cars, but nothing to indicate it's Scarlet. It's a bust. The only thing I found was her Mercedes going home earlier yesterday. That's it.

I move on to her phone, fingers flying on the keyboard as I go through the same processes as I've gone through countless times before with others. I look for vulnerabilities in the network, cracking my way in until I get what I want.

Only, it's not really working. I'm being blocked at every turn. This is . . . interesting.

Surprising.

She has countermeasures set up not only on her phone, but on her home network too.

Why?

I keep going. Keep pushing. Trying to find one tiny split in their shields.

Nothing.

Who is she? Why does she have shields set up? Good ones.

I'll find no explanation here. Only delays.

This whole fucking day has been filled with failures. And it's goddamn unacceptable.

I slam the side of my fist onto the wooden desk, and everything on it jitters. But anger isn't solving anything. It's a useless, pathetic emotion and one of the few I'm capable of tasting on my tongue.

What I need is unavailable. What I crave is pain. Blood. Sliced flesh and exposed muscles. The release they bring, the clarity of mind.

I power everything down for the final time, grab the puzzle box, and leave the office before I start scouring the dark web and wasting more of my goddamn time in search of a knave that needs a good fucking cleanse.

The late afternoon light streams through the tall stained-glass windows of my stone fortress. With a deep, centering breath, I sit in an armchair and inspect the object, turning it over and over in my hands until all the symbols and divots split away from the wood like glimmers of light. They line themselves before my eyes, turning into a map that leads me to my answer.

One by one I twist and turn, pressing and pulling them away until the box begins to open for me. I follow the map and, after half an hour of light swearing and annoyed admiration for the wretched puzzle, I'm done. The result is two elongated pyramids, roughly four or five inches in length, stuck together at the base, where a small latch sits. I waste no time opening it.

My brows narrow when I find only a small parchment inside. Not paper—parchment. I slowly unroll it and fall back into the armchair as I read the exquisite brown-ink calligraphy.

Power is a peculiar concept, laced with perception and illusion. We all fall victim to it. Sometimes, some of us take bigger bites than we can swallow. This time . . . it was you.
If I can steal from right under your nose . . . imagine what else I'm capable of, Carver.

P.S. If you haven't figured it out yet . . . start your car. You might be missing something.

I throw the parchment onto the coffee table, run toward the office to grab the keys, and burst through the back door where the Range is parked. Otto didn't mention anything amiss when he brought it to me. But then again, it's not his car. He wouldn't notice if something wasn't right.

Climbing into the driver's seat, I start the vehicle and wait for something to stand out. Everything looks fine at first glance. The lights are the same, and the dashboard behind the wheel hasn't changed. The main screen looks okay. I touch the screen, go into the menu, and slide through the various sections. Everything looks just as—

"Wait."

I click the search button in the navigation menu.

Empty.

No favorite locations have been set, and it's all factory settings, but I've searched in here before, and I know for a fact that it saves the search history.

I jump out of the car and rush back to the office when an idea hits me. Heading straight to the cabinet drawer that holds all my car-related miscellaneous items, I find the adapter that allows me to connect to its computer. I grab my laptop and return to the Range.

It takes a few minutes, but eventually, I find exactly what I suspected—nothing.

The location history of this car has been completely wiped. The worst thing is that I don't know exactly to what degree it saves it. I'm so focused on computers and phones, clearing my fucking car history hasn't been a priority.

Whoever broke in took all this information. All the locations this car has been to.

They could be anyone . . . clearly an enemy. Maybe someone from law enforcement, though they couldn't use this in an investigation, as it wouldn't hold up in court. I've taken this car to some of our private locations, like our underground concrete prison we use when we have a *client* that's not talkative enough or we want to silently dispose of. Or Midnight's parking lot. Meeting places with contacts. Jonathan "The Ghost" Rees and his HQ. I haven't always taken this car—I have two more—but I drive it enough that it's been to significant spots.

They have the locations of all those places now. They might not know what some mean, but they have them on the map.

I drag my fingers through my neat hair, pulling at the roots as I go through the next steps. Only, the next steps aren't coming to me. The solutions are muddled in my brain, and I can't pull them out of the muck.

Climbing out of the car, I pace around the driveway, trying to assess the impact of this predicament.

Already, I fucked up by not catching a woman who has watched me kill a man so many months ago. Now this.

God-fucking-damn it!

I should have predicted this. Prepared.

Only one thing left to do—adapt.

I walk back inside, through the foyer, then straight through the living space, passing everything until I reach the violin sitting on its mount next to the old organ. Nothing centers me and helps me focus like this exquisite piece.

I settle it in place and sink into that world where everything fits together neatly and all makes sense.

CHAPTER 8
Scarlet

The taste of salt in the air is one of my favorite things about Queenscove. That, and the rocky beach and cliffs at the westernmost part of the cove, where it curves out into the ocean. It's popularly called the Jurassic Crest because of the number of fossils and prehistoric bones that can be found there. Especially when bits of the cliff break away.

After I moved here, the walks I took on that rocky terrain in search of pieces of natural history grounded me.

Once my divorce is finalized, I'll go there with a bottle of expensive champagne and celebrate. All by my fucking self. That is, unless Carter Pierce makes good on his word and offs me.

"What are you daydreaming about?" Willow asks from the sunbed next to mine, hiding from the sun under her big beach hat.

"The future." I shrug.

She drops her sunglasses an inch and regards me with a cocked brow. "Don't fall into melancholy, please. Today has been a surprisingly good day."

It has indeed. We came to the beach early in the morning, lounged, read, drank, and swam with no care in the world. Willow is good like that, especially on that one day a month that marks yet another one that has passed since my life took a turn.

She doesn't do it because I'm sad about what happened. Yes, it was a betrayal, one that still stings, but at this point, my ego is the bruised one, not my heart. Willow tries to distract me from the annoying passage of time so I can try to forget I'm still tied to that cheating, blackmailing bastard.

"Shall we go for lunch now?" I ask. "Albeit a late one? I'm starving, and I'm almost dry."

"Yes, let me just pack these away. We're going to The Shack, right?"

It's the seafood restaurant at the edge of the beach, next to the best ice cream place in town. I might treat myself after lunch.

I rise, throwing my almost see-through beach dress over my two-piece bathing suit, and quickly pack everything into my beach bag. We walk through the hot sand for the ten minutes it takes to reach The Shack and climb the three steps onto the wooden terrace overlooking the beach. The pergola is covered in white veil-like fabric, and climbing plants circle every pillar, contributing to the cozy vibe.

But the food is the true star of the show. Fresh catches, delicious pairings, and yet, for some reason, it's not the most popular seafood place in the city. It's *my* freaking favorite, though.

"I have a craving for lobster. Want to share?" Willow asks.

"Sorry, babe. I haven't stopped thinking about the seafood soup. I'm gonna go for that."

"Ugh, you spoil my fun. But fine, I'll sacrifice my stomach and order a whole thing for myself." She feigns hardship as she sighs.

Snickering, I rise. "Can you order an iced tea for me, please? I'm just going to go wash my hands."

"Sure." She nods as she looks through the menu.

I slide my sandals on and hurry through the open double doors inside the beach-themed hut, then straight to the bathroom on the other side. After I do my business, I stare in the mirror as I wash my hands, noticing the blush over my nose, cheeks, and forehead. Faint freckles pop up, too. I should have been stricter with the damn SPF.

"Oh wow, I love that dress," a redheaded woman with wild, natural curls exclaims as she turns back from the hand dryer.

"Thank you," I say with a smile, appreciating her enthusiasm.

"Where from, if you don't mind?"

"Are you a tourist?"

"No," she says, laughing like I said something totally ridiculous.

Something about her feels awfully familiar. Maybe she visited Carmen's shop when I happened to be there.

"Then you know the secondhand-vintage shop on Hyacinth Lane?"

"Oh yes. Damn, you're lucky. It's so hard to snag the good pieces," she says as she moves to leave.

"I know, which is why I took this off my mom after she bought it."

"Oh, that's good! I like that!" she says, laughing right along with me just before she walks out the door. "Bye!"

I wave and smile. I swear this encounter gave me déjà vu from my university days, clubbing and striking one-night friendships with random girls in the bathroom. Usually over a cute lipstick or painful shoes.

The delicious scent of good food and the salty sea smacks into me as I walk out of the ladies' room and make my way through the busy restaurant. From the corner of my eye, I catch a spot of red, and I turn to find the woman from the bathroom. She's laughing and gesturing at the people sitting around her table.

Like the calm before a storm, all noise ceases, and all but one person blurs before me. Because there, at the same table, right across from her, sits Carter Pierce.

"I'll be damned," I mutter to myself, feeling the tug of a smile at my cheeks.

He's with a few other people, and as my feet remember they have to keep moving before I start drawing attention, I catch a glimpse of them all. I recognize each of them from the research I've done into Carter. Maddox Severin, Finnigan Hennessey and his purple-haired girlfriend, Evelyn Shaw, and Vincent "The Serpent" Sinclair.

The ball finally drops as I realize the redhead is his wife, Morrigan, former O'Rourke, part of one of Queenscove's elite families. Though only she and her brother stand today.

I'm only steps away from the door leading onto the terrace, but that burning ember inside my soul sends sparks of unfulfilled recklessness, and I feel compelled to oblige. I spin on my heels, stoking that ember until little flames ignite, and turn my smile into a devious grin as I walk right over to that table.

He's not facing me, so I get the pleasure of seeing his profile, looking as if it's carved from stone. His palms rest on his thighs as he quietly observes his friends.

But like any predator would, he senses my approach and turns, hazel eyes widening when they fall on me. My steps almost falter at his reaction, but I hold on to that reckless desire to catch the man off guard and walk until I'm only a few steps away.

"Mr. Pierce, good afternoon. What an absolute delight to run into you here." I greet him with my most charming smile, and the whole table turns their attention to me.

His gaze narrows and flickers toward his friends for a fraction of a second before he graces me with a strained, yet polite, nod. Last time he saw me, his blade was on my throat, leaving that sliver of a cut his eyes flicker to now. This moment right here is so fucking precious, I can barely contain my elation.

"Apologies for disturbing you." I address him, then swipe my gaze over the group, noting the surprised redhead. "I just saw you from across the room and thought it would be very rude of me not to say hello."

There's a brief pause when I actually doubt my actions, a slight awkwardness creeping in.

"Indeed. I hope you're enjoying your day at the beach." He finally speaks, all but spilling venom through that smoky tone.

I cock my head an inch, trying to ignore how he attempts discretion as his gaze roams down my body like he's mapping every inch of it beneath the sheer beach dress. Then he slams those beautiful eyes back onto mine.

"Very much so, thank you. After all, life is short and all that." I don't even try to hide the sarcasm.

"For some, shorter than others." He raises an eyebrow, mature creases forming on his forehead.

A crooked smile is all I give him in response before I turn to the others. "Here I am, talking about rudeness, and I haven't even introduced myself."

He shifts uncomfortably, chair scraping across the wooden floor as he clears his throat.

"I'm Scarlet Brasa-Glass. Nice to meet you all." I ignore him.

The redhead lets out a sound somewhere between a scoff and a yelp, while the others manage to maintain their composure, though not without exchanging surprised looks before they greet me politely.

He's told them about me.

"Scarlet, I'm not gonna beat around the bush. I feel this crazy need to ask you of your intentions, like I'm a parent meeting my daughter's new boyfriend. Only, well . . . you know." Morrigan speaks, eyebrows raised in both amusement and raw need to protect those she loves.

I cannot contain my laughter at her honesty as her husband gently rubs his temple with his pointer finger, holding in whatever line would have probably undermined his wife in public. But there's a lovely hint of pride in the black pits of his eyes. I like him already.

"Jesus fuck," Carter whispers, showing just a hint of exasperation, and I find his reaction so damn amusing.

"None of the intentions you're implying. If I had any, I wouldn't have waited six months to do something, until dear Mr. Pierce randomly saw me on the street." I shrug, holding the smile.

"I'm sure you can understand why it's a bit difficult for us to believe that," Finnigan Hennessey says.

"Actions, or lack thereof, speak louder than words in this situation. Right?" I ask.

Someone grunts, but my attention is back on Carter, caught in that hypnotic gaze that reminds me of carnivorous plants. Utterly beautiful, yet undoubtedly deadly.

Slowly, I bend over as he holds himself perfectly still,

until the heat of his cheek radiates against mine and my lips are a breath away from his ear.

"I was a good girl for you all this time," I whisper for only him to hear, "and you hurt my feelings, killer-boy."

I rise, taking in his clenched jaw, one tensely raised brow, and the feral look in his eyes. My gaze flickers toward the terrace, and I take a small step back, turning to address the whole table.

"Oh, it looks like my food just arrived." I enthusiastically rub my palms together. "Apologies for interrupting your lunch. It was nice meeting you all. Mr. Pierce . . . maybe we'll meet again."

Without waiting for an answer, I spin on my heels and walk away, a little bounce of glee in my step. A mad giddiness runs rampant through my nerves, and I have to suppress a screech of adrenaline.

A soft gasp leaves my throat as a cool hand wraps around my right wrist. I stop next to a wooden column, shells and dried flower garlands falling in waves around it, as a distinct shadow looms over me. His body feathers against mine, and deep notes of bergamot, lavender, and something different . . . fresh, but spicy . . . envelop me. Drown me.

"Pepper . . ." I whisper to myself.

I shove down the little voice inside my head that begs me to lean into him again.

"Good girls don't make a scene like you just did, kitten." His growly whisper turns my nerves to bolts of lightning. "There's no doubt about it and zero choice for you—we will meet again."

And just as quickly as he appeared behind me, he's gone. His scent evaporates, but his heat already penetrated my soul.

I'm rather shocked at the amount of words he spoke to me.

I don't turn to look at him. I'd rather not humor him

or feed into his ego. Instead, I hold on to the electrifying sensation peppered over my skin and walk toward the terrace.

I may have a problem—his threats are becoming addictive. Enticingly so.

CHAPTER 9
Carter

All afternoon and most of the evening, I tried and failed to get Scarlet's breathy, annoyingly sexy voice out of my head. Her whisper haunts me now. An ethereal chant playing on repeat.

I was a good girl for you . . .

Did she have any fucking clue what those words would do to me? How they would stroke that cold part of me that wants to spread her open, tie her up, and make her beg to become the exact opposite—a very, very bad girl? Just. For. Me.

I must be going mad.

Because even now, as I stare into the distance, unfocused on my surroundings, I'm utterly distracted by her scent. I can't pry it out of my mind or my senses—roses and lemon. Sweet and aromatically sour.

The soft, fair-skinned woman with eyes the color of dark

chocolate isn't just getting under my skin. She's tearing her way through. And I'm not putting up enough resistance.

Even when I force my thoughts in a different direction, my mind reels back to the way she looked in that restaurant. Fresh out of the ocean, salty hair falling in beach waves around her shoulders, sun-kissed cheeks with a soft dusting of freckles, not an ounce of makeup covering the soft lines around her eyes.

And that dress...

That damn dress that allowed everyone to see her slight curves beneath it, her toned legs that kept fucking going for miles, and lean arms that would look perfect when stretched high above her head, tied at the wrists.

"Boss? Boss?"

Fuck. I return my focus to the room, the sound of the evening clientele at Midnight assaulting my ears all at once.

"Yes, Tina," I say as she stands by my table, waiting.

"It's all done. All cars have been checked, history cleaned, and a program was written to never record any similar data in the future."

"Yours too?"

"Every single person associated with The Sanctum, Midnight, The Fightclub, our army, security, everyone. That includes personal cars," Tina confirms.

"You've done great work on it. That was really fast."

"With all due respect, your whole team was afraid you were gonna cut us open if we didn't get this done asap. It was incentive for them all." She snickers.

"Not you?" I cock my head, observing her as she responds.

"I know better."

She does. Tina is the best out of my entire tech team. She knows that betrayal is the only thing that would make me take out anyone from my team. Otherwise, I wouldn't sacrifice any of the nine, considering their skills and vows of silence.

"Nothing has changed? No other cars broken into?"

"No. We're all good," she answers. "Is there anything else?"

"No, Tina, thank you. Feel free to go home. You've been working overtime."

"None of us were going to stop until all checks were done. Regardless of whether you gave the order or not."

This is what taking care of one's employees gets you— loyalty.

I may not be an emotional man, but I understand the effects of nurture. And we—The Sanctum—have been feeding these relationships for a decade now, carefully crafting the right entourage for our business.

"Some sleep will be welcome for sure. Have a good night, boss."

I nod my goodbye, then rise, swiping my gaze over the strategically placed tables, attempting to recognize faces through the dim light. But I can't fucking focus, and I'm damn thirsty.

Grabbing my empty glass, I head behind the bar. Encased in a metallic-gold, stylized eyelid, the realistic eyeball above the bar follows me around the room. Beneath the art-deco starburst of gold slats that surrounds it sits the only drink that can handle the job of distracting my brain—absinthe.

I prepare my gold-filigree-encrusted glass, pour the inviting green liquid inside, then set the perforated spoon above it with a sugar cube on top.

"Bring the water drip to my table, please," I tell the bartender.

"Of course, Mr. Pierce."

As I walk back to my table, a familiar face heads my way.

"Carter, my boy. I missed you!" Jonathan exclaims, those first three words pulling me back into memories that rarely make their way into my consciousness nowadays.

My father—his best friend—used to call me that as he looked at me with hidden emotions I couldn't quite place. There was warmth in those words, though—a staggering contrast from my mother's tone, the woman who I now know is the reason why Jonathan and my father's friendship phased out. Not that it surprised me. They stopped meeting for years. Dad focused on me, and his friend on his business.

Then one day, when my father used those same endearing words as his last, I saw Jonathan for the first time in years.

We didn't talk. Didn't even interact. He kept his distance, sitting in the waiting room of the hospital wing until I was done. Almost a year later, just before I was about to leave for my second year of university, he made contact, and we've kept a relationship ever since.

I think he speaks those words—*Carter, my boy*—as much for him as he does for me. He cared about my father, and somehow, I think they make him feel closer to him. I'm not familiar with regrets, but he hasn't shied away from telling me how many he has for his broken friendship. I never needed a father figure after mine's passing, but Jonathan Rees has naturally become one without me even noticing.

With a twinkle in his bright eyes, he waits for me to place my drink on the table so he can pull me into a full body hug.

Outside his husband, he only reserves this behavior for me. And he's the only person I allow to act this way toward me.

He takes a seat in one of the armchairs, and I take the one right next to him.

"Jonathan, how are you?" I ask, noting a bit more salt than pepper in his hair these days.

Not that it deters from his exquisitely distinguished look in his three-piece, light-gray suit. A large oval ruby set on a gold brooch pinned to his chest adds a touch of extravagance to the whole ensemble.

"It's been too long, my boy. But I'm good, keeping busy as always," he says.

"Three weeks, yes. How was your first holiday in—"

"Five years. It was just as you would expect—stressful. Much to Anthony's annoyance. It wasn't easy, keeping my mind off the business. I'm not used to it."

"But all is working well?"

"Minus some minor kinks. But you know how it is. Some things only you can do."

I nod in acknowledgment. Takes a specific skill set to get some jobs done.

"All well with you?" He nods toward my drink. "I mostly see you drinking absinthe when you have a stubborn problem to solve."

He has no fucking idea.

The bartender comes to the table with my water drip, and I set it up over the sugar cube as Jonathan orders his drink.

"Stubborn indeed. Nothing I can't handle." I lean back in my armchair, propping an ankle over my knee as I settle my hands onto the carved wooden ends of the armrests. "You might want to check your ranks, though."

"Explain."

"While you were gone, word got around that *The Ghost* wasn't home. The Granges wanted to invade your territory and take over," I say, relaying the rumor.

Only close friends and old allies know that Jonathan is *The Ghost*. There are plenty inside his business that have never seen his face. He prefers running things from the shadows and doesn't feed into any rumors. The moniker was given by people utterly desperate to figure out who the mysterious, high-value smuggler running half the docks and all shipment train lines in Queenscove is. The nickname stuck.

"Excuse me? Why didn't my men tell me about this?" He leans forward, a vein in his throat pulsing to the surface.

"Because we took them out before the intention reached your borders."

"You did?" He cocks his head, relaxing back in his armchair.

I nod in response, noting the last of the sugar dissolving into my absinthe. The wait is worth it, though, when I take the first sip, assimilating the burn into my throat.

"Thank you, Carter. I appreciate that."

"You know The Sanctum and I will always have your back," I assure him.

He smiles, and a similar warmth to the one I once saw in my father's eyes brims in his.

"I'm even more shocked that they thought it would be so easy to simply swoop in and claim my operation and my men as their own," he says, shaking his head at the absurdity.

And I agree. Jonathan's business was built well over two decades ago, with roots embedded deep enough in the underworld that even his death wouldn't pry them out. There are men behind the helm, ready to take over and do him justice if that scenario ever happens.

Even if the Granges invaded his headquarters, even if they managed to kill some of his men, it wouldn't be enough.

It's irrelevant now, since their army is disjointed and dispersed and the two Grange brothers running it are ten feet deep underground.

What's more important is how they knew the boss was out of town. That was internal information. The Granges didn't mobilize themselves all of a sudden. No. That was an operation on standby.

"You know what it means," I say before taking another healthy sip of my aromatic drink.

"That I have a mole to track and bury." He nods as the

bartender returns with his drink. "Now, tell me what it is you wanted to talk to me about."

We spend the better part of the next couple of hours discussing business. Cillian O'Rourke arrives about halfway through since this meeting happened at his request.

The business in question is the one the Holt family left behind—the control of the other half of the docks. Jonathan handles half, plus the very profitable train-line connections that spread like spiderwebs from Queenscove all over the continent, facilitating very profitable criminal operations for other people.

Old-man Holt used to own the other half of the docks, though his operation was nowhere near as well-oiled as Jonathan's. After a string of betrayals and strategic deaths in the last couple of years, the docks are now under Cillian's control. It was never his intention or desire to handle the operations, but they basically fell into his lap.

After months of battling with the impact of the previous ownership's loss, he reached a more peaceful stage. But in order to make this business thrive, he requires experience he doesn't have.

Two hours or so later, Cillian and Jonathan strike a deal—a silent partnership that benefits them both. Morrigan's brother gets experienced support, a few profitable clients transferred to him, and more importantly, *The Ghost's* endorsement.

"He seems like a good kid," Jonathan says as he watches Cillian leave Midnight.

"He's proven himself to us."

"To his sister too, I hear."

I nod in acknowledgment. Morrigan was an island inside her own family for so long. A pawn in her father's master plan, until she struck a deal with Vincent. We didn't know

Cillian was working in the background until the moment was just right, and he helped get her out and take down everyone involved. Their own parents included.

"Thank you for hearing him out and taking him on," I say to him.

"It's for my benefit too. I waited years to have a decent *neighbor*. Having the opportunity to groom him is an added bonus. I get to shape him to my liking. Plus, he sounds like a decent man, unlike his late father."

"I'm glad it worked out for you."

"Now it's time for me to go. I have a mole to hunt down." He rises, gently spreading his arms for me to hug him once more. "I'll see you soon, my boy. Good luck with your own *problem*."

I swallow a rumbling grunt as that last word brings forth the mental image I just about managed to bury in the last hour or so. I briefly wrap my arms around Jonathan. Such an awkward, unnatural interaction. I understand its significance at a social level, but I feel only absence in the hollowness beneath my ribs that probably houses one's soul. I do it for Jonathan either way.

As he heads toward the exit, a cramping tightness swells through my hands, heating its way up my arms. And just like that, Scarlet's dark eyes pierce through the back of my mind once again.

This is getting ridiculous.

No matter what I do, she still finds her way back in. This should have been a clean, cutthroat resolution to a problem that has dragged on far too long.

I make my way toward the back entrance, since even Midnight, my sanctuary away from home, doesn't seem to be able to fix me.

Five long steps later and the reinforced back door stares back at me. Only, my hand hovers mid-air in front of the keypad as a frozen breath lodges behind my sternum.

Apprehension cuts up my spine, excruciatingly slow as it crests over each vertebra. My gaze turns toward the silent disturbance glimmering under the dim light in the corner of my eye. Before I change direction, I pause, holding my breath to listen for motion as I count ten of my heartbeats. Nothing.

Spinning on my heels, I rush toward the office door and stop a pace away from the silver object that caught my eye. Ringing fills my ears as all scenarios rush through my mind, and I wonder if I'll be lucky enough for this to be a simple object that fell out of one of my staff's pockets.

Only, as I squat down and get a better view of the shiny, grooved cylinder, I realize that the reality is so much more dire; it's another fucking puzzle box. Not only is it in my speakeasy that requires a membership and password to get into, but it's also in a secure fucking area.

Right in front of my goddamn office!

This. Is. War.

On a sharp breath, I grab the offending object and slam my way into the office. Fire and brimstone course through my veins with a vengeance that threatens to demolish this building around me.

They were here . . . in my motherfucking space. My goddamn sanctuary.

The desks shake as I drop into the chair and turn toward all my screens, angrily punching keys to get the hallway cameras up.

"This can't be . . ." I whisper to myself, strain tugging between my brows as my fingers fly over the keyboard, bringing more and more cameras up from all around the speakeasy.

But the result repeats itself. Over and over.

Until the air refuses to find its way back into my lungs and the blood in my veins reaches a threatening temperature.

They're wiped. Every single motherfucking camera in this joint is wiped clean for today.

I want to ask myself how it's possible, because I cannot fucking fathom who would have the guts to pull something like this. To mess with The Sanctum in our own fucking house. But I know exactly how it was done. I just didn't think someone in this city who's not under my wing would be this good at coding. Because they had to dig deep into my network and bypass so many walls, time would have been a problem. Which means they didn't do it here.

Somehow, someone hacked into this network remotely, then broke in.

My heartbeats run rampant behind my ribs, so loud I hear them in my ears. My stomach hollows, and blinding pressure presses against my temples. None of these visceral sensations stops there. With gritted teeth and curling fists, I realize that what I'm feeling is *fury*. Blood-red fury rushing like violent river rapids. I've experienced this before, but never like this. Never so strong.

My first thought is *her*—Scarlet.

Who the fuck else would dare mess with me? With my Sanctum!

No one is stupid enough.

Or maybe you just want it to be her.

"Fuck the puzzle box." *I'm going after her.*

Grabbing my keys, I shove off the chair and rush straight out the office door. I'm about to walk into the parking lot when I realize the dark-haired kitten is clouding my judgment, and I'm already making mistakes. I spin on my heels, and with determined steps I'm urging to move calmly as I walk back into the bustling speakeasy, I signal a waitress to follow me as I head behind the bar toward the bartender on duty.

"Did you see a solo person here today?" I ask them.

"Several," the waitress answers.

"Yes," the bartender agrees.

"Any of them suspicious? Any of them disappeared out of your sight and went toward the back door?"

"I didn't notice anything," the bartender explains, "but there were a few occasions when I was busy with customers and wasn't able to watch the door."

Pushing back a sigh, I try to rationalize with myself that killing him would be pointless since I can't blame him for serving our customers and tending the bar.

I turn my attention to the waitress, noting how tense she is as she fumbles with her hands.

"I haven't seen anything either. But I'll ask Heather, the other waitress."

"What about a woman on her own?" I ask them both.

This time they exchange looks for a moment. Their expressions aren't of knowing, but slight confusion and a touch of curiosity.

"Only Mrs. Reinhardt," the bartender says, but I doubt the former beauty-queen heiress in her late fifties is who I'm looking for.

"I served a blonde woman. Long, luscious waves. She looked to be in her forties, maybe."

Scarlet could have been wearing a wig, but no way she looks to be in her forties. Late twenties, at most, with soft, glowing skin, far too perfect to the touch.

Christ's sake!

"Okay. Go through all memberships scanned in the last four hours. Pinpoint the solo orders you remember, and text me those names." We don't use actual payments here. Our customers simply scan their membership card, and the money gets pulled out of the card or bank account they have on file. This will come in handy. "Do your best to identify *all* of them." I turn to leave, throwing them a knowing look over my shoulder.

Their widening eyes suggest they understand the importance of this.

And it is so fucking important. Because if I find out that wretched minx had anything to do with this, sinking my teeth into her will be so much sweeter.

If it wasn't her . . . Well, that's an even bigger problem, because I have no idea who it could be.

CHAPTER 10
Carter

After the briefest detour at my house to change into something less constricting, I followed the young crescent moon to Scarlet's family's estate. Recklessness burns through my bones, urging me to burst in and demand satisfaction for the fucking troubles she caused, regardless of the consequences and who could witness or record it. Such unfamiliar, stupid recklessness.

Unlike anything I've ever felt.

But I silence it with logic as I finish my check for perimeter cameras. I can't go around the whole thing since they have so much land here. I should be okay, because surprisingly, they have no surveillance here.

Bit odd for such a large estate.

But it's okay—I brought my own.

With one last look through the birches that shelter this

side of the property from the quiet road, I grab onto the thick wisteria branches and scale the brick wall. Before jumping to the other side, I peek over, noting the utter stillness between the multitude of trees and bushes dotted all around the grounds. No people in sight. No obvious cameras, either.

I throw the hood of my black sweatshirt over my head and jump down. I land on my feet on the thick grass, the unopened puzzle heavy in the pocket of my sweatpants.

After checking the satellite map once again, I rush forward, my steps crunching over fresh grass, dead leaves, and small sticks as I head toward the smaller cottage on the property. I hope my instincts are right and that's the home Scarlet lives in.

As I near the location, I soften my steps and stick to the trees' shadows, keeping my senses alert for movement and CCTV or hidden trail cams.

My spine stiffens when splashes sound in the distance, intensifying the tension in my muscles, which has only grown since I left the speakeasy. Anticipation weaves through the taut fibers beneath my skin, and unfamiliar heat spills into my chest. Though, it has a strange effect—my lips twitch. Upward.

Simmer the fuck down.

But I can't. It takes conscious effort to stay put and not rush toward the swashing noise and the dim light flickering maybe thirty feet away. A large pond comes into view, thick vegetation dotted around, and sleeping water lilies float on its disturbed surface. And the source sweeps into view—a woman floats on her back, spreading her arms wide around her body as she settles.

There she is.

Still body carried by the water, she relaxes as the ripple slows around her, an ethereal image forcing lead through my legs until my feet freeze in place.

I'm closer now. Close enough to see the moonlight shimmering in the water droplets over her round cheek, slightly parted, full lips, and softly upturned nose. And the rest of her is hard to ignore. Because Miss Scarlet Brasa-Glass is stark naked.

The dim light of the flickering candle set on the shore throws an empyrean glow over her curves, sloping over the water. And I map each and every one of them, from her full, soft breasts peeking above the surface, down the slight roundness of her abdomen, over hip bones continuing into beautifully taut thighs, and all the way down to her toes. I map them all, etching them deep into my memory.

Too many seconds pass as I watch her. They stretch and turn into minutes, and between those growing moments, my feet move. Unconscious actions bring me closer to her, because she appears clearer before me.

Too clear.

Too wet.

Too . . . immersing.

I squeeze my fist until my short nails dig into my palm and pull me out of whatever this strange fixation is. The sting turns to pain, and only then does it actually work, my mind reeling back to my purpose. Just about.

I was hoping I would get here and catch her just as she returned home, with some sort of clear indication of her nefarious whereabouts. Some clue that it was she who broke into my establishment and left yet another puzzle box in my private space.

But judging by the empty wineglass sitting next to the large candle, the two fingers of liquid left in the bottle, and the crumbs on the plate next to it, Miss Scarlet has been here for a while. Either she drinks and eats excessively fast, or . . . she somehow anticipated I would come here, scale her boundary wall, and stalk her in the night.

I almost scoff at that last theory. Could she have really thought I would do this?

It's a dangerous question to ask myself, because it leads to another. One that holds an even more dire implication: did I honestly think she was the one behind these strange intrusions, or was I looking for a justifiable reason to come after her?

Such a dangerous, dangerous premise.

It implies that being a witness to a kill at my hands isn't reason enough to come after her. Deeper than that, it suggests I might have changed my mind about her demise.

The thought gets lost as her arms glide high above her head, a gentle slosh following as she slowly pushes the water toward her feet and her body slides forward.

Rising, all but her shoulder hidden beneath the surface, she grabs something off the shore. A small flame pops up a moment later, just before a thick waft of smoke streams out of her mouth. By the way her head falls back after taking another long puff, and the fact that she doesn't immediately exhale, I can bet it's not a cigarette she's smoking.

She's so relaxed, so . . . serene. Worry-free.

There's no way she thought I would come for her tonight, willingly risking being caught in this position. One does not await death by skinny dipping and smoking a joint.

I lean against a tree, crossing one leg over the other, and run through all the reasons why I should be moving, not settling in. My fingers itch on my phone, and I bring it up, triggering the camera. I don't dare think twice as I slide over to video and press the big red button that sends an exhilarating feeling through my bones.

Three minutes pass. Then twelve. Twenty-three.

She floats. She swims. She throws her head back. Water drips over her lips. In the crook of her neck. Over the slopes of her breasts. Drops catch on the tips of her nipples. Down the slight swell of her belly and into the apex between her thighs that disappears just beneath the surface.

The joint is long finished, but the dim fog that has gathered over the surface of the pond looks like lingering smoke.

I've closed more of the distance between us, camera still aimed at this . . . creature. This calm, blissful creature made of velvet and sin.

Scarlet sinks beneath the ripple, then emerges two moments later toward the shore, moving at a slow, constant pace, inch by enthralling inch. She tips her head back gently, squeezing the water out of her long hair that looks black in this absent light. She lets it fall on the curve of her back, the tips dripping water onto the slope of her ass before she dips down and blows out the candle.

She grabs the glass and plate in one hand, then tips the wine bottle back and drinks the last few milliliters with the other. Just like nobody's watching . . .

One corner of my lips curves at the ungracious gesture. She makes it look sexy as hell. Especially in her sultry nakedness with her creamy, unmarked skin on full display. How perfect she would look against my heavily tattooed complexion.

She walks toward the old stone cottage, and I match her steps, keeping to the shadows of the trees. Low garden lights hidden within the flower beds dimly illuminate her path, and one antique outdoor lamp lights up her front door. She presses the handle, looking behind her for a moment before she steps inside and closes the door. Then the porch light goes off.

She doesn't notice me. Not in this darkness.

It pleases me, but it angers me, too. What if someone else was watching her? What if others have in the past?

I circle the house at a slow pace, looking for cameras that could catch me in the act. Once again, there are none.

What I do note are the dim lights turning on inside, window by window brightening as she walks through her house, stopping behind one that's frosted—the bathroom. I stand here, listening through the sounds of the crickets, until the toilet flushes and the shower runs.

My need to gather evidence justifies my next move. Inside this house, I could find an indication that she is the person who broke into my car. My bar. Or maybe at least some clues as to who Scarlet Brasa-Glass is, this mystery woman with no social-media presence and almost no trace online.

I use this reasoning as I head back to a dark window I noticed was slightly cracked. I keep using it as I open it and slowly lift myself until I can climb through. I use it again when my steps guide me through this dark room, toward a cracked door, and into the light.

The shower runs in the distance, and I walk into the main hallway of the house. I called it a cottage, but it's definitely bigger than that.

A disabled alarm blinks slowly by the front door, and I memorize the model for later, but that's not the first thing I notice in her space; it's the display tables. Old and new. High and low, sturdy and skinny, filled neatly with *everything*. Art in all of its forms. Sculptures. Gold and silver knick-knacks. And bones. So many bones. Anything from animal skulls to a human spine displayed in an artistic curve, the ends of each vertebra dipped in a gold metal.

What have I walked into?

As I peek into a couple of the rooms, I see even more interesting things—fossils. Out of all the things I thought I would find . . . none of these were on my list. And these are not just any fossils, but Mesozoic pieces displayed under paintings that look too expensive to be in the house of a *normal* woman. And I have yet to figure out what this one does for a living.

Judging by my surroundings, definitely not a mundane nine-to-five.

I walk deeper into the house, listening as the shower sounds shift with movement—she stepped in. I shouldn't, but I take it as an invitation to observe.

The door to the bathroom is already half open, steam rolling in gentle waves through the wide gap. I close the distance until I fill that space and lay my eyes on her once again, bathed in the dimmed wall light. Her head is under the spray, hands running slowly through her hair, creamy skin blurred by the steamed-up glass.

I stopped filming after she entered the house, but I can't help myself now. Not when she's so close. So oblivious to this predicament. I turn on the phone's camera once again, aiming it at her.

Something stirs within me as I watch her run her hands over the curves of her body as her head delicately falls back. A cruel tremor quakes from my chest straight down to my cock. My gaze widens, my brain having trouble finding the logic between my duty and physical reaction.

This shouldn't be happening. It can't keep happening.

This woman is black magic, crawling under my skin when I don't know a goddamn thing about her. When I'm supposed to fucking end her.

With gritted teeth, I take one step further into her space and reach into my belt holster for my favorite knife—four inches long, thin blade. I shift closer, eyes trained on her as she turns her back to me.

My hand flexes around the knife's hilt on the same rhythm as hers runs through her hair. This synchronization bothers me too . . . Hearts thrumming on the same beat.

And hers must stop.

Scarlet must die.

This was always the plan. Since the moment I lost her in that alley too many months ago.

I don't care if she's the person behind the puzzle boxes.

I don't care if I have many more questions that only she can answer now that I've seen the contents of her house.

I don't care if one side of my brain is telling me she's important somehow.

I have to kill her. If I don't, I fear she'll grow roots inside of me. It's already started, and I must sever them now. Only, a sharp, raking feeling tears down my throat, clawing through my chest until my lungs are shredded and my heart is caught in a tight, choking grip. Squeezing. Hard. My hands clench painfully around the phone and knife. My windpipe tightens as I take one step further, and the realization of what these feelings are slams through me—hesitation.

Not indecision, not avoidance, like what I've been doing so far, but pure hesitation. The type that brings doubt and ridiculous morality into play. The one that feeds curiosity and demands more.

Fuck.

Duty doesn't prevail. Not now, as I watch her wash herself, oblivious to my presence in her private space. She's so vulnerable. I could simply end her. Right here, right now.

I could do so many things to her.

Raw. Filthy. Utterly satisfying things.

Breaths rake out of me as I slide my knife into the holster, poking at my shattered resolve. I try to rationalize with myself and stop my retreat by ending the video and putting my phone away.

Reaching into my pocket, I pull out the cylindrical puzzle, keeping one eye on that shower and the woman inside it as I begin rotating the metal elements. I solved some of it as I was changing at home; maybe I'll get the rest done while she's washing herself.

Three more turns—her hands brush in circles over her breasts.

Two clicks—they run over her waist and belly.

Four rotations—her hand disappears between her legs as she widens them, rubbing between.

My cock stirs. As my fingers fly over the puzzle, I can only hope the clicks mean progress, not a trap.

Her movements are mechanical at first. Then they slow.

My hands still when the puzzle clicks open as a moan escapes Scarlet's mouth. I can't bring myself to look down at the contents, not when the woman takes her time between her legs.

But she moves on too suddenly, washing down her legs until she reaches her feet, and I'm slightly disappointed.

I let out a quiet breath that was painfully stuck in my lungs, then look at the solved puzzle to find a small roll of parchment. Unrolling it, I frown at what I find—a QR code and some senseless words.

No.

Not senseless at all.

A riddle.

Born in fire,
Fed by breath,
Warms in winter,
Dies a dark, slow death.

What the fuck?

I put away the box and pull out my phone to scan the QR code. A website pops up, nothing on it but one empty box with "password" written above it. I have to solve that damn riddle.

Returning my gaze to Scarlet, I run those words through my head. Fire. Breath—air. Warms in winter—actual campfire? Dies slow . . . Fire. Air blowing on it. Keeps you warm? Fizzles slow . . .

Ember?

I type in the word and when the website opens up, my spine snaps straight. Cocking my head, I scroll through what appear to be photos taken this evening in the speakeasy. Not just any photos, but of me, Jonathan, and Cillian during the business meeting.

This is not good. Not fucking good at all.

What are the chances this has been orchestrated by Scarlet? What interest would she have in the business deal I facilitated?

Sliding the phone into my pocket, I look up at the blurred version of the woman who's taking up too much real estate in my brain and reluctantly step back. Further and further, passing through the door once more, wondering just when the purpose I've been chasing for so many months has turned from murder for my own protection to stubborn curiosity. Not deep down at all, I know that's what brought me here tonight. Nothing else. Definitely not the desire to kill her.

Because I also brought a fucking surveillance camera with me. I knew my knife wouldn't take her life tonight. But I had to pretend. I had to fucking try to fool myself.

Moving fast, I find the master bedroom and walk past a few clothes scattered on the floor by an antique wardrobe that catches my eye. Other garments are thrown over its cracked-open door, and a bra hangs by its strap on the corner. Her four-poster wooden bed is unmade, and a pair of deep-red lace panties are casually thrown at the foot. This is definitely her bedroom.

I'm relieved to see a smoke detector fitted on the ceiling, similar enough to the one in my pocket, which doubles as a camera. Grabbing the chair from the vanity table, I climb up and make quick work of disconnecting the device before replacing it with mine. I check the feed, confirming it's all working, then climb down and put the chair back in its place in front of the vanity.

Yet another spot in this house that looks . . . interesting.

Right at the back, on a small ledge under the mirror, is a row of antique-looking vials. They've been tucked behind the expected makeup, brushes, and other beauty stuff. While the sizes vary from short and round to tall and thin, they all have one thing in common—the tiniest bit of liquid at the bottom.

Various oddities are dotted between the vials, like what looks like a dinosaur claw, a small painted bowl with tiny bones in it, and a white taxidermy mouse with a flower in his paw that looks almost . . . cute.

Stepping back, I shake my head, suppressing the need to look around for more clues about this woman.

The shower stops. The glass door swings open with a slight creak, and I can't trust myself to stay.

Not because I'll kill her, but because I'll find too many hedonistic ways to break her.

CHAPTER 11
Carter

The cold spray of the shower hits like frigid hale, but I have to put out this heat that has filled me with such fiery vengeance. I drove like a madman back home, speeding with all the windows down, hoping that the gushes of air would do the job.

They didn't.

This shower is not doing a better job.

Maybe . . .

Oh no, that's a bad fucking idea.

But maybe . . .

I could fight fire with fire.

I shake my head at this fucking idea, because I know it's both good and terrible. It could backfire. It could become addicting.

Stepping out of the spray, I grab my phone and prop it on

the four-foot-high divider wall before I walk back in. I'm not a fan of glass cages, so I had to have an open shower, with only this partial wall dividing it from the rest of the bathroom.

I open the spy-cam app, pulse speeding as I wait for Scarlet's bedroom to pop on screen. The image slams into my chest like a wild blaze, shooting straight to my cock. It's the only part of me that's moving. Throbbing. I refuse to move, especially blink.

Because this sinful woman is spread bare in the middle of her bed, fingers sunk deep inside her pussy, back arched, and features strained with euphoria.

And I have a front-row seat to this show.

"That's it, kitten, fuck that pussy raw."

I turn the volume up, and my bathroom fills with her moans and soft cries. She sounds disheveled and desperate, begging for more.

For deeper gratification. For that stretch that brings a taste of pain.

I fist my cock, bracing myself against the wall as I watch her, pumping myself until my movements turn harsh. Borderline desperate. I tighten my grip around the piercings, hissing through satisfying pain, my knees threatening to buckle with the onslaught of pleasure. Harder and faster, I run my hand over my length, eyes trained on the woman who is not so slowly turning my life upside down.

"Aah, fuck!" she curses, reaching to the side with her free hand.

My attention is stuck on the arc of her curves—the gentle swells of her breasts, the sinuous lines of her luscious thighs, and the tantalizing glimpse of her pussy, partially hidden beneath the movement of her hand.

I flinch as my phone vibrates loudly on the tiles, and a text pops up at the top of my screen.

Electric heat blooms behind my ribs, and I lean in to make sure it's definitely Scarlet's name there. I swipe down enough for the reply box to show up without opening the app. I don't want to miss a whimper or a squirm.

Be honest, killer-boy, how many times a day do you think of me?

A smirk pulls at the corner of my mouth. I don't have to imagine her thinking of me as she tries to make herself come. I get to witness it.

More than I should.

I didn't have to be that damn honest.

The message disappears off my screen and lights up hers. She scrambles for her phone, fingers still inside her aching pussy, the pad of her palm bearing down on her clit as she reads the text. Her heavy mewl lands right on the tip of my cock, precum coating it. I rub it over my length, imagining her spit coating every inch of me.

Another text flashes on my screen, and once again, I swipe on it.

Were you thinking of me tonight?

My dick has definitely taken over, because there's no way my brain thinks the next word is a good idea.

Yes.

Her pleasure-tainted cries imprint on my walls, filling the air around me and sinking into my lungs, my mind, my nerves. My very fucking soul demands more of them.

She types with one hand, and another text pops up.

Was I on my knees or on top?

Jesus, she's direct.
I like it.

On your back. Legs spread wide. My knife to your throat. Your blood running down my blade and between your tits. A thin thread down your belly...

This honesty can get me in fucking trouble. Only, on the feed on my phone, I don't see panic. No disgust. No fear. Unhinged desires painted in pleasure and elation are all I see on her stunning face.

What have I stumbled into? How is this woman real?

Most would fear my honest words. Would fucking run screaming. Yet there is Scarlet...smiling as she types the next text. She slows the thrust of her fingers, but the movements harden. Her rhythm grows passionate, finding those threads that bring true pleasure rather than frantic, desperate pleasure.

Down my belly...between the soft, wet seam of my pussy. Is that what you imagine, with your cock in your hand, late in the night? Does thinking of killing me make you hard, killer-boy?

I reply before I even finish reading it, pumping my cock harder, flicking the head with a tighter squeeze.

You're taking liberties...such a greedy little slut, aren't you? The thought of punishing you makes me hard, kitten.

"*Aaah* . . ." she moans so loud I'm compelled to join her, throwing my head back as my release inches much closer.

> Tell me more of this punishment.

> I would strip you naked. Sit you on my thigh, your side to my front, your ass hanging out. Your flimsy throat would be in my hand so I could feel your screams vibrate through my skin as I spanked you silly.

> Like a good little whore, you would beg me to turn your pain to pleasure as your slutty little pussy drenches my leg, grinding to chase that release that I wouldn't allow to come. I would slap your ass until thin threads of blood coat your creamy skin in crimson spiderwebs.

It's official. I am going mad.

I could have said anything else. Like cut her fucking throat. Torture her. At least maybe whip her. Use any other instrument that would keep me at arm's length from the reckless woman.

I could have.

But I wouldn't have dared. Because the moment I get my hands on her, I want to do anything in my power to feel every single thing she feels. Her pleasure, her pain, her desperation. All of it. I couldn't use an instrument and deny my own pleasure. My satisfaction.

"*Oh god, yes!*" she cries on a wanton moan, bending her legs for better access.

She rubs that bundle of nerves with the pad of her palm, finger-fucking her pussy in punishment, demanding the rapture-divining cliff to inch closer.

Is that a promise, killer-boy?

You'd like that, wouldn't you? Is your messy little cunt dripping thinking of all the pleasure I could drown you in?

Yes. Oh god, yesss!

The reply comes so quickly, I almost come on the fucking spot.

Are you filling your pussy with your fingers, imagining my fat cock pumping it full of cum?

"Oh god, oh god! Oh . . . that filthy, filthy mouth. Fuuuck!" she cries out as she reads the text.

I've created a monster. Two, maybe . . . because I struggle to recognize myself. I'm a creature of logic, but right now, I'm built of lust alone.

Please...

I read that text two dozen times at least. Over and over. Until my cock aches to burst, imagining Scarlet beneath me, begging me to let her come all over me. Begging for every inch. For my cock to stretch her, my cum to fill her perfect little cunt.

Come.

She reads my command, and the phone slides out of her hand as she braces herself against the headboard. Eyes squeezed shut, mouth wide, and head thrown back, she cries out as the orgasm hits her head-on.

Bliss coats her pleasure-laced screams as she writhes on her bed, legs shaking uncontrollably.

Then she screams *my name*.

My goddamn name.

"Jesus Christ, woman!" My balls draw up, and my load shoots out in heavy, explosive streams all over the fucking wall as Scarlet's voice echoes through my bathroom, crying out my name in pure ecstasy.

The threads of pleasure run deep, weaving around my goddamn soul as I step backward until my shoulder blades hit the cold wall.

This is a line I shouldn't have crossed. There's no coming back from this.

But I fucking needed this.

And I want so much more.

I was wrong before I opened the feed to her camera. This won't become addicting. Because it already is.

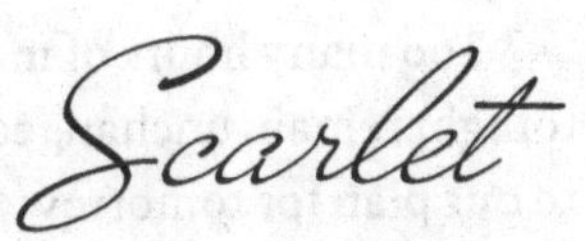

I WOKE UP WITH AN almost painful smile on my face this morning. The music was on, breakfast tasted amazing, and *all* the birds seemed to be singing in the garden. The day looked fucking promising.

If I didn't already have plans, I would have been at Carter's door after I woke up, confronting him about all the texts from last night. I would have made him face me rather than hide behind a screen. Maybe I would have jumped him and ground against his beautifully carved body hiding underneath those tailored three-piece suits.

No maybe; I would have *definitely* jumped him.

Maybe put a knife to his throat for daring to try to fucking kill me.

But that particular pleasure will have to wait.

Today is mostly a surveillance day. The primary focus is my next target. Dad and I have been on this guy for weeks now, and our window is opening tomorrow night. It's a bit of a different job than what we're used to, and not because our target will be at home. That just makes it so much more exciting. I love a good challenge that gets the adrenaline pumping and the blood pressure spiking.

Everything is organized, and there's no more planning to be done. Only surveillance of the man to ensure no changes to the plan are necessary.

I've been at it for hours, constantly carrying my laptop around. On the sofa. On the deck. While lifting weights in my spare bedroom. On the treadmill. In the natural pool out in the garden.

Too many hours of making sure his patterns and plan for tonight remain unchanged, and there won't be any disruption to our plan for tomorrow night.

But even with all the side activities I've been doing, I'm going fucking stir-crazy. As much as I enjoy this part of the job, I'm restless today. I can't stop thinking about a different plan I have, which has nothing to do with this heist. That prospect brings tingles right between my damn legs.

Until then, though . . . I need a break.

From the tray next to the laptop I perched on the banks of the pond's deep end, I grab a ready-rolled joint and light it up. Taking a deep, satisfying drag, I push away from the shore and float on my back.

The gentle ripple at the surface tickles my ears, and I let it carry me toward the middle of the natural pool. I close my eyes and sink into the taste of serenity the weed brings. There's nothing like it. Especially on days like this, when my limbs are itching, I can't sit still, and my mind runs a hundred miles per minute.

Weed was another of Dad's tips when my state of mind and the rambling voices in my head drove me to rashness. I remember that day vividly. It still makes me snort. It wasn't a surprise to me that my father was pretty open about anything on the other side of the law, though recreational weed is legal now.

The family business—stealing, heists, selling contraband—is something my brother and I were introduced to early on, once Dad felt we were mature enough to understand the implications and the responsibility we had to keeping our secret. Later on, he helped me with my problems . . . managing my anger, and how and where to focus all that aggression. Yet, being introduced to weed by my own father was more shocking than the stealing or killing. His calmness in high-stress situations suddenly made sense, though.

Joints aren't usually my go-to. I prefer gummies or cheese puffs. But I like a good smoke outside, where the scent doesn't stick to me, or before I take a shower. Mother would probably pop a fucking blood vessel if she knew.

I chuckle deeply at that thought, choking on smoke on the way out.

That woman hasn't graced my doorstep in a couple of years, thank fuck. To be fair, I didn't tell her I moved here, so who knows, maybe she has tried.

I flinch just as I exhale a long plume of smoke, my phone vibrating on the tray. Dropping my legs beneath the surface,

I swim toward the shore, but frown when I see that it's an unknown number calling me. I let it ring.

Once.

Twice.

Three times.

Cocking my head, I take another long drag from the spliff and watch the call end. Last time an unknown caller flashed on my screen, it was my soon-to-be ex and I ended up shattering my phone. I don't have a good feeling about this.

I stub the joint on the ashtray and continue staring at my phone like it's about to grow legs and jump at me. Then it kind of does, vibrating again and sending a tremor all through my flesh as that "unknown number" lights up my screen.

"Fuck it." I answer the call and pop it on speaker.

Only, I don't say a word, waiting to see what awaits on the other line.

A few seconds pass before I hear a long sigh.

"I know you're there."

Motherfucking Ariana. How fucking dare she call me.

"Then speak," I say.

"Look, I know what went on between us is unforgivable, okay? I know. And I'm sorry it happened as it did, and it ruined our friendship."

"You better hurry up this pathetic speech, babe. I have shit to do."

"I'm not gonna pretend I'm sorry for what I did, though. He and I are meant to be together, and I can't apologize for going for what I know is mine."

The fucking gall she has!

"But no matter what," Ariana continues, *"I still care about you."*

I scoff so hard I think I spit on my phone.

"Jesus Christ, what do you want? You're not fucking

fooling me with false declarations."

"Fine. Give him what he wants, Scarlet."

"Oh, spare me. I can't believe the bastard sent his girlfriend to collect for him."

She sighs before she continues. *"I'm the last resort before he comes at you. He's changing, Scar, and I don't want you to be in the crossfire. And he and I . . . we'll never be able to marry if he's legally tied to you."*

Marriage? What the actual fuck.

"First of all, don't ever dare to call me by my fucking nickname. You don't deserve it. Second of all—let him fucking come. What's he gonna do? Torture me to get his way?" I laugh. "We both know that's not gonna work on me. And threatening my fucking parents with violence is just plain disrespectful."

"That's not why I'm calling, Scarlet. I want to warn you. He has something on you . . . leverage."

Oh, give me a break.

"Fuck him and his leverage! We all have goddamn leverage on each other. Did he suddenly forget what he does for a living? I certainly didn't. He's not getting shit from me. He kissed my generosity goodbye the moment his lips touched yours. Now leave me the fuck alone, or I swear to God, when I'm done with him, I won't need a divorce anymore and you'll have to find someone else's husband to fuck."

I hang up, slamming my phone face down on the tray. Took some self-control not to throw that thing into the nearest tree and smash it to bits. Again.

"It was a good fucking day, and then they go and ruin it," I scream at myself as I get out of the pond, grab my stuff, and storm inside the house.

I'm throwing everything as I walk to my bedroom, struggling to forget about that wretched word seeping like tar through my thoughts—*leverage*.

There's no way he has something that can be proven. That can stick against me.

No fucking way.

"Ughh goddamn it!" I grab the closest thing to me and smash it against the wall in one swift move. It crashes and breaks into pieces that scatter all over the floor.

Shit, I liked that flamingo lamp . . .

I think it's time to cheer myself up. And I have just the solution.

CHAPTER 12
Carter

onathan's office in the back of his and his husband's antique shop has always been an oddly comforting place for me. Being surrounded by gold-framed old paintings, antiques, and books weathered by time gives me a deep sense of calm. Peace.

Not now, though. Not after watching the camera feed from Scarlet's bedroom earlier today. I'm biting the inside of my lip, I can't stop tapping my foot, and I'm itching to get out of here to find out what got her so angry.

This flip in attitude holds my thoughts hostage from my current environment. And it's been happening all day. The moment I opened my eyes, when the sun was still breaching the horizon, I picked up my phone to see what she was doing. I watched her sleep, sprawled right in the middle of the bed like she was taking advantage of every free inch the mattress had to offer.

While brushing my teeth, I still watched her. While I worked out in my gym. While taking my morning shower I used for much more than washing. Once again, with my hand firmly wrapped around my cock.

I couldn't. Fucking. Stop.

Then I powered on my system and opened her camera feed there. Not on one of the side screens, but dead center in front of me. Thirty-five inches of Scarlet.

She woke up like the sun rose only for her. Throwing the covers off, she revealed her naked body to me, save for a delicate scrap of fabric that covered the most intimate part of her. She turned on music via the speaker by the bed, and then the madwoman danced.

And I stopped working.

It was a spell.

Dark magic laced with creamy skin and the hypnotizing mystery of a woman. She was a kaleidoscope of color splashed all over my screen. I *had to* keep watching. It felt like a unicorn experience, one I hoped wouldn't be unique, but I couldn't blink in case its beauty never again graced my gaze.

Hair tied in two messy buns at the top of her head, she danced like the world was hers. She threw on some casual clothes, several times bumping, maybe a tad too hard, against the wood frame of her bed. It didn't seem to faze her or slow her down.

She was in and out of the feed throughout the day, cheerful and bright.

Until later on, when she rolled through like a fiery storm with thunderous eyes and strained muscles, throwing everything in her sight. She changed into plain black, tightening the buns at the top of her head before she disappeared. Too much time has passed since, and I can't fucking stop thinking about it all. About her.

I do have to admit . . . she's fucking beautiful when she bleeds fury. That visceral sentiment simply belongs on her features, in those dark eyes.

"You are very focused on that screen, my boy." Sitting in his leather chair at the other side of his desk, Jonathan startles me out of my train of thought. "More business distracting you?"

A scoff huffs from the seat next to me. "If business has dark hair and a pretty smile."

My head whips to Maddox in a heartbeat. Outing me to Jonathan isn't what sparks my anger. His comment about Scarlet's pretty smile does. He has no fucking business noticing her. I glower but keep my mouth shut.

"Oh, goody! Has it finally happened? A woman caught the infamous Carver's attention?" Jonathan sounds like a fucking schoolgirl excited for new gossip.

With one deep, slow breath, I focus on the man. "You're sure you have no thoughts on who could have wanted to watch us in Midnight? Considering the little *breach* you had?"

Jonathan cocks his head and narrows his eyes on me, stretching the silence for too many seconds. "The traitor has been disposed of, and he was swiftly joined by the very few men who shared his views. My little birds have been quiet since, and I haven't heard of any others who shared their views. I'm not saying there couldn't be more, but I'm inclined to believe that whoever took those photos of us in your establishment didn't come from my organization."

They could have come from ours.

The thought has been running wild through my mind. Do we have a traitor in our midst? Is someone on the inside playing us? And if so . . . with what purpose?

"I wonder if this was about Cillian," Maddox says. "He's

new in the business too. And he's no longer skirting on the border of the underworld. One foot stands firm in it."

I already ran through that scenario, and every exercise of logic I've done has ended in irrational answers. The conclusions make no sense.

And when an equation ends in a false value, the only rational explanation is that one of the variables is incorrect. Something isn't what it seems, and it's unacceptable that I haven't figured out what.

"Doesn't that make the photographer's timing surprisingly lucky?" Jonathan partially mirrors my thoughts.

I nod. "Nothing about this makes sense."

"The bottom line is that I'm not worried about this. I know my reaction and opinion matter to you. All of you. I appreciate you coming in person to discuss this issue. And I'm not worried about my privacy. Yes, I keep my identity as close as I can, but I'm more of a recluse than someone who demands anonymity. So, if they know the infamous Ghost is Jonathan Rees, fuck 'em." He shrugs and leans forward to grab the bottle of wine from the side of the desk so that he can pour himself another small glass.

I'm slightly uneasy. He and I may be close, but a threat to his business at my fault would be a direct affront. It could damage not just our personal connection, but the relationship between The Sanctum and The Ghost that we've been feeding and nurturing for a decade.

His reaction confuses me. Maybe I was wrong. Maybe it's not his business that comes first when it comes to him and me.

It drives my thoughts to dangerous territories. Am I putting too much stock in the importance of businesses and reputations rather than nurturing personal affairs? I've always seen personal connections as a byproduct of business dealings.

A necessity. Sometimes an advantage. But never a benefit.

Have I been cultivating deeper *friendships* without even realizing?

Would I benefit more from something even deeper than that?

I nod at him, unsure of it all. "As soon as I know more, I'll let you know."

He smiles, leaning back in his chair once again. "I know you will, Carter. You'll solve this mystery too, as you always do."

My phone vibrates in my jacket pocket, and I curse the interruption. But when I look at the screen, I see fucking fire and brimstone in my wake and almost knock the chair over when I rise.

"Apologies, but I have to cut this short."

"Carter, wha—"

"I have to go." I spin on my heels without even giving Jonathan a proper goodbye.

"Pierce! You can't keep doing that—shutting us out. What the fuck happened?" Maddox says.

I only half turn, but it's enough to see them both over my shoulder. "Someone broke into my house."

Maddox frowns, crossing his arms over his expansive chest, but Jonathan raises a curious eyebrow.

"It seems to me that there's one common denominator in these strange happenings," Jonathan says calmly.

I already know what his next word will be.

"You."

* * *

If I could fly through Queenscove's traffic, I would, but as it stands, I'm stuck at a red light. Less than a mile from my house. It takes a lot of self-control to stay put and not abandon my car in the middle of this damn boulevard.

If it wasn't for the motion sensors I kept separate from the main security system, I wouldn't have known of the break-in. I've cycled through every single camera I have in and around my house, and every single fucking one shows static.

Fucking static!

I'm done wondering who the hell has the skills for this, because I don't care anymore. I'm simply wondering who in their ever-loving mind has the audacity to break into *my* house.

My fucking house!

Muscles tighten around my bones, searing frost crystalizing in my veins as all those thoughts threaten to overwhelm me.

I am the Carver, and I swear to all the gods they're gonna end up praying to, I will make them pay in pounds of skin, bone, and muscle. Slice by motherfucking slice.

The light turns green, and I'm finally close enough to the start of the queue that I can pass through and get home. Three turns later and I'm flying through the wrought iron gates onto the cobbled drive. With a screech, the car stops in front of the stone steps nestled between the old trees and ancient graves rising from the thick grass—the former St. George's Church.

I bought this fourteenth-century stone building a few years ago and converted it into a house after it was left unused for half a decade. Not enough believers in this city for all the churches we have. I jumped on the opportunity right away. It felt like the ultimate fuck-you to my religious-fanatic mother who has sacrificed everything for her Christian god.

I rush up the steps and press the handle to the heavy metal-reinforced wooden door, but it won't budge. Maybe they got in through the side door. After quickly unlocking it, I burst inside the large entry foyer, gun drawn and aimed at my surroundings as I pass through the open-space main living area, the former church nave. I did save a couple of pews and used them for decor on the sides, in front of the floor-to-ceiling bookcases covering every single wall that doesn't contain a window.

There's no noise, no movement.

My gaze travels halfway up the bookcases, where the warm wooden balcony surrounds the entire open space, its footprint curving like the soft waves of the sea you can see from the East windows. There is no soul in sight.

I make quick work of going through the expansive space, checking behind every couch, behind the kitchen island, then in the former transepts that are now the bathroom, storage space, laundry room, and office.

My bedroom is the last place I check. Up three steps, which are bowed in the middle by the thousands of feet they have met, right where the chancel and its altar used to be. A beautiful sacrilege to its former god. It's empty here too.

The whole house is empty.

Going into the office, I power on my system, which always shows the cameras first, and frown when I see that they're back online. Whoever did this turned them back on.

Gun back in my holster, I stand in the middle of the room, eyes searching every nook and cranny. Nothing's amiss, so I move on to the few files and paperwork I have here.

I repeat this in the living area.

Then in all the other spaces, just to find absolutely nothing changed or missing. Even my invaluable Stradivarius violin sits untouched on its stand next to the old organ.

The last place to check is the bedroom. Against the wall to the right of the door I currently have my back to, on slim, black metal legs, sits a display counter—a shallow enclosure encased in UV-treated glass—and I tentatively step toward it.

With a deepening pit in my stomach, I dare gaze inside

it, and my heart threatens to stall in my chest. Because right there, inside that humidity-controlled environment, sits another goddamn puzzle box.

But that's not the main problem, which is that it sits *instead* of something else.

Something precious.

Something that was *mine*.

They stole from me. Whoever the hell this person is . . . they fucking stole from me.

Not just anything, but one of eighteen third-edition copies of La Commedia by Dante Alighieri from 1472. Seventeen are known to exist. My copy, obtained by the previous owner through various nefarious activities and at least three murders, is not recorded anywhere but in the initial printing records. It reached me through pure luck, after its owner met his demise at my hands. It sat beautifully displayed in my bedroom for three fucking years.

Until now.

I grab the puzzle and start twisting, pacing through the bedroom for the better part of half an hour, turning and pulling at the small metal protrusions emerging from the metal pyramid. The small carved symbols that cover its surface must mean something, but none of the languages I'm aware of use that alphabet. Eventually, the offending object opens for me.

There's no riddle here this time. Only one loosely rolled parchment, a website link written on it. I sit down at the edge of my bed and type the link on my phone, squeezing the device too tightly in my hand.

The result opens up in full screen on my phone, and I swallow dryly. It's me inside Metamorphosis. A close-up as I sit at the bar, observing the stage.

The photo was taken mere days ago, when I couldn't

bring myself to do anything but watch others. And even then, something about it felt off.

Jonathan was right—this isn't about him or Cillian.

It may be wishful thinking, but all my instincts point to Scarlet.

Maybe I'm wrong, but I'm not taking the chance anymore.

Before I leave, I check the camera feed from her bedroom. I find her once again filled with wondrous joy, dancing inside her house as she changes her clothes and bounces around the place.

Interesting time to change.

I waste no time walking into the early night. I climb inside the car within thirty seconds, and I'm through the gate before the minute strikes.

Driving like the asphalt's burning my tires, I weave through traffic, not caring if the side of the road I'm on is right or not. Ignoring speed limits and traffic signs, I drive with one objective in sight.

I don't want revenge, nor retribution. I want punishment.

After she confesses, of course.

I'm done pretending I still want to kill her. I don't. Not even a fucking little bit.

There are so many other filthy things I have in mind. None of them consensual. None of them hold an ounce of human decency. But if she's the culprit, she deserves them all.

I drive closer and closer to her house, planning every single detail of our encounter. Counting the ways I'll make the kitten beg me to either kill her or make her come. Maybe both. Maybe at the same time.

My phone startles me out of my fantasies. Maddox's name flashes on the screen, and I answer.

"I'm—"

"*You need to get to Midnight right now.*" The urgency mixed with fury in his tone furrows my brows.

"I'm in the middle of something. Is it—"

"Fucking urgent, Pierce. One of our girls was just delivered almost dead at our front door. With a message."

What the fuck?

The timing is goddamn ridiculous. I squeeze the steering wheel hard enough that pain radiates through my bones. I'm so close that I can see Scarlet's estate up ahead. So close to solving this fucking mystery.

But I sigh and turn the car around with a deafening screech.

"I'm on my way."

CHAPTER 13
Carter

One thin crimson line traces the dips and mounds of his abdominals. In and out. Over and down. From an inch above the navel up until it meets the sternum. Then I slide the blade to the right—mine, not his—stopping at the point where his ribs curve too much, before I move back down again, toward his hip bone.

The dark-red line is not as thin by the time I reach my destination. It thickens with every tiny blood vessel I sever, with every passing minute. More and more. Faster and faster.

Striking red.

Almost *scarlet*.

I slide the sharp surgical knife underneath the flap I created in this man's abdomen, popping out a corner so I can peel it down and fold it into his lap.

"Please, please stop . . ." he mutters. The scrap of fabric

covering his mouth muffles his voice.

It's not there to shut him up, but to keep his drool away from me.

I look away from the newly exposed muscle and a thin layer of fat attached to the peeled skin now almost completely folded over in his lap. Cocking my head, I meet his teary, bloodshot gaze, which is devoid of the hope his voice still seems to hold.

I have nothing to say to him. Never really do. Vincent is the one of us with the golden tongue that can make almost everyone talk. If that doesn't work, I come in. I'm the one with the scalpel, the knives, the pliers, and many other tools that don't require questions to be asked. Pain makes pretty much everyone talk, and I'm here to listen.

I've been doing this for years, though not to this particular man. I've only been at him for a couple of hours. At a grueling, calm pace that made him spill all his secrets. At least, the ones I'm interested in.

Back when I only had a few victims in my repertoire, I thought the infliction of pain itself pulled me in so fiercely that it made me want to do it slower, longer, and so much more often. I couldn't understand I didn't know myself then. It took a few years to see what fascinates me so—emotions.

Because pain brings forth emotions which are deeply visceral and amazingly unique. Like nothing I've ever seen. An opera of feelings within that rainbow of expressions and reactions.

It's not that I can't feel emotions myself. At a certain level, I do, but states of mind are what I feel the most, like anger, slight joy, contempt, annoyance.

But when I look in my victim's eyes, I find a deep fascination in the complexity of emotions looking back at me. It took me a long time to attempt pinpointing them through association with body language and physical reactions.

They're painted in colorful shades, cycling between hope, fear, regret, and maybe a tinge of love for someone he'll never see again. Probably many more emotions that I can't yet recognize.

Sometimes I carve for the sole purpose of feeding this need with unfamiliar emotions I cannot seem to experience or understand myself. I feed it because it's the only way I can step away from the dominant, inhuman part of me. The only way I can attempt to understand and perhaps relate to others. It's necessary in my line of work.

"Please . . . just kill me," the flayed man begs.

Strips of flesh are missing from his thighs, biceps, and now his abdomen. I cut him. I stabbed him. And yet he looks nothing like Diana, the escort from Katya's team that his associate dropped at our doorstep.

She was half-dead. Barely able to move or talk. Broken so deeply, we're not sure she's going to make it. But she's in surgery now, with doctors fixing her badly damaged spleen and internal bleeding.

Katya and some of the others are currently in the hospital waiting room. Finnigan and a couple of security guys are lurking in the hospital too. Staying close, just in case.

Somehow, through a blinking consciousness and barely any strength, Diana managed to give us a glimpse into what happened. The man dying before my eyes gave me the rest.

She was assigned to Frank Duval, a politician we've known to be dirty for a long time. But even as he's slowly digging his claws through so many pockets in Queenscove, obtaining proof of his dodgy dealings is almost impossible. He covers his tracks too well.

Our escorts are so much more than their given names. They're spies. Skilled ones at that. And even though they're part of our syndicate, they're our best kept secret. We've held that business separate from the very start. We protect them, take care of them, but their official leader is Ekaterina—Katya.

If Queenscove and beyond learned the escort firm is ours, they wouldn't use our services, and we wouldn't discover their secrets.

But Diana got caught tonight as she was cloning a phone. She thought she was safe, but Duval must have suspected something, or maybe it was pure dumb luck. He then brought in my little friend here, and together they proceeded to torture her for information. She begged and begged, she fought and resisted, but pain does terrible things to the human psyche. It twists it and bends it until you can't distinguish dream from reality.

The man bleeding before me said that she was barely conscious when she muttered our name . . . The Sanctum. She gave us away on a platter to Duval, and after seeing the state of her, I can't blame her.

Our escorts are trained in various skills, including combat and manipulation, but we don't expect them to be soldiers conditioned to torture methods. This should never have happened to her.

This asshole gave me every bit of information he had about an hour ago, but his pleas and pain have coaxed me on. Diana's agony too. This second hour has been for her and me. I needed to draw more out of him until that wretched, hungry creature within me grew satisfied.

And it finally is.

I, on the other hand, am exhausted.

Standing tall and straightening my back, I look at the man tied to the chair before me in the center of this cold, gray room glowing in nothing but artificial light. Bruises have developed, swollen cheeks and eye. Around the flayed skin and sliced muscles, the man is covered in blood on almost every inch of his body. Only the adrenaline I administered keeps him alert.

He's positively demonic.

Nothing like the arrogance he regarded me with when I found him smoking by the back entrance of a busy downtown bar. The guy who delivered Diana to us gave him away. He's currently lying dead on the floor a few feet to my left.

But I'm done. I got what I needed. I know who truly needs to pay.

Now, I need to sleep.

"I gave you . . . everything . . . you needed . . ." he begs me, fear radiating from his eyes, exhaustion from his voice. "Please, hel—"

In one swift motion, I swipe the surgical knife against his throat, turning on my heels just as the spray reaches me. I walk to the table and chairs sat by the entrance, stripping off the plastic overalls as he faintly heaves and gurgles.

I open the door to let the security guys in. Very few of them watch me when I *work*. Some can't fully stomach it and others don't care one bit, but I prefer the solitude. The quiet.

"You know what to do," I tell them.

They nod and get to work. A cleanup crew will be called, and our interrogation room will be clean in hours, the bodies disposed of.

I walk through the bright, long corridor leading up to the stairs and eventually out the main door of our underground facility. Climbing into my car, I crack my neck to relieve the tension, ignoring how faint the moonlight is and how close the sun is to the horizon.

It's been a long fucking night. So different from what I envisioned it would be.

I sigh, long and lazy, as I start the engine and pull onto the small road, following it until I reach the main one a couple of miles away.

I'm supposed to turn right to head home, yet my arms seem to have a mind of their own, because they turn the steering wheel left instead.

And I keep driving.

And driving.

Passing mansions, then houses, then palms, birches, and tall hedges.

Until Scarlet's stone garden wall comes into view.

I'm too tired to argue with my brain or whatever made this decision to come here. I open her bedroom feed on my phone, noticing once again how she sleeps like she wants to conquer the entire surface of her bed, before I scale the wall and jump into her garden.

Mindlessly, I walk through the trees on the expansive estate, toward her cottage by the pond, and straight to the first cracked window I see. It's not the only one. I have to thank the pleasant nighttime Queenscove breeze for this. Just like me, she seems to enjoy sleeping with it licking her skin.

I climb inside her house, walking through the hallway that takes me straight to her bedroom, and enter through the open doorway.

There she is—the reckless kitten I'm still convinced broke into my house—sleeping peacefully.

A white sheet covers her sprawled body, clinging to every enticing curve like she was made to be sculpted and displayed in a museum. Her dark hair is a starburst over the white pillowcase, her long, slender arms spread above her head, begging to be tied right there.

I'm fucked. Truly and utterly fucked.

I want to make her scream in pleasure, then torture her to pain.

I want her mouth around my cock and her beating heart bleeding in my hand.

I want to kill her and fuck her. Destroy her and own her.

I want it all.

But most of all, I want her.

She has to be mine. I don't fucking understand why, but I have to make her mine. She's a mystery I haven't solved, and goddamn it if I'm gonna let anyone else figure her out.

With slow, careful steps, I near her bed, bending over her sleeping form. She smells divine . . . sweet with a bitter note that pulls me in further. I imagine oleander as I draw in another breath of her, crimson petals falling over her form. That's how she smells—beautiful, but deadly.

I really shouldn't, but I can't help myself . . . so I reach over and ever so slowly brush the backs of my fingers against her cheek, humming low in my chest when the velvet feel of her sizzles against my skin.

I drag that feathery touch lower, against her neck, tracing the slope of her clavicle and down her chest, until I reach the seam of the sheet.

I suck in a breath, an electric burst sizzling low in my abdomen when goosebumps bloom over her flesh beneath my touch.

She doesn't stir, though. Not even a little bit.

Yet her lips seem to have parted slightly. Pale-berry, full, divine lips.

I've done many terrible, cruel things in my life, but denying a woman the opportunity to consent has never been one of them. Yet here I am, tracing the edge of the sheet covering Scarlet's breasts, pretending it's not moving lower with every stroke.

This right here is what will turn me into a true monster.

I stop, the back of my pointer finger lightly brushing just

above her sternum, and drag my gaze back up to her lips, soft cheeks, and thick lashes.

Then, at a grueling pace, I slide that digit down her sternum, dragging the sheet with it. This tortured movement draws down her abdomen, over her soft skin.

Goosebumps nettle over my skin like an omen designed for me alone. The moment I reach her belly button, my gaze still fixed on her face to observe her unconscious reactions, I stop. Nostrils flaring as I inhale a slow, strained breath, I splay my palm over her soft belly in a gentle touch.

She still doesn't stir. But I revel one more moment, then reluctantly move away.

I don't just step back. I turn altogether, walking out the door and back the way I came. I know that only a few more seconds in that room will break my resolve.

There are many things I want to take from her, but consent is not one of them. Which is surprising, since her life is on that list too.

What has Scarlet done to me?

CHAPTER 14

Scarlet

I had the strangest dream last night. Feverish. Surreal.

It was a feeling more than anything. It bred images in my mind, painted in deep red hues. Intertwined limbs, wrists bound with silk, wet lips parted in ecstasy, and a thin, dewy layer covering my naked, flushed body. His too. Because, of course it happened again, and the wretched Carter Pierce invaded another of my dreams.

Never before like this, though.

Since that first moment we met in that dark alley, he's been a constant presence once I fall asleep. But this was intimate on a different level.

He was naked, tattooed flesh steamed in that same thin dew, glistening with our hedonism. He was an angry god, and I was his willing subject.

Nothing I've done today has managed to pry those images out of my mind. Through breakfast, through work, through two cold showers. The second one had to happen after those images bled into a daydream involving Metamorphosis.

Jealousy sprouted at the thought of all those women who have felt his feverish power on their skin, in real life, with tears spawned from that transcendent collision between agony and rapture flowing down their cheeks. They are utterly unique, and I wish to capture them. I wish I could feel them. Understand their impact.

I spent all of my lunchtime, and the couple of hours after, reasoning with myself that maybe, just maybe . . . if I have this experience with Carter at the helm, I will feel it too.

I'm fucking desperate for it.

Feeling something would be better than feeling nothing at all.

In the end, I had to leave the damn house because I was driving myself nuts.

"I have a hazelnut oat cappuccino for Scarlet!" The barista shouts loud enough to pull me out of that deep hole I was about to fall into again.

I put my hand up and walk to the counter to grab my drink. Same one I order all the time. The one I ordered the day Carter and I finally saw each other for the first time since that night in the alley.

Same coffee shop too.

I can't help but grin. It was a great meet-cute. Unhinged. Perfect.

If I discount the very rude attempted murder later that day.

My phone chimes as I turn and head toward the exit.

Sleep well, kitten?

Ear to ear, the smirk extends. I can't freaking help it.

> Mmm...very well. Dreamy.

> How about you, killer-boy?

Do tell.

I definitely did not sleep as well as you.

> This is a story worth telling in person. *wink*

> What's keeping you up?

You'll get your wish soon enough, kitten.

A mild case of home invasion, among other things.

> Oh, goody, my prayers will finally be answered.

> Now who would dare break into The Carver's house?

Walking toward the café's exit, I tap my finger against the edge of the phone, watching those three dots appear and disappear as Carter types.

C: Who indeed...

C: I'll share my theory if you tell me your dreams.

I walk out onto the street, biting my lip as I begin to type. But I smash right into someone and barely manage to hold on to my coffee without spilling it.

"Oh god, I'm so sorry." I bounce back, fumbling to stick

my phone into my handbag. "That was totally my fault, I do apologi—"

That last word sticks in my throat like hot tar when I see the person I just bumped into—my soon-to-be motherfucking ex-husband. And look at that, he's hand in hand with his *new squeeze.*

What a fucking delight.

"I would say this is an interesting coincidence, but you live an hour and a half away. So . . ." I trail off, tension rippling through my muscles as I take them in.

"You would be right. There's no coincidence at all." A smug satisfaction laces through Bernard's eyes.

He steps forward and I step back, but I almost bump into the café's wall. Before he can corner me, I shift quickly to my right so my back is clear and I can escape if needed.

"You've been following me."

"You didn't give me any choice, Scarlet. If you don't see reason, I have to make you understand. In person."

"And you chose a busy café in which to throw your pathetic threats at me?"

I scoff, and his smug grin switches to disdain.

"You have a tendency to hole up in your hermit hide for weeks, and I can't afford to wait until you decide to crawl out of it," he says.

"Crawl indeed," Ariana adds. Her voice is so much more annoying than I ever noticed before. She cocks an eyebrow, looking me up and down with such an air of superiority. She's lucky I can't spit in her face right here, right now. Though a vague ache pulls at my heartstrings at what we once had.

Deceit, Scarlet, that's what you had. She was never your friend!

I don't know when my blood began to boil, but it's bubbling at the surface, and I'm squeezing my free fist hard enough that deep pressure blooms in my palm. This is not good. Not fucking good at all.

"Can you just get to the threat part of this conversation so I can carry on with my day?"

Bernard's expression darkens, the smugness making way for annoyance. "You're still my wife, Scarlet. You don't get to disrespect me."

I burst out laughing. I can't help myself. "Your wife? Fuck you and your delusional bullshit, asshole." My gaze flickers to Ariana. "You're insulting my poor excuse of a replacement, by the way. She doesn't look like she likes it when you call me 'your wife.'"

She hisses at me, her souring expression emphasizing wrinkles I never noticed before.

"Actually, say it again. She looks pretty when she's all hurt and angry," I say, unable to contain my amusement.

"You shut your mouth." Bernard steps right into my space, and my grin shakes. "Give me the stones, Scarlet, same monthly arrangement as before, or—"

"No. Go fuck yourself, Bernard. Along with your leverage. Shove it deep up your asshole until you can fucking taste it. Now, I have shit to do."

I turn to leave, but he wraps his hand around my wrist, the tightness so constricting that dangerous pressure grows beneath the skin. In moments like this one, it would be useful to be able to distinguish the sensation. Is it pain? Is he constricting my blood vessels? Is he breaking my fucking wrist?

I pull to get away, but he yanks me right back to face him.

"Give me the stones, Scarlet, or I'll deliver the Levain pendant back to its last owner and tell him your parents stole it. Along with the rest of their jewels."

"Nice try, but I know for a fact it's currently in a jewelry box in my safe." Only, I'm not as confident as I should be in those words, because Bernard's grin is far too smug.

He cocks his head, regarding me for a brief moment before he pulls out his phone. He swipes a couple of times on the screen, then shows it to me.

My spine stiffens, blood freezing in my veins.

"This proves nothing. It could have been taken when we were still together," I say, looking at the photo of the precious ruby pendant held in front of his arrogant face.

"Last night, actually." He shoves his phone back into his pocket, looking like he won this game I didn't know we were playing. "You'll find that the one in your safe is a pretty darn good replica I commissioned."

"You're bluffing," I challenge.

Disbelief melds with fury, and I want to clock him right here in the middle of the fucking street. He could still be lying to me, but somehow, I doubt he would look so goddamn confident if he was.

"Not at all. But you'll have your confirmation when you go home," he says.

I won't need it; he's not lying about this. As much as I wish he was. The Levain pendant is one of the few pieces my father and I have stolen that's too beautiful to break apart and too unique to sell without getting us in serious trouble. I took inventory of everything when I moved out, but in the madness of it all, I didn't check each goddamn piece in detail. It never crossed my mind this asshole would pull something like it. A fake? Really?

This is bad. Real bad.

"Why did you do this, Bernard?"

"I suggested it, actually." Ariana crosses her arms against her chest, pursing her lips.

"You?" I should be surprised, but these two assholes were going at it behind my back long before I found out.

"Leverage," Bernard explains. "I had other plans with it, but I knew there would come a time when you would refuse to give me my stones."

"*Your* stones? You're fucking delusional. I can't believe you planned for me to discover you were cheating."

"I didn't plan for that, actually," he says, tightening his hold on my wrist.

I'm confused. "You were going to blackmail me while we were still together?"

"Controlling you would have been slightly easier, but I would say I'm doing pretty damn good even now that we're separated."

His victorious grin disgusts me.

"You piece of shit, you have no idea what you've just done," I say, trying to yank my wrist free of his bruising hold. "And it's not a separation. I fucking dumped you, you swine."

The air shifts against the back of my neck. Rich notes of bergamot and lavender snake through my senses a moment before a chilling, smoky voice speaks behind me.

"I will break your ribs open and tear your heart out if you don't take your hands off her."

No fucking way!

Bernard's hold loosens, and I can finally pull my wrist away and take a step back. But I falter when a hand slides over the small of my back and wraps around my waist. My spine snaps straight, and an apprehensive shiver runs over it.

I'm pressed against the towering body standing next to me, and his marvelous scent is hypnotizing. Is it really him? I force composure as I tilt my head with such calmness. I'm proud of myself.

And I'm right—Carter Pierce holds me against him, regarding my *husband* with a cold, eerie gaze that seeps bone-deep. I'm curious about the effect it has on Bernard, but I can't tear my eyes off of the carved, sharp features of the man who tightens his grip on me like I'm about to bolt.

Then he looks down, and something so much more visceral bleeds through his expression. It shines a lot like possessiveness.

I think his scent got to my head.

"Hello, Scarlet." A sly smirk ghosts across his lips, and I think I'm melting. Just a little.

Who am I kidding? I'm at the brink of becoming nothing more than a puddle.

He dips down before I get a chance to greet him, and I'm fucking startled silly when his nose slides over that sensitive spot where my ear meets my jaw. The gentle touch rips an embarrassing giggle out of me.

It freaking tickles.

For one brief moment, he stalls.

Only one, devoid of breath and heartbeats, before he presses his lips there.

The tickle dissipates completely, heat pooling low in my belly, a shiver breaking over my skin as my muscles seize. When he rises, I'm pretty sure all the air in the world is sucked out, because there's none in my damn lungs.

What the hell just happened?

"I know we were supposed to meet at my place, but I thought I would pick you up instead, love."

His place . . . pick me—love?

My brain is short-circuiting.

"Oh my god, you're . . ." Ariana gasps.

I quickly recover, leaning into him as I plaster my most charming smile on my lips. "Always so thoughtful, baby. Thank you."

It's not hard work. At all. Not when he looks at me like he's putting no effort into this. It comes all too naturally.

His gaze flickers down to my hand, and every muscle in

his face and throat tightens at once.

I follow his line of sight, noticing the angry red darkening around my wrist. *For fuck's sake, now I need to get that checked out.*

"I'm okay," I wrap my arm around his waist and hold him to me.

He doesn't recoil. Doesn't stiffen. He already holds me near enough to him that I couldn't possibly tug him any closer. His icy, furious stare finds mine again, but there's no threat. Not directed at me, anyway. Right there, in that peering blue inside the hazel of his eyes, there is softness bred of possessiveness. It's all mine, and I'm not even sure he knows it's there.

"Now, love, please introduce me to the man who dared lay a fucking finger on you." He turns his menacing attention on Bernard, and I hear a shift before me.

I almost forgot he was there.

"Right, yes. This is Bernard Camora, my ex-husband," I say, noticing Ariana's gaze roaming all over Carter.

I wanna clock her right in the fucking face just for daring to admire him.

"Not ex. I *am* your husband," the asshole contends.

Excuse me? Is he whipping his dick out? This isn't a fucking pissing contest.

I turn to him, ready to make a nasty remark, but falter when his foul expression makes me smirk. His face seems almost red, his gaze switching between Carter and me. If we're comparing, Carter fucking won. He's taller, gorgeous, richer, and so much more powerful.

And right now . . . he's pretending to be mine. Fucking delightful.

"If Scarlet says ex, you are her ex." Carter replies before I bother to, and something swells not just in my belly, but in my damn soul too.

Settle. He's acting . . . just acting.

"And who might *you* be?" Bernard sounds bitter, fitting his sullen look. If he's not careful, one might mistake that for jealousy.

"Carter Pierce," he says.

His name alone is enough explanation. The confidence he exudes is nothing short of insanity. Yet, it works.

"And you are with . . . *her?*" Ariana asks, pointing up and down my body like I'm the ugly duckling that could never snag a man like Carter. I can't help feeling just a tad inferior.

Bernard narrows his eyes, and ever so slowly, something akin to recognition seeps through. He blinks a few times, then pulls his shoulders back as he crosses his arms, and I have a feeling he's about to dig his own grave just by his expression.

"Look, no offense pal—"

Oh, here we go.

"Scarlet and I have *private* business to discuss. So, if you don't mind . . ."

Does he have a death wish?

I can't exhale as I look up at Carter to see how that indignation landed. He cocks his head, hand tightening around my waist as he nestles me deeper into him. Okay, that's . . . surprisingly nice. Warm. *Comforting.*

"I mind." He leaves no space for argument. "I don't take lightly another man touching what is *mine.*"

My heart stalls beneath my ribs, goosebumps spreading over my skin as his last word echoes through my thoughts in that growling voice.

Calm down, Scarlet, he's only pretending.

"But hurting her? Marking her skin?" Carter continues, shaking his head at such a slow, torturous pace. Violent threats lie in the wake of each movement. "That has *dire* consequences."

Bernard scoffs, but his gaze becomes unsettled.

"Consequen—"

"I'm not done." Carter's tone turns to gravel as it darkens, and he takes one small step forward, guiding me with him. "I know you are aware of who I am. You've also heard rumors. Correct?"

My ex purses his lips, indignation way too clear in his eyes as his nostrils flare. He's aware.

"Let me clear them up for you—they are wrong. Who I am, what I do, is *much* worse than any rumor that graced your ears. I don't plan on wasting my time with you. As it stands, you are insignificant. However—"

I'm pulled forward once again, his chest only a foot away from Bernard as he looks down at him.

"If even the tip of your finger grazes a single hair on Scarlet's body ever again, I won't just give you a glimpse into what I do. I will make you my masterpiece. I will carve you, Camora. So slowly, your screams will last for hours on end. They will imprint into my mind, and turn into a haunting. And I'll use them as my motherfucking lullaby every single night to soothe me to sleep."

Fuck me . . .

Gorgeously perfect. And Bernard is close to shaking. Hell, I am too.

I wanted this man before, but now? Now I'll raze anything standing in my way.

"I'll speak to you soon, Scarlet," my ex says.

"You're not getting what you want, Bernard. And it would be prudent to return what you stole," I say.

His brows knit together in a menacing promise that makes me uneasy. If he truly goes to Anders, the former owner of the Levain pendant and a major player in the West Coast mafia, Dad and Carmen are dead.

The fact that he's threatening them, not me, pisses me off

even more. He knows I care more for their safety than mine. But if he thinks he can do that and still get what he wants, then he truly is an idiot.

Bernard turns around, dragging Ariana with him, and walks away. Slowly. Sneaking angry looks behind him.

In one swift motion, Carter turns, crushing me against his front as I gasp and grab onto his waist. I don't need to steady myself; he holds me tight enough with just that one hand splayed over the small of my back. So tight. And so very close.

I can't help but acknowledge every single part of me pressed against each part of him. His strong abdomen against the butterflies in my stomach. My perked nipples against his taut torso. His hardening cock against my belly and the fire growing there.

"You know, I can stand up for myself," I all but whisper, growing hotter under his intense gaze.

He tilts his head, throwing a brief, nonchalant look toward Bernard and Ariana. A faint trace of a smirk wrinkles his cheek as he dips down. "I thought I did a much better job."

The world grows silent as his soft, warm lips brush against my cheek. So close to my ear, lightning bursts down the side of my neck and straight between my thighs like liquid thunder.

"You're a great actor, killer-boy. But the gig has ended."

My voice was supposed to sound antagonistic. Sarcastic, even. Instead, it's breathy, drowned in lust and desperate desire.

His lips burn a path across my cheek, and I suck in a wanton breath as he reaches dangerously close to the corner of my mouth.

"Has it?" he says. "They're still watching."

Then, I hope they never stop.

Carter presses a soft, almost sensual, uncharacteristic kiss to that spot not quite at the corner of my lips, and nothing could have fucking stopped the moan that spilled from between them.

A rumbling growl vibrates through his throat in response, and a breath catches in mine when his hand grabs it, holding me firmly in place. It's as if he's simultaneously keeping me from running away and from moving any closer. And I oblige, relaxing into the possessiveness of his grip.

"Since they're watching . . ." I whisper.

I run my hands over his back, one going between the shoulder blades, but the other . . . Well, we have to make it believable, right? I slide it right down over his ass, and swallow down a groan at the tight mass I'm met with there.

His grip on my throat tightens, and pressure grows at the back of it. But fuck me, because it pools right between my thighs.

This is *amazing!*

"What do you think you're doing?" He brushes his lips against my cheek one last time before he rises, his eyes regarding me with cold curiosity.

"Making it believable." I give his ass cheek a good squeeze and a playful tap, a grin pulling at my cheeks when he cocks his brow.

He throws another look Bernard's way, then, just as quickly as he came onto me, he lets go and takes a step back.

My body already misses the feel of his.

But his absence makes way for that cold-stoned anger brought on by Bernard and Ariana to come back. The reckless kind I learned to harness and focus.

Bernard crossed a line today. I could have handled his attempted blackmail when it was directed at me only, but what he just pulled is one step too fucking far.

He will pay for his goddamn sin.

But I need to clear my head so I can plan this retribution.

And I have something prepared just perfect for the job.

"See you later, killer-boy." I turn, rushing toward my car.

"Wait!" he calls after me, but I'm already too far away.

I look over my shoulder as I weave between the people on the sidewalk. "No time, *boyfriend*. I have things to do."

People to kill.

CHAPTER 15
Scarlet

Sometimes I wonder how my life would have turned out if I was normal. Or better yet, average. If my body worked like others do. If my mind didn't follow this unconventional path. And if my mental health wasn't battered so early on.

I've made peace with most of that, no matter how much I get lost in thought about it. What I wonder now is if any or all of the above are the explanation for my *mood*.

That's what my brother calls it. *"Oh, Scar, you're in that mood again, aren't you?"*

It's not how I would describe my rage-filled, recklessly explosive, and wildly destructive temper that takes over in certain situations, but I appreciate him, Dad, and Carmen for not judging me. Not to my face, at least.

None of them have a moral leg to stand on, anyway, but

neither do they have this thundering need inside their souls that requires feeding on human tears to survive.

None of them do what I do.

They don't have to see pain.

Bend it to their will.

Harness it.

I do.

"P—please . . . you don't need . . . to do this." The plea comes out slow, slurred.

Just like all the others before it.

These people never learn. It makes me wonder if I give off a merciful-woman vibe. Maybe I need to pick a bigger sledgehammer.

Yup. That must be it.

My cheeks strain with a wide grin as I turn away from the heavy-duty steel worktable Mr. Cohen currently lies on, fully strapped in. Though, he's only tied up so he doesn't accidentally fall on his face while I fucking punish every single bone in his body.

With the drug currently running through his system, he wouldn't be going far, even without the straps. Benzodiazepine is a marvelous substance. It gives me the opportunity to subdue a full-grown man who's much stronger than me, while keeping their ability to speak and feel pain. Well, kind of speak.

But the pain part is the most important one. I need them to feel it *all.*

I grab the red-handled, eight-pound sledgehammer, balancing it in both my hands as I return to the worktable.

"Much better, right?" I carefully swing the tool up and rest it on my shoulder, looking the asshole in the eyes the whole time.

He blinks between me and the offending article, gaze

widening with every passing second. "No, oh God. What are you—"

"See, Mr. Cohen, I have an anger-management problem. Had it since I can remember. But it's not just any ol' anger issue. It's one of those that could get me locked up. When it overcomes me, the only way to appease it is to make people like you hurt. Bad." I pause, watching him begin to tremble.

Though, with the effects of the drugs, it looks more like a pathetic, weak twitch.

"The reason why it would get me locked up, not exclusively in a prison, but in one of those darling places for the criminally insane, is because beating you isn't what tickles my nervous system. Your pain is. Your tears."

The man begins to whimper, a soft, pitiful sound that stops the moment I cock my head. He shakes his, defiance breaking through his gaze.

"No . . . I won—no tears," he mutters.

I shake my head, snickering. "That's what this is for." I raise the sledgehammer high above my head, waggling my brows as I swing it onto his thigh.

The thump comes before the stomach-curdling splintering.

A visceral scream rips out of his throat, bouncing against the concrete walls. Pain penetrates his expression, and my gaze fixates on his eyes. On the glassy sheen thickly covering them, the trembling lids, and the angry blood vessels webbing through the white. I can even see the agony in the irises. A window to a pain-laced soul.

Such a special, special thing, pain is.

A vulnerability that clouds the mind. The judgment.

It spikes emotions and turns you against even the people you love.

It's a unique physical reaction. Because no other has such

effects over the human mind, the body, and the soul.

Not just his—mine too.

His response to pain is a soothing song to my aching, explosive soul.

After raising the sledgehammer, I bring it down on Cohen's knee in one clean strike, with much more determination in my swing.

Bones crack on vicious notes, sending a deafening vibration through my chest. His scream doesn't follow immediately. An imploding shriek comes first—the rejection of defeat. For one second, Cohen thought he could do it, but when pain comes, it seems to erase their minds. Pain becomes all they know. All they can process.

But his screams are my focus now. They fill me with mad need.

It's funny, really, how much these bellows and cries used to annoy me. No matter if I knew the theory of it all, there was a clear disconnect in my mind between the concept of pain and this irrational, pointless noise. It's hard to understand, let alone feel compassion for something you will never relate to.

Years have passed since I began this *therapy*, and their wails have become my soundtrack. I'm learning. Associating. Adjusting.

"Please, Lord, plea—Sav—" he begs, slurred words joined by more whimpers deeply etched with pain.

"There's no salvation for you here."

Raising the sledgehammer, I let the man see it for a few excruciating moments, right up there, about to crash down on his bones once more. You'd think that seeing what's coming makes it easier. Gives you time to prepare for it.

Spoiler alert—it doesn't.

His screams fall into a constant, defeated cry, head lolling to the side as he sinks into the agony of his broken bones. And just like that, defeat comes. Tears stream steadily from his eyes.

I rest the sledgehammer against the wall and grab the green glass vial from a nearby table. The vial is a pretty little thing, made of thin, delicate glass, narrow at the mouth and bottom, round and fat in the middle. It has a tall stopper, long and thin—it looks like an old perfume bottle.

I remove the stopper as I reach the man, holding his head to the side as I place the open vial at the corner of his eye.

He's too blinded by his suffering to understand what I'm doing. Or even acknowledge it. He simply cries, body cracked open to make way for his broken soul.

And it will be broken.

Men like him deserve so much more.

"This is what happens, Cohen. This is the consequence of your crimes. All of them."

His cries grow as he appears to register my calm words.

"You hurt the innocent. The voiceless ones. Hunt them for sport. Torture them. Parade them like trophies in narcissistic photos on social media. Then chop off their heads and display them on your walls."

His body trembles as he tries to pull his head out of my grip. "It's . . . called hun—hunting."

"No, my darling, it's called murder. Hunting is what animals do when they seek prey they plan to feed themselves and families with. Hunting is what human animals do when they have the same need, and they honor every part of that soul. Use it, so no part is wasted. So it didn't die in vain. Animals are different from us, but we have a different type of intelligence—we understand suffering, both physical and emotional. We understand torture, and that a kill for a purpose like this must be quick."

Satisfied with the amount of tears I collected from him, I

close the vial and place it back on the table. When I return to Cohen, I grab the sledgehammer again, and without warning, I bring it down on his hip, grunting sharply when it shatters beneath my rage.

"You don't. You choose cruelty."

Smash.

"You choose pain and waste."

Smash.

"You choose selfishness and ego."

Smash.

"And I choose the same for you."

Two more times, I bring down the tool on both his ankles. His screams lose themselves somewhere in the background, where I don't really give a shit about them anymore.

That pain in his expression, the violent twitch of his body as his nerves and heart acknowledge and try to live through it, has me transfixed.

"Then you had to come back from your bloody safaris and hurt animals here." I shake my head. "Tsk, tsk, tsk. Lion cubs are not pets, motherfucker. And they're certainly not fucking punching bags. I know what you've done. I've seen the mangled little bodies. I've seen the photos you took as fucking trophies. I saw your smile as you held that poor soul. I wretched and vomited through it all, but I still looked. I looked because I had to feel that horror in the pit of my soul and decide what punishment is the most appropriate for you." One deep breath later, I say the next words with a wide grin on my lips. "Well, I have decided, darling. And I still don't think the punishment fits the crime."

He opens his mouth, attempting to form words, but somewhere before my eyes, red seeps in, emotions spiking with the thought of the other reason I'm here. The man I would love to do this to too. The emotional pain he causes me. The fucking heartache as he threatens my parents. The absolute rage at the audacity to cheat on me with my best friend and then refuse the divorce. All of it blows into me all at once, and when I smash that sledgehammer into Cohen's shoulder, the wail that rips out of him is so loud, so visceral, so charged and guttural, it makes me pause. Not stop completely, but admire.

There it is . . . that splendid moment when humanity is gone and all that's left is a meat-sack of pure agony. I harness it carefully, storing all the small reactions in my imaginary filing cabinet.

Maybe I should write a horror novel someday. I will have a detailed list of physical reactions to pain and fear to choose from—no need to scour the internet for examples.

But my rage is not gone yet.

The moment to admire is over.

Mad shrieks, erratic swings of the heavy mallet, unhinged movements come together in a dance of violence. I smash joints first, then the big bones. Before I bring the mallet down on his sternum, I hold his crumpling gaze for enough time that the death skirting his eyes imprints in my mind. That defeat. The fear. The hope for the end of pain. A heady, addictive mix.

Then I crush him.

Ribs snap and pierce his organs, a soundless scream catches in his throat, and finally, the blood comes. He coughs it out in thick ribbons, and as I watch death clouding his eyes, thicker and thicker, my rage dying with him, my chest lighter, I still think this man hasn't suffered enough.

There's a special place in hell for people who abuse animals. And since I need an outlet for my explosive rage, years back, I made it my mission to send them all there.

* * *

"Are you okay, Scar?" my brother cocks his head in that annoying, concerned way. He pushes the wooden box holding Cohen's body into the cremator, feeding him to the fire.

The asshole wasn't a big man, so in about three hours at around fourteen hundred degrees Fahrenheit, he will be ash. Whatever remains, goes in the cremulator, and soon we'll have nothing but dust. I'll sprinkle it on the fucking highway. He doesn't deserve to *rest* anywhere else.

"Marc, you know I'm always good after."

He shakes his head. "That's not what I mean. The whole ex-refusing-to-be-an-ex thing." He starts inspecting the space carefully, probably looking for evidence we might have accidentally dropped.

This cremation room is used for burning, so it should be clean. I do my business downstairs, deep in the crematorium's labyrinth of a storage cellar. My brother's business offers privacy since he doesn't work for funerals, but medical waste, decommissioned science donations, finished body farm experiments, and other strange purposes.

But it's not the only reason I like it; half of that cellar isn't in the official plans. That includes the escape tunnel built in my *murder* room. Hopefully there will never be a need for it, but its existence greatly calms me.

"Please don't remind me of him. He's the reason I'm here now," I say.

"I know you don't like it, but I need to know. Did he hurt you? You're my sister, Scar. You know I'd do anything for you."

"And I appreciate that. I love you for it. But don't worry, Bernard will pay eventually. I just have to be smart about it. Plan. And no, he did not hurt me," I reassure him.

Only, his gaze flickers to my exposed wrist that has caught a bit of color since my bitch of an ex grabbed me too hard.

"Oh, that?" I shrug. "He grabbed my wrist, but he's been

taken care of. Carter surely did—"

Shit.

Mentioning that name was a huge fucking mistake.

"Carter?" Marc tilts his head, the scrutiny blatant.

"New friend. Anyway, he was threatened, quite graphically, if I might say so myself. So, I'm sure he'll leave me alone for a while. Long enough for me to formulate a plan that will secure my freedom from him and his family's consequences," I explain, removing the coveralls I'm wearing and throwing them into the same flames Cohen burns in before Marc shuts the heavy door.

"Scar."

"Yes?"

"You're grinning like a teenager in love."

What?

"No, I'm not! Stop it. I'm just feeling better after murdering this asshole." I gesture a bit too enthusiastically at the cremator.

"Who's Carter?"

"Seriously. Just leave it. It's not important."

"Does he know what you do? What we *all* do?" he insists.

"We're not that close. Like I said, he's just a new friend."

Who wants to punish me, potentially fuck me, and murder me.

"Also," I continue, "why would you assume I would share what either of us does? The only reason Bernard knew of the family business was because of his father's connection with Dad. Even then, I never shared *this*." I gesture wildly around us. "Only the family knows. Clearly, I'm not going to share this with one of the lead—"

Fucking hell, Scarlet, shut your damn mouth!

I take a deep breath in before I continue.

"My new friend."

"One of the what?" Marc raises an eyebrow, the corner of his lip twitching upward.

"I have to get home. I have a job tonight."

If he keeps pushing, I'm gonna end up accidentally telling him who I'm talking about. He has this knack of getting all the gritty details out of me. If he finds out I have a weird involvement with one of the men at the head of The Sanctum, he's gonna fucking flip. Then he'll tell Dad.

I may be an independent woman, despite living on my dad's land, but I don't like upsetting him.

"For what it's worth, I'm glad there was someone there to threaten that piece of shit. Especially if he dared put his hands on you." He walks over and pulls me into a tight hug. "Now, go start the cleanup in your little murder den. I'll join in a minute once all is set up here."

"Love you, big brother."

"Love you too."

The gods blessed me, really. For someone like me to be born into a family who accepts me, understands me, and helps me is quite a lucky thing. Well, most of the family, anyway, minus the one who calls herself my mother. My brother was the one trying to fight my battle when I was a kid. It was he who saw my inner rage first. It was also he who outed my mother to Dad when he realized what she was doing.

I'm lucky.

And Bernard Camora is not fucking taking this away from me.

I'll crush him before he gets the chance.

CHAPTER 16
Carter

I almost gave up on finding Scarlet after she left me worked up and confused in front of that coffee shop. I've been keeping myself busy by studying the man who put Diana in the hospital, and formulating a plan of action with Vincent, Finnigan, and Maddox.

Katya joined us too, though most of her contribution has centered around the many ways she would like to kill the man.

None were quick. Or clean.

Or sane, for that matter.

And none of us questioned her.

The escorts are hers and, no matter how stern Katya is, she would give her life for each and every one of them. She feels responsible, probably because of the time she spends with them. Maybe she cares for other reasons too, though I never felt the need to intrude and find out.

Katya left Midnight not long ago. Off to a meeting with her team, after which she'll take them into hiding at a secure location. She's worried the rest of them will be in danger too.

Vincent and Finnigan have left as well. Paying a visit to one of our *friends* to do some homework on Duval.

We have to do damage control. Or rather, *I* have to do it, since Maddox is currently downstairs in The Fightclub's gym, burning through the frustration that seems to be plaguing him more and more these days.

My tech team is on it, though, sinking their nimble fingers in all the right keyholes so we can monitor the situation. Duval has a choice—render our escort business useless by spreading the word that it belongs to us or keep this precious information to himself and use it.

The second option can actually do so much more damage, depending on what his approach would be. A smart man would attempt blackmail. An even smarter one . . . a takeover.

The escort business was never ours to begin with. It was Katya's long before we became The Sanctum, but at a much smaller scale. Finnigan's brother, Ronan, who laid the foundation for our operation, helped her. Stood by her. And eventually, they joined forces to elevate that side of the business to benefit both them and us. It's been years since those ownership lines blurred, and though Katya leads them and we respect her wholeheartedly, the escort business, as it stands today, fully belongs to The Sanctum.

Which is why damage control is necessary. But it's the last thing I want to do right now, and I'm so goddamn distracted.

The velvet softness of her skin.

The feel of her pressed tight against me.

That intoxicating rose-and-lemon scent.

It's haunting. So much so that I've been checking her

bedroom camera feed every thirty minutes. At first. It turned into twenty. Then ten.

Fuck, I must be going mad, but I can't get Scarlet out of my head.

I want to see her. Touch her. Breathe her in.

I want to make her scream and cry. Whimper and beg.

I want to consume her.

Yet, one question constantly blares in my mind: is she or is she not the person who dared break into my car, my bar, and my motherfucking house?

Two questions, actually—why?

I need those answers as desperately as I need to lay eyes on her again. If only I could fucking find her.

But I need to stay focused, take care of our business. Duval is hurt now. I anticipate an escalation soon, since I truly don't believe he'll leave things as they are.

He's too proud. Too competitive. We've been watching him for years, since he interfered in a real estate purchase that would have granted us a second legal business in Queenscove—a grand hotel. Hospitality is great, especially in this touristy city, but it would have been another way for us to spy on people. Observe. Find out precious information we can use against them or that we can trade.

But Duval was desperate to get his hands on it. He greased too many hands, played too many of his cards, and we stood no chance. He bought it instead.

Nothing looks more suspicious than a politician being able to afford something like that, but that's what happens to people in power. They don't get questioned.

My phone vibrates on the table, and I answer when one of my tech's numbers pops up.

"Yes, Tina."

"Sorry to bother you. There's a situation at the warehouse.

They just received a strange package."

It's not technically a warehouse. We call it that, as it's more generic than holding cells, torture room, and arms deposit. And most of it is underground.

"What do you mean by package?"

"They said some courier kid came over with a large box with your name on it. They stopped him for questioning, and the poor bastard was shitting himself. Told security he got paid five hundred by this guy in a black hoodie. Didn't get a good look, as his face was concealed."

My mind goes straight to the person on the CCTV tapes who broke into my car. Could it be?

"Did they open it?" I ask.

"Of course not. It's for you."

"I'm on my way."

I hang up, rising and rushing toward the back door. But as I walk through, I almost crash into Maddox.

"Where are you running off to?" he asks, brow raised as he regards me.

"Warehouse. They received a suspicious package."

"We don't receive packages there." He cocks his head, crossing his arms over his expansive chest.

"Precisely."

"I'm coming with you."

I want to protest and tell him to stay here. What if it's yet another puzzle box? What if it hides other photos of me in *interesting* situations? But protesting means revealing a vulnerability that has been growing since my car was broken into. And there is no way I'm showing that.

I let him join, riding together a few miles out of Queenscove, where our warehouse is tucked away in the middle of nowhere.

* * *

"Carter, what the hell is that?" Maddox asks, his brows creating angry welts between them as he regards the wooden-and-metal object.

Answering would mean admitting that for the last week or two, I've been manipulated by someone. Sent on a *treasure* hunt that I followed like a good little puppy.

Instead, I turn the hexagonal prism in my hands to find out its secrets, noting how much more complex and beautiful it looks compared to the last ones.

What an odd thought.

Beautiful.

But I push it back in the expansive chamber of my brain where I shove all thoughts and sensations I don't want to process.

Or don't know how.

"It's another puzzle box, isn't it?" Maddox says.

I continue my quest to open it, pressing and pulling the delicate divots and shards that appear. Flipping it over and over until, finally, I can see the scroll inside.

Only, I can't reach it.

"I can't . . . fuck!" It looks like it should open, but it's not fucking letting me. There must be another trick to it. "I think—there!" I exclaim as I find the smallest of divots in the brushed metal.

Piercing pain slices through my finger when I press it, and I hiss as I pull it back.

"What happened?" Maddox leans closer, looking at the string of blood flowing from the tip of my finger.

"It pricked me," I whisper in disbelief.

"Look, it's open."

I'm worried it might have injected me with something, but

as I look at the small, crimson-covered metal shard popping out right under the divot I pressed, I realize it's much more sinister than that. This was a blood sacrifice. A minuscule sacrifice, but a sacrifice, nonetheless. The small shard is strategically placed to release just as you press the button.

I put away the box inside my armrest and unroll the small parchment I grabbed from inside it.

"You seemed awfully enthusiastic solving that puzzle box."

I whip my head around, holding his honey-laced gaze dripping with challenge. One of his eyebrows arches so high that it risks joining his buzz-cut hairline. But he doesn't press further. I'm grateful. I've beaten myself up plenty already for this clear failure on my part.

"Any more clues about who's doing this?"

"Just hunches," I offer, because it's true.

I want it to be Scarlet, but there's no proof pointing to her. And I'm struggling to distinguish the buzzing in my gut—is it instinct or wishful thinking?

I turn my attention to the scroll, noting the shortened link and one oddly familiar line.

And I was told about this torture, that it was the Hell of carnal sins when reasons give way to . . .

"Desire . . ." I whisper on an awe-stricken breath.

"What?"

"It's from Dante's *Divine Comedy*. The last word of that sentence is 'desire.'" I pluck my phone from my jacket's inner pocket, fingers rushing over the screen as I type in the website link and then the password on the prompt.

"That's your—"

"Mhm." I watch the camera feed of my own fucking house.

The lights turn on, bathing the large living space in a soft glow. The same hooded figure I've seen in the CCTV footage after my car was broken into appears in the shot. They're wearing black sweatpants and a bulky sweatshirt. It's hard to tell if it's a man or woman. Their steps are light as they casually stroll through my house without a care in the world. No rush. No pressure.

We watch in silence as they walk through the space, running one gloved hand over various surfaces and objects. But it's only a taunt. Their path has been clearly planned, the direction set since the moment they walked in.

They stop in front of my violin. My Crimson Stradivarius.

No.

They lean over it, a tortured bend at the hips.

Do not fucking touch that.

They run one finger over the tuned strings, stopping for a single moment, before they wrap their hand around its neck and lift it off of its stand.

Put that down, goddammit!

But they do no such thing. Instead, with a spring in their steps and eyes trained on their phone, they walk in the direction of the camera I'm staring through. Then stop. Dead center in the frame, tucking the phone away.

My heart rushes on maddening beats as they reach up and pull off their face-covering, but the hood obstructs part of my view, and the downward angle doesn't allow me to see their face. Thumps reverberate through my chest. Its beats echo in my ears, and I'm shifting to the edge of the seat.

Then that organ stalls behind my ribs as the hood falls back in an excruciating movement, revealing exactly what I wanted. *Hoped.* Fucking wished for.

Scarlet Brasa-Glass stands in my goddamn house, a serene, taunting smile curving her pretty fucking lips and crinkling her dark eyes. A whirlwind of unexplainable sensations ravages my thoughts, my muscles, and worst of all, my soul. That in itself is inexplicable. How can one feel their soul? Or effects on it? It's senseless. It does not exist.

Yet . . . it shivers and writhes beneath my ribs and deep within my consciousness, fighting to break free like a chained creature that has been waiting to be fed for eons. And there, smirking inside my house, blowing a sultry, deviously taunting kiss toward the camera before she skips out of frame, is its first, only, and last meal.

"Holy shit . . ." Maddox whispers next to me.

Holy shit indeed.

The kitten has been playing with me all along, jeering with such expert precision and skill that I don't know if I'm supposed to be furious or awestruck. I'm both. And more than that . . . I'm fucking hard.

Not all the way, but goddamn it, this—her—she gave me a fucking semi. But she stole from me. I would have overlooked *The Divine Comedy*, but my violin? My fucking precious Crimson masterpiece?

That has crossed a line carved with bones and drawn in blood, and she's not getting away this time.

Scarlet won't die, not unless she damaged my violin, but she'll be punished until she's a begging, sopping mess, crying for reprieve. Because I need to know *why*.

Why taunt me?

Why break into my car, my bar, my fucking house?

Why follow me? Steal from me?

And on top of it all . . . *how*?

I have thick, high walls drawn in code, and I cannot think what skill level she has to match me so very well. What does she do for a living that she never sparkled on my radar? Where has she been hiding?

"I'm dropping you off," I tell Maddox as I cross the seatbelt over my body and start the car before rushing onto the road.

"Is she a threat, Carter? To you?"

I ponder the question for a few long moments, stepping harder on the gas, the angry engine rumbling through my thoughts.

"None of what she did was an attack. On us or me." I'm not making excuses. It's true. There have been no actions beyond these taunts.

I could argue that breaking into my spaces and hacking into my systems are attacks in themselves, but logic prevails here; she hasn't actually done anything. Definitely not to The Sanctum.

This has all been about me.

And it fucking nags me to no end that I haven't figured out why.

Maddox chuckles, a low, vibrating sound that startles me. I glance his way just as he shakes his head, suppressing a grin.

"What?" I say.

"You don't see it, do you?"

"See what?"

He's laughing now, a gruff rumble as he presses a large hand over his belly. "She likes you."

I frown, tightening my grip on the steering wheel. "You think she did this because she likes me?" That's preposterous.

"It's fucking obvious. Didn't you see that *sultry* smile on her? The kiss she blew? If that doesn't spell *'come hither,'* I'm not sure what does."

Come hither?

Christ, I thought I was the only one going mad, but maybe he is too.

"You need to get laid, Maddox. Clearly, you're seeing mixed signals all over the place."

He's not all that wrong, though, because I know she likes me. Well, she may not like me, but she is attracted to me. That, I can fucking guarantee.

"Don't worry, I'm all set in that department," he says.

Once again, I whip my head around, glancing at him before looking back at the road. "With?"

I have one obvious answer in mind, but I'm surprised he managed to hide it.

"Just a woman I met in The Fightclub."

There's no way it's who I'm thinking of. She never stepped foot down there. But this makes it even more shocking.

"So . . . it's a new thing?" I ask.

"A couple of weeks."

So not a one-time thing. Strange. But I nod, shifting my attention back to the road ahead and the problem at hand.

I wish I could get there faster, but the wretched kitten knew what she was doing by leaving the puzzle where she did. It's out of town, on the opposite side from her house. I'll even reach Midnight before my house. But I speed through the easing late-evening traffic, counting the fucking miles before we get to the speakeasy.

They trickle down, one by one, minute by minute, until finally, we're in the center of Queenscove. Midnight is nearby, hidden in one of the old alleyways.

"Be careful, Carter. And . . . have fun." Maddox swings the car door shut on a rumbling chuckle before I get to argue.

But I think I will.

I deserve some fucking fun.

CHAPTER 17
Scarlet

The familiar threads of adrenaline bloom through my muscles, anticipation putting a slight bounce in my step. Sexual frustration does too.

Since Carter touched me, held me, and warmed my aching body, I've been burning deep inside. It was all fake. Just a game. But fuck, it felt like he wanted more.

After I took out my anger on Cohen, who's nothing but a pile of ash now, I had to feed this blazing need. Perfect time for my final strike on Carter.

Playing with him has been exceedingly fun. My last move wasn't supposed to be today, but I got impatient after the feel of his lips against my skin. For my last move, I knew I wanted to steal something important to him, but I didn't know what that would be. Last night, I sneaked into his CCTV, and, by sheer luck, I caught him playing the violin. I saw it in his house, but for whatever reason, it didn't even cross my mind he knew how to play.

My decision was made the moment I saw him with it perched on his shoulder. I was mesmerized by the fluidity of his movements, by the beauty with which he played those chords. I had to stop watching. Somehow it felt wrong to be behind a screen instead of experiencing this in person.

So that was it—the violin was my final target, to make sure I pissed him off really good. I would have loved to see the look on his face when he saw the recording of me in his house. I would have followed him so I could get the opportunity, but there was no time. Tonight, Dad and I have an important job—and I'm gonna be late.

I make quick work of getting dressed, pulling on a sports bra, a long-sleeved, form-fitting T-shirt, and yoga pants. Matching my dark outfit, I slide on the usual black converse I regularly clean and keep away for jobs.

My phone vibrates, and Dad's name flashes on the screen. I answer on the second ring.

"*Evening, sweet pea.*"

"Hey, Dad."

"*Are you ready?*"

"Yes. Grabbing my laptop and my other phone now, and I'm out the door," I answer.

"*I'll wait at the end of your drive.*"

I hang up, grab two hair ties, and part my thick hair in the middle before I roll the length into two space buns on the sides of the top of my head. After one last fit check in the mirror, I turn off the lights and walk out through the back door in the kitchen, watching Dad's headlights come down the long, winding driveway that connects our houses.

Setting my "work phone" in the holder after I get in my car, I press on his other number as we both pull onto the road through the automatic gate.

"I checked traffic, it's all clear," I tell him.

"And our target?"

"Calm, but last time I checked, he kept looking at his watch."

"Perfect. It's a forty-five-minute drive, plus the car change in Cranwick. We should be there around the same time his date arrives. Then, in and out in fifteen minutes," Dad says, confirming the plan.

"I bet I can be in and out in ten."

With a hearty, rugged laugh, he guides the car along the dark roads out of Queenscove. *"Fifteen was already stretching it, but as you wish. I bet you dinner for a week."*

"And dessert," I add. "Homemade unicorn cake." I follow his car as he takes a left onto the regional highway. We're avoiding all the big interstates since most are monitored by cameras.

"I don't know what a unicorn cake is, but since I'm not losing, I don't need to. You better clear your schedule, sweet pea. You're gonna be doing a lot of cooking."

It's my turn to laugh because he will absolutely have to learn what the rainbow cake with a fondant unicorn on top is. I admit, ten minutes might be a stretch to get into Randy Wayne's mansion, navigate my way around the gargantuan space, and come out with our assets, but I love a good challenge.

The rest of the ride goes smoothly. The roads are surprisingly lively, and we like it this way. We don't attract attention when there's a stream of constant, albeit calm, traffic.

We stop in Cranwick, about fifteen minutes away from our destination, to pick up our second cars from their hiding spot. We drove them to the back of the abandoned gas station three nights ago for this purpose. On every job we do, no matter where it is, we change cars to these two that can't be traced back to us. Plus, they're so generic, so mind-numbingly normal, they don't stand out at all.

We reach Randy Wayne's estate through the road at the back of the property, in the small woodland that borders it on three sides. His need for privacy is our advantage.

I call Dad as I pull my laptop from the padded briefcase I placed in the footwell. A few years back, I accidentally broke the laptop screen on my way to a job. When I hit a pothole, it fell against the hard case of a toolkit. The bag it was in didn't help, and it fucked the entire job since I use it to control alarm systems and CCTV. So padded briefcases are my go-to now.

"What's the status?" Dad asks over the speaker.

My fingertips fly over the keyboard as I make my way back into Wayne's home security system, which I already hacked two months ago when we started researching this job.

"His date arrived," I confirm as I find the man in the grand foyer of his mansion.

I turn up the volume and listen to their conversation—small talk. Awkward. Not because he doesn't know the escort he hired, but because he's itching to get her down to his secret room in the basement. Every three weeks, he does this. He sends his wife and kids on a luxurious shopping trip somewhere far away from here so he can indulge in his secret desires. She's a dominatrix, and he's addicted to the degradation she offers.

I had the *pleasure* of seeing it all when I realized he has a separate security system for the basement and his secret room. It was all the insight I needed to figure out the best time to break into his house. I know how long he's going to be in there, and I also know he sends all the staff home the day the dominatrix comes. While he's busy in his little dungeon, the rest of the house is dead quiet.

Mine to play in.

"They're going downstairs," I tell Dad.

"Get ready."

I follow them on the CCTV as they reach the basement. His steps quicken when he nears the fake shelves that hide his secret room. I keep watching as they walk in, close the door behind them, and turn on the red lights inside, revealing an assortment of instruments and props.

My feet start to itch as I mindlessly tap my fingers on the side of the laptop, impatience riddling me even though I know I have to give them a few minutes to make sure they're deep into their play.

"Come on . . . come on . . ." I whisper.

"How long have they been in?" Dad asks as I chew on my lip.

"Four minutes."

"Give them five more."

The moment the man is butt naked, kneeling with his cheek stuck to the floor and legs spread by a bar, I know it's time.

Fuck yes!

Fingers flying on the keyboard, I disable his entire home security system, cheeks pulling into a victorious smile when it's all done.

"We're on!" I announce, ending the call and slamming the laptop shut.

I hide it in its case under the seat, pull my gloves on, strap on the hip pack with all my tools and the phone, double-check my hair is in place, and climb out of the car. There's such a spring in my step that my grin hurts my face, and Dad's shaking his head as he follows.

"Ten minutes, old man. Ten minutes," I say over my shoulder as I push back the ivy that has started growing over the garden gate. It covers the access pad now.

"Time starts now," he says as I connect my modified

keypad reader to the device.

I count the seconds in my head, cracking my neck as I wait for the numbers to be revealed.

Finally!

I could scream in excitement, but I quickly punch in the revealed numbers and crack open the gate.

Hiding in the shadows of the trees, I sprint through the estate's sprawling garden on light feet. I've done this so many times, it's second nature to move like I'm gliding over the ground. I have the back door unlocked and my lock picks back in the hip pack before Dad reaches me. I remove my shoes and hand them to him.

We step into the house, listening for a few seconds before I make a beeline to the other side and straight into Wayne's office. As planned, Dad waits by the basement access, just in case the owner's activities finish earlier than planned.

I cross through the atmospherically lit hallway, through too many formal rooms I bet no one in this house uses, and reach the office. As slowly as I possibly can, I crack open the heavy padded wooden door and walk into the dark space. The moon is on the other side of the house, so it's pitch black here and I can't see a fucking thing.

Be patient, Scarlet. Breathe.

Patience is not my fucking virtue. It never has been. Manic is more my jam. But I force myself.

Breathing in slowly, eyes aimed at the darkest corner of this room, I count to six, my gaze adjusting to the new conditions.

I know what to expect here—a trigger in the bookcase, which opens a heavy metal door to a panic room. The challenge is opening that without making any noise.

I find the right book after three tries, and something clicks.

Fuck, that was loud.

Pressing my hand to my hip pack, I wait for a vibration from my phone, but nothing comes. I let out a relieved breath and slip my fingers into the small crack behind the bookcase, slowly sliding the heavy door open.

My fingers itch to pull faster, but I can't rush this.

Eventually, the gap is big enough for me to slip through, and right there, on a fucking marble pedestal, laid on a delicate metal stand in the center of the back wall, sits my target.

Christ, that dagger is beautiful.

The long, slim blade carved from ivory is set in a pale gold hilt sculpted in the shape of a human spine. The hilt curves at the end, where a blood-red ruby is set. The sacrificial dagger was made to hurt the person who clutched it, thus symbolizing the price the soul pays for taking a life.

There's something disturbingly pure about that.

I walk over to the pedestal, inspecting all around it to make sure there's no trap. In all my research over the last weeks, nothing was revealed, but I have to make sure.

I find nothing.

Wayne certainly didn't expect anyone would break into his house to steal it, which is surprising, since he bragged to all the wrong people about getting his hands on the artifact.

I grab the dagger, smiling when the slightly sharpened vertebra of the gold spine digs into my palm. What an odd feeling. Satisfying, somehow.

As quickly as possible, I walk out, close the heavy door behind me, and make sure everything is exactly as it was when I came in. On hurried steps, almost tiptoeing in my soft socks over the wooden floor, I head back through the oversized, dimly lit spaces until I reach Dad again.

"Eight minutes," he whispers.

"Better not slow me down, then." I wiggle my eyebrows as I beckon him back the way we came.

The adrenaline rush hits like lightning in a warm summer storm, and I'm skipping and pirouetting my way through the shadows of the adolescent trees scattered through the garden.

There's only one other feeling that compares to the marvelous sense of achievement brought on by stealing something someone's going to be so unbelievably pissed about losing, and that's watching pain fall in streams of tears out of an asshole's eyes.

That particular feeling is unique. Unbeatable. And disturbingly esoteric.

"Damn. Nine minutes and fifty-something seconds." Dad shakes his head, scoffing with a smile on his lips. "I'm going to have to learn what a unicorn cake is, aren't I?"

I jump up and down like a lunatic with my hands in the air before I bow in mock acceptance of his unspoken praise.

"Time to go." I spin on my heels to head to my car.

The adrenaline wave I'm riding is exhilarating, and I revel in it as we head out of town to end our mission.

We have a good deed to do.

CHAPTER 18
Carter

I can count on the fingers of one hand the number of times I've been surprised in all my conscious years, and I'll still have fingers left.

What I'm witnessing currently is one of those moments. And potentially the most surprising of them all.

Because Miss Scarlet Brasa-Glass currently jumps like a madwoman—a painfully fascinating, stunning madwoman—with what I can only presume is the Baldvain sacrificial dagger clutched in her hand.

Sweet Mary, mother of Jesus . . .

"She stole it," I whisper to myself, watching from within the shadows of the forest as she hands the dagger to her father and heads back to her car.

This impromptu trip has been surreal, to say the least.

After I dropped off Maddox, I was about to rush to my

house, but I had to pause and remind myself that Scarlet has been messing with my mind, clouding it, masterfully switching my attention and turning me rash. I opened that link once more and confirmed my suspicion. The video was a recording. A recent one, judging by the lack of light streaming through the windows.

I changed my route to Scarlet's house in an instant. Just as I was setting off, the spy-cam app alerted me to movement. The wretched little kitten was strutting inside her bedroom, all sunshine and butterflies as she turned on the music and started dancing around as she undressed. She was already hypnotizing me with her swaying hips, arms high above her head as she moved to a rhythm I didn't even register.

I couldn't keep watching. Not when I knew breaking into my home, again, and stealing from me prompted the excitement.

Speed limits became guidance as I drove through Queenscove, toward her house. I was fucking ready to confront the kitten.

Only, even the best laid plans don't work out. By the time I parked behind her property and scaled the wall, her car was following another out of her drive. I didn't debate it as I went after them, following at a healthy distance.

When they finally reached their destination in Cranwick, the wealthy part of town with expensive mansions spaced far apart, I hid in the woodland shadows that surround the property. It's then that I realized Scarlet was with her father. The confusion grew, but I had a feeling all my questions would be answered soon.

She was so excited as she expertly broke into someone's garden. A secure place, too. The itch to follow her and learn more burned deep, but I couldn't. I kept an eye out while researching the property owner on my phone, trying to figure out why she's here.

Things started falling into place when I discovered it's Randy Wayne's house. I've heard of him. He's a wannabe interloper, dealing in hard drugs at a medium scale, but that's not the reason why the man reached my radar—that Baldvain dagger is.

The one Scarlet is currently holding proudly in her delicate hands as she jumps around after rushing out of the man's estate.

A precious, ancient artifact from the Bronze Age. A sacrificial blade used by the Baldvain civilization, lost over a hundred years ago. The ruby on its hilt is worth more than some people can fathom, but the whole dagger itself is priceless in cultural value.

Wayne bought it for millions on the black-market, after it was randomly found in a storage unit. Then the fucking idiot made the mistake of bragging about it.

It's irrelevant now, because it looks like he's no longer its owner.

Watching Scarlet victoriously celebrate stealing the blade from this idiot gives me a strange sense of satisfaction and uneasy anticipation.

As she and her father climb back into their cars, I run back to mine and follow them once again, trying to keep a healthy distance now that the night has grown quieter.

After about twenty minutes of driving, we stop once more. This time, not in the expensive suburbs or the outskirts, but right in the center of the next town over. I park in the shadows, tucked around the corner where I can still get a view of their cars.

"Where are you going?" I whisper to myself.

Scarlet's father steps out of his car, hood pulled well over his eyes as he takes a left and disappears between two towering buildings.

I look for Scarlet, who parked a couple cars back from him on the same street, but she makes no attempt to climb out or follow.

What's happening here?

Pulling my phone out, I open the maps app, hoping that one bar of signal can do the job and update my location, but that damn loading wheel keeps going and going, and a familiar strain tugs at my temples.

I could turn on my dashboard and access the car's GPS, but that damn thing will light me up like a Christmas tree and risk attracting attention. In a flash, the map on my phone jumps and the location updates just as a bright beam lights up the night before me.

"Shit!" I drop the phone on the passenger seat when Scarlet's car joins the main road, following her father's vehicle.

Whatever they were doing, they were damn fast.

I stay as far away as I can, following them back to where they left their cars, and the road becomes familiar once they make the switch. We're heading back to Queenscove.

Only, as they pull onto the main road and reach the first junction, Scarlet's father drives in the expected direction, but not her. She makes a left instead, and I don't even debate my next step. I follow her, wondering where she could possibly be going now, well after midnight.

Unless she's seeing a man.

Maybe that's where she went after she left me in front of the coffee shop, and why I couldn't find her until she went home tonight, too happy and excited.

My grip tightens on the steering wheel, chest strained, as tension builds between my brows.

No, no way. There was no indication in all the digging I've done about any other new boyfriend since her separation.

She could have found one since.

This bothers me so much more than it should. The idea of her with another man brings a strange, empty-yet-overflowing sickly sensation in my stomach. The idea of Scarlet with another man simply doesn't fit. It can't.

She fucking can't.

I keep following the woman, trying to figure out where I'm being led. I've never been around here, but it looks like she knows exactly where she's going, taking deliberate turns along the way.

We're well out of the city now, the roads quiet, thick clouds closing in and swallowing the moonlight.

I'm staying as far back as I can, but Scarlet speeds up dangerously. She races into the distance and takes the next left, about a quarter of a mile out.

"She knows. Fuck!" I snap at myself. My foot sinks onto the gas pedal to catch up to her.

No point in hiding anymore. Clearly, I haven't done a great job at it.

Her car is fast, though, and by the time I get remotely close to her, we're driving through a lush laurel forest, the darkness thick as smoke here.

I'm about to be thankful she's still sticking to the main road when the reckless woman takes a sharp right and disappears down a forest track, headlights flashing between the trees.

The moment I turn onto the track, lightning cuts across the dark sky like an omen, illuminating the menacing clouds.

One, two, three, fo—

Thunder shatters the night, its boom swallowing my engine's rumble moments before thick ribbons of rain drench my windshield. I almost skid, startled by the sudden downpour, but Scarlet hasn't really slowed down.

I'm driving like a maniac to keep up with her, the bumper and underside shield scraping over the mounds in the middle of the road created by years of heavy vehicles running through.

Yet, it's her I'm more worried about. A crippling thought pierces my mind—she doesn't know who she's running from. If panic or fear kick-started the need to escape, she could make mistakes in this worsening weather.

I need to stop this.

I flash my lights like a white fucking flag, hoping she'll get the memo and slow down. But it's no use. The only time she actually hits the brakes is when there's something on the dirt road, and each time, I notice the slight skid of her wheels. This rain has come too fast. The road is drenched, puddles already formed.

Fuck it, I'll stop and turn around. At least then she'll calm down. Because at this point, I'm worried she's gonna fucking kill herself trying to escape me.

I slow down gently, trying to avoid that fate myself, when Scarlet brakes and turns, drifting in a surprisingly masterful way to the right and disappearing through the trees. When I pass that point, her headlights disappear down that narrow track.

Braking to a stop, I drop my head back, expelling a heavy breath I've been forcing down. The rain doesn't fall. It pours. Buckets bash my car like it owes it something.

This doesn't change anything—I'll still confront her, demand an explanation. *Punish her.*

But I can drive back to her house and wait for her there. Maybe kidnap her, tie her up in my church. Force her to reveal all her dirty secrets.

Like why she's breaking into criminals' houses and stealing precious items in the dead of night. Why she's nowhere to be found online and has almost no virtual footprint. What was she doing when she came into the fetish club to take those photos of me? And . . . why exactly she isn't yet divorced from that asshole of a man.

I haven't figured out why I want to ask that last question. It brings nothing to the current predicament, but for whatever reason, I find it important to know.

Deeply lost in thought, I hear the car coming at me from behind before I see it. Its headlights are off.

I press my foot on the gas when I realize she has no intention of stopping, but my damn wheels skid into the mud, taking too long to get a fucking move on.

The rain is too thick, the road too slippery with mud and gravel, and I barely catch some speed when Scarlet's car slams into me from behind, propelling me forward.

"Fuck me, woman!"

Damn, she's mad.

She doesn't relent. Her headlights flash, blinding me in the rearview mirror, and I have the pleasure of watching them approach at speed just before she rams into me once more. I clench the steering wheel, attempting to keep the car steady as it skids left and right.

Really mad.

But I'm fucking annoyed now too. I brace against the steering wheel and slam my foot on the brake. Metal shrieks against metal as she crashes into me, and pain blooms in my neck from the strain.

My dashboard lights glitch dangerously, but the car still moves when I press the gas, so I ignore it. I look over my shoulder, trying to catch a glimpse of her.

Is she okay?

Tightness grips my chest in a cold vise. Only one of her headlights works, and at the same time I notice movement in my mirror, she accelerates once again.

For some odd reason, I feel a tug at the corner of my lips as that vise eases behind my ribs, and I accelerate more as she nears me.

All those flashing lights definitely mean something, because even though I catch some speed, it's not nearly enough to put distance between us. At the same time, lightning strikes in front of us, closer than I've ever witnessed it before, and the tree it hits falls in a flaming heap onto the dirt road.

I slam the brake, hoping my foot can find another magic length to this damn pedal before I crash into that broken tree. I pull the steering wheel to the left to avoid a head-on collision. My wheels catch on something hard, and my ass hurts as I bump the seat, the seat belt cutting into my shoulder.

In a blinding light, with a deafening crash against my side, my world spins off of its axis. Over and over. The car tightens around me, changing shape as pain stings through my neck and white fabric blows around me, cushioning my body.

"Holy . . . fuck." I blow out a loud, thick breath like I'm using it to figure out if my lungs still work and my heart is beating.

It's definitely still beating because I can hear it in my fucking ears and feel its thump in the backs of my eyes.

I'm upside down.

Lovely.

Where's Scarlet?

The thought rams into me harder than anything else tonight, and I rush to crush down the airbags surrounding me, fumbling for my seatbelt. But the fucking thing either isn't responding, or my movements are too frantic.

I try to brace my feet to push myself up and release the tension on it.

"Goddamn it, unclip, you bastard!" I rage, screaming into this damn storm I can now feel through my smashed window. "Fuck! Scarlet!"

I need to get to her.

"Yes?"

CHAPTER 19
Scarlet

"Scarlet!"

The visceral notes in that scream make me pause.

Concern at the edge of desperation weaves through, and I frown, utterly confused since that certainly does not sound like who I thought it would be.

Who the fuck is in this car?

"Yes?" I bend down to look through the broken window.

"Jesus Christ, woman!" The answer comes out startled.

"It was you?" I shriek when I'm met with motherfucking Carter Pierce hanging by his seatbelt. "For fuck's sake! What the hell are you doing here? I thought you were—"

Bernard. I genuinely thought it was him trying to scare me off.

"How many houses have you broken into tonight?" The pause in his words is charged with dark promises. "Who were you expecting?"

"Just two," I say, the giddiness in my tone shielding the slight unease I feel.

He doesn't reply, only pins me down with that frigid stare of his.

"I'd ask why you're following me, but I guess you're much quicker at solving puzzles than I thought."

Over the heavy rain, I'm not sure I heard it right, but I could have sworn he growled.

"Yes, I've become quite experienced," he mutters.

If looks could cut, his would have me split in half.

This impromptu meeting is inconvenient. I had a plan, a good one I've been working on since I decided to fuck with him. It would have ended beautifully, and potentially peacefully too. Now . . . I have to adapt.

"Bet you had a bit of fun, though." I wink.

He narrows his eyes for a split second and shakes his head. "A hand, if you will?"

"Now, why should I help you? You want to kill me, after all."

"May I point out that I stopped following you, and *you* rammed into me?"

Fair, but still.

"Promise you won't kill me," I say.

His answer is a deep, malevolent growl buried so low in his chest, it threatens to shake the earth beneath my feet.

"Pro—"

"I promise."

Okay, that was easier than I thought it would be.

"Say please," I push, pursing my lips.

He narrows his eyes on me, but from this upside-down angle, he looks fucking hilarious.

"Scarlet." A threatening rumble laces his tone, hitting low and deep inside my belly, with a fiery undertone.

"Yes, Carter."

His nostrils flare as he blinks slowly, running his tongue over his top teeth. "Would you *please* give me a hand?"

"Sure thing!" I drop to my knees, giggling and grinning from ear to ear, much to his exasperation. "Here, I'll brace you."

I slide my shoulder under his, ignoring the jarring pressure in my torso as I push up with as much force as I can muster, until I hear a click.

"Got it."

He didn't need to say it. His weight barrels down on me, and I scamper backward, falling on my ass. He thuds to the floor—well, technically it's the ceiling of his car—before he slides out, caking his suit in mud. My ass is soaking in it too, since I'm in a whole puddle of it.

I could probably wash myself off in this rain, the downpour's so heavy.

He rises, attempting to swipe the mud off of his trousers before he straightens, towering before me. Wet, disheveled strands of hair fall on the right side of his head. His suit clings to raw, taut muscles, his eyes wild with something I can't quite put my finger on. Lightning splits the sky behind him, rumbling clouds explode, and before them, Carter looks like the vicious god ruling them all.

My chest rises and falls on heavy, ragged breaths, and water runs over my face as I seem to be stuck to this spot.

He reaches for me, his hand outstretched, and all I can do is stare at it, wondering if it means more than I think it does.

Finally, I grab it, but when he pulls me up, I slide in the mud and land right against him. Our bodies are lined up, his arms wrapped around me, and my inability to breathe has nothing to do with how tightly he holds me.

"All good?" he asks in a whisper.

Rain slides off of him and onto me. The droplets from his

hair hit my lips as I hold his malice-laced gaze. I would take it personally, but that's his usual expression—cold, devoid of emotions, yet so stunningly beautiful with those hazel eyes drenched in that saturated blue.

It feels too good in his arms—warm, entrapped by the possession I'm sure I'm imagining—but I manage a nod in response.

He seems unaffected as he looks past me, toward my mangled car, and frowns. I know, it's bad. Really bad. Yet somehow, seeing *him* here, not Bernard, has made some of that anger toward my ruined, beloved car die down.

"What the fuck were you thinking, Scarlet? What if I was someone else?"

His borderline scolding startles me, and I recoil, head tipping slightly back as I study the phenomenon.

"Umm . . ."

"Umm . . . what if I was undercover police?" he asks.

I frown, lips parting and ready to fight back. Only, like a fish out of water, I shut them and open them all over again as I realize . . . *what if?* It never crossed my mind.

"I didn't—look, I thought you were someone else."

"Who?" A frown deepens the ridge between his brows.

"It doesn't matter. Can we please get out of this rain?"

I push against him, but the vise around me tightens, arms pressing me harder into him. I should protest more, or at all, but he's warm. Surprisingly inviting.

He holds my gaze, looking into my eyes for too many charged moments for me to still believe I'm imagining things. Right here, trapped in his gaze, it feels like I'm skirting the edge of a cliff—perilous, addictive, utterly hedonistic—yet I'm home at the same time.

"I'll call for someone to pick us up." He breaks the moment, releasing me.

Picking the pieces of my broken hope off the ground, I nod, and he turns around, dropping to his knees to search through his upside-down car. A shiver pierces my flesh, the absence of his body against mine quite unwelcome.

I turn and go to look for my phone too. I slip several times on the mud and drenched gravel, but thank the gods my car is still the right way up.

"Fuck." Carter's swear filters through the battering rain.

"What?" I call out.

There's a pause before footsteps near.

"No signal."

Fuck indeed.

That's not good. Not good at all.

A faint thread of unease snakes around my guts, and I take one controlled, deep breath to dissolve it.

It's fine. It's. Fine.

Finally, I find the device under the passenger seat. The screen is cracked, but it still allows me to see the unfortunate situation we're in.

"Scarlet . . . what is—"

"Oh, no. Oh no! I don't have any signal either." I clutch the phone tightly in my hand, that thread of unease coming back with a vengeance, morphing into panic, multiplying, and gripping my insides.

I'm already pacing, feet slapping through the mud as I bite my lip, pressure forming in my temples.

"Scarlet." Carter's tone is nothing but wind weaving through the thick raindrops.

"We're stuck here. No cars. No phone. In the middle of the woods," I mutter to myself, pacing from one end of the car to the other. "*Fuck.* And there's this damn storm. The cold. Oh god, what will—"

"Scarlet!" He's on me. Strong hands clutch my shoulders

as he turns me to face him.

But I don't see him. Only a smudge of his beautiful, brutal face. I did this. I brought us here. Caused the crash. Forced us into this situation. I doomed us.

"Look at me!" With his guttural bellow, my focus snaps.

I see him, his eyes shadowed as he looks down at me. My cheeks almost warm as he holds them, forcing my full attention on him.

He doesn't add to the command, yet I don't falter either, because it lingers in my mind. My muscles. Somewhere deep in my soul too.

There's an intimate quality to this moment. Our silence carries through the deafening storm, leaving room for a truth I didn't allow myself space to acknowledge before. I am obsessed with this man, yes, but more than that . . . I like him. Really like him.

His thumbs move, brushing slowly, his gaze charged with a restraint that might crack soon, as he forces them away from where his digits reach dangerously close to my lips.

"Scarlet . . ."

"Yes . . ."

One second, I'm convinced he might feel the same, and the next, he blinks and the slight spark I saw through the darkness snaps out of his gaze.

"You're bleeding."

"Huh?" I have to blink away the stupor I've been trapped in, because his words don't fully register.

"You're bleeding." He looks between us, then lets go of me, taking half a step back before he drops to one knee.

I could get used to this. I snicker to myself.

He fumbles with his phone, the flashlight too bright as he turns it on and aims it at me.

"Oh." I reach over to where the damage is, but he grabs

my wrists, pulling it away.

"You're dirty. Do not touch it."

Shit, of course.

"Oh god, where is that from?" My hands tremble as I look down, but in this darkness and with all the pouring rain, I can't see shit.

I can't even see blood, only the slight rip in my dark T-shirt, but with the panic threads now gone and Carter's intoxicating gaze away from mine, my brain finally focuses on that feeling it's been pushing back.

I am hurt. This fucking night just keeps getting worse.

Though, with this man kneeling at my feet, head tipping back to look at me with a sinfully cocked eyebrow, it might not be that bad after all.

"You're running on adrenaline, aren't you?"

Sure, that's it.

He can't yet know why my reaction is not quite . . . normal.

On a series of quick, jerky nods, I begin to fumble with my fingers. "Is it—is it in my back?"

His head bobs up and down slowly. "I saw it when you were looking for your phone. Don't look," he says as I'm about to pivot. "It's very close to your waist, so it's unlikely it hit anything important, but I should pull it out."

"I thought you're always supposed to leave that stuff in," I argue.

"Not always."

I frown. "What is it?"

He rises, placing one hand on the small of my back, bringing me even closer to him as I crane my head to catch more of those droplets that fall off of him.

"What are you doing?" I whisper, but before the last word leaves my lips, something scrapes through my insides, and I flinch against him.

He brings his other hand between us, and I grab the bloody object as he steps back.

"You've got to be fucking kidding me." It's my goddamn pencil.

Of all the things that could have impaled me during the car crash, the pencil out of my toolbox was it.

"Hands up," Carter orders me.

I frown at my extended arms, wondering why I didn't even question his command.

He stands before me and wraps his suit jacket around me, tying it tight around my waist.

"It will keep pressure on the wound."

"Thanks."

He cocks his head, scrutinizing every bit of me. "Are you okay?"

"I'll be fine. Thank you." I strain my voice, trying out the fake gestures I've learned over the years—jerky movements, biting my lip, repeated blinking, and heavy breaths.

He doesn't question me further. Instead, he looks at his phone, slides his fingers over the screen, and shakes his head.

"Do you have any idea where we are?" He shows me the map app.

I pinch the image and move it about until I find the rough area. I'm familiar with it. In my research for this job—or any job—I map out all the routes of escape or distraction. This was one of them. Though, I'm not one hundred percent sure where exactly in the forest we are. And I know for a fact we're not close enough to civilization to walk through this raging storm in the middle of the night.

"There." He taps on a brown blob on the screen. "It's a cabin of some sort. And I think we're around here." He points to a spot that's not quite that far. At least, not on his screen.

"Are you sure about this?"

"Do you have any other ideas, Scarlet? Because we sure as fuck can't walk back to Queenscove, and going back to the main road will take much longer than reaching this cabin."

"Wow . . . not sure you've ever spoken so many words in a row to me before." I take a dig at him.

His nostrils flare as he fixates on me. My breath catches in my chest. Without another word, he turns and walks back to his car, kneeling inside it again. He still says nothing as he rises and walks away, passing the tree line and moving into the forest.

"Wait!" I stop him, running back to the car to grab the briefcase with my laptop.

It's slightly banged up, but I'm confident it's fine. He looks at me, then the case, but turns around without asking about it.

Why do I have a feeling I'm in for a hard, brutal night?
Because you basically asked for it, silly woman.

CHAPTER 20
Scarlet

I'm not sure how long we've been walking, but I'm convinced of one thing—Carter Pierce was born in utter silence.

It's the only explanation for how comfortable he is with this lengthy silence.

He found out I've been breaking into his car, business, and house. That I've been following him. Messing with him. I stole from him. Caused this car crash. Stranded us in the middle of a forest during a damn monsoon. And he hasn't spoken one word to me since we began walking.

Either he's using this time to plan a fantastic revenge, or . . .

I got nothing.

I'm uncomfortable. Nervous. And, frankly . . . cold. This damn storm isn't doing me any favors.

The ground beneath my feet is so wet, there's no crunch

when I step over the leaves, twigs, and whatever else lies on this forest floor. It's dangerously slippery, and the last thing I need right now is to get injured. Again.

The dull throb in my side seems to intensify at times, and I can't help but feel a little worried. I don't care much when I hurt myself, but I'm not usually stuck in the middle of nowhere with no access to medical care.

I need a distraction.

"Can you slow down, please?" He's only a couple of paces ahead, but in the heavy downpour, my words don't travel. "Carter!" I shout.

He whips around, his gaze urgently searching the forest before he finally settles on me.

"Are you okay?" he asks, the words low yet alert.

"I just wanted you to slow down."

"We can't."

"Well, I can't walk as fast as you. You're taller. You cover more distance with your gigantic steps, and I'm slipping all over the place."

It's too dark here to read his expression, but my imagination runs wild. Is he scowling? Rolling his eyes? Or maybe he's sweetly sympathetic.

I almost audibly scoff at the ridiculousness of the latter.

Carter turns and continues walking. No answer. No acknowledgment. I smile when his pace slows, allowing me to catch up. But he's still quiet, focused on our non-existent path ahead or his phone, and I'm getting more fidgety by the minute.

"Okay, can we get this over with?" I plant my feet in the mud, clutching my temples before I throw my hands to the sides as he turns excruciatingly slowly toward me. "I can't take this anymore! This charged . . . silence. Just lay it on me!"

Lightning cuts across the sky, catching the exact moment Carter cocks a naturally sculpted eyebrow that fuels my frustration further.

"Seriously. Let's get this out of the way," I insist.

"I'm good."

Frowning, I recoil, shaking my head in disbelief. "You—what? You're *good?*" I exclaim, rushing after him when he dares to turn around and walk away again.

Thunder blasts through the night, the wretched rain punishing my skin as I grab his forearm to stop him.

"Cut the bullshit, killer-boy. There's no way you're not bothered by this, regardless of your promise to let me live."

His eyes move from my hand clutching his forearm to my body, traveling upward until they meet mine. If looks could draw pain, his would douse me in it. I'm a sucker for a challenge and I refuse to let go, though I'm a little hurt he's so bothered by my touch.

"Do not call me that infernal name," he seethes.

Tilting my head, I playfully cock an eyebrow. This is it. My opening to get him talking.

"Would you prefer I text it to you? You sure do like it when I text you. When I tease you." I step in front of him, splaying my palm over his chest, searching for his heartbeat. "Call you that *infernal* name with my hands buried deep between my thighs. Touching. Stroking. Thrusting."

My other hand is still tightly wrapped around his forearm, and I tip my head back to catch his gaze, despite the heavy raindrops.

"Where's that man from the texts? The one who wanted to strip me. Spank me. Make my slutty little pussy drench him." I drag my hand down his chest, over his abs flexing beneath my touch, until I hit the buckle of his belt and pause.

His nostrils flare, yet tensing his muscles is the only movement he dares.

"Where's the man who wanted to make me bleed and

come?" I reach lower and press my hand over his strained length. "Who imagined pushing this fat cock inside of me?"

He tries to shield the hitch in his breath, but his body betrays him, cock twitching and hardening under my touch, the hollowness beneath his cheekbones deepening.

"Where's the man who asked if I slept well? Hmm?" I give him one hard squeeze as I lean into him. "Where are you, killer-boy?"

I could have blinked and missed it if it wasn't for the air rushing over my skin, the rough bark digging into my back, the breath ripped out of my lungs, or his menacing grip around my wrist. It took one swift move to back me against a tree with one hand immobilized above my head as his body traps me here.

"Carter—"

He wraps his hand around my throat, trapping any remaining words there as it tightens.

"Stop. Fucking. Talking," he says through gritted teeth, his intense gaze boring into mine.

I dig my fingernails into his forearm, shuffling against the tree as I struggle through the pressure intensifying in my throat. But with it, something stronger blooms behind my ribs. It threatens to spread. Lower.

"Is this what you were so desperate for?" His grasp clenches my throat. "Punishment?"

I writhe against his body, clawing up his arm as the strain grows, spreads up to my temple, and settles behind my eyes. A mesmerizing, borderline-terrifying dizziness follows. The air becomes grit as it barely manages to pass through my airways, and I squirm harder against him.

"Well, here we are, kitten. Your life in my hand, your punishment, my own dirty pleasure. Because, trust me"—he leans in further, his whisper laced with vengeful lust—"all I dream of recently is punishing you. I knew from the moment my car was broken into that you were the culprit. But *you*, wretched little thing, you made me doubt my instincts. Sent me on false trails. Derailed me. *That* is what I most want to punish you for."

His body lines up with mine, his cock nestled against my lower belly, right in that spot above the pubic bone that brings a strange kind of pleasure. His grip on my throat clenches tighter. My body fights back on its own. My chest fills with terror as the strain increases until it threatens to crack me open.

What little air was able to pass through has now converged at the base of my throat. Lodged tight.

Almost . . .

Almost *painful*.

And something magnificent blooms through every single nerve and fiber of my being.

CHAPTER 21
Carter

If it wasn't for the sharpness in the hitch of my breath, the slight ache in my chest, and the strain in the widening of my eyes, I wouldn't be able to accept the shock rippling through me right now.

Pure, untainted shock.

I didn't miss the moment threads of fear filtered through her pretty eyes. Mere heartbeats after delightful beats of panic vibrated through her pulse, straight into my touch.

But neither of those visceral feelings looks back at me now.

Delight. Pure and utter delight shines in a maniacal grin that brightens every feature of her stunning face. Except her eyes. They darken with a powerful need I'm convinced I'm the first to satisfy.

I don't know what to do with this. I've never seen such

satisfaction in response to pain. To the promise of punishment and the prospect of death. It's only ever been play. A game.

But Scarlet knows death is something I can certainly deliver, and though I've promised I would spare her now, the fact that I'm capable of it seems enough.

Yet here she is . . . pulse slowing beneath my touch, skin wet and hot against mine, one soft, delicate hand making my cock harder than I think I've ever been. Like a pathetic, lovesick puppy, I can't stop gawking at her.

On this perilous precipice she's drawing pleasure from, malice sharpening her soft features, she's the most beautiful thing I've ever seen.

The *only* beautiful thing I ever want to see again.

Though, I have a feeling nothing will ever compare from now on.

Scarlet is ruining me.

The maniacal grin begins to falter as the sparkle in her eyes dims ever so slightly, her hand on my length easing its grip. But I want to capture this moment fully. Imprint it on my skin. Learn its flavor and remember it forever.

So, I do.

I descend onto her with the same force as this punishing storm, crushing my mouth to hers like her flavor could escape me if I didn't. Lips soften as the shock makes way for indulgence, and they draw me in like sirens at sea.

Goddamn it, she's exquisite.

She tastes of everything I've ever enjoyed and nothing I've ever encountered, all at once. Wildflowers in bloom and destruction bred from fire. She tastes like she's the end of all I've known and the beginning of my new favorite experience. Honey and spice layered beautifully.

Her lips part fully, letting me in when I release her throat, and she draws in a deep breath like she pulls the life force directly from my lungs. She presses against me, greedily demanding more, tongues clashing as we explore each other with vicious need.

Scarlet's moan trembles against my lips, my tongue, and yanks an unfamiliar, foreign growl from deep within my chest. It's charged with a need and ardor never before heard in my voice.

My cock strains heavily against the seam of my trousers, and I rip Scarlet's hand away, ignoring her disappointed plea as I grab her ass and yank her upward. She takes but a moment before she catches on and throws her legs around my hips. The wanton cry that spills from her lips tastes so fucking sweet, my knees threaten to buckle. My cock nestles against that warm spot between her inviting thighs, lined up so perfectly with the covered seam of her pussy. She grinds against me, seeking pleasure with delightful desperation.

Hooking her free arm around my neck, she pulls me harder against her before she breaks our kiss to let words pass.

"If I knew earlier this is how you punish . . ." She trails off as she strokes my tongue with hers, lips clashing in a wild, hypnotic kiss.

It's not how I punish, but it's certainly a punishment. Only, it's me at the receiving end, because this is not enough. I want every single bit of her aligned with me. Her naked skin against mine, my lips on her softness, her softness on every inch of my body. And the worst thing is . . . I never want it to end.

Ever.

But it has to. Right?

There will come a time when she realizes that my darkness is too devoid of stars for her.

I can't learn to be around her. I can't allow myself to get used to her.

Because she'll leave.

But I certainly can indulge.

"Grind on my cock like that, kitten, and you'll learn just how far off from punishment this is." I break the kiss, licking the raindrops off her lips between every other word.

"I think you're all talk, killer-boy. A pretty mouth that spills sweet promises it can't deliver."

My body stills, muscles straining under the wet clothes, yet my cock hardens even more than I thought possible at the blatant challenge. The gall of this woman. The women I *play* with would never. The cane would meet their ass, their thighs.

But Scarlet is not a woman I play with. She doesn't know the rules. If she ever finds herself strapped to one of my benches, I'm afraid the rules will go out the window and a line I've never crossed will turn to ash.

What if, though . . .

I release her wrist, drawing my palm down to her ribs, thumb dangerously close to her breast.

"You're making one dire mistake," I say, grinding my cock against her pussy.

A strained moan escapes her, taking control as she rolls her hips, seeking more pleasure. I oblige, pressing my aching hardness onto her, pumping my hips as she feeds off of this chaste pleasure.

"Punishment is not bred only of agony, kitten." I dip in, gently scraping my teeth over the crook of her neck, licking my way to the sensitive spot behind her ear before I bite and suck as she shudders in bliss. "Sometimes, it's born of the deprivation of pleasure."

I drop Scarlet back on her feet and peel myself away from her awfully inviting body.

Even in this faint moonlight, I can see the heavy raindrops slipping through the angry crease formed between her brows, dropping off of her parted lips as she regards me in utter outrage.

"I can't believe you just did that," she murmurs.

"Come on now. We need to find the cabin."

I don't even bother to acknowledge her shock, no matter how hard my cock is or how twitchy my fingers are to find that soft, warm spot between her thighs.

"Don't you fucking walk away from me, Carter Pierce!" she yells, then grabs my wrist, yanking me backward. Or attempting to.

I halt and look over my shoulder. "Don't be a brat, Scarlet."

"I'm not a damn brat! I just can't believe you just—" She's smoldering so beautifully. "Finish what you started, killer-boy."

"You're not used to being denied what you want, are you? Grew up a bit too spoiled, kitten?"

She stops dead in her tracks, tightening her grip until my wrist bone screams at me in a heated ache and she rips her hand away. The outrage is completely wiped off of her features as she fixes me with an irritated, fiery gaze.

"Don't you dare speak of my upbringing like you know anything about it." She's seething, her entire stance tensing with words clearly heavy with more than just memories.

Frowning, I cock my head, studying her demeanor and reaction. She's not just upset—she looks almost haunted by fresh ghosts of her past—and the need to figure her out grows to a dangerous level. Something happened to her.

Embers sizzle behind my ribs, and an aching hollowness strains in the pit of my stomach. As I try to decipher those odd sensations, another more disturbing involuntary reaction follows—a threatening rumble, deep in my chest. Close to the same spot where Scarlet's essence seems to be settling in.

What the fuck was that?

I'm fighting the urge to trap her, peel off all those layers, and find out what happened to her and who hurt her. My thoughts are interrupted by her shadow flying past me.

"You coming?" she all but growls, already a few steps ahead.

"You're going the wrong way," I call out, proceeding to walk in the right direction.

I hear her follow, but I don't turn. As much as the bratty behavior intrigues me, I'm fucking soaked, caked in mud, and cold. And we're just over halfway to the cabin. It better have a damn roof.

Scarlet pops up next to me, falling into step. I glance down at where my jacket is tied around her waist, but in this lack of light, it's impossible to tell how much blood soaks it. We need to get to that cabin as soon as possible. Though a fucking hospital would have been better.

"How are you feeling?"

"Fine." Her answer is clipped. Cold.

I frown, turning my full attention to her. "I mean your . . ." I point to the spot where she's wounded.

She turns frazzled, wrapping her arms around herself as she avoids eye contact and focuses forward.

"Like I said, fine." Her tone brightens, but there's something slightly off about it. "Don't worry, I'm not gonna cry about it."

Clearly.

We walk in silence the rest of the way there. Mainly out of necessity, since the storm thickens. Water bashes us with the help of the intensifying wind, filling our mouths with water every time we try to speak, but I don't miss the stolen glances, just as she doesn't miss mine.

I wish I could find out what's going through her head. If I ask, she'll probably just glare at me, but I have so many questions. About her. What she stole tonight. What her father did with it. If this is a regular occurrence. What she does for a living. Why she fucked with me. And so much more.

All those questions will have to wait.

"There!" she screeches. She leaps toward the cabin, which appears in a clearing barely bigger than it.

It's a small wooden building, slightly crooked, with only one window on this side next to its old, slanted door. The glass is still there, though, and that's a good sign for now.

"Scarlet! Stop!" My sharp, guttural shout cuts through the heavy downpour as I rush toward her, managing to block her way into the cabin. "Stay here."

"What? Why?" she asks, frowning. She recoils slightly as my stern gaze lands on hers.

"I'll check it out first."

Cocking an eyebrow, she considers my words, then nods, stepping back. I turn around and press the wooden door's rusty, heavy handle. After turning on the light on my phone, I aim it inside.

The space is tight. Really tight. A basic kitchenette covers half the left wall, with a large storage chest filling the rest. As I step inside, I spot a wood-burning stove tucked behind the door, wood stacked high in the corner, and across from it, a small bed squeezed into the farthest nook.

One ridiculously small bed.

"Oh shit . . ." I mutter under my breath.

"What was that?"

"Nothing. It's all clear," I announce, making room for her as I walk further into the vacant space.

"Damn, when do you think someone came here last?" She swipes her finger over the kitchen counter.

"Hard to say. Dust settles fast in a place like this."

Especially when the narrow cracks between the wall boards let the wind howl through. There aren't many, but the leaking roof near the wooden chest doesn't help. A puddle is already forming on the floor.

Scarlet stops before the blanket-covered wooden bed, the moments she takes to stare at it stretching uncomfortably. Her shoulders tense, mirroring my own uneasiness—we'll have to share.

I'm bracing for a flurry of complaints—demands too—yet the woman startles me as she claps her hands together and turns on her heels with a spring in her step.

"Right, please pick up that bucket and come with me." As she walks past me, she points to the old tin vessel tucked away beside the kitchenette, then disappears out the front door. "Chop, chop, killer-boy!" she calls out, impatient.

Tension builds in my temples. This damn woman raises my blood pressure so much that I might end up in the hospital before the night ends. Yet, intrigue takes over, and for once, I do as I'm told.

"Right, let's see . . ." she mutters to herself as she bounces around me in the rain, attention focused on my clothes.

She takes the bucket from my hands, places it in the corner where the water drains off the roof, then hurries back to me. I flinch when she touches my back, brushing her delicate hands over my muscles as I frown, confused. But I tense further when they're on my ass.

Is she wiping me?

She sighs, the sound sharp, and mutters something I can't distinguish.

In the next second, she pops up before disappearing again, bouncing around me as she studies me. I'm too mesmerized to question her, realizing she's trying to remove the mud from my clothes with quick and unsteady movements. But I'm more caught up in her slightly unhinged perkiness and the unexpected care she's showing.

She's a motherfucking ray of sunshine in this apocalyptic storm.

One moment, she's behind me. The next, she's crouched at my feet, swiping frantically at my trousers.

"Scarlet, stop th—"

"This isn't working." She shakes her head, rising to her feet, and I don't even think she heard me. "Right. Off with them."

I frown as she cranes her neck to fix me with her dark gaze. She doesn't offer an explanation. She removes my jacket from around her waist and dumps it into the bucket, ignoring my protests completely when I try to explain she needs to keep it against her wound.

The woman hushes me, demanding I strip as her T-shirt flies over her head. She's already kicked her shoes off, and she's pushing her leggings down.

She's an unhinged, blood-boiling, stubborn little woman, and I can't even argue with her. I'm forced to watch the strings of blood flow out of the small wound on her side, mixing with rainwater as she ignores the damn thing completely and demands I hand her my shirt and trousers. I oblige, then bring my gun and holster inside the old cabin, taking the opportunity to look for a first-aid kit in the few storage spaces.

"Bingo!" I exclaim as I finally find a weathered tin stocked pretty well with everything from gauze to painkillers.

Someone's definitely using this cabin. What a surprise they're gonna get next time they come here.

I want to look in the large chest, but the ache in the pit of my stomach calls me outside. To her. I need to make sure she's safe.

So I hurry back out, gauze and tape in hand.

"What are you doing?" she asks when I grab her arm and pull her to her feet, turning her side to me.

"You're bleeding."

"We already knew that, genius."

Her insult drifts over my head as I focus all my attention on patching her up. It's temporary. I'll have to replace it when she moves her ass back inside the shelter. But at least it will put some pressure on the wound.

She squats down the moment the bandage is on, and my attention is once again pulled to her actions. To the care with which she rinses the mud off our clothes passing one by one through that small bucket before she attempts to squeeze the better part of the water out.

I tell myself that I'm *relenting* when I begin to pluck them out of her tired hands and wring out the excess water, but the reality is that there wasn't much protest in my intention. I help her with each garment, taking them inside one by one and temporarily laying them on the wooden chest. There are only five pieces of clothing, but the repetition grows curiously comforting. Domestic, somehow. And the empty bucket sends an odd, disappointing sensation through my stomach.

I walk out of the cabin but halt, mesmerized. The kitten stands a few feet away, arms spread wide, head craned back, closed eyes aimed at the sky as she takes in every heavy drop battering her almost naked body. The cotton panties cling to every curve, sports bra tight against breasts I've already admired, and she makes no attempt to come out of the deluge.

I've already crossed half the distance before I realize my legs are acting on their own, pulled in by this ethereal image. My fingers itch to trail down her skin, and deep in my chest blooms a need to feel what she feels right now. The rawness of whatever emotion drives her to stand there and absorb the chaos of this ruthless storm.

The beauty in her burrows deep beyond her soft skin, and it compels me to attempt to experience the world through her eyes.

Maybe she hears my steps, maybe her instincts alert her to a predator closing in, but she straightens and turns to me slowly. Charged moments pass, stretching the silence that has been remarkably comforting between us, and just like this cloudburst, the reality I've been shoving into the deep corners of my mind assaults me.

Scarlet can't be someone I simply play with in Metamorphosis. Definitely not a quick fuck, or a singular, all-night-long conquest. She can't be part of my life temporarily. If I let Scarlet in . . . she will never be rid of me. Nor I of her.

The slight shake in her flesh is the only thing capable of pulling me out of this train of thought, and I urge her toward the cabin, refusing to walk in before she's safe inside.

I shut the door behind me, annoyed that apart from an old lock a strong wind could break through, not much else keeps us secure in here.

With the lights from our phones turned on, we make our way through the tight space. She moves the bucket below the spot where the roof leaks, and I scramble to make a fire in the old stove. Luckily, all we need is already here. The cabin is well stocked by whoever uses it. Yet, with my thoughts distracted by Scarlet's current state, it still takes me a few attempts to get the fire going. Though, my lack of experience contributes to it too.

But it's on, lighting up the space as well. When I turn, warm light bathes Scarlet, shining and sparkling over her wet skin as she stands next to the bed, arms wrapped tightly around herself.

Her clattering teeth make me anxious, but her lack of interest in the wound soaking the bandage concerns me more. I've been watching her, and I wonder if she either has a really high tolerance for pain, or she just masks it extremely well.

The latter raises too many questions that threaten to

turn me violent, especially combined with her sharp retort regarding her upbringing.

She turns toward the bed, cocking her head.

"Do I dare?" she asks, bending over to lift the blanket that covers it.

"Not yet. Sit," I tell her, walking toward the wooden chest to look for something that could help me take care of her.

"I'm fine," she argues.

"I said *sit.*"

Her eyes widen, the protest shining bright in her fire-lit gaze, but something else, something more *primal,* glows just a bit brighter. Then she sits, hands clasped together in her lap, attention fixed on me, complete absence of protest, but the defiance is there . . . in the goosebumps marring her skin.

That does something to me. Her obedience to my words. The responsiveness. It makes me wonder how else I could bend her to my will.

It makes my cock twitch. Hard. It heats my blood and brings to the surface cravings I've been ignoring. Desires that exist for her and her alone.

I don't know if the stove is doing its job or it's me who's suddenly hot, but it takes me a moment to gather myself and turn back to the task at hand.

"This is useful." I pull out the rack I find folded and tucked next to the wooden chest.

"What's that?"

"A clothes rack. To dry them." I unfold it and set it in front of the door, next to the stove, before I grab our wet clothes and hang them there.

Scarlet wants to help, but I stop her. She's done enough.

With a screech, the lid of the wooden chest gives way as I lift it open, revealing all sorts of treasures inside. A weathered fur, a couple of blankets, a pillow, and a few towels. I'm not sure how clean they are, but they'll be perfect to attempt to dry our hair with, Scarlet's especially.

I grab the pillow, blankets, and towels, running one of the latter quickly through my hair before I set them all next to her on the bed.

"I can do it." Scarlet attempts to stop me as I capture her hair in the towel and squeeze the water out.

But I respond with a stern look that settles her instantly. Calmly, I massage her hair, her scalp, allowing myself a few extra moments.

When most of the excess water is absorbed, I gently pat down her skin, then tend to her wound once more.

"It's bleeding, but it's not too bad."

"Thank you," she murmurs.

Yet again, I don't hear the little strain in her voice that I'd expect from someone in pain. Or at least discomfort.

"Up," I order.

She cocks an eyebrow, and I don't miss how she sheepishly chews on her bottom lip before she does as she's told. I drape a blanket over her shoulders, wrapping her tightly in it, then peel off the cover so that I can inspect the bed.

"It's clean," she exclaims.

"I think whoever uses this brings clean linen with them and takes away the used one each time, based on the contents of that chest."

"We'll have to make it up to them."

I nod in agreement.

"Take off your underwear and slide in."

"My underwear?"

"It's wet." I briefly turn to her, cocking an eyebrow as I grab the towel and dry myself before laying it over the lid of the chest.

I put the pillow in place, carefully folding the second towel over it to avoid getting it too wet, then gesture for Scarlet to get in. She listens, jumping in and setting all blankets over her shivering body.

"What about you?" she asks.

I'm already pulling down my boxers, reveling in her sharp intake of breath as I hang them next to her underwear on the drying rack. When I turn and walk toward the small bed, her eyes widen, but fuck, her mouth is wider. A little pride blooms inside me. Way down low, it hardens too, and I can't help grin.

"What about me?" I respond as I lift the blankets and slide in.

"You're serious!" She yelps as my cold skin makes contact with hers.

"It's either this or one of us will be extremely uncomfortable, and potentially cold, on the dirty, wet, wooden floor. And it's not going to be me." I shift on my side, tucking the blankets behind me.

We're facing each other, burnished flames dancing over her features as she attempts to keep her naked body away from mine. But the bed is too small, and I may not be as big as Maddox, but I fill this pretty damn well.

"You're shaking, kitten." I tease. "You won't be going on the floor either."

"Yes, I will. Right in front of that stove."

I roll my eyes and lift the blankets to make a little space. "Turn around."

"What?"

"Turn around, Scarlet. Back to me."

I poke her with my knee, suppressing a laugh when she slaps my bare chest.

"What's your intention, killer-boy?" She flips over, and I tuck a bit of the blanket between my cock and her ass, attempting to be the good guy here.

"To keep you from freezing."

She groans deep in her chest when I wrap her in my arms and press her against me, muscles softening as our joined bodies begin to produce a bit of heat.

"Better?"

Silence stretches.

Finally, she nods.

But those quiet seconds allowed my thoughts to drift toward an answer . . . *I'm not better.*

Fuck, I'm much more than that.

In this foreign, unfamiliar place, in a stranger's bed, with Scarlet tucked within my arms, I think I found home.

I'm done pretending I'm not ready to fuck this woman into oblivion. I need to get her out of my fucking system or fuck her deep enough in there that she can't pry herself out.

And I don't want her out of my system.

CHAPTER 22
Scarlet

Rain mercilessly batters the cabin's roof, filling the silence that stretches between our slightly out-of-sync breaths.

The blanket he tucked between his cock and my ass wouldn't provide us with modesty, even if he wasn't half hard. The slight bulge pressing into me drives my thoughts to dangerous, delicious places.

I caught a really good look at what hangs between Carter's legs when he undressed, and . . . it truly hangs. So much so that I had to lick a little drool at the corner of my mouth.

He's been the main character of so many of my dreams in the last few months, but, my lord, even I didn't imagine the carved masterpiece I'm currently held flush against.

I'm afraid to breathe, in case it causes me to accidentally grind against him, yet I'm not sure why. It's not like I've hidden my attraction for the man. Maybe it's this night, this small bed, or the fact that there is quite literally nowhere to run, that messes with my head. With my guts.

My muscles started relaxing once our bodies began warming each other, but damn, they've tensed back up now that I feel his taut skin and how his heartbeats vibrate through my flesh and join mine. Even his chaste hold on my shoulder seems to itch to slide somewhere more intriguing.

The breath I pull into my lungs weighs me down. It sizzles in the air around us, charged with an intensity that seeps through my skin, goosebumps rippling all the way up my back. My back rolls, and my ass pushes against him involuntarily.

I swallow my apology when I hear him suck in a breath.

"Would you have done it?" I blurt out, rolling my eyes at myself. "Would you have really killed me?"

"If you were a threat to me or The Sanctum, yes."

"Just like that?"

"Yes." His bluntness sends shivers down my spine.

"And you've decided I'm not a threat." I purposefully phrase it as a statement, not a question. Maybe it's wishful thinking for the sake of self-preservation.

"You made me promise not to kill you."

That's definitely not what I needed to hear, and I tense further.

"So, you do think I'm a threat."

"Only tonight, I found out it was you who stole from me, infiltrated my business, and invaded my home. I don't know why yet. You tell me, *kitten*, are you a threat?"

His hand tightens on my shoulder, body pressing more firmly against mine, and with his cock hard against my ass, I can't fucking think straight. I imagine him ripping the blanket away and sinking his length so far between my ass cheeks that

I scream louder than this storm from the hedonistic intrusion.

Fuck, I can't think straight!

With a clumsy, rushed turn, I face him. His arm is still wrapped around me, palm now laid on my back, and if I thought I couldn't think straight before, well . . . this was a big mistake. Flames dance through his devilish eyes, making his carved cheekbones harsher in this light, and . . . the blanket no longer separates us.

He holds my stare. I hold his.

My breath stalls in my lungs. The warm tip of his cock twitches against my belly.

The stove must have warmed up the cabin because my skin grows damp. And deep between my joined thighs, it turns . . . slippery.

"I'm not a threat to you," I whisper, but it comes out breathy. *Needy.*

Carter's empty eyes remain unchanged. Unaffected. And slight disappointment prickles in my chest.

"And my Sanctum?" Right there, in his low, smoky tone of voice, I can hear that he's not all that unaffected.

"It was never about them. But you already knew that," I murmur.

No answer comes, but in his eyes, I notice a spark that has nothing to do with the flames.

"You ruined my last plan," I tell him.

"How? You successfully stole my violin."

I uncross my arms tucked tight to my chest and lay one hand over his waist, reveling in the noticeable hitch in his breath and the goosebumps suddenly peppering his skin.

"I may be a thief, but I wasn't going to keep the things I stole from you. You were supposed to come after me at my house. Not here. But you figured out the puzzle much faster than I thought you would."

"I'm a pretty smart guy," he says with a sinful smirk that makes me even wetter.

"Clearly."

"And what then? At your house?"

"We would have hashed it out over a glass of exquisite wine. Talked about how exciting this little game has been. I would have convinced you to stop this nonsense about killing me. And we would have called a truce while enjoying a nice swim in my pond. I have a very nice pond." I flutter my eyebrows, grinning suggestively.

"And you think that would have been enough to convince me? Wine and a swim? After everything you put me through?"

"My charming personality too." I answer with that same smile on my lips.

"Charming, indeed." Laced with sarcasm, it doesn't sound like a compliment at all.

He lifts an eyebrow when I shift closer. My breasts press against his heavily tattooed chest, and his entire cock lines up against my pubic bone. But I recoil slightly; something cold and hard digs into me.

"You okay, kitten?"

I'm not sure.

"Wha—what is that?"

"Jacob's ladder."

I frown, utterly confused by his response, but only for a couple of seconds. Because the penny drops and a random memory filters through—cock piercings. Rungs of a ladder running up the underside of his penis.

Sweet Mary mother of God.

Okay, okay. Focus, Scarlet. You're better than this.

"Let me ask you this," I say, lifting my leg to splay it over his. Turns out I am, in fact, not better than this. "What would you be killing me for? Watching you murder a man? Or stealing your precious violin?"

The first answer comes from his fingers digging into my shoulder blade and the slight pressure building there.

The second is his hardening cock, no longer half-mast against my pelvis.

And the third is deeper. Darker. His eyes turn menacing, like they absorb all light cast onto them from the flames at the opposite side of the room.

His palm settles on the small of my back, the tips of his fingers tickle my cheeks, and he presses me against him, holding me firm. I almost forget what my question was, because his cock is nestled onto the slippery seam of my sex, piercings sat comfortably against that sensitive part of me. A flurry of electric tingles bursts from my clit, spreading through my body on a shiver.

"You tease me, Scarlet." He drawls my name like it was born on his tongue. "Forgetting that you're trapped here, all alone, with the predator you've been carelessly poking at for weeks." He mercilessly grinds against my center, pinning me against the onslaught of pleasure when I try to pull back.

Fully distracted by the ecstasy in my core, I don't react in time as he flips us over and tucks me under his towering body. I'm drenched in darkness beneath this feral man, folding my leg over his that he shoves beneath. At this angle, the torture comes from his thick length assaulting the drenched seam of my center, warming metal rolling against my pulsing clit.

"Look at you now, kitten. Pinned beneath my body, your warm little cunt weeping for me. So very greedy, aren't you?"

He bucks his hips, and the moan I've been keeping tucked away in my chest explodes out of me as I sink further into the pillow.

"That's it. Show your true colors, Scarlet girl. Show me just how much you want my cock to teach you how to harness rough pain into mind-bending pleasure. Is that why you're so wet for me, little whore?"

I shake my head because opening my mouth might only reveal another desperate moan.

"I like a fighter, and I yearn to punish a filthy little brat like you."

He rewards me with another grind of his hips. This time, the tip of his cock catches on my aching clit, sending my whole body into a violent shake. His breath tickles the crook of my neck as his teeth scrape the sensitive parts of my ear.

"I could have both, you know. I could shove my cock so deep into your messy, needy cunt and break your pretty little neck at the same time. Right here, in the middle of this forest . . . and no one would know. No one would find you. I would probably fill you with my cum, regardless."

One hand drags over the base of my throat, leaving goosebumps in its wake as a strained whimper breaks out of me.

"Or maybe I'll keep you alive until that final moment, when your last breath strangles my cock and every bit of my cum fills you."

"Fuck . . ." I moan, wondering just how sick I am to get so fucking horny at the thought of my death. But the mental image of this man fucking me raw, straight into oblivion, is the hottest thing I've ever pictured in my head.

"You would like that, wouldn't you?" He licks the side of my throat, grinding his cock through the wet seam of my core, the tip teasing my entrance but never penetrating. "Dirty little slut, you would love to be utterly helpless as you squeeze my cock and I do the same to this delicate throat. Such filthy"— he licks the edge of my jaw up to my chin, and the breath stalls in my throat—"filthy desires you have, kitten."

"Yes," I whisper so low that I'm not sure he heard me.

"Tell me why you fucked with me, my business . . . my home. Tell me why you played me when I so very graciously spared your life."

That sentence pulls me right out of my pleasure-laced stupor. I pull out the knife I tucked between the mattress and wall and put all my force into flipping us over. We fall with a violent thud onto the wooden floor, wrapped in a mess of blankets, and I revel in the surprise I finally see in Carter's eyes.

He grips my hips as I straddle him, glancing down, but he can only feel the blade I hold to his throat.

"Now, where did you get that little thing from?" he asks, quirking an eyebrow.

"I swiped it from the kitchen when I was taking my underwear off. A girl has to protect herself when a *predator* is in her bed," I taunt.

"And you say you're not a threat to me."

"I may just be when you dare to fucking claim that you 'so very graciously spared' my life, asshole!"

"You're alive, aren't you?"

Does he have selective memory loss?

"Not because you didn't try! Someone else stopped you, otherwise I would have been dead in the middle of a jewelry store!" I'm raging, balancing the tip of the knife in the same spot he sliced the skin on my throat.

But I can't control my hips from rolling onto his cock, torturing him with pleasure just as he tortured me. Fuck, it feels so good. I don't blame him for wondering how it would feel to fuck me and kill me at the same time. Especially now, when I know piercings adorn his beautiful length.

The man dares to chuckle, actually fucking chuckle, and digs his fingers into my flesh as he pushes his cock against my pussy.

"Ah, that little thing. Is that why you're so tightly wound, kitten?"

Excuse me?

"**Y**ou almost fucking killed me! Do you have any idea how angry that made me? You left a damn scar on me!" Scarlet roars on top of me. The flames dancing behind her give her a delightful, feral quality.

My answer comes with the press of my hips, cock straining against her weeping pussy, pulling a strangled moan out of her pretty little throat that bears my mark. *Gorgeous*.

Yet, she doesn't falter.

"That's why I did it all. It was my goddamn revenge. You needed to understand you may be the lion of this jungle, but it's the fucking lioness who controls the kingdom. There are consequences, even for your mighty actions, *killer-boy*."

Well, I'll be damned. I hurt her feelings, and this devious, intriguing cat-and-mouse game was her revenge.

This kitten isn't going anywhere.

I'll fucking chain her to me if that's what it takes to keep her to myself for the rest of my days. She's the unhinged little beast to the hungry creature living beneath my skin.

"Stop fucking smiling and apologize!" She slaps my chest, seething as she leans forward to get better leverage with that knife against my throat.

My cock springs up as her pussy lifts off of it, the tip lining up damn near perfectly with her drenched seam. I think I may be seeing stars, because even that warmth shoots electric pleasure straight into my balls. Scarlet's eyes drift closed for a few delicious moments, and a twitch pulses into the tip of my shaft.

"If it's an apology you're begging for, it's not going to come," I tease.

"You fucking bastard!"

A sharp hiss tears from my throat as a sting sears across it, my hips jerking up involuntarily, clutching hers tighter. Stars explode behind my eyes. Because that single, hitched motion drove my cock deep into Scarlet's unbelievable cunt. Three of the four rungs of my ladder vanish inside her.

Crying out, she hurls the knife to the side, bracing herself against my chest with one hand while the other locks tightly around my wrist as I clutch her hip.

Fuck, I think I dreamed of this moment. Of her tight walls strangling every inch of me. Sweet whimpers as she impales herself on me. Only, I'm sure I imagined it without the blood currently flowing out of the cut in my throat. She could have actually killed me, and I didn't even take her seriously.

"Oh, fuck!" She slaps my chest, attempting to lift herself off my cock. The friction derails her efforts, and she whimpers as her head falls back, a sensual motion that holds my gaze hostage.

Sliding her hand off my throat, she pulls back to straighten, and her gaze widens as one more rung slides inside her sweet, pulsing cunt. She brushes her palm against her belly, and when I notice the blood left in its wake, a feral instinct blooms within me. A primal need that never surfaced because no target was ever worth it.

It is now—Scarlet is worth it.

"You look good against my pale skin." That unhinged grin of hers is back, painting her features in pixie delight as she looks at her bloodied hand.

I grind my teeth when she adds more, gently rubbing her hand over the cut on the base of my throat. I should be pissed she sliced through one of my tattoos, but I'm strangely calm and proud to bear her mark.

"What are you—?"

The question catches in my throat when she lifts off my cock until only the tip remains. She grabs it with that drenched hand and paints it in violent shades of *scarlet* like my dick belongs to her.

When she lowers herself on my bloodied cock, taking on each piercing one by one, counting silently until she's balls fucking deep, I think nirvana herself gazes upon me, because I'm about to fucking come. And I realize I may really be right— my cock definitely belongs to her.

"Jesus Christ, woman!" I dig my fingers into her flesh, guiding her as I piston my hips to meet hers.

That feral creature beneath my flesh brims with each glimpse of my blood-coated length.

"Mooore," I growl.

And with that grin pulling at her lips, she adds more blood between thrusts. But she doesn't stop there. She spreads it all around her pussy, using it to rub her clit as she throws her head back and revels in the filth of it.

"My dirty little whore. You look so fucking beautiful just like this, painted in the color that bears your name." I slide my hands down her thighs, rejecting the instinct to take control. "That's it, kitten. Fuck my cock like your sweet cunt owns every inch of it."

She moans in response, grabbing onto my forearm to brace herself as she bounces on my shaft. The slapping of our skins forms my new favorite melody. Abstaining from coming is a fucking Olympic sport, and I may just be a gold medalist, because it's damn near impossible with a pussy like Scarlet's wrapped around my cock.

I'm done for.

"You're so goddamn good at this, kitten," I rasp.

"Oh, Carter . . ." She whispers my name like a ritualistic chant. And I'll happily be her god if this is how she worships at my altar.

"Take everything you need from me. Take it all."

A full-body shiver ripples through her, strangling my shaft as she collapses onto my chest. I grab the back of her neck with one hand, wrapping the other around her hip to hold her still and take over. Jerking my hips to meet hers, I roll them slightly at the end when her whimpers grow with the movement. Over and over, I fuck her twitching cunt, reveling in every single mewl that falls from between her pretty lips.

"This . . . is too much. So much . . ." she whispers breathlessly, as if this onslaught of pleasure is a true assault.

"It's not nearly enough, love."

I pump my hips, grinding my pelvis against her clit until every inch of her blooms in goosebumps and her moans turn into lust-filled cries.

"Bend back, Scarlet."

"Wh-what?"

I guide her up, ignoring her protests as she clings to me.

"Brace yourself backward."

She frowns but follows the order and leans back, steadying herself on the floor next to my thighs.

"Holy fuck!" she exclaims as the angle allows my cock to grind harder against that magical spot inside her core. "Oh, Carter."

"Keep saying my name just like that, in that slutty, breathy tone, and I'll ruin this pretty pussy, Scarlet."

She cries out as she slams her hips down, rolling them as she all but uses me to get off.

"Ruin me . . ." she whispers.

I take control, wrapping my hands around her hips and holding her only a couple of inches above me, then fucking her like her life depends on it. I pump my hips upward, easing out before I ram right back in, repeating the movements as she whimpers and chants a series of curse words in her melodic voice.

Her legs tighten around mine, breasts blooming in delightful goosebumps, core pulsing faster as a full-body shiver ripples through her.

"Oh, fuck, Carter . . . I—fuck! I don—"

She doesn't need to ask for it. I know what she needs.

I release one hand from her hip, bringing two knuckles to her clit and bearing down on it. It takes three rolls before spasms shake her entire body. She cries out as she drenches me with her pleasure.

I've never experienced a woman reveling in her orgasm quite like this. I'm so fucking fascinated by the way she squeezes my shaft, so enraptured by the pleasure she douses me in, I almost forget to pull out. I scramble to lift her off, but she frantically shakes her head, slamming down on me and trapping my cock inside of her.

"Scarlet, I—"

"Come!" she rasps.

And by God, I do.

My cock spasms almost violently within her choking pussy, and I spill inside of her. Ribbons of cum jerk in her warmth, and I swear I feel it rippling through my lower belly, my lower back, and up my fucking spine.

She collapses onto me, whispering something about having the contraceptive implant as she buries her head in the crook of my shoulder. I almost chuckle at the practicality infiltrating her ecstasy. She still trembles softly with her orgasm, and I'm barely reeling back from mine.

I find myself with my arms circling her, one hand on the back of her neck, holding her to make sure she doesn't get away from me. But I pull her head back just enough to see her pleasure-tainted features.

Her eyes flutter open, a dark abyss pulling me in, and I crush my lips against hers like she's my only lifeline as I lose myself in her darkness. The kiss lacks the hungry violence I was expecting. It's doused in lazy passion, in comfort and indulgence. And I drown myself in it as I delve into her inviting mouth, stroking her tongue with mine, sucking her lush lips, and tasting every sweet, soft part of her.

When we break for air, it's lighter. Colorful, somehow. And I know it's she who is changing my atmosphere.

"This was a mistake," she whispers.

"Why?" I ask. Her words cut unexpectedly.

"Because you're the first man to ever make me feel this way. To . . . make me come."

"Oh." Now that is truly shocking. Too many thoughts go through my head, ranging from How the fuck is it possible? to Hell yes, I'm the first to have the privilege.

"Either me and you are it for the end of times," she adds, "or . . . I don't know how to go on without feeling this . . . bliss ever again." The truth dances with the flames in her eyes.

It may be the lingering orgasm messing with my brain, but there's no fucking way any other man gets this privilege from now on. All of her orgasms are *mine*.

"You can't expect to tell me I'm basically your first and think there's any fucking chance for anyone else to touch you, Scarlet. Consider this first orgasm my mark on you. No one gets to touch you ever again."

I don't miss the hitch in her breath, and I could have sworn my heart beat just a little faster.

"That's quite a caveman thing to say," she says.

"I don't care if you don't like it."

"I didn't say I don't, killer-boy." She rises just enough to better pin me with her intense gaze. "Just remember one thing; if your mark is on me, mine is on you. And I'll gut any woman who dares to fucking touch you. Make sure you're okay with that, otherwise there's gonna be a whole lot of blood on your hands." Her tone is laced with honey, sunshine, and bloody butterflies. So colorful and sweet you could miss the blatant, disturbing threat.

I take in her violent, utterly possessive words, and I could have sworn my cock, which is still inside of her, twitched. Christ . . . she really is an unhinged little beast.

"Kitten, you wouldn't hurt a fly," I tease.

"That's true—I wouldn't hurt a fly. Or most animals, for that matter. But humans are a whole different story." That feral look gleams in her eyes, bringing forth a feeling so deeply familiar I could be looking into a mirror.

She's speaking the truth. I just know it in my gut.

"You're not fucking with me, are you?"

She slowly shakes her head. "Tell me your preferred *poison*, and I'll tell you mine."

She's serious. But this is it, my opportunity to learn more about her.

"You know mine already."

"Carving?" she asks, though it's more rhetorical.

I nod.

"It's long. Drawn out. Effective for extracting information."

"It is," I agree. "It's useful, but it's not why I do it."

"Why, then?"

I reluctantly pull my cock out of her, ignoring her protest as I shift her to the side and rise to grab a towel, then sit down next to her.

"When I carve into them, when I flay them alive," I say, pushing her thighs apart to wipe her clean, "it's to observe the array of emotions passing through them. It's fascinating to see which one settles in, because it's always different. I do it to see their reactions to each one, to feel their screams against my eardrums and experience their fear, their regret, their desperation. It's enthralling."

She's propped up on her elbows, observing me as I finish cleaning the blood and cum from us both. I throw the towel to the side, and she cocks her head, heavy with unspoken words. I feel analyzed.

I rise to my feet, then help her up. She silently protests when I nudge her into bed, grabbing the first-aid kit to gently clean the cut on my throat first. When she's done, she happily jumps onto the mattress, lying patiently as I give each blanket a little shake before I lay it on top of her.

A strange sensation passes through my gut. It takes me a moment, but I identify the signs. I wish I wouldn't, because this is vulnerability. *I am feeling* vulnerable.

A small shockwave ripples through me. Intense, yet oddly comforting in its novelty. I don't push it back but embrace it as I slide into bed next to Scarlet. I wrap her in my arms, our legs a tangled mess.

"You don't really feel much, do you?"

Her question echoes through the chambers of my mind.

"Not really, no."

I expected her expression to change, for me to see some form of a negative shift in her features. But there's none. She just nods.

"Does that bother you?" I ask.

She ponders for a moment. "Do you feel any emotions?"

"Complex emotions are foreign. I can understand anger, frustration, all those interesting ones you *graced* me with lately. I can feel a sort of basic joy, satisfaction."

"What about . . . um . . . care?"

"To a certain level. I understand that the people close to me are there for a reason. They would put their life in danger for me, so logically, I would do the same for them. They are my people, who I trust completely for all logical reasons, and maybe some illogical ones, so if this is care, then yes. I can feel care."

She chews on her lip, blinking a bit more rapidly.

"Anything more *intense* than that?"

"Not yet."

But I know the words are a lie before they even spill from my mouth. Blatant fucking lie. Because right here, with Scarlet wrapped tightly in my arms, unfamiliar, *new*, raw emotions riddle me to my fucking bones.

And goddamn it, they feel good.

CHAPTER 24
Scarlet

I try to squash and shove away the disappointment that attempts to make a home in my soul. He can't feel what I desperately need him to for us to be . . . us. Carter can't feel love.

He said it himself—care is a logical reaction that he understands, but anything more intense is simply unfamiliar to him. How can I be with a man who would never love me?

No. Not "would," but "could." He *could* never love me.

One can argue that his love is the last thing I should want since he clearly lacks certain parts of his humanity. I've looked into it before, back when I was trying to understand my own murderous tendencies. I would have preferred to be like what I think he may be—a psychopath—but sadly, I discovered I'm simply evil. Or maybe he's not a psychopath and he has alexithymia, an odd, fascinating condition I discovered as I fell into that research hole for weeks.

I'm curious. I've seen the emptiness peering back at me.

It's as if his eyes are made of precious stones—beautiful, but cold. Like all emotions were stripped long ago, yet they still linger deep in the untouchable abyss of his soul. Because he looks like he was born of despair that finally accepted its condition.

I think there's more to him than a simple diagnosis, and I shove back that intrusive voice that tells me he'll never be able to give me what I want, because I crave to peel his layers and find out more about him.

Especially when he's so keen to keep me.

"And you, Scarlet?" he asks, pulling me out of my thoughts. "What's your *poison*?"

Only my family knows my deepest, darkest secret—my need to inflict pain on others. I even kept it away from Bernard, and I can't pinpoint why I didn't feel like I could share it with him. Now I know that deep down, I never trusted him.

Yet, as I stare into Carter's devastatingly beautiful gaze, something clicks.

"Pain," I rasp.

Fuck, it feels good to say it. It feels even better to see the slight twitch in his eyes, like surprise and intrigue mars them.

"Brutal, raw pain is my poison." I exhale a breath of relief. "I *love* seeing how it lands."

"Really?" he asks, genuine interest in his voice. No judgment. No horror.

"Oh, yeah! Their reactions to it are addictive. And I— What are you doing?"

Carter slides down my body, his lips dragging over my breasts, reaching my peaked nipple. He sucks on it until pleasure ripples deep in my belly.

"Continue, Scarlet. Tell me more." He dives beneath the

blankets, tongue and teeth brushing around my belly button, over to the sensitive dip next to my hip bones, before he continues down.

I yelp when he grips my hips and yanks me sideways so I'm on my back. He situates himself right between my thighs, breath close to that aching spot that still bears traces of him.

"Carter, I—Aaah!" I cry out when he pushes his tongue inside my core, regardless of his cum still coating my walls, then sucks my clit like he genuinely wants to take my breath away.

No warning. No teasing.

"Tell. Me. More," he orders, punctuating each word with another stroke of his tongue.

"Oh, fuck." A few centering inhales are required to find some stray brain cells through the mind-bending zaps of pleasure. "I-I love how crushing their bones twists their vocal cords."

I grip his hair with one hand, steadying myself on the wall behind me with the other, my breaths sawing out of me as hard as his tongue presses inside.

"How the indignation and . . . ego shining in their eyes turns into a sheer veil they think I can't see through," I continue.

Fuck, he's *so good* at this. A surge of pleasure crests inside of me, tearing at my walls to rip their way out as he builds the pleasure higher and higher, stroking my clit tortuously slowly with his thumb.

The peak is in sight once more.

Just at the edge of rational thought and pure, unkempt oblivion.

"What else?" he presses, before he licks me with the flat of his tongue. My back arches off the bed in response.

"It-it's a marvelous thing," I blurt out between whimpers, "affecting the body—Ah." I cry out when his tongue dives back inside me, eating me out like a man starved. "And the mind. It quickly makes an atheist choose a god to believe in."

He chuckles against my sex, sending tingling vibrations through it, and I press him harder against me, fingers tangled in his hair as I moan.

"So wet. So greedy. So *perfect*," he praises, voice low, husky. "My wild fucking girl."

"Aaah!" Pleasure arrows deep in my core as he plunges his fingers inside.

"This pussy is mine now." He lays his claim as a current strikes through my body with each powerful thrust of his fingers.

Yours . . .

I don't know if I spoke that word or just thought it. He growls against my folds, hungry and demanding.

"What else do you love about inflicting pain, kitten?"

But I'm struggling to form words when his digits stroke the most forbidden parts of me on a maddening rhythm that threatens to rip away any semblance of sanity.

"It's a beast . . . lying dormant inside people." My back arches high, nails scraping against the wall above my head with the pleasure rippling from the clit he so expertly sucks. "And when it gets a voice . . . it devours their humanity. Powerful enough that it even turns them against the ones they love the most."

Memories flash in my mind of people who had fallen victim to me. Beautiful moments of agony I carefully mapped out and learned. Enjoyed. Now they mix with this exquisite assault led by Carter's tongue and fingers. The combination is exquisite.

He knew exactly what he was doing when he slid under the covers.

A trap I launched myself into.

But I wouldn't crawl out, even if I could. The ecstasy is

addictive, cresting higher and higher, and I *need* to find out where it takes me. It feels different from before, when he fucked me so very well and gave me my first ever orgasm by a man.

"One more," he whispers.

My pussy stretches with a further intrusion. A fullness that makes me writhe with the wanton pleasure it brings. With erratic breaths, I roll my hips like I'm fucking myself with Carter's fingers.

"Yes, just like that, my greedy little whore. You're so fucking wet for me." His smoky praises work on me just as well as his fingers, and I would crawl at his feet if he'd keep talking to me like that. "Pain is a wonderful thing, love. What do you like most about inflicting it?"

"Their tears." I don't waste a breath with my reply. "Blood, screams, or death are not the peak of it all—tears are."

He rolls his fingers against that sensitive spot that has never felt another person's touch before. My ex is completely clueless, clearly, and the few before him never took the time.

"They're the tangible relinquishment of hope in the face of agony," I add between heaving breaths.

His tongue presses against my clit as his lips latch onto it, pleasure brimming at an untouchable edge I want to dive off of as I curl my toes and dig my heels into the mattress.

"They're the omen of finality," I whimper. "The ode to pain."

With that last word and one final roll of his digits, I explode around them in bursting stars and ripples of ecstasy coiling inside my sex, my belly, through my spine, gripping my nipples and tearing out of my throat in a primal scream that puts the thunderous storm to shame.

"And I collect them all . . ." I whisper through the orgasm's shattering waves.

Carter

THROUGH THE FASCINATION AT SCARLET'S violent orgasm, quivering body, and pleasure-laced features, my mind snaps to that moment in her house when I saw some delicate vials under the vanity mirror. Are those it? The tears she collects?

She's such a weird creature.

And here I am, fucking mesmerized by her.

"I don't know how you did that. Twice," she murmurs in a lazy, well-fucked voice as I crawl up her body and lie next to her.

"Almost make you squirt?"

"Sorry, what?" she exclaims with widening eyes.

I pull my hand from under the cover, her wetness all but dripping off of the three fingers I fucked her with, though my entire hand is coated. Half my face too.

"Oh my god . . ." she whispers. "Let me get you a towel."

"I'll get it, love." I slide two of those fingers between my lips, sucking her sweet flavor off of them on a long groan.

"Holy fuck," she all but moans.

I cock an eyebrow, then slide out of bed to grab the discarded towel, wipe myself, and slide back in.

"And you really never orgasmed before by another person?" I ask.

Shaking her head, she looks sheepish for the first time since I met her.

"No wonder you're divorcing Camora."

She bursts into chesty laughter, and I'm transfixed. God, the more time I spend with this woman, the more I find new things to be enthralled by.

"If only that would have been the reason. But others before him were just as unsuccessful. I thought I was to blame."

The mention of the other people she's been with makes me want to track them all down and beat the memories of Scarlet right out of their brains.

"What was the reason?" Finally, I get to know why she's divorcing Camora.

"I found out he was cheating on me, for quite a while. That night, actually . . . when you and I first met."

"And that night you were . . . ?"

"Trying not to kill them both," she answers bluntly.

I think I understand. She was removing herself from the situation.

"Walking alone through the dark alleys wasn't the most *brilliant* idea, though," I say.

"Actually, it was. You see, murder for me is not a sick craving to satisfy my bloodlust. It's an almost involuntary reaction to fury. My wild fits of rage are rash. Destructive. And chasing an adrenaline-fueled high in the absence of a kill is the only way to calm my nerves."

"You willingly put yourself in danger to spare that fucking asshole?" I seethe between clenched teeth.

She has no response to that. Just stares at me as the dying embers of the fire sparkle over her features.

"When we return home, I'll take him out for you."

"Y-you would do that? For me?" She's taken aback, gaze wide and starry-eyed.

I nod, the words somehow too heavy to be spoken. Admission of my possessiveness over her is too difficult. But it's here, scratching beneath the surface, begging to crowd her against the wall completely and fuck her yet again.

"He's not worth the muscle strain. Once the divorce is done, he'll be out of my life," she says. "Then he can live happily ever after with my *former* best friend while I mind my own business far away from them."

"He fucked your best friend?" That is low.

She nods, a hint of sadness clouding her gaze.

"He didn't just fuck her. He had an affair. Someone like me doesn't make friends easily. But she and I clicked long ago, when we were teenagers. Anyway, it's all dust in the wind now."

It isn't, though. The hurt still brims in her eyes, her emotions a pain-filled shield she's throwing around her.

"Why isn't he granting you the divorce?" I ask.

Rolling her eyes, she sighs. "He's blackmailing me."

"All the more reason for me to kill him. What is he blackmailing you with?"

"Jewels."

I frown, but something clicks into place. "This has to do with your business, doesn't it? Like whatever you were doing tonight."

"Yes."

"Is that what you normally steal? Why your stepmother owns a jewelry store?"

"Normally, but not always," she says.

"You didn't steal jewelry tonight," I acknowledge, already knowing the answer.

That mad grin returns to her soft lips, eyes narrowing in mischief as she shakes her head.

"Is it in that briefcase you insisted on taking out of your car?" I ask, intrigued to see the famous dagger.

"No. And thank you for reminding me of my lovely Agatha. My poor, precious girl."

I cock an eyebrow. "Agatha?"

"Pretty name for a pretty girl—my car. God, I'm gonna miss her."

She's so fucking strange. And I want her even more for it. But sadness taints her eyes, and there's something fascinatingly tragic about it. It makes me want to fix everything for her and make sure that wretched emotion never shares the same atmosphere as her.

"What did you do with the dagger, then?" I'm intrigued, but I also want to distract her from the car she's clearly very sad about.

"Donated it to a museum," she says with a wide, proud grin. "Slid it into their mailbox with a note. Oh, to be a fly on the wall when Wayne not only finds out his precious conquest was taken from him, but that it magically appeared in a museum and he can't do anything about it."

Soft wrinkles crease the skin around her eyes, alongside the pure joy shining in them, and I'm . . . enthralled.

"Impressive."

That timid smile returns, and I can't help but wonder if, in this growing darkness, I'm missing flushed cheeks too.

"What's in the briefcase, then?"

"My laptop." She shrugs.

"Wait. Is it satellite?"

She shakes her head. "We wouldn't be here if it was. Just a standard laptop, I'm afraid, but I do some of my best coding work on it and I don't want to lose it."

Fair enough. I should be disappointed, but I think I'd be pissed if anyone dared to save us right now.

"How did you hone these skills?" I ask. "I'm not saying coding and hacking are difficult, but still. I have a feeling it's not a skill passed on from your father."

"You'd be surprised by the things he's passed on to me. I joined his business, not the other way around."

Clever way of avoiding a straight answer. But I have time, and it seems that nothing excites me more now than discovering this woman.

With the tips of my fingers, I draw lazy circles over the velvety skin of her back as she carries on telling me her life story, filled with intentional gaps she carefully skirts around. Enough time passes as we talk that I have to add wood to the fire.

I thought we would be dead asleep by now, but I can't stop asking questions and she's had no issue answering them.

I've learned that she's been doing this for about eight years, but she trained long before that. Jewelry is officially their primary business. The unofficial endeavor revolves around stealing art, contraband being her favorite, with its poetic justice.

I also found out that after she broke into my car, she went up a building via the fire escape, walked over the connected roofs of a couple other buildings, then went inside and disappeared via a ride she booked. Finally, an answer to that mystery.

Her father has been at this for the better part of three decades, and the fact that he's still here, having never seen the inside of a cell, is fascinating.

"We're not perfect, Carter. Yes, we've never been caught or found, but that doesn't mean we haven't come close." She shrugs. "I think the worst was when we were *claiming* a Dubois painting a couple of years back. A small portrait called 'Daydreams in G Minor' of—"

"His wife playing the violin." I finish the sentence, wide eyed. "I can't believe that was you."

"You heard of the heist."

"Heard of it? Love, you stole it before I had a chance to buy it off of Grange."

She bursts out laughing. A loud, full-belly cackle that shows zero remorse.

"Now that's irony," she says, snickering. "I heard he had a buyer, so I decided to move in before the transaction. Didn't know it was you. Apologies, dear sir. Did you want it for yourself?"

"I'm a collector." I nod, refusing to reveal more. Like my frustration over that painting.

"Oh, I know you are. Been to your place. Remember?" she teases.

And it works. I'm thoroughly teased and willing for more.

"It's not fair, though," she continues. "You know so much about me, yet you haven't revealed anything about you."

"Fair? Kitten, you should know plenty. You've been watching me for a while. Actually, for how long have you known it was me in the alley?"

"Pretty much since I saw you, but I confirmed it the next day. I knew already you were part of The Sanctum, but you're certainly the only one who dresses dapper, and with such attention to detail. You weren't hard to pinpoint."

Fuck, it's even worse than I thought. She's known the entire time, and I've been thoroughly in the dark.

"Then you've had plenty of time to do your research," I argue.

Scarlet scoffs, smirking as she shakes her head. "You and I both know that you are more than capable of controlling the information present online. I only saw what you wanted people to see. Yes, fair enough, I got into Metamorphosis and . . . saw plenty in there."

I recoil slightly. *Plenty?* What the fuck does that mean?

"I have indeed researched deeper, and my skills allowed me better access, but . . . I haven't scratched the surface. And

I would like to *carve* right into it and learn just who you are. Give me something good. Personal. *Vulnerable.*"

Her request lands like a challenge. She knows by now I don't do personal. I certainly don't do vulnerable. But she holds my gaze in a vise that tightens somewhere behind my ribs, prying open all those things the creature that lives there chews on every single day of my life. She wants them out, and I can't think of anything worse.

She'll run away.

She'll hide from me.

And I'll lose her before I truly figure out how I can have her. Protect her from me. *Keep her.*

"The violin you stole from me is called 'The Crimson Violin.' It's the most precious thing I own. I would *kill* for it."

She narrows her eyes, expression falling gently from amusement to slight worry.

"Does that mean that you still want to kill me?" she murmurs.

The answers spill inside my mind before her sentence is finished. Voicing it wouldn't scare her—but it scares me. Because I wouldn't kill her. I would kill *for her.*

It's too soon.

Too fast.

Too much.

Strains grip my chest, deep beneath my ribs, twisting and churning, fluttering lower around muscles, sinews, and hollow parts of my abdomen. A peculiar physical reaction to a sensation that has been blooming viciously in the intangible parts of me.

"I expect you haven't damaged it, and you will return it to me. So, no. I do not want to kill you anymore, Scarlet."

Her gaze brightens, and the quirk of a smile softens her features and relaxes her.

"If it's so precious, how come you don't display it in a case? Keep it safer?"

"The true crime would be to own but not play her. I couldn't do it to her. Not after what she's been through."

"She . . ." Scarlet whispers.

"You've never heard of it, have you?"

She shakes her head slowly.

"It is said her owner was a masterful violinist. Back in a time when women were considered inept for such artistic endeavors, and limited to singing, she prevailed. Society tried endlessly to reject her, but she didn't care. She continued to play for herself and whoever came to hear her song. Her husband adored her. Cherished every part of her and encouraged her talent. But as with every old story, or legend, tragedy strikes. Their house was broken into, the violinist was attacked and murdered, and her husband was powerless to stop it. Her blood was spilled all over her precious violin. Filled with pain and fresh grief, he began wiping it off, only the well-used instrument had lost so much of its lacquer that bare wood covered much of it."

"Oh my god . . ." Scarlet whispers, transfixed.

"Yes. It's stained with her blood. He added more when his morbid inspiration struck. Rubbed it in until most of the violin turned crimson. He even sanded the remaining lacquered areas and stained it there too."

"That's why it looks almost patchy. Weathered."

"And that's why I and many others refer to her as a 'she.' She's not the best Stradivarius out there, nor the most famous, but she is the most tragic. And not playing it would be even worse."

Scarlet nods, sadness brimming in her eyes as she looks down, drifting thoughts likely taking her to that love so tragically lost.

"What happened to him? To the husband?" she asks.

"He fell deep into his own art afterward. His style changed and twisted. Became raw and dark. From realistic, vivid, and soft paintings, he fell into the clutches of the morbid chiaroscuro."

"Wait a damn minute!"

I smirk, seeing the understanding in her widening gaze.

"Holy fuck." She rises to sit, blankets falling off her naked body now bathed in the warm hues of the fire.

I can't help myself. I reach over and drag a finger from the base of her neck, following a slow path between her breasts, and stop right above her navel.

"Yes, kitten." I confirm her loud thoughts. "*She* is Veralin Dubois. The painter's wife."

"Oh, god." She crashes back to the bed, and I cover her with the blankets as the sadness takes full control of her beautiful features. She curls into me, naked body flush against mine as she grieves their story. "I can't fathom such raw loss. The agony he must have felt. The violin . . ."

"I know." I pinch her chin between my thumb and finger and bring her attention to me, peppering kisses over her soft lips. "But he immortalized her into the centuries. Carried her memory well beyond their deaths."

Scarlet smiles gently, making her look much younger, softer, so much more delicate and in need of protection. *My protection.*

"Now tell me, kitten. What's one of the most precious things you own?" I attempt distraction, and it seems to work as she giggles.

"An almost complete triceratops skeleton."

My mouth falls open, eyes straining as I wait for her to tell me she's fucking with me.

But it never comes.

"You're serious," I whisper.

"Yup!"

A ray of fucking sunshine stares back at me.

"It's a beautiful specimen." She shifts and settles on her back. "My pride and joy, standing at just over eight feet tall. I bought her a couple years back, and she's currently in storage until I get my own place, fit for her."

"It does sound like *she* should be displayed," I agree.

Though, when I see her like this, starry-eyed, daydreaming of things she loves, I would agree with my own murder just to keep her in this state.

I'm so thoroughly fucked, my world is spinning.

"It would look mighty pretty in the center of that great big church of yours, stained-glass sunshine raining down on it," Scarlet says, laughing. The whimsical sound shoots straight to my cock. "I didn't mean—" She covers her mouth, eyes widening in horror. "I didn't suggest living there or . . . I know this is only one night and—oh god." She pulls the blanket over her head in clear mortification.

But the surprise she sees in my eyes is not what she thinks it is. Because that might not have been what she was suggesting, but fuck if Scarlet wouldn't look *mighty pretty* in that great big church of mine.

For the first time, the solitude I've always thrived in doesn't feel as attractive anymore.

CHAPTER 25
Scarlet

Our clothes are dry, the storm quieted down sometime in the middle of the night, and the rain stopped before Carter and I woke up, limbs entangled as we nested in that small bed.

I think he woke up before me. His eyes bore no trace of sleep when I opened mine and found him watching me. I would have thought it creepy if it wasn't downright flattering. The usual chill in his gaze was still present, the emptiness still looked back at me, but there was a comforting familiarity in it. A kindred malice that felt like home.

Today seems different. Like last night's storm cleansed the negative, unsettled tension between us.

Conflict remains, but it's internal. Because the end of this mad chase and the explosive sex left me with . . . feelings. Thick and heavy feelings, all for the man that quietly walks beside me now.

I never thought that one night could shift the earth as much as it did, but it left space for desires, doubts, and a longing for things that could probably never be.

As we walk shoulder to shoulder through the wet, calm woods and steal hopeful glances, I can't help but wonder if he's going to bring up what happens next.

Is this a one-off?

Do we shake hands and part ways now that he declared he no longer wishes to kill me? Or do we . . . see where this road takes us?

Don't be stupid, Scar. This road leads nowhere.

He can't love you, and you can't give him what all men seem to want.

I sigh, disguising it as strain from all the walking, as I turn my attention to anything but the man beside me.

"Careful," he urges, arms wrapping around me as my feet catch on something and I lose my balance.

"Shit. Sorry." I grip him as he steadies me when I almost trip on a fallen branch. It wasn't small, either.

I really need to pay more attention rather than think of all the ways a relationship between us lacks *all* the potential.

But his careful touch is warm, possessive, and so fucking inviting. How could I not think of it?

He doesn't release me when I look into his eyes with the same hope that burns in my chest. He pulls me closer, brushes the fallen strands of hair off my cheek, and tucks them behind my ear. Such gentleness for a man with a nickname that inspires bloodshed.

Swiping the tip of his thumb over my bottom lip, hunger fills his eyes, and I have only a second to take a breath before he crushes his mouth to mine.

In my chest, buried in that cavity that stalls my breath

when he touches me, fire burns with furious fervor. With one hand on the small of my back, he presses me against his taut body, and I all but melt into him. Our tongues stroke each other, lips gripping every ounce of passion the other has to offer, and fuck if I don't want him to take me right here, right now. Bury me in the mud and offer me to the fairy gods that lie in wait.

I'll be his sacrifice, dying thoroughly fucked and perfectly spent.

When he comes up for air, panting heavily, I swear I see humanity in his hypnotizing hazel eyes. For one brief moment, when his gaze is so focused on me, our impossible future flashes before my eyes.

"We—"

Both our heads snap to the side when his phone vibrates in his other hand. It's a rude interruption, and I hate to say it's a necessary one.

"One text got through. Let's keep going," he says as he grabs my hand and guides me on an invisible path he mapped out.

The more ground we cover, the more his phone vibrates. His head isn't buried in it, though, and his steps aren't mindless. He makes sure I'm able to keep up, holding branches away from striking me.

"Fuck," he mutters under his breath.

"Everything okay?"

The seconds stretch, and I can't tell if he's simmering or genuinely doesn't know if things are good.

"I think the—"

His phone rings, interrupting him yet again, and I resist the vivid urge to roll my eyes. He apologizes before he picks up, but we carry on walking, regardless.

"It's a long story. I'll pin my location to Brendan. Come

get us . . . Yes, *us*."

Another pause stretches out.

"Like I said, long story . . . The very same."

Another pause.

"Crashed."

Annoyance strains his brows as he listens to whatever is said on the other line.

"Finnigan, you're wasting my time. Come get us."

He hangs up, rolling his eyes as his neck cracks in two places.

"You sound like you need a massage," I say.

"Or a hundred," he mutters. "Are you offering?"

I smirk, wiggling my brows when he looks at me. "If it gets you naked under me, you bet I am."

That does it. His brows relax, his eyes soften, and a sinful smirk pulls at the corner of his lips. For a man who doesn't feel complex emotions, he sure does master all the simple ones.

"Talk like that and we'll never leave this forest."

"Look at me like that and I'll make sure we get lost," I counter.

He scoffs playfully, shaking his head as he turns the attention back to our path.

The notifications keep coming on Carter's phone. I can't tell if something happened while we were off-grid or if this is just his norm.

I wonder what I'll be met with when I charge mine. It died during the night, and I really want to believe no one noticed I didn't return from the heist. I'm not quite convinced.

When I split up from dad last night, I told him over the phone that I was going for a bit of a drive. It's not unusual for us to take different routes after a heist. I didn't want to worry him, not unless whoever was clearly following us went after him instead of me.

Technically, he has no reason to check up on me and

notice I haven't returned. We may live on the same land, but we give each other plenty of space. I'm holding my fingers crossed that no one has attempted to call me since.

"Something happened?" I ask.

"Not quite." He keeps his answer too short for this to be a back and forth.

"Is everyone okay?"

"Yes."

I want to protest his clipped answers, but I notice something.

"We made it!" I exclaim, jumping around and pointing toward the dirt road that finally appears between the old trees.

"You'll break an ankle, love," he says, but that vicious smile touches his eyes too, and I know he's enjoying it.

"You can send our location now."

"Already sent when I ended the call." Looking down at his phone, he swipes a few times. "Updated," he confirms.

"Perfect. Then they'll come get us." I turn to him, throwing my arms around his neck. "And you'll be free of me, killer-boy," I whisper

He wraps one hand around my middle, the other firmly gripping my neck, fingers tangled in my hair, and he holds me to him like the world might get swept from under our feet.

"Now, why would I want that?"

There it goes again—my breath stalling in my chest, tugging at my ribs to free itself.

"Kiss me . . ." I whisper.

And he does.

Soft and slow, hard and fast, hungrily and lazily, all at once. I swear the sun has changed position while he feasted on me and I reveled in him. Days could pass and I would be happy right here, lips raw and awfully parched.

We don't come up for air when the silence breaks, a rumble vibrating in the distance. We indulge until the last moment, when the engine disturbs the forest around us and eyes threaten to fall on us.

With great reluctance, he rips his lips off of mine, releasing me without stepping away.

Even if he stops looking at me like he is now, with silent, earth-trembling intensity, I'll still feel it deep in the fibers of my muscles, tightening around my bones, and stealing every ounce of breath away.

Tires skid on the gravel road. His gaze stays firm on mine. Car doors slam shut. Our heartbeats remain in sync. Steps crunch on the gravel. Our breaths entangle tightly.

"You scare me, Scarlet."

My lips part and surprise rushes out of me, throwing my world into an uncontrollable rotation. His words flow through the wind, and I want to chase them back. Make sure I heard them right and that they weren't a beautiful breeze sweeping by.

"Pierce!" a rough, deep voice booms, shaking the trees.

Carter sighs, though it looks more like he's preparing himself. "Shall we?"

I nod, and we both turn and head straight toward the two men standing by the flat gray SUV—Maddox Severin and Vincent Sinclair.

"I thought Finnigan was coming," Carter says as we reach them.

"He's with Evelyn and Maya," Maddox answers.

"Fair enough." He turns to me. "I believe you know Scarlet Brasa-Glass."

"Gentlemen."

They both nod at me, and Maddox moves to open the back door, politely showing me in. For such a brutal, scarred, and slightly terrifying man, he gives an oddly calm vibe. I bet he could wring my neck in one slight move with that gigantic hand of his, though.

I look at Carter, and when he nods, I climb into the backseat, relaxing into it when he enters on the other side, the other two following at the front.

"Tell me everything that happened," Carter almost orders.

I catch Vincent glancing toward me before he and Maddox exchange looks.

"Don't get shy on my account, boys. I know the rules. Get killed if I spill the beans, blah, blah, blah." I gesture with my hands, laughing. "Plus, Carter has plenty of leverage on me, since he knows all my dirty little secrets."

I turn to him, smirking knowingly. He cocks an eyebrow and settles into his seat.

"She's fine. Tell me what Duval did."

Duval . . . hmm.

A few more seconds pass. Reluctance lingers in the air as Maddox drives along the forest road, toward the civilization I'm uneager to return to.

"Maddox had his fight last night. The Fightclub was packed. Our guys noticed Duval and called us," Vincent begins. "We couldn't make a fuss, so we waited until the night was over, making sure he never left our sight. But once Finn and I appeared, we didn't leave his, either. He waited until the fight was over, the bets were paid, and half the patrons left."

"And?" Carter's getting eager to reach the climax of this little story.

"He was talking a lot without saying much, lackeys in tow for a show of power. Eventually, he said he realized that the girls have dropped off the face of the earth. Apparently, he's been talking with other people who are familiar with them, and he deduced they've gone into hiding."

Girls? Like family? Friends? Business partners?

My curiosity spikes.

"Watch this." Vincent hands him a phone. "Brendan said you would want to see it for yourself."

I don't pry, but the volume is loud enough for me to hear bits and pieces.

"Don't worry, I've kept your secret safe. But that's why I'm here. Your secret will remain secure if you agree to a business deal."

"Mr. Duval, we don't respond well to threats, and we certainly don't cut business deals with people who threaten us."

"But here's the catch, Mr. Sinclair. If you don't agree, I will take you down, brick by brick. Legally and illegally. And when I'm done with you, I will find the rest of your Sanctum. I'll leave your women and children alive. Destitute. Broken."

I don't hear the next parts over Carter's growl and the engine's rumbling.

"You've got to be fucking kidding me." Carter runs a hand through his hair and passes the phone back to Vincent.

"We told him to fuck off," Maddox says. "The fact that he thought we would just hand him that business makes me wonder just how screwed in the head he is."

"I guess you have to be some degree of fucked up to reach so high up on the political scale," Carter mutters.

I can't help but wonder if I can be of assistance.

Maybe I can prove myself to Carter's Sanctum and gain some brownie points of trust.

"Scarlet?" Vincent says.

"Yeah?"

"You might want to prepare yourself."

I frown, confused.

"When Carter disappeared, which is something he

would never, ever do, we got worried. My wife acted on a hunch—an impressive one, it seems—and went to your stepmother's shop."

My heart stalls in my chest. When we moved here, my family told me to stay off of The Sanctum's radar. And here I am, in their fucking bed.

"Your family knows."

Shit.

CHAPTER 26

Carter

Scarlet insisted we drop her off at the head of her driveway. After Vincent's revelation, and also after noticing her brother's car in her drive, she said The Sanctum appearing at her door might be overkill.

I was reluctant to leave her but had to trust her reassurance that she's fine. They'd probably be just as worried about her as my own "family" has been about me.

So that's what we did—dropped her off in her driveway, then drove to my house.

I took my sweet time in the shower, enjoying every drop of hot water coming out of that tap. But now, as I finish dressing in my bedroom, I hear so much more chatter in my living area than when I came in.

They're all here. Morrigan, Evelyn, and Finnigan have joined Vincent and Maddox.

"Oh, fuck, you're okay!" Morrigan throws herself at me, arms wrapped around my back as she pulls me into a tight hug. A surprising one.

She's a passionate woman, I know that, but the heat she puts into this embrace, the relieved tone of her voice, it all suggests a level of interest more . . . familial.

"You got us all so worried," she says as she pulls away. "She better have been worth it," she whispers to me alone, wiggling her brows.

She definitely was, but I'm not entirely sure why Morrigan is so sure my interaction with Scarlet wasn't innocent.

I stay silent and walk toward the sofa, then drop onto the soft cushion. Strangely, I miss the cabin's hard bed.

It's not the bed you miss, Carter.

I shush the voice in my head and turn my attention to the guys. "So, Duval wants the escort service?"

They all exchange telling looks, but no one answers me.

"There's an elephant in the room, Carter. We all want to know one thing," Morrigan says first.

"My personal life doesn't take precedence over what's going on in The Sanctum."

"So, she *is* part of your personal life." Finnigan wiggles his brows, elbowing Morrigan gently.

I swear these two have been a nightmare since they started getting used to each other. Always in cahoots.

"The Sanctum is under attack, Hennessey. Focus."

He cocks a brow, exchanging looks with Evelyn, who chews on her bottom lip. Sometimes I think they don't just share a bed, but a brain too. The looks passing between them seem like entire conversations.

"Otto's fine. We visited him in jail. The accusations are bogus, and we have a genuine alibi for him. Duval just wanted to put on a show of power. Demonstrate what he can achieve,"

Vincent offers.

"Having him arrested for murder seems excessive," I say.

"Yeah. Good thing it wasn't one of the real murders he's committed." He shakes his head.

True. Otto is part of our army. One of our best guys. Many bullets have flown from his guns and into our enemies.

"When is he getting released?" I ask.

"Paperwork is being done as we speak," Vincent answers. "Richard is handling it, but even with his impressive lawyer skills, it still took him a while to dig through the bureaucratic nightmare of a hole Duval threw Otto into. He almost got rerouted to a high-security prison for no reason other than to make it harder for us to get him out and to show just what he can do."

"Duval's not going to stop, that's clear. The question is, when is he going to hit next?" My question lingers heavily in the air.

None of us has an answer.

"We have to stay close. All of us. Hackers, army, escorts, fucking bartenders. We need to protect them all," Vincent states, his black gaze stern as it passes through the room.

We nod in unison.

"Metamorphosis too." Maddox turns to Morrigan. "Loreley . . ." He almost whispers her name, like speaking too loudly would make it real.

"Yes. She'll be ecstatic to hear that my association with The Sanctum is putting her in danger. Yet again," the redhead says, rolling her eyes.

"Unfair. Last time, it was her crazy, fucked-up ex-boyfriend and his jealousy of you," Finnigan counters, a smug grin on his face.

"Okay, yeah. Fair," she says. "It was the association with you a little, though."

"Sure," Maddox says. "I'll give you that."

Finnigan laughs, but Maddox looks painfully unimpressed. Regardless of what woman he's seeing right now, I wonder if he'll end up making it his mission to keep Loreley safe anyway.

"We'll send a team to Loreley's building," I say. "That will cover her, Metamorphosis, and the café."

Morrigan nods, satisfied.

"A few guys at Evelyn's bakery too." Finnigan turns to his girlfriend, who nods in agreement.

"Vincent, what do you think of bringing Mamaw June to our house?" Evelyn asks. "She can keep an eye on Maya, and considering our location, it's easy to station up on the dunes and see someone coming toward the beach for a few miles."

"I'll ask her. Mom's pretty stubborn, as you know, but she'll hear Maya's name and come running." He chuckles.

"It's a good place to take anyone, really. You're right about the dunes. Great place for an ambush, with how secluded it is," Maddox says. These two are more like brother and sister than friends, and always on each other's backs.

"Okay. If anyone else wants to go there, we'll do that. My tech team is pretty secluded already, but I'll send a unit to stay with them," I add. "Everyone else has been debriefed on the situation, right?"

Vincent nods.

"Then we'll update them on our decision. The team leaders can decide if they want to pull our men together or not. If they can, of course."

"Yeah, it will be hard to pull together hundreds of people, but as long as they stay vigilant, they should be good. Otto was targeted because of his almost constant presence with us, but our soldiers aren't well known at all. They should be safe."

I agree. But the tech team will still be working overtime to monitor the situation.

"Great. I need some food now. Let's go eat." My stomach is rumbling, and I would very much like to demolish a steak right about now.

"Eat out? Really?" Evelyn cocks an eyebrow.

"What's he going to do?" I counter. "Attack us in a restaurant?"

Morrigan rises from her armchair, yanking on the hem of her T-shirt with a smug look on her face. "Let him fucking try."

She's a firecracker. We've seen her in action, and I have a feeling she would get along really well with Scarlet. Maybe a bit too well. I might have to keep an eye on that, because those two could get into a lot of trouble.

I frown at my train of thought. I'm already envisioning Scarlet within my *family*. This is . . . strange.

We all rise, getting ready to leave, but Morrigan pulls me to the side and leans against the kitchen counter, slightly out of earshot.

"Are you sure you're okay?" she asks.

I frown at the question. Of course I am. Why wouldn't I be? Her worry surprises me, nonetheless. Twice today, she expressed her concern toward my wellbeing.

"I don't know what happened last night," she insists, "but you seem . . . different."

"How so?" I ask.

"Rattled, somehow."

"I'm fine, Morrigan. I didn't get hurt during the accident. Only a bit of whiplash and some bruises."

She cocks an eyebrow, crossing her arms against her chest. "And what happened after?"

Scarlet's throat in my hand as I crowded her against a tree? Her naked body wrapped around mine as I sank my cock inside her incredible pussy? Holding her as she slept soundly in my arms?

Yeah. Rattled sounds about right.

"I'm all good," I insist, keeping everything else to myself. "Come, let's go eat," I say, moving to head off.

"Scarlet has a membership at Metamorphosis," Morrigan says, stopping me.

I look over my shoulder. I'm aware she does, considering she came to take photos of me and entrance at the club is well policed.

"I looked into it," she continues. "She's had one for about three months."

Now I turn to her. I don't think I'm masking my shock very well, but I hope I'm hiding this simmering heat filling both my chest and my temples and somehow shooting down to my knuckles.

Three months?

What has Scarlet been doing at Metamorphosis all this time?

And more importantly . . . who?

Scarlet

"YOU'RE OKAY!" CARMEN EXCLAIMS AS she bursts out of my house, wrapping me in a tight hug. She pulls back and holds my shoulders to inspect me. "Aren't you?" She frowns.

"Just a bit grimy. But I'm fine," I assure her with a smile, but it falls fast when I see both my dad and big brother standing in my doorway.

"Did he hurt you?" Dad asks.

Frowning, I walk up the steps, desperate to get in and take a hot shower. "Did who hurt me?"

"Scar, come on. Pierce! Did he fucking hurt you?" Marc exclaims, impatient.

"Yeah, and then he was a gentleman and brought me home." I laugh and push through. I don't hear anyone following. "Well, come on, then. In or out?" I shout over my shoulder.

Finally, they walk in and settle in the cozy living room.

"How did you get involved with The Sanctum, Scarlet? I know this is your life, I know you're an adult and you can do whatever you want, but how is it that I only warned you of one single thing when you moved to Queenscove, and yet you ended up straight in their clutches?" Dad rubs a hand over his face and sighs.

I'm gonna need a smoke to handle this conversation.

After walking over to the teak sideboard underneath the TV, I open a drawer, pull a joint from the cigarette tin, light it up, and take one long drag.

My head falls back as the smoke penetrates my lungs and almost instantly helps chill me out. Almost.

"You have to understand that going to the shop this morning and having Morrigan Sinclair, *The Serpent's* wife, waiting for me to open up was a bit surprising," Carmen says as she leans forward on the sofa. "Finding out she was there because she was looking for her missing friend and thought he would be with you was anxiety inducing. But Carter Pierce? *The* Carter Pierce? Now, *that* was shocking."

I take another drag of smoke, and the living room fills with the weed scent that always seems to take the edge off. It helps me think. And right now, it's allowing me to understand they were simply worried.

"The Carver, Scar? Really?" Marc rises, pacing before he plucks the joint out of my hand and takes a drag. He rarely joins in with me. He *must* be pissed.

"I'm sorry I worried you. Obviously, I didn't mean to. There was no signal, and by morning, my phone died. It was unintentional," I explain.

"Did you split up with me last night because of him?" Dad asks.

I nod my reply. No way do I want to get into the details of him following us, because that would require an explanation of our very weird *relationship*.

"When did this start?" Carmen asks.

"I met him when I moved here. But we've been talking for a month, maybe two." I haven't kept track. It's probably been less, but so much has happened that it feels like a short lifetime.

"He's your *boyfriend?*" Marc says that word with wide eyes.

"No—I don't know. We haven't talked about that." Or anything, for that matter.

We just fucked once, and he ate me out after. And that's no way to describe us to my fucking family.

"This is a different world, Scarlet. More complex than ours, and so much more dangerous. These men aren't criminals like us, so I can't help but worry," he says.

"Like *us?*" I scoff. "We both know neither of you are criminals like me." I point around the room.

Silence falls as I take the joint from my brother and take a puff, savoring it as my family settles into the thought that actually, with my violent tendencies, I'm not all that different from any of The Sanctum. It may be a daunting thought for them, but it's a comforting one for me. My family accepts me, but with Carter, it feels like I can truly be myself.

"We just want to make sure you're safe. Happy. Unharmed," Carmen assures me, her features softening.

"I'm all good. Apart from being assaulted by a pencil, I'm fine."

"What?" Marc recoils slightly.

"When I crashed, this random pencil flew out of my toolbox and stabbed me. I'm fine." I hold out my hand, stopping them as they rise. Worry laces their eyes. "Carter cleaned me up and patched me. We had a first-aid kit. It didn't hit anything major. And yes, I will go to the doctor and get it checked out."

Dad takes such a long breath in that I can see the wheels spinning as he attempts to stay calm.

"You crashed? Was it because of him?" he asks.

I shake my head. "Nah. I caused it. The rain was so thick, I skidded and actually crashed into him."

"What exactly happened last night?" Dad frowns.

"I'll tell you after I have a shower. But before I do . . . do you remember Martin Duval?"

"From the sapphire job we did a couple of years ago?" Dad says. "That was, what, about fifty miles from here?"

"Yeah. Frank Duval's son, the councilman. What do you remember about them?"

CHAPTER 27
Scarlet

Crashing onto the bed, I ask my speaker to play my favorite playlist at a soft volume as I stare at the ceiling. The light is dim, the color changed to red, and my spent body can't even muster the strength to get under the covers.

I drag in a breath, holding it in for long enough to rid myself of this dull, lingering anxiety. My fists tighten around the sheet, and I attempt to pinpoint the root cause of it as I try some breathing exercises.

It doesn't work. I'm not even sure it's anxiety related. I'm just . . . unsettled.

All day was spent either with my family or in the hospital, getting professionally patched up and going through all the usual tests I'm required to go through. It's fucking exhausting. I've dreamed of my comfortable, fluffy bed since the moment

I came back this morning, but now it's not doing anything to relax me.

I need . . . something.

But I don't freaking know what.

My phone vibrates on the nightstand, and I sigh. My family's probably checking up on me. I love them, but I'm not going to fucking break.

Yet, sometimes I really want to.

Enjoying your big, soft bed yet, kitten?

I brighten up in an instant. It's not my family at all, but Carter. The number of times I wanted to text him today but held back. I don't know what the social standard is for what we've done. But I've itched so bad all day.

Big beds are overrated.

No, not yet. You?

Me neither. Something's missing.

A smile tugs at my lips, and I wanna squeal and kick my feet. Maybe I'm reading too much into it, but fuck it, I'm gonna choose to believe I'm the one missing from his bed.

Is everything okay? Everyone okay?

Yes. Things are getting complicated, but yes.

How are you? Did you go to the doctor?

Okay, this is cute. He's checking up on me. If I'm reading too much into it, then my heart will be fucked. Even Bernard wasn't really that bothered with my health at the start. He would say I've been living with my condition my whole life, no point making a fuss about it. Granted, Carter knows nothing. Yet. But still.

> Went. Got checked. Patched up, though they praised your skills and said there's no trace of infection considering the circumstances. All good.

> I hope you're not just saying that for my benefit. If you need a better doctor, say the word.

> Do you need a car?

> Why? You gonna give me one?

I laugh as I type that text, and his reply comes instantly.

> Yes.

I choke on my own spit and have to sit up to recover. Breaths saw out of my lungs as I reread that single word like the letters will magically change to "Don't be fucking stupid. I was going to give you my dealer's number."

But they don't change.

"*Yes.*" One word. Heavy with implications I must be reading too much into.

> You're quite familiar with one of them. ;) You can come see the rest and take your pick.

> And don't worry, GPS has been disabled on all of them. No one's going to track you.

I burst out laughing, falling back on the bed and rolling as I hold my belly.

A very generous offer, sir. I'll let you know if I'll take you up on it.

Impressed to see you've learned your lesson.

I still have to teach you yours.

Blinking repeatedly, I clutch my phone tighter as deep in my belly, a fire stirs.

If you must. What would this lesson consist of?

A punishment.

Does it involve me dead and buried six feet deep out in the sticks?

It involves a spreader bar against your ankles, your wrists tied to the ceiling to keep you nice and immobile as I do whatever the fuck I deem appropriate to you.

My soul must have left my body because I'm looking down at my flushed face right now, at the desire sparkling in my eyes and the wanton need that fills me as I bite and lick my lips.

Well, I guess... if I must. Lessons are important, right?

Exceptionally important.

When would this lesson take place?

Tomorrow evening. I'll give you the details tomorrow. But only if you're a good girl and go to sleep now.

And if I don't?

I'll be the only one enjoying your lesson.

I must be sick in the head because that prospect intrigues me even more. He won't kill me, I know that. He won't beat me up like some wife-beater, either.

What would he do to me that only he would enjoy?

My phone vibrates in my hand as I daydream of horribly dirty things.

Sleep, kitten.

Maybe I wasn't replying because I listened and fell asleep. You don't know.

I do know. See you tomorrow, kitten.

Sleep tight, killer-boy.

Slowly, I slide under the covers, my lids finally heavy and chest light, and as I drift off to dreamland, I realize all the anxiety's gone. But I don't have time to process why as sleep takes me.

* * *

I run back inside my house on eager steps, holding tightly to the large, shallow square box the courier handed to me. The bronze silk ribbon looks beautifully decadent against the red, and I'm dying to crack it open.

I tried really hard to not wait around on Carter. I didn't want to be that woman, waiting endlessly on a man.

Clearly, he also didn't want to be that man, because he

texted me mid-morning to tell me something's coming at eight pm. It didn't stop me from checking the time far too often all day.

He didn't tell me what he planned, but I've been hoping tirelessly that those fantasies I've been plagued with, of pain and subdued violence, would come true.

Setting the box on the coffee table, I pull on the delicate ribbon and lift the lid. A white card sits on bronze tissue paper, my name written beautifully in cursive on it, and I turn it to find a short message.

> *Put this outfit on and be ready by 8:30pm. A car will*
> *come to pick you up for Metamorphosis.*
> *Looking forward to your lesson.*
>
> *Yours,*
> *C*

Mine . . .

I peel off the tissue paper, and on top of another layer sits something made more of straps than fabric. I'm suddenly hot. I may have been to Metamorphosis a few times, but never have I worn something like this. Revealing outfits that made me feel confident as fuck, yes, but never just . . . risqué lingerie.

I lift it via the bra straps and cock my head. Okay, it's actually quite pretty. It's a dark-red teddy made of lace and satin straps that I'll have to figure out in a minute when I pull it on.

I lay it to the side as I remove the rest of the tissue paper to discover a heap of lace the same color as the teddy. When I lift it, I find the softest sheer lace dress I've ever touched. It's a simple design, with an exposed back and a tie behind the neck.

I'm not sure what I expected when I read the note, but this is not it. Maybe I thought Carter would choose metal and leather. Something harsh. More . . . hardcore.

This is soft. Delicate. Elegantly depraved.

Like Midnight.

It makes sense, really.

I double-check the box, wondering if I'm missing a mask since they're mandatory for Metamorphosis, but there's nothing in there. I shrug and run into the bedroom with the items, less anxious now to try them out, since I know a dress will partially cover the lingerie.

It takes me a moment, but I pull the teddy on. I have to take a moment as I stare at myself in the mirror. I'm no stranger to sexy lingerie, and I'm familiar with the confidence it gives me, but nothing I own looks quite like this.

The lace triangles, tied with satin straps behind my back and neck, barely cover my breasts. The crotchless lace panties are connected to the bra by satin straps that mimic a sunburst, gathered together at the top of the panties and spreading as they reach the bottom of the bra. And the stark contrast between the dark-red garment against my creamy skin is striking.

With much more confidence, I pull the long dress on. The lace is slightly elastic and the cut quite relaxed, falling delicately over my hips. The fabric tightens toward my knees, then flares again until it reaches the floor. I quickly tie it behind my neck before I turn to the mirror once more.

My mouth falls open as I stare at myself. The sheer dark-red lace melts into the teddy it lies on top of, clinging to my slight curves and looking almost liquid in its intricate, delicate pattern. Because both the dress and teddy are lace of a similar pattern, you can't even tell if I'm wearing underwear or not. It's making me stare longer to find its edges and shape.

When I turn, I notice how the open back falls until it reaches the small of my back, just above the top of the panties that don't leave much to the imagination.

I can't stop gawking at myself.

But within those beautiful feelings, doubt sneaks through. Carter's good at this. Too good. How many before me have enjoyed this treatment?

Stepping back from the mirror, I sit back on the bed and clutch my hands on my lap, fiddling with my fingers.

He's no saint, Scarlet. You've known this for a while. Seen it with your own eyes in the very place he's taking you tonight. You wanted this. Now, here you are.

I take one deep breath, trying to embrace the voice of reason echoing inside my mind. I did. I've wanted this for so long. I was fucking ready to beg him to give me what I so desperately need.

He's the only one I would trust to even attempt it.

A car pulls in at the end of my drive, and the driver calls the intercom on my gate as I brush my loose hair for the hundredth time.

"Here goes nothing," I whisper to myself, swiping the crimson lipstick over my lips one last time before dropping it into my small satin satchel.

You better be eager and ready, love, because I'm going to fucking ruin you.

Carter's text reaches me as the man who looks more like a gorilla than a driver pulls out of my street.

I'm ready.

What are your hard limits?

No electric shocks. No metal clamps. No needles. Oh, and no pumps.

Got it. Pick your safe words.

No safe words.

That's not how this works and you know it.

Fine. Pumpkin. Don't expect me to use it.

I see your lessons need to be much more intense than I thought.

Don't hold back on me, Carter. I want all of you! The good, the bad... the Carver.

You scare me, Scarlet.

He said this to me before, when the guys rescued us, and I still don't really know what he means.

Why?

You push me to bring forth what I constantly hold at bay.

You're scared of yourself.

I'm perfectly aware of who I am. But I'm not sure I'll like that reflection in your eyes.

All of you, Carter. And I promise I'll give you all of me too.

He doesn't reply anymore. I check my phone the whole way to Metamorphosis, but to no avail.

As Lee opens the back door for me and helps me climb out of the car, I thank him and head toward the club's entrance. The eyes that fall on me as I walk over are impossible to miss, even behind their masks. I fastened mine inside the car, so no one could see my face, but I have a feeling my face is not where they're looking.

More and more of them notice me as I go through the usual checks and pass the reception foyer decorated in decadent dark velvet and bathed in a sultry golden light. Then I climb down the steps into the darkness of Metamorphosis, where one truly becomes either the real version of themselves or someone else entirely. Who will I be after tonight?

I stop close to the bottom of the stairs, looking around for a familiar body or mask, but the club is already busy and the man who should be waiting for me either isn't or I can't recognize him.

On anxious steps, I try not to trip on my excessively high heels as I head for an empty space at the end of the bar. At the start of the evening, most seats tend to be taken, everyone still a bit *stiff*. I don't blame them. It's exactly how I'm feeling— riddled with nervous energy.

"A necromancer, please." I order my go-to cocktail from the bartender and pull out my phone. I shoot a text to Carter, letting him know I'm here.

My drink comes before any reply from him, and I lean against the bar, gaze searching nervously around the club for any trace of the man. I've seen his mask before, and I would recognize it now, but no one stands out.

A few people thought I was paying them attention and came to talk to me, so many more than when I usually come in here. This dress is like a fucking beacon, yet it's not attracting the one man I'm dying to see me in it.

"Hello there."

"Hello." I turn to find a familiar white mask covering two-thirds of the man's face.

We've spoken before. Of course, no names were exchanged, but we recognize each other from the masks. I've never seen him play, or cared to, for that matter, but he's been fairly okay company. Polite.

Tonight, though, he sits much closer to my personal space.

"Are you enjoying your night?"

"I've only just arrived. You?" I ask, pulling away slightly.

"Much more now. I must say, you look absolutely ravishing tonight."

"Oh, thanks." I guess I didn't all the other nights?

"There's something different about you." He touches my arm, fingers sliding a bit too gently down it. "Tell me, what are you looking for tonight?"

"Actually, I'm—"

"Love . . ." The air shifts as the deep whisper spills into my ear, its warmth brushing over it as he presses against my back.

One word, lost through the sultry music filling this expansive space, yet I know without a shadow of a doubt it's Carter.

"She's with me." He stakes his claim, circling his arm around my waist and forcing the other guy's hand from my elbow.

The man sighs, pursing his lips. "Next time, make sure she wears a bracelet." And with that salty comment, he turns and leaves.

I realize I'm clutching the bracelet tightly in my fist, completely forgotten.

"Another punishment on the list for you, kitten? Maybe it will remind you to wear the appropriate bracelet so people know you are *taken*." He emphasizes each syllable of that word as he presses me harder against him. "I like when other people admire what is mine, but never touch. You understand that, Scarlet? *Never touch.* Though, when it comes to you, I'm not sure I can even stand their stares."

I lean back into him, brushing my hand over his as I drop my head to his shoulder. "What if they touch? What would you want to do to them?"

His lips brush softly against the top of my ear as he whispers in an erotic tone, "Carve their backs open, wrap my hand around their spine, and rip it. Right. The fuck. *Out.*"

The moan spilling from my tongue is nothing short of erotic with a disturbing edge. But Carter doesn't run. Doesn't recoil. He embraces me tighter, running his free hand over my arm, interlacing his fingers with mine like he's making sure I won't run.

I wouldn't.

No other *sane* man would accept me.

Not like he seems to.

"Time to finish your drink, kitten."

Mindlessly, I lift my glass from the bar, sipping slowly until half the drink is gone, burning beautifully down my throat.

He spins me around to face him, then pulls the drink from my hand, swirling it as he smells it.

"Mmm . . ." He hums deep in his chest, recognition hitting his gaze. It's filled with a killer, seductive energy as he takes in the scent.

Then the wretched man turns the glass and presses his lips right where my red lipstick stains it, and as I bite my lip, panties getting increasingly damp, he drinks the whole thing.

He places the glass on the bar as he takes a step back, his gaze falling down to my feet. It trails up my body, leaving raw goosebumps in its wake. My nipples uncomfortably graze the lace as they peak. By the time his eyes find mine again, I'm panting, flushed, and embarrassingly wet.

This man . . .

His chest rises and falls on heavy, labored breaths, but his gaze is the loudest. In his cold, murderous eyes, a creature lurks. Primal and feral as it surfaces just enough to glimpse its hunger. And it's looking right at me.

I don't need his words of appreciation. The way he looks at me in this outfit he picked tells me all I need to know.

He closes the distance between us, reaching up and brushing a thumb over my parted lips. "Ready?"

I lick my bottom lip, hoping to still get a taste of him. Disappointingly, there's nothing.

"I'm just going to run to the ladies' room."

I need a fucking minute to recover from his intensity, otherwise I'll turn into a puddle and disintegrate the moment I step into that playroom.

He nods and I all but run to the bathroom. I take a moment on the toilet, doing some breathing exercises to manage this nervous energy riddling me. I'm not sure if they work, but at least I can think a little straighter. When I look into the mirror, the woman staring back at me is almost unrecognizable. Wanton need painted all over her flushed cheeks. But nervousness still coats her gaze.

I've never done this before. Never stepped foot in a playroom. Never engaged sexually with anyone here. Or in public. Ever.

You can do this, Scar.

I take one deep breath as I fix my lipstick, then walk out of the bathroom, heading straight to the bar.

What the fuck?

Standing in front of Carter, far too close for comfort, is a blonde woman. She sensually brushes her hand up and down his bicep, body language screaming, *Fuck my brains out!* Though, her black latex teddy and thigh-high boots would have been enough. His hands may be shoved in his trouser pockets, but his white shirtsleeves are rolled up on his forearms, meaning his "taken" bracelet is clear as fucking day.

Who is this bitch?

But as she turns her head to the side, giggling in an

attempt to look even sexier, I recognize her. I've seen her with Carter. Here. Playing.

My teeth grit together, fists tightening as I watch her drag that wandering hand up his shoulder. The moment it reaches skin, I catch him recoiling and grabbing her wrist.

"Oh no you fucking don't," I seethe.

I'm maybe twenty feet away, but it takes no time to close the distance, swipe the cocktail umbrella out of someone's drink, and stick it straight in the bitch's throat.

"You have five seconds to get your hand off of him, or I'll slice it off your arm and slap you to death with it," I say.

She stills, but I push the umbrella's stick just a little. I don't care if I pierce her skin. She's lucky I'm not sticking it straight in her fucking jugular and painting this whole bar in her blood.

Blondie yelps and steps away, touching her throat as she turns to me with a scared yet disgusted expression. "You're fucking crazy!"

I step right into Carter's space but keep my gaze trained on her as a devious grin pulls on my lips.

"Certifiably insane," I agree, to her utter horror.

"You deserve better, Carter." She composes herself, expression turning smug as she purses her lips.

When I make to go for her again, she jumps and quickly turns on her heels, disappearing through the crowd.

I turn to Carter, who watches me with subdued amusement, one sinfully cocked eyebrow threatening to melt me right here, right now.

"I'll kill the next one," I say. "Rip her heart out and display it on your bookshelf in formaldehyde."

I turn, a grin pulling at my cheeks, and walk toward our booked playroom, Carter right on my heels.

CHAPTER 28
Carter

I grab the waters and straws I ordered when she was in the bathroom, then follow Scarlet through the club. Her alluring hips swing as she walks toward the playroom we booked. At this point, I don't even care where she leads me. I'll probably follow, regardless.

How well this kitten played me since we met in that dark alley. The extent of her game became clear to me as she carefully stepped down the stairs into the club. She looked exquisite in the outfit I purchased for her, but it's the mask that clued me in.

I've seen her before. Even had her in my arms once when she tripped as she walked by me. She was stunning, sinful body chaste in that modest dress, but it wasn't what attracted me to her. Her scent did. So intriguing. So . . . tortuously familiar.

Now I know why.

I follow her without a second thought, the creature lurking beneath my surface trying to claw out and snap at all the men drooling over her as she passes them.

I'll fill Scarlet with my cum until it drips on her thighs and the corner of her fucking lips so that every single goddamn man in this club can smell me on her and know that *she. Is. Mine!*

Too many eyes watch us as we stop by the playroom door. They eagerly wait for us to go inside so they can crowd by the window. They know me. They've seen me here before. But they haven't seen Scarlet, and they've had their greedy eyes on her since the moment she stepped foot down those stairs.

I have a feeling she's about to erase my memories of the other women who've been in this position before her.

Surprisingly, that thought doesn't put me off.

I open the door for her and let her pass before I shut it behind me, observing her calculated steps as she clutches her fingers and fails to mask her evident nervousness. People outside already move before the window, but I grab the small remote and press the button to close the curtains. For now.

Silence falls without their loud stares as I turn to Scarlet.

Goddamn, she's fucking ravishing, and my mouth goes dry in an instant. I stalk toward her, circling her waist, palm splayed on the bare middle of her back, sensing the instant goosebumps that bloom beneath it.

"You make this dress look like the most precious, expensive of gowns." I pull her against me, running my hand up her spine, reveling in her shiver.

"It's a beautiful dress..."

I shake my head. "No. *You* are beautiful, Scarlet."

"Thank you." She almost whispers her reply, and I wonder if there's a blush on her cheeks behind the mask.

"Now..." I let go, pacing around her, pretending to plan an attack I've mapped out in my mind already. I stop behind her, brushing the hair away from her neck, and plant a chaste kiss right there. "What do you want from me tonight, love?"

Her breasts rise and fall on heavy breaths, head dropping slightly to the side, and I accept the invite, swiping my tongue over that sensitive skin.

"Make me hurt."

I stop, waiting for something else to follow. Laughter, maybe.

"Teach me a lesson," she adds.

"I'm not sure you know what you're asking for."

She turns to me, standing so close that her heat warms me as she pins me with her mask-shadowed gaze. "Punish me," she whispers.

I step away, putting much needed space between us as heat floods my chest. That request uses the same words I've heard from others before, yet they're inherently different.

This is a challenge wrapped in quiet desperation, and the visceral need in those words seems to speak directly to the creature beneath my flesh.

Scarlet closes the distance between us once more.

"All of you . . ." In a hushed tone, she repeats the same words she texted to me earlier.

Cracking my neck from side to side, I straighten with the shiver that runs up my spine, then walk toward the wall that holds so many instruments to choose from. I don't linger, knowing exactly what I want to go for—the spreader bar. At least for her ankles.

I can feel her eyes on me as I set up; she's trying to figure out what I have planned for her.

"Come here."

She moves quickly, following my cues as I strap her wrists to the chain fixed to the ceiling, her arms extended high above her head.

"You don't want rules." I don't ask, just confirm as I fix the spreader bar to the floor, adjusting it to her, but I don't strap her in yet.

"This is not BDSM, Carter. We both know it."

"Why?" I step away to admire her there.

"Does it matter?" She shifts her weight from one leg to the other.

I suppose it doesn't. But I want to know. She had very few hard limits, which makes me even more curious about those she does have.

Lifting the remote, I turn to her. "Have they watched you before?"

She shakes her head, that trace of shyness brightening her gaze.

"Use your words, kitten."

"No."

"Have you *played* here before?" Something twists in my stomach as I ask the question.

"Never."

Relief cools my insides; I won't have to build a list of men to kill.

Cocking my head, I ask an even more important question. "Have you played . . . ever?"

She hesitates, shifting her weight from one foot to the other.

"Words, Scarlet."

"No."

Fuck me sideways. And she wants me to destroy her. No rules. No holding back.

What the fuck?

"Don't you dare pussy out on me," she warns, head tilting down as her menacing gaze bores into me.

"You're in no position to order me around." My blood

boils as I close the distance, slap her thigh, and revel in her yelp. "Now keep your mouth shut, little slut, unless you want to scream, answer my questions, or speak your safe word."

"Yes," she whimpers.

"Yes?"

"Sir."

Good fucking girl.

"Curtains open or closed?" I ask.

"Whatever you wish."

I walk to the window and stop. "Do you want to see yourself, or them?"

"Whatever you wish," she repeats. How annoying.

Out of spite, I open the curtains as they are, mirror deactivated. The crowd hasn't left. More have joined, and they stare at Scarlet like she's fucking dessert, even though their evening is just starting.

I walk around, stopping behind her, close enough to hear her ragged breaths. This is definitely not BDSM. If it was, we would thrive on comfort, even if discomfort was the sub's request. We would thrive on rules, prior approvals, and mountains of consent. Normally, I would ask her if she was ready.

Not now.

I pull on the small ribbon behind her neck, watching the crowd as the dress falls and gathers on her hips. I enjoy their approving gazes as Scarlet's breath hitches. Then I walk to the wall and table that hold the myriad toys, turning to admire her in the teddy I got her. My mouth fucking waters, but I pause when my gaze falls on the small, thin bandage on the side of her abdomen. I didn't forget, but with the brutal requests she's making, it feels like she has.

She said she's fine, but I have to keep an even closer eye on her.

"Have I told you I have a thing for stretching?" It's a

rhetorical question. I know I haven't.

I pick up the inflatable dildo to see if she squirms. She doesn't. Maybe the pastel-colored tentacle toy? She tenses but looks more intrigued than apprehensive. Putting it down, I go for what I wanted in the first place—the thigh-strapped pussy spreader. She attempts to close her legs, and I know I have a winner.

The next thing I grab is the metal cat-claw scratcher I thoroughly enjoy. I slide it over my middle finger, testing it on my palm to ensure it's the right sharpness without cutting through.

I show her the spreader, giving her one more opportunity to think twice about this. She doesn't say a thing, and I'm both disappointed and excited all at once. I pull gently on her dress, watching it pool on the floor at her feet.

She's fucking gorgeous, and seeing those pussy lips peeking through the crotchless panties makes me fucking hard. I grab the dress, take it to the leather bench, then walk back, circling her like she's prey. Beautifully exposed without being fully naked, she makes the lace teddy look stunning.

In the past, the women I brought here stripped completely, but I couldn't bring myself to request this of Scarlet. I'm telling myself that it's for her comfort, but . . . it might be for mine.

I adjust the room's color temperature to a warm, comforting glow, then turn on music using the tablet on the table. A sultry song starts, and I watch in delight as Scarlet squirms in her bindings.

"I think it's time, kitten," I say as I swipe my metal-clawed finger down her cleavage, leaving a pink weal down her chest.

The first of many.

I drop down on one knee, face to face with her sweet, beautiful cunt. I allow myself one extra second before I strap her ankles to the spreader bar. A grin threatens to pull at my cheeks; she can't fucking move—can barely protest. She's fully at my mercy.

With each of my movements, her breathing becomes more labored, her gaze filled with nervous, impatient energy. She licks her lips like all the water in her body pools in one specific spot, draining her. Her pretty cunt is already wet. I can fucking see it.

With her eyes trained on me, I suck two fingers between my lips, then glide them through the slick seam of her pussy, enjoying her muted gasp. Once more, I tease her, dragging those digits over her entrance but never entering her, even as she squirms for it.

Perfect.

I pluck from my pocket one of the leather-strapped spreader clamp sets, and her lips part in slight shock when I gently pinch the top side of her right labia and fit one of the clamps on it. I check the tightness and gently adjust before I circle the strap around her thigh and repeat the action further down. I adjust the strap until one side of her core is beautifully spread, then grab the other clamp set, fit it on her left labia and around her thigh, and spread her core until she's fully open.

I exhale slowly, blowing all that air over her opening, watching how it pulses and begs to be filled. She moans something filthy under her breath, and I bring that metal-clawed middle finger to her pussy. I scratch the sharp end on the inside of her labia, marveling at the goosebumps that bloom over her thighs and belly.

Her gaze flickers to the crowd gathered by the window as I continue the sharp exploration on her sensitive inner thigh. Holding her gaze, I press the tip deeper as I bear down on that sensitive bundle of nerves with two fingers. She cries out and the thinnest trace of blood appears from the scratch, but she doesn't protest one bit.

I repeat the motions on the other thigh, scraping the claw gently in a spiral motion before I press it harder, applying more pressure on her clit at the same time.

Her velvet-soft, creamy skin looks beautiful with the trickles of crimson staining it. She's a stark contrast to my heavily tattooed skin, and I'm thoroughly enjoying her untouched quality—minus some faded scars I've noticed on her back. But I'll keep those questions for later.

I rise, walking behind her as I drag the claw over her skin. Red scratches rise in my wake, some deeper, with tiny droplets of blood welling over them. Wherever I go, she turns her head in my direction, seeking me, desperate to hold my gaze. She's slightly uncomfortable with all the others watching her, even though they have no idea who she is with that mask on.

I stride to the wall and grab my favorite riding crop—smooth on one side of the clapper, with small stainless-steel spikes on the other. Starting with the smooth side, I slap her thighs as I search her gaze for limits she doesn't voice. I increase the force, but she barely flinches.

I snap it over her inner thigh, where she's much more sensitive. Again, she takes it well. Repeating the motion, I hit harder this time, and she gasps, flinching, but I can tell she can take more. Then I drag the clapper over her exposed pussy, stopping right over her slick hole, and slap her once more.

"Aaah!" The moan ripping out of her mouth is nothing short of visceral. Vivid.

I drag the leather over her clit, and when I whip it, she cries out for a god I don't recognize.

"More," she urges.

Fuck, she's exquisite. My cock responds to her demands, desperate to feel her again.

I turn the crop around, the small spikes now the stars

of the show as I whip them over her thigh. She attempts to jump within her bonds but fails, and I reach over from behind her, sliding a finger through her exposed center, snapping the spiked crop against the front of her thigh again. Her core twitches, slick pleasure coating my finger.

I drag those spikes up her body and plunge three digits inside her warmth. She cries out, squeezing them, writhing even harder when I slap the leather against her mound.

My fingers thrust and roll in and out of her as I slap the clapper against her flesh on the same rhythm. She moans louder, trying to push against my hand and fuck herself with it, her gaze constantly seeking me over her shoulder.

Only, it's the pleasure she's wholly focused on. No pain clouds her gaze. No tears. No soft pleas chanted from her lips.

And that's what *I* need from her.

I drag the metal claw over Scarlet's skin, reveling in the arch of her body, muscles pulling against the leather straps. Then I snap the spiked crop against her thigh, harder than I've ever done before with any sub. She cries out, breathing quickening, lips parting with little gasps that make my cock ache.

She's not showing it, but I must have hurt her. I peek over and droplets of blood seep rapidly from the graze I left over her ribs. She might have enjoyed it, but my stomach drops just enough to make me uneasy.

Her gaze flickers to the viewing window again. Frowning, I turn to the crowd, walk over there, and in one swift motion, I pull the curtains shut.

"Better?"

She nods with jerky, rushed movements.

"Why didn't you say anything?" I ask.

"I-I know you like it. I thought it's what you want."

"You silly, silly girl." I rip off our masks, grasp her jaw in my hand, and hold her attention hostage. "It's you I want."

Her eyes widen, lips parting in surprise as her gaze flickers between my eyes and my mouth. She wants a kiss, but I release her without gracing her with one. Instead, I give her one more painful whip of the crop, and her body jumps in response, as much as the restraints allow.

"Look at you," I murmur, circling her with patient steps. "You take it so beautifully, kitten. But let's see how much you can really endure."

I flick the riding crop against her inner thigh, and the spikes leave a delicate constellation of marks. Her body jolts, her head tipping back as she moans—a sound that's almost too pretty. Too deliberate. It fuels something dark and unrelenting in me.

Switching the crop to my left hand, I let the claw glide up her ribcage, just barely breaking the skin. Her chest heaves, and I drag the claw higher, over her nipple, circling it before flicking the point directly against the sensitive bud. Her cry is sharp, a perfect symphony of pleasure and pain—or so it seems.

I strike again, and the crop lands on her exposed cunt this time. The spikes leave tiny indentations on her soft flesh, the perfect contrast to the slick arousal coating her. Another cry spills from her lips, and her hips jerk forward.

I don't stop. I scratch the claw down her stomach hard enough to leave shallow, stinging cuts. The crop's spikes bite into her outer thigh, then her inner, and then directly over her clit. Each strike is deliberate. Calculated. My gaze fixes on her face, searching for the cracks.

Her cries grow louder, more breathless, her body shuddering with every touch, but something about her reactions doesn't sit right. Her moans are flawless, her trembles almost too perfect. I switch back to the crop only and slide my fingers inside her inviting warmth, fucking her with them simultaneously.

Pleasure and pain are a wonderful combination, and yet, she only seems to respond to one of them.

Pressing the tip of the crop against her clit, I thrust three digits into her, hard, relentless, curling just enough to make her body tighten around me. I strike her inner thigh again, harder this time, and watch her jolt against the restraints. Her head snaps up, and she gasps loudly, a cry spilling from her lips that feels . . . off.

She's *performing*.

I pull my fingers out, my pace slowing, my movements deliberate. My gaze locks on hers, and my free hand grips her jaw, forcing her to meet my eyes.

"You're lying to me, kitten."

Her breath catches, her mask of pain faltering for the first time.

"N-no." Her faint voice trembles, not with fear, but with effort.

Cocking my head, I watch her as I lower my hand to find one of the crimson welts on her skin and trace it with my thumb. "You're faking it."

She hesitates, her lips parting and closing, but no words come out.

"Scarlet." My tone sharpens, brooking no argument.

Finally, she exhales, her composure shifting to straighten, mask falling like she flipped a switch. "I can't feel pain," she says softly. The admission shatters like glass between us. "I have CIP—congenital insensitivity to pain. I can't feel it, Carter. I never have."

I freeze, the words sinking in, my mind dissecting their meaning with clinical precision. The world narrows to just her words, and the implications slice through me.

No pain.

None of the usual methods I use to break people will work

on her. None of the responses I feed on will ever come from her.

How fascinating.

She breaks people to see the pain strung through their eyes, and I break them to rip out their emotional responses. We both feed on opposite sides of the spectrum. Sides we will never relate to.

For a moment, I wonder if we're too different. But I quickly realize . . . we're exactly what each other is missing.

Stepping closer, I grip her chin firmly, forcing her to look at me. Her pupils are blown wide, her lips swollen, begging to be kissed.

"Why?"

"I wanted—" Her voice breaks and she shakes her head. "I wanted to feel something, Carter. Anything. I wanted what I see in others when they're with you. The pleasure born out of pain, that visceral sensation that seems to send them to another world."

The words stab at something deep inside me, unfamiliar and sharp. I've built my world on pain, on control, on feeding off the reactions I draw from others. Learning from them. And yet, here she is. Unyielding. Untouchable in the way I know best— and somehow still the most *real* thing I've ever encountered.

I drag my thumb over the curve of her lip again, my grip on her jaw tightening just enough to hold her steady and crush my lips to hers in a bruising kiss that imprints on both of us.

"You don't need what I've given others. What you get from me from now on, Scarlet, will only ever be yours. I'll give you pleasure that will make you fucking proud you can't feel pain." I kiss her again, punctuating those words to make sure they sink in. "Only yours. Only for you."

She nods, her breath shallow, her body straining against the bonds like she's trying to reach me. I release her slowly out of them, then hold her to make sure she can stand.

Maybe she can't feel pain, but her body still bears the effects of it. I sit her down, clean every single welt I left on her body. I rub soothing lotion on each red mark the crop left. She quietly shifts and turns as she drinks her water, letting me take care of her.

The more we sit in silence, the more my mind reels. I knew she was fascinating, but fuck me, the universe had something in store for me. I have some research to do.

But first, I need to take her home.

CHAPTER 29
Scarlet

I didn't know what I would feel once I finally revealed to him what is both my strength and my weakness. Turns out, it's relief.

Only, as Carter clutches the wheel, driving us away from Metamorphosis, he looks anything but relieved. He's sterner and stiller than usual, his gaze cold and penetrating.

In an instant, I deflate when the reason for his cold demeanor crosses my mind—his desire is to inflict pain. He draws pleasure from it. And I can't offer him that.

And it's not the only thing I can't offer him . . .

He probably feels cheated, led on.

"Look, I'm sorry. I know I'm not what you expected or wanted. It was something I *needed* to explore, even knowing that I would never feel what I was supposed to. But I wanted to see if I could feel its impact differently, maybe in thrill, emotions, or . . . fuck. I don't know. I just knew I wouldn't trust anyone but you to explore this with. I'm sorry I led you on and disappointed you," I blurt out in one breath.

I'm pressed back in my seat as he slams his foot on the gas, driving furiously toward the outskirts of Queenscove.

"Jeez, no need to kill me. Just drop me off and you won't have to deal with me again," I say, rolling my eyes. But disappointment and regret riddle me.

His hand lands on my thigh in a bruising grip, pulling my attention to him. "I'm taking you to your house because I know you'll be more comfortable in your own space after tonight. Otherwise, I wouldn't hesitate to take you to mine and never fucking let you go. Ever."

My eyes bulge. Is he for real?

"But I can't be what you want, Carter."

"And what do you think I want?" he asks.

"Someone who can *play* with you and give you what you need—pain. Physical and mental reactions to it. I will never be that."

He shakes his head, driving like a madman through the quieter streets as we near the outskirts. "No. You will never be that."

His words hit me straight in the chest.

"Because you are different. So much more than all the women before you."

Umm . . . what?

"You think you're not what I *need*, but you are exactly that. My life, this game, has become repetitive. Dull. But you, kitten, you revived it all. You throw me off my game completely. You intrigue me. You have no limit. Well, you do, but I can't tell what it is, and now I have to be the one to find it for you. You've made everything so much more interesting than I ever thought it could be."

Christ, this is dangerous. So fucking dangerous. Because his words imply so much permanence between us. A constant, recurring presence in each other's lives, long-term. And it fucking terrifies me.

"Then why do you look so mad about it all?" I ask.

"Because I could have hurt you badly. Much more than I ever intended, and neither of us would have had any idea. Fuck, Scarlet, it could have been really bad if I didn't notice that something was off."

"So . . . you're mad because you could have hurt me, in a scenario where the intention was exactly that."

Tires screech as the car comes to a stop in front of my gate. *When the hell did we cross all this distance?* He waits for me to press in a code, then drives in. The metal gate closes behind us.

"Hurt, Scarlet, not maim. Not permanently damage. *Not. Fucking. Kill.*" He parks next to my house. He kills the engine, climbs out of the car, and walks to my side before I get a chance to react.

As he opens the door and guides me out, his words linger in the air between us.

"You're not an enemy I was looking to torture, regardless of the punishment you told me you wanted," he says. "Whatever I was doing to you, it's meant to be pleasure bred of pain. Controlled. Enjoyable, even in its darkness."

He walks toward my house, then stops by the front door and waits for me to unlock it before he waltzes right in like he owns the place. He doesn't wait, doesn't pause. He just goes straight to my living room as if he knows exactly where it is.

"Control," I mutter, ignoring the voice in my head that screams at me to ask him why he's so comfortable in my home when this is his first time here.

"Yes. All of this is about control."

"Why *do* you do it? Go to Metamorphosis and dominate these women?"

He settles into my sofa, resting his ankle over his knee as he spreads his arms over the back of it. His eyes remain on me as I grab a joint, light up, and take a seat on the armchair to his right.

"Mental release. The silence that comes after exerting this control. In my line of work, I let loose, I carve and slice with no restrictions or consequences. But there . . . the restraint, the rules, the hold the subs have on me. These things give me the structure that I need after drawing so much blood and inflicting all that suffering."

"And how do I fit in there?" I ask, drawing in a long puff of smoke.

"The control I must exert with you is exhilarating. Scarlet, you are the single most intriguing and coveted thing in my life now. An enigma that is all mine."

I recoil at that last choice of words—enigma. I've heard that before. Not a single positive followed after.

But Carter is different. He has to be.

"Is that it? You want me because I suddenly became more interesting to you?"

"I wanted you before. You know that. Don't twist this." He scoots closer, leaning over and plucking the joint from my fingers. "You simply added more to that pot of desire. And not just that, but my desire to keep you safe."

He takes a hit, sucking in slowly, and fuck me if it's not the most seductive gesture I've ever seen. His head falls back as he exhales, and I realize my mouth has fallen open.

I've tried so hard to ignore this, but right here, in my home, where he seems to fit so very well, I can't deny how much I want this man. Not just to fuck or play with, but . . . him. *All of him.*

I was afraid of falling, but it's too late. I'm deep in that crevasse. What a fucking mistake this is.

What will he do when he finds out everything I can't offer him? What I'll never be willing to give? Would he ever be okay with just the two of us?

"Now, we've talked enough of pain." He takes another puff, hands the spliff back to me, and takes my hand. "I think I owe you some pleasure."

I can't help the curious smile as I let him guide me through my own house, walking us out the back door that overlooks the pond. Without a second thought, he grabs a blanket out of the basket perched on the small porch and heads straight for the water.

"Carter?"

He glances at me before he gives the blanket one shake and lays it on the ground.

"You seem to be awfully familiar with my house."

I could be on the fucking moon and there's no way I could miss the devious grin touching his eyes.

He doesn't grace me with an answer as he walks over to me, grabs the spliff, and takes a smoke. Then he places it between my lips to do the same before he stubs it in the grass. He reaches behind my neck and unties my dress for the second time tonight, helping it down after it falls to my hips. I step out of it, and there's no hesitation as he undoes the teddy too, taking it off, along with my shoes, and leaving me naked before him.

"You can't distract me from your answer with my own nakedness." I say to him.

A ghost of a smile touches his lips, and one by one, he unbuttons his waistcoat, peeling it off before he follows up with his white shirt. I don't plan on helping at all. I sit on the blanket he laid for us and admire the excruciatingly beautiful view as I prop myself on my forearms.

When his heavily tattooed torso is revealed, my mouth goes dry. Yet, not as fucking dry as when he unbuckles his belt. With his eyes trained on me, he grabs the buckle and pulls the damned thing out in one swift motion. It's so unbearably hot that I can't keep myself from squeezing my thighs together. And he notices, snapping the belt in the air once, watching me flinch with a grin on his lips before he drops it on the ground.

His shoes, socks, trousers, and boxers follow only seconds later, and finally . . . Carter Pierce's tattooed body is stark naked in my garden, in all his damn glory, the Jacob's ladder on his half-hard cock on full display.

I cannot with this man. He's too much and not enough, all at once. I want to crawl under his skin and make a home there, because I struggle to get enough of him.

"Tell me why—"

"Because I've been here before, kitten." He drops to his knees on the blanket, shoving my legs open so he can situate himself between them. "I've walked through your house . . ." He licks a path from my navel to between my breasts, continuing upward until he reaches my throat and swallows my incoming protest.

He's been in my house?

He kisses me slowly, tongue swiping inside my mouth, pushing me to my back when I try to pull away. It's clear this is on his terms. Once more, this man is staking his claim, only this time, his possessiveness is directed at me.

"I have watched you from the shadows of your own home," he whispers on a ragged breath before he plunges between my lips.

"Aaah!" I cry out when his fingers glide down my wetness and push past my folds to enter me.

"Was there as you showered without one single care in

the world. And you had no idea."

The words he speaks stimulate me almost as much as his fingers. The prospect of this particular man standing in my home without my knowledge makes me sickeningly hot.

"Such a fucking stalker," I whimper, accusing him as I buck my hips downward and seek more pleasure.

"You made me into one." He sinks his teeth into my neck, dragging his tongue over the marks, even though all I felt was intriguing pressure.

"For how long?"

"Not long enough." He ends the confession with a hungry kiss, demanding in every way.

When he breaks away, he slides next to me and turns me on my side so that I'm facing away from him, but before I know it, he grabs me by my waist and flips us over. I'm lying on top of him, my back to his front as he bends his legs. His cock rests on my pubic bone, and the warmth against my clit makes me squirm for more.

Carter's hands roam over my body, caressing every inch of me like he's mapping it to make sure it's fully imprinted in his memory.

He grabs my neck, holding it without tightening his grip, and rolls my nipple between his fingers, pinching it playfully before he moves to the other one. He takes his time when he notices me squirming, then slides his other hand down my abdomen until he reaches the empty part of me that craves him the most.

Two digits slide on either side of my clit, rubbing between my lips, ignoring my weeping center.

"Oh, Carter, please. Please fuck me!" I cry out, rolling my hips against his, urging his fingers or his cock or anything, at this point, to slide inside my aching pussy.

Though, I would prefer it if he would refresh my memory

about how good his piercings feel.

"Mmm . . ." he growls into my ear. "You begging for me is my new favorite thing to hear."

"Then end my suffering, please," I plead yet again as he strokes my pussy, teasing every part of it but the one that could give me the bliss I yearn for.

He chuckles, and I melt deeper into him. That sound reaches parts of me that never lit up for anyone else before.

"This messy little pussy is already dripping at the thought of my cock pumping it full of cum."

"Yes, it is! It's weeping for all of you. Your fingers, your piercings, your beautiful fucking cock, just—aaah!" I end that sentence on a wanton cry as his cock impales me, piercings forcing their way in, one by one. Each one brings more bliss.

"My greedy little whore, you take me so well. Every fucking inch of my cock belongs right here, inside your eager little pussy."

He slides in and out of me, one hand wrapped around my middle as his other caresses my breasts, taking control and fucking me on a grueling rhythm.

At this angle, each piercing on his cock rubs against that magical spot inside of me, one by one pushing me deeper into a place where desire is the air that I breathe and need dominates every fiber of my being.

His lips slide over my ear, hand squeezes my breasts, pinching my nipples as he strokes my walls. I'm completely powerless. High on pleasure. High on him.

"Your cock . . . fuck—Your piercings . . . they rub right . . ." I struggle to form the words. To get the idea out of my head.

Our bodies melt together, damp skins gliding against each other. We pant and moan in unison as he fucks me slow and deep. It's nothing like I expected sex with the Carver to be. This is sensual. Perfectly esoteric. And utterly transcendent.

Then it turns into more.

Because as his strokes intensify, his fingers bear down on my clit, circling it rapidly, building on the pressure. High.

Fuck—too high!

It pools too low, his cock and piercings assaulting parts of me that seem to have a different effect.

"Carter—oh, fuck, you need to stop."

But he strokes the bundle of nerves harder, putting even more pressure. My skin prickles, and my toes curl.

"I think I'm gonna—"

Pleasure collides with all my senses, gushing out of me in endless, uncontrollable streams. I'm coming. My body shakes as Carter holds me to him and ribbons of his hot cum shoot inside me, his rhythm slowing as he nurses our orgasms.

I'm just at the edge of mindless body trembling as he holds me safely to him.

"Did I just . . . ?"

"Squirt? Yes, kitten. Yes, you fucking did." Pride laces his voice.

But I was about to ask if I peed myself. For a few moments there, that's what I thought was going to happen.

Then ecstasy rolled in waves through me, and I swear, even my body is in disbelief that it was able to do that.

A man has never even given me an orgasm before Carter. And now . . . I squirted at his hands. And cock.

I'm ruined.

CHAPTER 30
Carter

Scarlet told me she's not sure how to process what I just did to her, but as I watch her walk back from her cottage after running to the bathroom, stark naked, bare feet sinking into the grass, I struggle to process what she's doing to me.

Slow, sultry sex isn't my thing. Visualizing a future with a woman isn't either. But here I am, imagining this dark-haired woman in my home, in my bed, on my lap, in my kitchen, reading next to her, cooking and goddamn murdering together. I can see all of this happening. It's almost palpable.

She plops down on the blanket, nestling into my side as she wraps her limbs around my body. There's no protest on my part as I lay here naked, stretched out, arms braced behind my head as I watch the stars flicker across the dark sky, thinking of Scarlet's damn dinosaur displayed in the middle of my church. The thought doesn't just intrigue me—it excites me.

"How was your childhood, growing up with your condition?" I ask, something inside of me desperate to learn more about her.

She sighs, fingernails digging into the skin covering my ribs. "Likely much more different than yours."

That wouldn't be hard to achieve . . .

"Tell me about it."

"It's not really pretty. But not entirely bad, either. I have my dad to thank for the latter," she confesses.

"Your mother for the former?"

"And then some. She's a crazy fucking bitch."

Well then, it sounds like we have that in common. Maybe our childhoods weren't so different after all.

"I don't remember finding out I can't feel pain, or hot and cold sensations. I just remember it always being a thing in my life. My mom told me about the moment they realized I wasn't 'normal.' Repeatedly." The exasperation in her tone shelters buried vulnerability. "Apparently, I was playing with my brother. I only just started walking, and I fell and cut myself on these big decorative rocks they had around a garden bed. I was bleeding, but I kept playing and didn't shed one tear. That's what started it all."

"It must have been quite difficult to play with other children, where hurting yourself is normal."

"It wasn't difficult at all, because I was never really allowed to play with other kids, not without very strict supervision. Every minor injury, scrape, or stub ended in a doctor's visit since we had no way of knowing how bad it was. I didn't really understand, either. It's hard to, when 'pain' is just a word to you. It bears no consequence or physical reaction, and it certainly doesn't strike fear." She lets out a deep breath, mindlessly scraping her manicured fingernails over my ribs.

Goosebumps break out all over my body.

"I didn't make things easy, either. I was a wild child, even after I started understanding what could happen after seeing it happen to others. With time, things got even worse. Eventually, I wasn't allowed to leave the house. That's how I got good at hacking. I've never really been a teenager. The only reason I remained in school was because of my father's insistence on it. But outside of it, I was to *stay safe* and locked inside." She creates air quotes with her fingers.

"Fuck, I'm sorry, love."

"It wasn't even the worst of it." She pauses, untangling herself from my body and lying on her back as she rests her head in the crook of my armpit. "Paranoia and delusion set in eventually. Mom became consumed by the idea that I would hurt myself and die. Then she found some crazy-ass doctor who believed CIP could be cured by targeting the brain and spine with electroshock therapy and other deeply invasive procedures. It never crossed her mind that the guy could be as delusional as her or be feeding his own fucked-up agenda."

My muscles tense with every word she speaks, the conversation falling in a direction that I certainly didn't expect.

They hurt her.

They fucking hurt her!

"What did they do to you, Scarlet?" I ask between gritted teeth.

"Experimented," she says, too lightheartedly. Like she's repeated it to herself so much that it became mundane. "Mostly electroshock therapy, though there wasn't anything therapeutic about it. They strapped me to a table, face down, and shocked my spine. My neck. My head. Pierced me with needles, cut me and pretended they were making progress. My mother was so fucking stupid. She believed it."

My blood boils by the time she speaks the last word. Now some of her hard limits make so much sense.

"Are they still alive?" I ask.

"The doctor and his assistant, or my mom?"

"All of them."

"Dad chased Mom away when he found out what she was doing to me. She was brilliant at sneaking around and kept it away from him for months. She threatened me in order to keep my mouth shut. Bribed me too, promising freedom once I was *cured*. Dad was livid. I really thought he was going to kill her, but he punished himself most of all. To this day, I'm not sure he forgave himself. And the doctor and his assistant are dead."

I'm pleased yet disappointed at the same time, because I would have preferred to be the one to take the assholes' lives.

"I'm sorry, Scarlet. I'm sorry this was your childhood, that you had to live through such trauma."

She shrugs. "I made peace with it long ago, I guess. Certain feelings resurface every now and then, but whatever they did to me, whatever my mom did, was emotional. Their experiments felt like I was outside of my body, looking down. Almost foreign. But emotionally . . . they stripped me bare." She trails off, her voice distant, a soft whisper in the breeze. "Sometimes I wonder if I'm even entitled to have those feelings, since I never truly suffered. I don't know. It's strange, I guess."

The fact that she's been made to feel like she can't be traumatized, can't suffer as a result of what she was put through, angers me even more. I'm not good with the emotional side, but I know physical pain, and I certainly understand betrayal and madness at the hands of someone who should care for you unconditionally.

If I ever run into that goddamn woman who calls herself

her mother, I will strip her of her skin while she begs for mercy. Scratch that. I *will* find her, and I'll enjoy watching her beg for her life.

"I've been thinking of dropping her last name. Glass is hers. She insisted on a double barrel since my parents were never married." She snickers under her breath as she continues. "Bitch was fucking livid when Dad married Carmen. And so fast as well, considering that she tried for years to get him to ask her. I guess he had a feeling about her."

That he certainly did. Not that I'm not pissed that he didn't realize what she was doing earlier. Though, I guess I can certainly relate to that. And I don't blame my father, either.

What I don't quite understand is why she's still holding on to her mother's name. For a woman who means nothing to her, this feels strange. Is there any hope left there?

"How was your father with you?"

"Brilliant." Her voice turns bubbly, light. "He wanted me to understand my condition. Learn to live with it safely without being isolated. He taught me anatomy in a way that made me understand what happens in the body rather than shoving 'pain' in my face. He was cautious, but he didn't keep me from situations where I could get hurt. He taught me to be smart about it. My brother, Marc, joined in too. He's fiercely protective of me. He was the one who saw the first signs of what Mom was doing, and there isn't much he wouldn't do to protect me."

I can relate to that. This need to burn the world to the ground to keep her safe seems to be growing in strength inside of me.

"And they accept the murderous part of you too?"

"Yes. I think Dad believes it's a consequence of Mom's actions. Maybe Marc thinks so too. Once again, Dad taught me how to do it safely, after I went batshit crazy once. Or twice," she says with a giggle. "And Marc owns a crematorium. Well, I'm sure you can figure out how that's helpful."

How fascinating. "Is it?"

Did I speak those words out loud?

"I mean, I know I'm lucky to have people around me who didn't instantly throw me in jail or some insane asylum," she continues, "but they're not like me . . . and sometimes I hate that they have to put up with me."

Frowning, I mull over her words, trying to identify the underlying emotions and figure out their logical impact.

Loneliness.

That's it. They accept her, but they will never relate to her psyche. My heart thumps faster, louder in my chest, as the revelation sinks in. Is this why she's been so keen on me? The need for a kindred spirit she wouldn't feel so lonely with?

"Once again, you know so much of me, killer-boy, yet I don't know anything of you." Scarlet pulls me out of my creeping thoughts.

"What would you like to know?"

"It's only fair that I learn of your childhood. I have a feeling that growing up without the ability to understand complex emotions is not all that different from growing up without feeling pain."

I tighten my interlocked fingers, mulling over her words. "Maybe not. I can only see it from my perspective since I can't relate to anyone else. I realized early on that I wasn't like other people. Not just kids. All people. It didn't take long, and my parents acted on their suspicions. The first discovery was my intelligence level. I scored remarkably high, and they hoped that was the explanation for everything."

Scarlet rises and turns, propping herself on her elbow as she watches me, long fingers caressing my chest.

"But it wasn't . . ." she whispers.

I shake my head, gaze fixed on her mesmerizing, dark eyes. "The second discovery, after further doctor visits, was my low emotional intelligence. Looking back, it's rather amusing how she skirted around the words 'lacks empathy' as she explained it to my parents. The third one was a hunch. The doctor whispered the word to them—psychopathy. But I was too young for such a diagnosis, so she couldn't brand me with it. There were other possible explanations, but I didn't dwell on any of them."

Scarlet doesn't flinch at my words, though part of me expected her to recoil as I spoke them. Her eyes don't shift away from me. They don't fill with indecision or fear, and her touch never falters.

Why?

Any sane being would walk away right about now.

"Did they treat you differently after receiving those results?" she asks.

"Yes and no. Similar to you, my mother didn't take it very well, and my father insisted on understanding me. But there's no trauma there."

For the first time, in the face of Scarlet's confessions to me, I hear the lie in that last sentence.

"Do they know . . . everything?" She cocks an eyebrow.

"You mean my predilection for slicing into people so I can experience that complex range of emotions I'm not able to otherwise?"

She smiles, and once again, I'm fascinated by her lack of negative reaction. Talking to her is . . . easy. Unrestricted. No mask needed.

"My need surfaced early on. What I have become . . . my father knew parts of it, before he died."

"I'm so sorry, Carter. That must have been . . . difficult." She chooses her words so well.

And she's right on the money too, because losing my father was indeed difficult. Frustrating for such a man in my complex world to be taken by a mundane illness. There was anger. Even more so at my lack of grief. *Difficult* is the right word.

Sadness breaches her gaze. It doesn't shine. It's a dull ache, reflected in the slight crease of her brows, the curve of her lips, and her slowing breaths. *That* is empathy, and as much as I appreciate it coming from her, I'm grateful I don't get to experience the oddity for myself. It looks tedious. Exhausting. Highly unnecessary.

"And your mother?" she asks.

"Still alive. Living up north. And no, she knows nothing of me."

She smiles, something interesting flickering through her gaze. "You know you're not that bad, right? I remember what you were doing the first time we met. You guys might be a feared criminal organization, or whatever you call yourselves, but what you were fighting for then was good."

"I know," I agree. "But I could have just as easily been a lone serial killer seeking only my pleasure."

"What stopped you?"

"It was a choice, Scarlet. I do not need to be . . . stopped."

I don't miss how my words sink in, the gentle realization of what I'm capable of but choose not to do. I'm still a serial killer, but my chosen family weaved a moral compass through my cruelty.

Would she run away if I became something else?

Something worse?

Myself?

CHAPTER 31
Scarlet

"I've been meaning to ask you," Carter calls out from the bedroom as I lock the large safe room leading from my office. "I found your sealed record from when you were sixteen."

Oh, there we go. This should be fun.

I walk out of the office and toward the bedroom, where we retired when the night was getting a bit too old and we were growing quite hungry. We ate the leftover pasta I thought he might be too fussy to eat, since he seems more like a "gourmet meals" kind of man. Yet, he enjoyed it without an issue. He wasn't even too good to eat in bed with me.

"What about it?"

"What did the kid do?" he asks.

"I caught him when he kicked a dog. He was about to repeat the action and beat up the poor thing. So, I beat him up instead. With my shoe."

"With your . . . what?"

"There was nothing on hand." I shrug. "It was spontaneous. I wasn't prepared. I was wearing these combat-style platform boots, really thick and heavy, and I beat the crap out of him with it." I reach the bedroom and stand in its doorway. "I have something for you."

He lifts his head from where he's lying on the bed, and I swear his gaze brightens.

"The Crimson Violin." He rises to sit, and I walk to him, handing him his precious instrument. He turns it in his hands, inspecting it.

"Don't worry. I took good care of it."

He gives me this look that screams, *"I'll be the judge of that."*

"You're quite fond of animals?" he asks, setting the violin next to the bed once satisfied.

"Very. Every single person I've killed so far has harmed animals to some degree. I love picking the smug ones." I grin as I climb next to him under the covers. "The rich ones who kill endangered species for clout, the ones who experiment on them, the assholes who are simply cruel, and the ones who have been reported for suspected animal abuse but the authorities either didn't have enough evidence or couldn't be bothered. I get so much fucking satisfaction from it."

"Because they're bad people, or because of your love for animals? Would you get the same satisfaction if you killed a murderer? Or a rapist?"

"Maybe. I never tried nor cared to. Don't get me wrong, they need punishment too, but . . . animals are voiceless. Some of them love unconditionally, no matter what you do to them. They'll fear you and still hope you'll pet them. Love them. Trust them. I dream of smashing their abuser's bones as they scream for mercy. I get fucking hot just thinking about that justice."

He brushes a strand of wavy hair off of my face, a trace of a smile in his peculiar hazel eyes. It's like looking at an eclipse—so incredibly rare and beautiful.

"How do you find them?"

"I have a list," I answer.

"And you pick one from the list every . . . week?"

I scoff. "I wish, but no. I have to be careful. I research and watch my targets for a while, and when that angry beast inside of me begs for blood and violence, like when Bernard showed up at the fucking café, I pick one from that list. Doing it more often would require more resources. It's too risky."

"Interesting. I can certainly help if you'd like to *indulge* more. I can protect you if you'd like me to."

I draw back slightly, caught off guard by the offer. "Umm . . . thank you."

I don't know what else to say. I'm almost speechless.

He shrugs, settling deeper into the pillow, like what he just told me didn't mean the world. "I understand you, Scarlet. And I appreciate what you do, how you channel that reckless energy. If I can help keep you off either your victims' or authorities' radar, of course I will."

I burst out laughing because the surreal quality of this moment is really getting to me. "Well, in that case, seriously, thank you."

"My pleasure." He smiles, a faint dimple appearing in his gaunt cheek.

Fuck, he's such a beautiful roman, with the longer hair at the top of his head falling lazily to the side. The sexual tension still lingers in the air, yet its hunger has subsided. Silence settles. Comfort too.

We lazily gaze into each other's eyes, like we can learn all those unsaid things about ourselves if we don't ask the questions out loud.

Our steady breaths are the only sounds in my dimly lit bedroom. Strangely heartening. Effortless.

The adrenaline drains slowly, and tiredness follows, weighing down my lids, but I'm reluctant to close my eyes. Like he would disappear if I fell asleep.

"Would you play for me?"

He watches me for a few seconds before he turns and grabs the violin off of the floor, then props himself against the headboard.

I interrupt him when he opens his mouth to ask a question I anticipate. "Something that . . . consumes you."

He nods, unfocusing his gaze as he allows himself a moment to think.

The room is bathed in a soft, muted glow as he rests the violin on his collarbone, relaxing into the hold and setting his jaw on the chin rest. It was hard to visualize a hardened and cold man like him playing such a delicate instrument, but here he is, his composure unraveling bit by bit as his fingers settle on the strings. Hidden layers come to life before me.

Lifting the bow, he draws it across the strings with a grace I didn't know he had in him. The first note hums low and deep, vibrating in the quiet space between us. I feel the sound more than hear it at first. It reaches inside me, finding sensitive places I forgot existed. His eyes fall shut, lashes casting soft shadows on his carved cheekbones as stray strands of hair fall over his features, and for the first time since I've known him, he looks . . . serene.

Each stroke of the bow is fluid. He's carving emotion out of thin air, each note a revelation that technically doesn't exist within him.

Yet here they are, emotions on full display.

His hands move deftly, guiding the violin with an

entrancing confidence. The faint sway of his body pulls me into his rhythm. An enthralling melody spills from his fingertips. Sharp at times. Piercing. Then it falls to a murmur. Gentle. Almost shy. Right there, in those movements, in his strained expression, I see how fiercely he guards himself. His soul. His trust. Maybe his heart too.

My chest tightens with a strange ache. I hadn't expected this side of him—the unconscious vulnerability, the soul he hides beneath every harsh line, every cold glance. Yet here he is, exposing himself in a way his words and logical mind never could.

I couldn't look away, even if I tried. His brow furrows as he leans into a haunting note, his jaw clenched with concentration, his fingers coaxing out sounds that are both raw and impossibly tender. The music swells and fills every corner of the room. I'm holding my breath, fearing he'll stop if I exhale too loudly.

This moment, this version of him—it's utterly ravishing. A man unraveling, yet completely in control.

When he opens his eyes, there's a flicker of something unguarded in his gaze. Just for me. And I realize that I've seen him, truly, maybe for the first time.

A loud, distant knock startles me awake from potentially the best sleep of my fucking life. It takes me a second to acknowledge where I am, but fuck is it amazing to wake up with Scarlet next to me, with her delicate, warm hand resting on my chest.

"Love," I whisper, pressing a kiss to her forehead.

The knock sounds louder the second time around.

"Mmm . . ." she moans, nestling into me and making me want to scream at whoever the fuck dares disturb us.

But I can't. This is her house. And . . . shit, that could be her family.

Who am I kidding? It could only be her family.

"Scarlet, someone's at the door."

Her eyes flutter open, an endearing smile slowly settling on her lips. The third round of knocking startles her, and her eyes go wide as she rushes out of bed.

"Fuck. Sorry." She runs her hands through her hair and slaps her face a few times, her sleepy look fucking adorable as she attempts to wake herself. "Okay, I'm going . . ." She rushes toward the open bedroom door.

"Kitten!" I call after her.

She stops and whips around.

A grin tugs at my cheeks as I gesture down her body. "Maybe throw something on before you answer the door?"

"Shit. Oh, for fuck's sake. At least you're discovering early on that I certainly am not a morning person."

I chuckle as I watch her fumble around for a robe, and then I start getting dressed too. She disappears out the door as I finish, and voices drift in from the living room. One of them—male—sounds rather urgent. Barefoot, and with my shirt annoyingly untucked, I walk out of the bedroom to be by her side.

A man stands in Scarlet's house, hands settled on his hips, stance a little bit too aggressive for my taste.

With heavy steps, I head straight to her as she fumbles

with the espresso machine on a small coffee station. But I slow down when I recognize the resemblance. Short stature, mahogany-brown hair, dark-brown eyes that look so much like hers. He's taller, older too, but he's definitely her brother.

"Who exactly are you?" he asks.

"Don't be fucking rude, Marc. I told you he's here." Scarlet slaps his shoulder after she turns the espresso machine on, and it rumbles away. She steps next to me when I'm close enough, wrapping her arm around mine. "Carter, this is my *very rude* brother, Marc."

Neither of us makes any movement toward a polite introduction.

"Oh, for god's sake, play nice." Scarlet says.

Logically, if I want to keep this woman in my life, starting on the right foot with her family is imperative.

I reach out to him, my hand hanging for a handshake. "Nice to meet you. Carter Pierce."

He looks between my hand and his sister, lips pursed and shoulders tense, before he finally gives in and shakes it. "Marc Brasa." He introduces himself without their mother's last name.

How interesting.

"Congratulations, you're officially adults," Scarlet says. "What's up? Why are you here?"

"Just checking up on you." He shrugs, walking over to sit on the couch.

She rolls her eyes and turns to the freshly brewed coffee, pulling the cup out and setting it on the side.

"Convenient timing," she mutters under her breath. "How do you want yours?" she asks me, yet she sounds slightly unsettled.

Instinctively, I reach over and brush my palm up and down her spine. Her smile settles a little further.

"Sorry about this," she whispers. "So, what coffee do you want?"

"How about you go sit down, and I'll handle this."

"Umm—"

I nod, gesturing toward the couch. She takes a slow, deep breath, then agrees, her stance slightly more relaxed as she grabs the cup and heads toward her brother.

"I'm okay, Marc. I know you have . . . concerns, but everything's fine."

"I'd rather be the judge of that, if you don't mind," he says.

"I do mind, actually," Scarlet snaps back.

Before her brother can say anything else, another knock rattles the door.

"Fucking shitballs, what now?" she exclaims.

I grab the two espressos I brewed and set them on the table before I take a seat in the high-back armchair by the unlit fireplace.

When Scarlet returns, her father stands tall in the room, the resemblance between him and his children uncanny, though his eyes are green instead of their brown. He's not a built man, more on the slender, wiry side, but he's tall, with a lot of white hair sneaking through the same dark-brown as Scarlet's.

"Carter, just in case you felt like meeting one member of my family was not enough this fine morning, this is my father." She walks straight to the couch and plops down on it. "I feel like a fucking child," she sighs.

I rise, walking over to the man who meets me halfway. "Carter Pierce. Nice to meet you, sir."

His eyes narrow on me. "Arias Brasa. You'll excuse me for barging in. My wife is on her way too, actually, but I'm sure you can understand why we're a bit . . . anxious for Scarlet."

"Anxious? You're being rude, Dad!" she protests.

"I understand." I nod.

I draw up short. This is a completely new situation for me. Unprecedented.

We all sit around the coffee table, sizing each other up. Maybe they thought they could intimidate me. Or that my reputation would be an exaggeration. They can't, and it isn't.

"Jeez, y'all are close to having a pissing contest," Scarlet complains.

"Well, last time you were with Carter, you totaled your car in the middle of a forest and went MIA all night, darling," her father says.

"Actually, she totaled my car too," I add.

He bursts out laughing, just as I hear the front door and a woman's voice as she announces herself.

"I see the ice was broken," a short woman with shoulder-length, dark, curly hair says as she walks in. "Hi, I'm Carmen. That one's better half." She points to her husband.

Arias's whole demeanor lights up with her in the room, and Scarlet laughs next to me.

"Pleased to meet you, Carmen. I'm—"

"Carter Pierce. Don't you worry, I know all about you."

I turn to Scarlet, but she shrugs and shakes her head.

"I'm not sure what these boys told you, but I'm just gonna say this. To both of you." Carmen props herself on the armrest of her husband's seat, crossing her legs and staring between us. "I know what organization you're not only part of, but founded, Carter. I know of the danger that surrounds you. Well, a part of it, anyway. But I also know Scarlet and her predilection for it. Truthfully, this"—she points between us—"connection you two have doesn't surprise me one bit. I really want to tell you that if you put Scarlet in any danger, we'll kill ourselves and take you down with us to avenge her. However, in reality, we know that no one can make her do anything she doesn't want to. Stubborn like her father. Wherever she sees danger, she dives in headfirst. All I'm going to say to both of you is . . . be careful. Seriously. Be careful. And I hope you told this man about your CIP, because he'll have to keep an eye on your reckless ass."

This time around, both men burst into playful laughter, and Scarlet joins in too. The atmosphere turns lighter, the mood almost fully flipped. Even with Marc still watching me like a hawk.

For the next hour or so, I sit almost entirely in silence, observing these familial interactions. How homey and comfortable they are with each other. An ease I've never experienced within my own family. Not the blood relations, anyway.

Logically, I can't miss something I never knew, yet as I watch them laugh and talk, make coffees and sort out breakfast as they throw around inside jokes from their past or the siblings' childhoods, I realize that my logic is flawed. I missed out. And I'll never have this for myself.

Was it all my fault?

Did I ruin my parents?

An early memory of my mother slips through my mind.

"You're good, darling. God plants the seeds of good in each of us. Yours is in there too."

"If that's true, then why do I want to do such bad things?"

"Because of that terrible creature within you. The one we will soon rip out and send back to hell."

If it wasn't for me, my mother wouldn't have gone on the path she went on. My parents could have still been together now. Happily, maybe.

As I witness Scarlet's sunshine, how she casts her light on everyone around her with her perky, carefree attitude, I can't understand how she could ever care about someone like me.

CHAPTER 32
Carter

Standing by the bar in Midnight, I nurse a drink after an exhausting day and an even more mentally draining evening.

Finnigan's ear is to the phone, a stupid grin plastered all over his pretty-boy face. He's likely talking to Evelyn, and I realize…I risk turning into him. Sans the stupid grin, obviously. But what I'm feeling on the inside seems awfully similar.

We had a lot of work to do today—damage control, research, planning and plotting, and meetings with all our team leaders—yet my thoughts strayed constantly to the dark-haired woman who has invaded my life and made herself at home in it.

Because of what happened within The Sanctum, she knew I'd be busy since leaving her house late yesterday morning, and I wasn't sure for how long. She's been a good girl, giving me space without question so I can work with the guys through this whole Duval mess.

But I haven't been good at all.

I find myself picking up the phone and texting her in every free moment I have.

It's odd. Illogical. Yet what would make even less sense would be stopping my behavior.

"We'll get him soon. You always find something." Maddox walks next to me, taking a long swig from his beer bottle.

I don't turn as I take a sip of my drink, looking at Vincent, observing the deepening shade beneath his eyes. This situation has been getting to all of us. Though, lately it's felt like one thing after the other.

"You won't admit it, but I know you're frustrated. Worried. You'll find something," Vincent says.

His words are almost meaningless. This bastard politician has taken so many precautions over the years, and nothing I've found so far is big enough to take him down. Even killing him isn't an easy solution, because his absence would be noticeable. Plus, he could have set contingencies in place, directing authorities to us in the event of his death.

"Carter?" Maddox asks.

"I'm fine. And yes, I will find him, if only—" My phone rings, interrupting me.

It's Scarlet.

But she never calls, only texts.

I swipe the screen to answer. "Hello—"

"Midnight! Open the front door!" she screams over the phone. "Nooow!"

There's a lot of shuffling and commotion in the background. A woman's anxious scream. I break into a sprint toward the door and just as I unlock it, a crash sounds on the other side. A split second later, Scarlet and Katya burst in.

"Incoming!"

"There's at least five of them!" Katya shouts as she hurries toward the back of the barroom.

None of us have time for questions as six men storm in, ready for a fight.

I catch one in a headlock and slam his head against the wall, repeating the action three more times until he passes out. Then I rush to Scarlet, seeing red when a man goes to attack her. Finnigan, Vincent, and Maddox are all busy with their own targets, but someone grabs me before I can reach her.

The man's grip on my shoulder is iron. He yanks me backward, and I stumble behind the bar. Bottles rattle and glass clinks as my spine collides with the bar's polished edge, but I don't have time to process the sting of pain. His fist flies toward my face, and I jerk my head to the side, just missing the punch. He grunts when I retaliate with an elbow to his ribs, but he doesn't let up. I'm rewarded with a jab to my side, a sharp pain bursting behind my ribs, but I shove through it with gritted teeth.

I pick up the bottle to my left—a thick, dark glass, nearly full. I seize it and swing it into his temple. The man staggers, dazed, his hands slipping from me. Not enough. I bring the bottle down on his head again, and the glass shatters on impact. Shards slice into his scalp. Blood mixes with the amber liquid dripping down his face, but the bald bastard won't go down.

He lunges at me, and we're grappling, fists colliding, breaths harsh and ragged. With my back bent against the bar, I reach behind me and fumble around with blind fingers until my hand lands on a short-bladed knife. It's flimsy, but I twist it in my hand and ram it upward, jamming it beneath his ribs. He gasps, eyes wide, pain flashing across his face. Twisting the blade deeper, I feel it hit flesh and muscle as I drive it upward with every ounce of strength I have.

The asshole jerks, chokes, and his body slackens as his grip loosens. Stepping back, I let him fall to the floor and whip around to find Scarlet.

The sounds of chaos begin to dim, and I see her, her expression hard but fierce as she wrestles her attacker. I rush to her at the same time as my brothers, also done with their own attackers.

But we all stall; it doesn't look like Scarlet needs any help at all. The man she's fighting falls to his knees as she breaks a chair over his head, already looking like he drew the short end of the stick with my mad kitten. She's not satisfied, though. She grabs a broken chair leg and slams it against his ear in an unhinged rush.

She looks lost in the flow of violence and pain. Utterly in her element as she breaks that chair leg in half. She raises another chair, continuing the job as she practically scolds the guy.

"This will teach you!"

Crack!

"Not to attack!"

Crack!

"Women!"

Crack!

"You fucking asshole!" She punctuates the last sentence with a violent, final swing of the wood across his temple, and the man falls motionless to the ground.

"Jesus Christ," Maddox says next to me. "She's—"

"Exquisite," I finish for him, utterly mesmerized and fascinated by the savagely sexy creature before me.

"Umm . . . sure. Let's go with that," he mutters.

I rush to her, grabbing her face in my hands. "Are you hurt?"

She cocks an eyebrow, and I shake my head to clear the fog. Of course she wouldn't really know.

"She saved me!" Katya says through strained breaths.

"Sorry?"

"Your girl saved my life." She pants, leaning over to brace herself with her knees as she attempts to recover. "I was driving over and noticed I was being followed. I realized I couldn't get in the back parking lot in good time with the gate and all, and I was about to take a different turn when the assholes rammed into me. After I crashed, I ran out without a second thought and headed straight to the main entrance. But they followed." She puts her hand up, unable to continue.

"I was coming to see you when I saw her running through these backstreets, kind of panicked," Scarlet recounts. "She looked familiar, I guess, and when I saw the guys chasing her and where she was headed, I kind of connected the dots. When I got to her, one guy was trying to get her in the back of the car and one other was climbing out to help him. I jumped the first one, got her loose, and I called you as we ran."

I shake my head at Scarlet, both in awe of her courage to help a perfect stranger and fucking furious with her for putting herself in such danger. Stepping back, I look her over and swipe blood from wherever it's splattered to confirm it's not coming from her. She protests, but I ignore her.

"I'll take you into the office, or maybe a hospital to make sure nothing's—"

"Carter, later."

"You know better than me why this is necessary."

"Your friends are *staring* at us," she whispers through clenched teeth, eyes wandering sheepishly to the side.

I straighten and turn to them. Each and every one of them is wide-eyed, staring at us like they're witnessing divinity. Or an abomination. I rub my fingers together, a tickle running from my spine to the back of my neck.

"I have CIP," Scarlet says, breaking through the tension.

"Congenital insensitivity to pain. I can't feel it, so if I get injured, I have no clue whatsoever. Unless I break my leg or something and fall on my face," she says with an awkward laugh. "Or I'm actively bleeding out and I notice it. So yeah, that's why he's checking me over."

They all react to the revelation, the mood lightening ever so slightly. But their gazes still flicker in my direction, an all-knowing amusement looking back at me. If I don't run away now, they're going to flood me with questions.

"Thank you." Katya steps forward and grabs Scarlet's hands.

"Glad I could be of help." She shrugs with a wide grin on her pretty lips.

They introduce themselves as Maddox steps next to me and leans over. "It seems I'm the last one standing, brother," he whispers hoarsely.

I look over my shoulder, and his scarred, cocked eyebrow says so much more than his tongue. I open my mouth, ready to protest, but Scarlet's voice pulls my attention, and I turn to her. Her porcelain skin is stained with the blood of the man laying lifeless at her feet, addicting smile tugging at her full lips like she didn't just beat that life out of him minutes ago. Almost like she was made just for me.

"I have something for you." Scarlet steps forward, drawing my attention. "For all of you." Her gaze swipes over my brothers and me.

I frown as she walks over to the messenger bag she threw to the side and places it on a chair with a loud *thump*.

"Your little *predicament* regarding Frank Duval stuck with me," she says.

"How does she know about that?" Finnigan steps forward, turning to me. "Carter, please tell me you're not st—"

Vincent intervenes. "She was in the car with us when we

went on the forest rescue mission, Finn. Madds and I were debriefing Carter on the situation that unfolded during his absence."

"For god's sake." The blond man swipes a hand over his face. "Might as well give her a key to our office."

"No need. I could make my own if I needed access." Scarlet cocks her head, a mad smile pulling at her cheeks. "But you have nothing of interest to me, and I also don't *work* in my backyard. I understand your concern, though." She pulls a stack of papers from her bag and slaps them on the table. "Anyway. I'm not gonna go into the details of what I do for a living, but a while back, I had some *dealings* with a certain Martin Duval—Frank's son. Because of the nature of my family business, we keep an eye on our 'business partners' for some time after. We've heard some things. Rumor has it that father and son have been silently feuding over money and how they share the family business. I had a thought."

Scarlet pauses for a few moments as she pulls out more paperwork, then places a USB stick on top. I swear I can hear my blood pumping in my ears as I connect the dots.

"I wondered if the son was taking things into his own hands and plotting behind his dad's back. So, I paid Martin Duval a visit. Granted, he wasn't at home at the time, but I confirmed my suspicions and discovered he's an idiot." She slaps the stack of paperwork, looking quite smug and proud of herself. "This, gentlemen, is stark evidence of bribery, dodgy planning permissions on protected land, money laundering, and illegal dumping of toxic waste. And it incriminates Martin, Frank, his wife, and a handful of politicians."

"You're saying you broke into Martin Duval's house . . . and stole all this? To help us?" Finnigan asks.

"Yup." She picks up the USB stick and looks at it. "The icing on the cake is this little baby—footage of Frank Duval, in his own office, plotting to undercut his shady investors. Extremely dangerous investors who would hate to find out they're being played. But it's clear the kid is planning something against his dad."

"How did you know it was Frank's office?" I ask, shoving my hands into my trouser pockets to keep myself from strangling the woman.

"Because I went there as well, to check for more dirt on the man. So, I recognized it. Keep up, killer-boy."

"Killer-what?" Finn exclaims, bursting out laughing.

I swipe a hand over my face, scratching my chin as I imagine all the ways I'll punish her for this. I think I'll start making a list.

"Scarlet, you should not have put yourself in danger. Twice." I step forward, undecided if I should strangle or kiss her.

She shrugs, placing the USB stick back on the pile and sliding it closer to us.

"I was bored, and I knew there could be something there that would help you all. It felt ridiculous not to do this. Plus, I knew it would be easier for me to break in without them realizing what hit them."

Bored. She was fucking bored, so she broke into the homes of two dangerous men to help our organization. Jesus fuck, what did I get myself into?

"Can I leave this with you?" I turn to the others.

Vincent nods. "See you tomorrow?"

"Yes. I need to make sure she's not hurt. Though I can't guarantee I'll be able to contain myself after what she just pulled."

The man snickers as he shakes his head, walking over to pick up all the evidence Scarlet brought.

"Thank you." Maddox steps forward, and we all turn to him. "We appreciate your help."

"I certainly do. That bastard put one of my girls in the hospital and sent these assholes after me. So, thank you," Katya says, joining in.

"Let's go, Scarlet." I grab her hand and pull her toward the back rooms so we can head to my car. "Oh, and the guy by the door is still alive. See what you can get out of him."

"With pleasure." Vincent's expression turns into the serpent he truly is, and he stalks toward the man as we pass through the door.

This night has certainly taken a turn. And maybe not quite for the worst.

CHAPTER 33
Scarlet

How I would have loved a carefree life. But I had to decide all those years ago to marry this motherfucker who's refusing my divorce. I've been spending the last two days with my head buried in my computer, trying to dig up dirt on my soon-to-be ex-husband.

Well, it's technically been a day and a few hours, but who's counting? Willow even checked up on me and brought me some cake to make me feel better.

After I gave The Sanctum the information I had on Duval, Carter swept me away, back to his home, to check me over for hidden injuries. While he was busy stripping me down to my underwear and palpating every bone and muscle in my body, I was feeling really proud of myself. I needed an in with his brothers in arms. Because regardless of their syndicate, they are friends first. Maybe even family. I need them to trust me.

I'm not 100% there yet, but damn it, I'm in.

Once I pulled myself out of that giddiness, I was in awe. I kept hoping Carter's fingers would slip beneath my underwear instead of the clinical inspection I was receiving. Yet, he was getting me hot in a different way. He was careful. Delicate. And so thorough. Lifting my limbs and checking my joints like most doctors have been doing my whole life.

When I asked him about it, he said he's been doing a lot of reading and learning about my condition. He even briefly spoke with a doctor who specializes in the subject so he would know what to look for. How to look. He did all of that . . . for me. So he could be prepared, since he knew that I couldn't stay out of trouble.

How could I not be in awe of this? I wished it was just carnal excitement I was feeling . . . but it's so much deeper than that.

And I'm afraid I might have to let him go.

It's my own fault. I saw us getting closer, more comfortable, and I didn't want to ruin it with serious talks about the future. I want more time with him before I reveal I'll never give him what men inherently need—a child.

You assume, Scarlet. Is Carter really the brooding kind?

That little voice in my head gives me some hope. But I know it's one of the reasons Bernard cheated on me. It was during our relationship that I decided I didn't want children. I'd been on the fence for years before that, but I was too young to form a decision. So many times my ex belittled me for robbing him of the opportunity to perpetuate his family name. Spread his seed and all that bullshit.

It's his right, of course. But I thought we could work through it like two decent people. Resolve it amicably. I was convinced he kept putting off the serious conversations because he was changing his mind too and wanted to stay together. Turns out he was just stalling, not because he planned to force it on me and get me pregnant, but because he had a more pressing interest.

Of which he reminded me over the phone yesterday evening as I was driving home from Carter's. The only thing that kept me calm during the ride was the fact that I was in one of Carter's cars. The man wasn't joking when he said he'd give me one from his collection.

I wanted the pretty metallic-silver baby ripped right out of the '50s, but thought the vintage Mercedes would turn too many heads. I went for the BMW instead. The M2 drives like a beast, and it did a decent job at centering my nerves during the angry phone call with Bernard.

So here I am, doing more digging into the man. I taught him too much during our time together. Too many countermeasures to protect himself from online attacks. I made my own damn life hard. But I think I'm getting close.

I know he wants the jewels I used to give him, but I haven't found out why he *needs* them. That's where I'll find my leverage on him.

Fingers flying over the keyboard and mouse, I finally see a small light at the end of this tunnel I've been navigating for months, eyes widening with each step that takes me closer to it.

"Fuck yeah!" I shout. "This is what I'm talking about!"

I'm finally in the Camoras' bank accounts. One by one, I manage to get into the brothers' personal and joint accounts where clean money is thrown into. Most of their business is conducted in cash, and their ledgers are kept under lock and key, but what I'm seeing here still paints a confusing picture.

"This doesn't look right." Bernard is . . . penniless.

Not just that, but the joint accounts look odd.

"Been busy, darling?"

I jump in my chair, whipping around just to be met by the asshole himself.

"What the fuck are you doing here, Bernard? And how did you get in?" I rise, trying to glance around for anything that could be used as a weapon. My hand glides over a pen and I clutch it in my palm.

"I didn't like the way you talked to me last night. I thought it was time for this game to get serious."

"Get the fuck away from me!" I shout, jabbing the pen in his side when he rushes toward me.

He recoils in pain, and I take the moment to push him off and sprint away. I'm barely out the door when I'm flung backward by the collar of my hoodie, and he wraps his arms around me. I grab onto his sleeve, clutching his cufflink and pulling at it to get him off me, but I just rip it in the process. I reach for the back of his neck, slamming my other elbow into his ribs, but the pained grunts don't weaken him when I try to flip him over.

"You're gonna pay for this, Bernard!" I rage at him, jabbing him over and over in his side.

"Not if you pay first."

A cloth appears in my line of sight, and I whip my head around, trying to get away from the sweet-smelling thing. He forces it onto my face and covers my nose. Holding my breath only keeps me away from its effects for so long. Eventually, I take a breath, and my muscles lose their strength, my limbs tremble, and my vision blurs. Darkness pulls me in.

Carter

SOMETHING ISN'T RIGHT. MY LAST three texts to Scarlet were left unread. She hasn't done that once since we met.

Now, as I stare at the camera feed from her bedroom and call her, I can hear the faint ringtone far in the background. She doesn't answer. Maybe she's just in the garden. Or her parent's house.

Maybe.

Tension builds in my brow as a strain pulls behind my ribs with breaths that start to weigh me down. I knew I should have put cameras throughout her whole goddamn house.

"What the hell are you looking at?"

Maddox.

I don't have time to hide Scarlet's bedroom feed or lie to him. Closing down everything as fast as I can, I rise and hurry out the office door, headed straight toward Midnight's parking lot.

He's on my heels, his heavy, booted steps unmissable as he follows me out. I'm too focused, too busy running through various scenarios in my head, each one more vomit inducing than the other.

I climb into the car, starting the engine as I hear the passenger door slam shut. A towering shadow sits next to me.

Maybe she's in the shower. Or out for a swim in the

pond. She could be hanging out with her family. Maybe I'm panicking for nothing.

Or maybe Duval found out she broke into his house.

My pulse rings in my ears, hands clutched painfully tight around the leather steering wheel as I drive over there. I don't even register the traffic lights. Did I pass any reds? Honks blare around me. Deep colors that remind me of her name flash. Maddox mutters curses under his breath. That feral creature inside of me rages, clawing at my insides to come out and shred this city to ribbons so it can find her. The gas pedal is maxed out, the world is a blur around me, but through it, I see my target.

We're close. So close.

Maddox doesn't utter a word as I slow down and pull into her drive—the gate is wide open. That makes me even more uneasy. When I climb out of the car and sprint toward her front door, he follows in silence. When I find it locked and go around the back, sighing when I don't see her calmly swimming in the pond, he's still on my heels.

I walk into her house, pausing for a few moments to listen, but it's deathly quiet. The blood rushing through my veins is clouding my sanity. Instead of quietly observing to make sure I don't miss something, I'm itching to rage and rush, turning this place over to find her. I shake my head, aggressively rubbing a hand over my jaw in an attempt to calm myself, then carry on through Scarlet's home.

Maddox's steps branch away from mine as he quietly understands what we're doing here.

I don't find her in the bathroom. Her bedroom is as empty as it was on the camera feed. And her kitchen lights are on, a half-eaten meal on the table, but no beautiful, brown-haired woman sitting there.

"Carter."

I snap my head toward the urgent sound of my name and find Maddox in the office. A rushed glance into the dimly lit space doesn't reveal much, only a slightly messy office, but I notice that some things were knocked over on her desk; the chair is slid a bit too far from it, and her screens are still on.

Maddox looks at me, a frown pulling tight at his brows, his scar looking so much more jagged and beastly in this light.

"Do you think it was Duval?" he asks.

I turn the lights on fully, stepping further into the room without answering, swiping my gaze in every nook like it could fucking speak to me. Something glints on the floor under the desk, a dark stain under it, and I pull a tissue from the box sitting on it, reaching over to grab it.

"Is that blood?" Maddox cocks his head at the pen I'm holding. Drops of crimson stain the white tissue.

It sure fucking is. And I don't know if it's hers or her attacker's. I leave the offending item on the desk, and my gaze catches on the screen—bank accounts.

Is she still looking into Duval? Everyone was quite appreciative of her assistance. It brought us so many more steps closer to nailing the guy, and our plan is well and fully underway now. But she didn't need to do anything else. She's done enough. Certainly more than I did . . . to my utter surprise.

Scrolling up in one of the windows, the name makes me recoil—Camora. She's looking into her ex. Cycling through the windows, I notice how empty his account is. I thought the Camoras were doing well for themselves, but as I look further into a joint account, an image starts to form. Connections grip each other like thin strings coiling together, matching transactions between accounts, sums adding up and routed around to confuse and deflect. But I see them. Plain as day. Bernard's been stealing from his family and taking out the money in cash.

"Carter!"

I turn toward Maddox's urgent tone, and his expression gives me instant hope as he hands over the small object he holds in his hand—a cufflink, with ripped shirt fabric still attached.

"Does that mean anything to you?"

Yes, it fucking does. Because it has a monogram on it. Two cursive letters wound together, forming two damning initials—BC.

"Bernard motherfucking Camora," I say through gritted teeth.

"Her ex?"

I nod my response, slide the object into my waistcoat pocket, and walk out the door. Maddox follows with determined steps.

"Where are we heading?" he asks once we're in the car.

"The Camoras."

He nods and picks up his phone, thick fingers working over the touchscreen as I drive off. I swipe the car screen, picking Tina's name from my team, and she answers in two rings.

"Are you home?" I shoot the question, interrupting her greeting.

"Yeah, is every—"

"I need you."

"Go."

"We talked about the Camora family, the loan sharks in Bonray. I need you to see if you can track Bernard Camora. Also look for the other brothers and tell me if they're at their HQ. The address is in their file on our server. Text that to me."

"Are you heading that way?" Tina asks.

"Yes."

She shuffles in the background and seconds later, the distinctive keyboard clacks fill the car. There's something oddly comforting about that mechanical sound. It calms my nerves and helps the cogs in my brain turn more smoothly.

"Address sent. I'll let the others know and call when I have something."

She hangs up without another word.

Maddox picks up my vibrating phone and pops the address into the satnav. The screen says an hour and a half to our destination, but at night, with clear roads and my fucking car . . . there's no way I don't get there in an hour.

And when I do, I'll eviscerate the motherfucker.

CHAPTER 34
Carter

One hour and four minutes. I fucking floored it all the way to Bonray, home of the Camoras' HQ.

I'm not sure what I was expecting, but a dive bar at the border of the shady part of town seems appropriate. My leg's been twitching for the last ten minutes, and the air in the car is too constricting as I'm forced to wait here for the others. Maddox called the other guys and took care of everything as I was driving. I'm grateful, because I fear what I'll do if it's just us two.

Three SUVs pull up in the dim parking lot, and Vincent, Finnigan, and a whole security team climb out as I exit the car, itching to walk in.

Fucking finally!

"Tina confirmed the other two brothers, Lucas and Alvaro Camora, should still be here. She tracked a few CCTV feeds in the area, and their cars were seen coming this way, but not leaving," I confirm to the whole team. "No sign of Bernard, but maybe the brothers will know."

"How do you wanna do this?" Finnigan asks.

"Storm in, kill everyone but the Camoras, and cut them up for information," I answer in one breath.

"I'm serious," he pushes, rolling his eyes.

I'm fucking serious too.

"We don't want to intimidate them too much. At least not right at the start," Vincent says, his gaze narrowed on mine for enough time to read the seriousness of my words. "The four of us will go in, plus four of you." He points at our team.

I nod in approval when he cocks an eyebrow at me.

"Briana." He turns to the team leader. "Walk in after us and keep an eye out in case the rest of the team should join us."

"I'll take Kyle with me. A couple is more believable in a dump like this," Briana says.

"Let's go." I walk away from them, too eager to get the hell in and find out where Scarlet is.

When we pass through the door, it's clear we're not gonna blend in. Maybe the security team, since they're dressed more casually, but Vincent, Finnigan, and I stick out like a sore thumb. Maddox is usually in tall boots, cargo trousers tucked in, and a T-shirt stretched out over his expansive torso, but with his stature and graveness, he sticks out regardless.

The barroom is not even half full, and every person in here watches us, most of them openly, as we walk toward the bartender.

"We need a word with your bosses," I say.

The bartender's gaze swipes over our group, growing more and more insecure as he goes along.

"I know we're a good-looking bunch, but would you mind admiring us *after* you let your bosses know we want a word?

Thanks," Finnigan says.

"And who are you?" he asks, feigning boredom.

"Tell them Scarlet's future husband is here to talk." Though they come out of my mouth, the words startle me.

The bartender cocks an eyebrow and drops the cloth he pretended to wipe the bar top with, then turns to pick up the phone at the end of the bar. Too many gazes burn my flesh, but I couldn't give less of a shit about their opinions right now. I wouldn't go through this for just anyone.

The bartender mutters something on the phone before he hangs up and turns to us.

"Through there." He points to the door on the right-hand side of the bar. "The door at the end of the corridor."

I turn on my heels and storm through with sure, determined steps. A shorter, fuller man, with curly brown hair brushing against his ears, waits in the open doorway, arms crossed against his chest. He straightens instantly when more of us keep walking into the narrow corridor.

"Scarlet's *future husband*, I presume?" His tone bears traces of amusement, but I think our presence wiped most of it off.

"Carter Pierce." I introduce myself and look inside the office, at the second man, who has risen from behind the wooden desk. No sign of Bernard, though. "Where's your brother?"

We step into the office, crowding inside the room.

"Well, I'm Alvaro," the first man says, "and this is my brother, Lucas. But I presume it's not this brother you're asking for."

"Nice to meet you, I guess," Lucas adds.

"Our apologies. Circumstances ask for some urgency, I'm afraid," Vincent says. "This is Finnigan Hennessey and Maddox Severin, and I am Vincent Sinclair."

"From . . . Queenscove?" he asks, cocking his head. But I

don't miss the slight tremor in his gaze at the revelation.

"The very same," Finnigan answers.

"And why are you looking for our brother?" Lucas asks.

"He attacked Scarlet and kidnapped her out of her home tonight," Vincent says. "We need to find him."

Alvaro frowns, whipping his head toward his brother as they exchange confused, irritated looks.

"You're sure of this?" he asks.

I step forward and pull the cufflink out of my waistcoat pocket, the ripped shirt fabric still attached, then place it on his desk.

"This was on the floor of her ransacked office," I say. "There was some blood too."

The taller, leaner man leans over the desk and picks up the object, rolling his eyes and sighing. His exasperation speaks volumes. Why do I have the feeling there's not much love lost between the brothers?

"We need to know where he could have taken her. Now." I drop my gaze when the fire inside of me threatens to spill over.

"Look, we—"

"You might also want to do a sweep of all your bank accounts," I say, needing to throw another incentive in there. "Scarlet's PC was still turned on when we found it. In an attempt to convince your brother to grant her the divorce, she's been looking into all of your finances. I only glanced at the records, and I could tell right away. He's moving money around. Money he himself no longer has."

"Are you suggesting he's stealing from us?" Lucas asks, disbelief pulling at his brows.

"I'm not suggesting it. I'm telling you."

He exchanges a look with his brother which lasts more seconds than I'm willing to waste right now.

"I have an idea." Alvaro steps forward. "Our mother's old

house at the edge of town, next to the small forest there.”

"Take us." I don't wait for any response, finally seeing some goddamn light as I turn around and head straight for the exit.

Only a minute passes before the man walks out and heads to the parking lot. "Follow me."

* * *

House is too big of a word for the ruin that welcomes us at the edge of the Bonray woods. But it could be a fucking shed for all I care, because a shiny car sits at its entrance, and I would bet my left nut that it belongs to the asshole I'm searching for.

We sneak around, trying to keep quieter than the whistling wind. Voices come from inside, through the broken windows of the small, abandoned cottage.

"Your fucking gambling addiction is not my goddamn problem. Get it through your thick skull, Bernard. I am not giving you any more stones!" Scarlet's yell is a caress over my soul.

"Just . . . I'll give you the damn divorce, Scarlet. Just give me stones from your next few jobs, and I'll sign the papers." His harsh tone disguises the desperation. Not very well, though.

"Where will it end, huh? You have a problem, and I may not be a gambler, but I bet that this *arrangement* will never end. You'll keep stealing from your business, you'll keep going into debt, and you'll keep harassing me for precious stones. It. Will. Never. End!"

"For fuck's sake, Scarlet! Just give me what I need. They'll fucking kill me if I don't repay the debt."

"Nah, I'm good. Feel free to kill me, then take it from your business account. Again. I'm sure your brothers won't mind." The last line is sprinkled with so much sarcasm.

"Motherfucker," Alvaro whispers next to me.

I raise my hand and signal everyone to go in as Bernard shouts and rages inside. As I storm through the door, I spot Scarlet tied to a chair. When she sees me, her face lights up like a thousand suns shone their rays on her, and her soon-to-be-dead ex recoils in surprise a few feet away. More at his brother than us.

The man looks wrong . . . red, bloodshot eyes. Either he's on drugs or he hasn't slept in a week.

I look Scarlet up and down, searching for spots of blood on her pastel-purple jumpsuit as the tension in my forehead seems to bleed out of me. When I reach her eyes, they're soft, strangely cheerful, with a touch of sweet madness as she quirks her lips.

"I'm not hurt, Carter." She answers the question I couldn't bring myself to ask.

I nod, then turn my attention to her ex.

"Do you remember what I told you last time you dared touch Scarlet?" My voice doesn't quite sound like my own—a harsh, guttural tone as I stalk toward my target.

He reluctantly steps back, holding a knife up like he's about to slice some damn bread. Fucking pathetic. When Maddox goes to untie Scarlet, the asshole attempts a step toward her, but one growl from me and he stalls, knife tensing in his grip.

"Answer the fucking question," I demand. "Do you remember what I told you?"

He nods his head, the movement staggered as his gaze trembles.

"Good. Then you know what follows."

The moment unfolds in a flurry. His eyes bulge as an

animalistic panic overtakes him. A shriek cuts through the tension beside me as his arm swings out, knife glinting in the harsh light, aimed directly at me. But his gaze shifts, drawn past me, to where a flash of wild, walnut-brown hair barrels forward. A fierce blur of fury rushes at him head-on. She's fast. Pure defiance and rage leave us no time to react as she tackles Bernard to the ground.

Her rage would make her look unorganized if it wasn't for the strategic movements. She forces the knife out of his hand and swipes it away before she plants her knees on his forearms.

The first swing of her fist lands with a blood-curdling crack, and Bernard's nose explodes as it bends.

"What a stupid fucking woman I've been." She punctuates each word with another strike to the man's face. "First, to choose *you!*" Another swing to his ear makes the man cry out in agony. "Second, to give you the impression that I'm fucking weak."

She wraps her hands around his throat, the muscles in her slender arms showing just how powerful she built herself to be as she holds the flailing man down.

"Carter," she says through gritted teeth, and I'm right there, hand gently gripping her shoulder. "Take me away before I kill him."

Bending down, I wrap my hands under her armpits, and with some resistance, I lift her off of him, bringing her to my chest as I step away. She circles my waist and looks up at me with a chaste smile that seems both victorious and defeated.

"Thank you for not stopping me," she says.

I wanted to. A primal need, which lay dormant within me until I met her, urged me to protect her. To keep her away from harm. But logic sneaked through. Scarlet is who she is because of the strength she honed all on her own. I won't treat her like a damsel in distress. Not unless she wants me to.

I plant a kiss on her forehead before turning to Alvaro Camora.

He steps forward as his brother peels himself off the ground. "You've been busy, brother. Stealing from the family business to feed your own addiction. More than one, considering how you look."

"It's not like that," Bernard says. "It's fine. I can pay it all back and—"

"And our reputation? The people you owe money to know you're a Camora. What a fucking disgrace you turn us into when we're trying to honor Dad's legacy! Build up the business he left us!" With each sentence, Alvaro's tone grows louder, anger streaming through the vowels.

"It's my business too. I can still—"

"He's turning in his fucking grave!" The gravelly rage falls silent in the next moment as Alvaro pulls out his gun, and on a shattering pop, a bullet splits his brother's skull.

"Nooo!" Scarlet rips out of my hold, hands pressed against her temples as she rushes toward her ex's body.

Her screams are agonizing, her reaction tearing at the muscle hidden behind my ribs that, until now, I thought was only there to pump blood through my body.

But fuck, it hurts as it fills me with new and unwelcome sentiments. My chest aches, pressure building within it as my stomach hollows.

Was I that utterly wrong about her?

I can't fucking move. I can't breathe.

"He was an asshole, Scarlet. You know that," Alvaro says, attempting to calm her.

"I fucking know that!" she shrieks, the words soothing something within me. "I'm crying because now I can't get a fucking divorce! Not with this motherfucker six feet under in an unmarked grave! What the hell do I do? I have to wait years until we can declare him missing or some shit."

My fucking Scarlet! My unhinged kitten.

I'm on her before she's finished her rant, one hand on the back of her neck as I yank her into an all-consuming kiss. My lips crash onto hers, tongue forcing its way inside her sweet mouth, devouring her essence like it's my life force. And goddamn it, it is.

The sheer relief washes over me like a warm summer storm.

"I'll get you divorced by the end of the week, kitten," I promise her as I reluctantly break away from her soft lips.

Her gaze widens, happiness exploding like fireworks in her coffee-colored eyes. "Really?"

"You have my word. Having a judge in our pocket pays off."

"Fuck yeah! Oh my god, I fucking lo—" She halts the rest of the sentence, eyes bulging, mouth still open as her creamy cheeks turn lobster red.

She wasn't about to say what I think she was about to say. Was she?

That word has floated around me my whole life. An odd word that can only make sense along with the associated sentiment. A sentiment I could never understand. Not when it turned people into irrational, mad, blind fools who forget themselves and instead live for someone else.

I could never understand why people yearn so deeply to hear those words aimed at them.

Yet, as I stare into Scarlet's eyes, I see a future that was never in the books for me before, and I can't help but be curious how that word would land if spoken to me.

She clears her throat and takes a step back, turning to Alvaro. "Why did you kill him? He's your brother."

The man shrugs. "This way, the business is split in two, not three, and a thief is out."

"That simple?" I ask.

"Yes. He was dead weight. No pun intended." He snickers. "He's been causing nothing but trouble, and we had a feeling he's been doing something shifty on the side. I guess it's time to rehire the accountant we fired. I'm thinking the three of us can do it all ourselves. Maybe it's our own fault. But, anyway, you're free, Scarlet."

"What about Ariana?" she asks.

"Yeah, she'll be a tough one. But we'll spin the gambling debt around and tell her he skipped town. Took a boat out and fled the continent."

"I still need to go to his house tonight. He stole something from me, and I need it back. Ariana will know of it too. I can't risk it," Scarlet says.

"Go, then. Just make it look like an ambush or something. She'll fold fast. I mean . . . you already know the woman." Alvaro shrugs.

"Do we have to make sure you'll tell your brother the truth about who killed Bernard?" I ask, itching to end this conversation and leave. "Because if you dare blame it on Scarlet or us, we'll be back, and the Camoras will be nothing but a word in the wind."

"Um, no. You're good." The man twitches.

"Good." I wrap my arm around Scarlet's back, pulling her attention to me. "Let's take you home."

"Ariana first!" she squeaks.

"Of course, love."

She smiles as I guide her out of the cabin. Everyone follows as we head back to our cars.

The things I'll do to this woman once I get her in my fucking house. She'll have me imprinted on her body for eternity.

CHAPTER 35
Scarlet

"I stand by what I said when I wanted to crawl under the covers and die—Tabitha would look fucking fantastic in the middle of your church." I walk through the expansive space as Carter flips various switches and bathes the converted holy ground in an ethereal light.

"Tabitha?" He cocks an eyebrow in amusement.

"I didn't tell you she has a name, did I?"

He shakes his head as he walks into the kitchen area, and my feet follow without question. "So, you like to name things."

"Only things I love," I point out, popping the velvet box that holds the Levain pendant onto the counter.

"What else have you named?" he asks as he pulls out bottles and pours various things into a shaker.

"Christ, what haven't I? I have some fossils that I love, a couple of skulls that were my first—Margaret and Daisy— and one of my favorites is Marvin."

Carter bursts out into the purest laughter, so uncharacteristic, and it does something magical to my insides.

"Marvin?" He turns to me, pressing a hand to his stomach.

"Yup. He's a little white mouse I keep on my dressing table. Stop laughing at him. He's adorable."

"Oh, I know Marvin."

I frown, but a moment later, I remember what a stalker Carter is. "Just how much of my house did you inspect?"

"Enough to know you have a thing for bones and strange things. And I didn't know then, but apparently, human tears too."

"And you have a problem with that?" I cross my arms over my chest, cocking an eyebrow as he comes to me, attempting to hand me a drink.

"Not a one, kitten. It makes me want to crack my way into your mind to figure out what other surprises lie there."

"And I'm the weird one," I mutter as I grab the drink and follow him out.

"Your words, not mine. Now, I have to check a few things in my office. You can go ahead and snoop around or join me there."

"Oh, don't worry, killer-boy, I've done my share of snooping around your place too," I say with a wide grin that seems to please him. "I could do with some more, but right now, I want to celebrate my fucking freedom from that asshole. I'm joining you."

With a devastating quirk in his lips, he wraps his hand around my waist and pulls me into his body.

"You may be free of him, love, but you're all mine," he claims in a husky voice that ripples dangerously through me, and I can't help but melt into his body.

He kisses me until I'm out of breath, then moves away, just as my thoughts stray in a sadder direction. Eventually, I'll have to tell him why he might not really want me . . . but for now, I'm going to be an asshole and enjoy this moment.

Carter sits on his intricate chair, his office resembling something from a government facility, with all the screens and gadgets. Though, it's quite cozy here too, with the deep armchair in the corner and the ancient brick walls.

Cameras pop onto the screen. I recognize some places, and others, I've seen only in my research of Carter. He doesn't ignore me. Instead, he keeps my excitement going, discussing the cheesy idea of a divorce shower with a few friends. Just like those bridal showers some people get, only I'm gonna be celebrating my fantastic, albeit bloody, separation.

From pacing to cozying up in the armchair to more pacing, I eventually perch on his thigh. He cycles through all those cameras, accessing past footage too, seemingly satisfied with his findings. Or lack thereof, I guess.

"Almost done, love. With Duval around, and the move we made on him, we're expecting retaliation."

"I thought you have a team of tech people who handles this stuff."

"Yes, we do, but the situation is so charged now. I would rather be the extra pair of eyes."

Most leaders would delegate and wipe their hands of the problem. I appreciate this difference.

"What's that folder?" I point to a lonely icon named "S" on one of the screens.

Carter pauses, mouse stuck in the middle of the image, his body going slightly rigid beneath me. He drags the cursor to the file and double-clicks the folder, and I lean over, my ass sliding deeper into his lap as I attempt to distinguish the images in the small thumbnails.

"No fucking way!" I exclaim. "That's my fucking bedroom!" I whip my head around, meeting his gaze.

The slightest tinge of guilt meets me, but it's not enough for him to actually look like he's sorry.

"You have a camera in my bedroom, Carter?"

He nods, lips tugging into a suggestive grin. "And I don't intend on taking it out."

"But . . . I do stuff in there."

"Oh, I know." He raises his brows. I didn't know his face was capable of that.

"I didn't mean *that*. I meant . . . girl stuff. You can't—Wait, what?" I recoil, but he wraps his arm around my middle, tugging me against him. I'm fully seated now, feet off the ground.

He opens one video, and I'm stunned into silence as I watch myself drop the towel after coming out of the shower, happily naked without knowing he was stalking me. In another video, I'm simply sleeping. Peaceful. Oblivious. And in the third one . . . I'm splayed on my bed, legs bent and open wide, my hand deep between my thighs, fingers sunk deep inside my core.

My mouth drops open, yet I can't get any words out.

Holy hell, he's been watching me get myself off. Right here . . . in this office. And he saved the footage.

I'm astonished. Slightly appalled. And . . . turned on.

My hips involuntarily adjust on his lap, moisture gathering between my thighs, right in that spot that presses against the growing bulge beneath it. With his hand around my belly, he holds me firmly as he flexes upward, and the slightest whimper escapes my throat when his cock puts just the right amount of pressure on my sex.

"Do you like that, kitten?"

I lean into his whisper, pressing my back to his front

and leaning my head against his shoulder. His warmth is addicting. His touch even more so, as he slides his hand over my stomach until he reaches my breast, massaging it with a deliciously firm touch.

"Yes . . ." I answer.

"Look at yourself. Look how fucking hypnotizing you are as you drive your fingers into your addictive little cunt." He pinches my nipple through the fabric, rolling it between his fingers.

Logically, I know I should feel an ache, a slight pain, or maybe a deeper one, but I'm overcome with longing instead. An intense need to feel him do to me what I'm doing to myself on that screen.

"Such a beautiful little slut you are, putting on such a magnificent show without even knowing." He captures my earlobe between his teeth, sucking it into his mouth before he swipes his tongue over the edge and plants shivers and goosebumps all over my flesh.

"I didn't know . . ." I moan.

"Yet, you wanted it to be me. Didn't you? Look how fucking wet you got for me. Whimpering my name under your breath like you were praying I would appear out of the shadows and fuck you senseless."

Reaching under my blouse, he tugs down my bra and captures my breast in his large palm, kneading it into a bundle of pleasure as his other hand finds the heat between my legs.

I roll my hips against his bulge as he rubs the pad of his palm over the fabric covering that heated part of me, threatening to drive me wild.

"Play the next video, my filthy little girl."

Clumsily, I slap my hand on the desk and find the mouse, then skip to the next video.

"Oh, god," I whisper as he applies more pressure to my clit.

"Look how soundly you sleep as I stand right next to you. It was such a delightful surprise to find out you slept naked."

Heat pools between my legs, and I wonder just how fucked up in the head I am to find a video of me sleeping while the man who touches me right now stands next to my bed. Watching me. And . . . oh god, he reaches over, touching my skin, hooking his finger on the edge of the sheet and . . .

"Carter," I whimper as he slides his hand beneath the hem of my sweatpants to find the sopping mess.

"Beautiful, isn't it?"

I nod erratically, unable to take my eyes off of the screen. But then the video ends with him turning away.

"Y-you stopped."

"I did."

"Why? Oh god." I grind my aching core against his hard length, seeking the pressure that drives me wild. "Why didn't you do it? Touch me? Stroke me? Fuck me?"

Fingers sliding down further, he finds that warm part of me that weeps only for him and circles my clit with just the right speed to turn me into a whimpering mess.

"I wanted to, so fucking bad," he groans into my ear.

"But . . . ?" I ask as I lift my ass so he can lower my sweatpants.

As he slides two long fingers through my folds, his thumb bears down on the sensitive bundle of nerves. A hoarse moan rips through my throat as he enters me. He pulls out, repeating the motion until the sopping sounds urge him to slip a third finger in.

"A question slipped through my mind." His breaths come fast, matching mine. "What if you would have hated me for it? If I did that to you, what if you never allowed me to touch you again?"

I wouldn't have hated him, but I appreciate him more for

this logic.

He finger fucks me faster, his strokes punishing in their lustful viciousness, and I prop my knees against the edge of his desk, needing the leverage.

"Tell me what you want, kitten," he orders in his smoky tone I dream of too often.

But my mouth is filled to the brim with moans and soft, needy breaths. There's no space for words to form in a rational order.

A wanton cry rips from my throat when he pulls out his fingers, but my protest is shattered when the cruel man slaps my pussy into obedience. I jump out of my skin, but I'm ready to grab his hand and shove his fingers back inside of me, because . . . God fucking damn it, that was hot.

"Answer me, Scarlet."

He smacks my aching core once more, and the words spill out of my mouth without one ounce of my brain involved.

"Make me come, Carter! Drench every single inch of this goddamn desk with my pleasure! And when you're done, I want your magnificent cock down my throat."

His lust-filled groan vibrates against my body as his fingers impale me down to the last knuckles. I can't rationalize the onslaught of pleasure. How this man manages to touch the sensitive parts of me all at once, stroking inside of me, harsh yet skillful, rubbing his thumb against my clit, as his other hand is still busy with my breasts. I thought men couldn't multitask.

Heat and tremors curl my toes, pooling deep inside my core. Waves of them fill me as I reach back, bracing myself around his neck. He releases my breasts and slides his hand low on my belly, and when he presses his palm there, rolling his fingers against that spot that makes my eyes roll to the back of my head, I'm sure Valhalla, Nirvana, and the goddamn

Heavens open up for me all at once.

I scream through my orgasm in melodious waves as the pleasure gushes out of me. He wraps one arm around me, slowing his strokes against my sensitive core, whispering praises and dirty words into my ear as ecstasy coils around my insides. My heartbeat rages in my ears, my breaths rushed and incomplete, and my legs tremble so badly that Carter has to help me lower them.

I don't even care how drenched I am. How drenched he is. Or if I ruined his PC setup. I'm in fucking heaven and I'm not even a believer.

When air finally penetrates my lungs and manages to fill them without my pulse raging in my temples, I let myself slide off of his lap and onto my knees, then turn to face him. His legs are spread wide, strong arms casually rested on the armrests. When he slumps in the seat with his head cocked as he watches me kneel for him, he looks like a fucking god.

My fucking god!

I waste no time unbuckling his belt before I unbutton his trousers and pull down his boxers. My mouth pools with saliva at the sight before me. He's long and perfectly thick without being overwhelming. Veins bulge under velvety skin, and with those frenum piercings forming that exquisite Jacob's ladder, he looks positively menacing. I'm fucking drooling.

"I've been dying to do this." I hold his gaze as I swipe my tongue from the base of his cock, over the dips and mounds of all seven rungs, until I reach the thick tip and suck him into my mouth.

I moan at the saltiness of his precum. At the same time, he groans and tangles his fingers within my hair, holding me tightly as his cock twitches against my tongue. His feral gaze looks at me with more than passion. More than just carnal pleasure. There's a hunger in there that's mine and mine alone.

I tug against his hold, uncaring of the amount of hair he'll pull out, and take him deeper. The balls of the piercings roll against my tongue. I count each rung I manage to swallow, but I choke before I reach the fourth. I pull out on a sloppy sound, saliva connecting my lips to the tip of him. Carter licks his lips, eyes deeply fixed on mine.

"Again," he growls.

With a lascivious grin that touches my eyes more than my lips, I swallow him, head bobbing up and down with a sultry rhythm that pulls a melodious range of groans from his gorgeous lips.

"You're such a good fucking girl. Soon you'll swallow every single fucking rung in that dirty little mouth of yours."

I moan against his cock, sending vibrations straight down to his balls.

"Get me nice and sloppy, ready to fuck your pussy until you're begging for my cum to fill you."

Pulling him out on a loud *pop*, I spit on his cock and grin when he groans deep in his chest, then swallow him once more. I grab hold of his balls, kneading as I press them against his cock. I press the tips of my fingers to his perineum, massaging the muscle as I swallow him to the back of my throat.

"The fuck are you doing to me, Scarlet?" The smoky moan brings a strange sort of pride as I repeat the motions, reveling in every twitch and flex of his cock against my lips.

His balls tighten in my hand, cock rock-hard inside my mouth, and his grip on my hair stalls my efforts.

"That's enough."

I attempt to shake my head, but I can barely manage.

"Don't you dare make me come, Scarlet. I want to be inside you when I do. I want to fill that pussy until I spill out and mark every single bit of you as mine." He yanks my head away from his cock, and I reluctantly let go.

Less than ten seconds later, I'm on my feet, in his arms, and thrown onto his bed. In one quick stroke, he rips out his belt, vicious gaze trained on me like I'm his prize. He orders me to undress just as he does, then slides between my legs. Towering over me as he sits on his haunches, he rubs his cock against the wet seam of my core.

"Spread that pretty cunt for me, kitten, so I can remind it that it's mine."

Skin bursting into goosebumps, I reach down and follow his order. The man gives me one devastating look, which I feel deep in my belly as he grabs my hips. Then he spits on my pussy, marking me further, and sheathes himself so deeply that stars dance behind my eyes and my back arches off of the bed.

And once again, Valhalla, Nirvana, and the fucking Heavens look upon me.

CHAPTER 36
Scarlet

Tangled around each other, Carter holds me to his chest, where we occupy less than half of his ridiculous bed. Silence fell steadily after my third mind-blowing orgasm of the night. It's comfortable. So comfortable that anxiety has been brewing inside me.

The little voice in my head started out no louder than a breeze, but now it whispers louder, ripping this moment away from me.

"Something's bothering you."

I flinch at his statement. "I'm fi—"

"I can tell, Scarlet."

I sigh, pulling back slightly so I can see his beautiful face. He looks even better with unkempt hair.

"How?"

"You've tensed up, and your toes fidget like crazy."

For fuck's sake, leave it to my body to betray me.

"What is it?" he insists.

"It's just something I've been putting off. I shouldn't have, I know. It's so fucking unfair to you. But . . ." I rise to sit next to him, folding my legs beneath me. "I couldn't let go of you, of how you make me feel, how I am when I'm around you. I just needed a little bit more before I had to let it all go."

He frowns, his expression turning grave. "What the fuck are you talking about, Scarlet?"

I rub a hand over my forehead, then clutch my fingers in my lap as I take a deep breath. "I want this. Us. Whatever this is. I want you so bad that I fucking ache every single day. My blood screams for you inside my veins, and sometimes I can't stand it. And again, it's fucking unfair for me to confess this, but I need to get it out."

"Scarlet." His growl is a rumbling warning.

"I can't give you kids." I sigh, the words a heavy load I'm relieved to let go of. Now that they're out, more come in waves. "It's not a fertility issue. I simply don't want them. My genes are wrong. As much as my condition sometimes feels like a superpower, and as different as I am from my mother, I cannot bring myself to risk cursing a child with this. Or worse . . . with my mother's sickness."

I take a deep breath, gathering more of my stray thoughts.

"I lied to you before. I don't have a contraceptive implant. I had a hysterectomy a few years ago. I made sure it would be impossible for me to get pregnant. Since then, I realized I don't want kids at all, even adopted. They're not an option for me. And I know this discussion is premature. You might have not even thought of a future with me, but . . . it doesn't matter. I just need you to know now, this is it. This is all you get. Just me . . . I can't offer you anything else."

When I end my word vomit, Carter rises slowly, his

expression completely unreadable. Any moment now, he's going to tell me to fuck off out of his bed, out of his house, for forcing him to get close to me when I'm not willing to offer him this. But I'll never back down, no matter how much I want this man.

He grips my lower jaw between his thumb and index finger, dipping down and shocking me when he presses his lips to mine with such pressure. The kiss is bruising. Deep and charged with unspoken words with significant meanings I don't yet understand.

Pulling back, his hand still on my face, he presses one last kiss to my forehead. "Thank you."

"What?" I frown, confused.

"I didn't know until now what that gnawing, sickening feeling inside of me was. It's been eating at me for days . . . maybe longer. It has grown roots I haven't been able to rip out. But I understand now."

My eyes sting, vision blurring as tears form and my throat tightens. I thought I was ready for this. Goddamn it, I was wrong.

Carter brushes a finger over the contour of my cheek, his lips shifting into a soft, slight smile. "I don't want any children either, Scarlet."

Like a punch to the gut, the breath expels out of me, and the tears that drop onto my cheeks no longer come from fear.

"Are you serious?" I ask, clutching his face in my hands. "You're not just saying it? For me?"

He shakes his head. "That feeling eating at me seems to have been . . . worry. Fear. Probably for the same reason you've been afraid to confess this. I understand now, and whatever this is between us, I see it clearer."

"Oh god!" I exclaim, rushing to crush my lips against his in a bruising kiss I break only to pepper all over his face.

His chest shakes with a silent snicker.

"Why no kids?" I ask, curiosity taking over.

He shrugs and lies back on the bed, folding an arm to brace it behind his head. "They're not my thing. I've been around them, so the opinion is informed. Finnigan has his girlfriend's little sister, who they had to legally adopt, and Ronan, his brother, has Aaro, his boy. I found that I can't connect with a child beyond pleasantries. The appeal isn't there. The patience or understanding either. They're just these small creatures I'm waiting to grow a brain so I can have a rational conversation."

I was too focused on men's biological needs and failed to apply that theory to Carter. Though I can still see him as a father to some degree, the alternative makes much more sense, considering his inability to properly process emotions or empathy.

"I didn't think about it that way at all, but taking into account your *personality,* I can see now how kids might have a hard time fitting in."

"Yes, my *personality* certainly has something to do with it. My blood too." He takes a deep breath before he continues. "You've been honest with me, so logically, I owe you the same."

I shift slightly, getting more comfortable as my confusion grows.

"My reasons are similar to yours. My genes are rotten. My father was the only good one between us three, and even he died of a disease that can be congenital. I'm comfortable with the way I'm built, with how my mind works, because I physically don't know anything else."

He pauses, gaze unfocusing for a few moments that allow too much worry to build inside of me.

"But there are times, rare times, when I'm surrounded by my *brothers,* our friends, and in their eyes, I see a spark. I saw it in you too, with your family, this glimmer that spreads over your skin, brightening every fiber that forms you. That feeling is not hard to recognize—happiness. One that can only come from the ability to feel things that I will never fully understand. And in those moments, that hollowness within me becomes more noticeable."

That makes me feel so sad for him.

"It would be unfair to impart this feeling. I may consider myself at an advantage, like you do, but I won't risk spreading this to others. So, years ago, I got a vasectomy, but even those can fail sometimes, which is why I still like to make sure to wear a condom or that my partners use contraception."

He ends that deep confession in such a clinical tone, I'm startled.

"Funny . . . You can't feel the emotional pains, and I can't feel the physical ones. Both advantages we would never want to curse others with."

He nods. "And then, just as with you, there's my mother . . ." His tone doesn't shift from its almost monotone quality, but it's the way he trails off that straightens my spine to attention. "She used to drag me to church every Sunday when I was a small boy. She became more unsettled and forced Wednesday on me too. Then Friday. I understood later on that it was because of me."

He pauses for a few moments, gaze lost in a memory he's not sharing.

"The older I got, the deeper her beliefs burrowed, and the more evil she saw in me. Her faith turned radical, her Christianity a fully formed extremist beast that held no sense of logic. She didn't believe that I, her son, was evil. She was convinced evil existed within me, a creature controlling me, taking over. And where there's one, there are many. She found the right fanatic wack jobs to fuel her delusions. Priests who convinced her they could get the evil creature out.”

“No . . .” I whisper, hoping this confession isn't going where I think it is as worry for that little boy tightens around my heart.

“I was too young, somewhat sheltered, and didn't fully understand what they were doing to me. The tightly tied ropes, the Latin chants, the crucifixes they waved around, and the water they kept splashing me with were simply confusing. Slightly annoying. I don't even remember being scared.”

I watch every twitch in his features, every wrinkle forming as he recounts the horrendous things he experienced as a child, yet none betray emotions he may be hiding. Maybe all I really want is to stare into a mirror. Maybe I'm hoping that, despite everything I know of him, *he does* actually feel something. That *he is*, in fact, affected. But he continues his recount in the same calm voice, with the same relaxed expression, not one shift in his perfectly set features.

“It wasn't long until I began to understand. When the violence escalated and started leaving marks on my body. Of course, none of it worked. The evil was still within me, and she saw more of it every day, overtaking me. When the priest's exorcisms proved ineffective, she took matters into her own hands. She was so far gone by that point. Delusions convinced her that water is what cleanses us, washes off our sins through baptism, and sends the evil away. More than once, she forced me into the tub, taking matters into her own hands until the water breached my airways.”

“She was fucking drowning you?” I hate that I interrupted him, but the outrage tears through me, viciously stinging my eyes and tightening my chest.

“As she told my father when he caught her and found out everything, she was, in fact, *cleansing the evil* out of me. Of course, there was no demon, no despicable creature, no foreign evil. It's always been me."

And there, with that last statement, there's a small crack in the mask. A strain in his eyes, many more blinks than necessary, gaze flickering, yanking at my heart.

"It's funny, isn't it?" He turns to me as a tear slides down my cheek. He watches it, following its path before reaching over to capture it. Bringing his finger to his mouth, he sucks my sadness between his lips, attempting to make it go away.

"What's funny?" My voice trembles.

"How powerless we find ourselves before our parents. How much we want to trust them."

My gaze drifts into nothingness, shoulders slumping as his words sink in, along with the countless memories weighing them down.

"What happened after your dad found out?"

"He kicked her out without a second thought. She's with some cult somewhere. The wrong parent died, unfortunately."

My heart breaks for him, even if his is made of stone.

"I can't believe she tried to exorcise you. You w-were just a little boy . . ."

Carter shrugs like it's all dust in the wind. Experiences that happened to someone else, not his own tragic background. It fucking infuriates me. But most of all, it fills me with horrible sadness.

I climb onto him, regardless of how detached he is, and slide my hands under his neck. I wrap myself around him. Maybe he doesn't need this, maybe he just doesn't know he does, but I certainly do. I bury my face in the soft crook of his shoulder, spilling tears for both him and me, for the parents who failed us, for the people who didn't know what was being done to us, and for the childhoods tainted by madness.

"I'm sorry, baby. I'm sorry," I whisper against his warm skin.

Seconds flow one by one, each lighter than the one before. His arms wrap around my body and startle me. I squeeze him harder. And so does he, his breaths falling heavier after the shift in his rigid soul. Maybe it's for me, but hopefully a little bit for himself too.

If all our other moments before didn't cement my feelings, this one etched them in every inch of my being. He may not be able to give me his, but Carter Pierce has my heart.

CHAPTER 37
Scarlet

This time around, I made sure to let my family know I'm alive. They would have certainly noticed my absence since I've been living it up at Carter's for two days now. My clothes have been sitting clean in his dryer since yesterday, yet he seems perfectly happy for me to wear his. Even his boxer shorts.

Though I've spent much more time out of them. Splayed on his bed. Bent over his kitchen counter. On my knees in his shower. And on all fours in the middle of his church. But I also curled into him as I answered more of his burning questions about my life. I stood quietly as he washed my long hair in the shower. And danced through his kitchen as he cooked some delicious fillet steaks for us.

We've had moments. More in the last forty-eight hours than I thought possible. It's interesting how much you can learn about a person once you remove all the bullshit rules people have about dating, when you remove all the worry about what someone's gonna think about you, and when you simply stop giving a shit and allow someone in.

There is one thing I didn't ask, and he also didn't share—why he lives in a church. I have two theories—what he does in here is his way of desecrating everything his mother stood for, or it's his subconscious way of being close to the mother he was supposed to have.

I don't want to ask him about it. I think I prefer holding on to my theories.

An angry vibration startles me fully awake from the nap I fell into after yet another orgasm that left me spent. Technically, I regained consciousness a few minutes ago, but the slumber felt so good that I refused to open my eyes or move.

Deep burnt-orange hues litter the sky, slipping through one of the few windows that isn't stained glass.

How long did I nap for?

I turn around in bed to search for Carter, the question sitting on the tip of my tongue, but I almost choke on it when I see the man. He's sitting up, bare torso leaned against the headboard as he reads a weathered book, a pair of rounded square-framed glasses perched on his nose.

Goddamn those retro-looking glasses!

Goddamn this man!

And goddamn that stray strand of hair brushing against the frames!

I didn't think it was possible for him to get any fucking hotter. The tattoos were enough. The perfectly carved features were already too much. But the fucking glasses? That's just excessive.

He's oblivious to my inner turmoil as he quirks the corner

of his lip, throwing a soft "good evening" at me as he leans over his nightstand to pick up his phone.

After a few moments of reading, he taps his thumbs on the screen, replying to the message. The conversation carries on until he pauses, waiting for the other person to reply.

His expression is unchanged and I'm not sure if it's my curiosity or my jealousy gnawing at me, but I'm fucking itching to know what the message is about.

Finally, he puts down the phone and places the book next to it, but when he's about to slide those glasses off, I jump up and slide right onto his lap.

"Don't you fucking dare." I catch his wrist, bringing it down to my bare behind.

He gives it a tight squeeze before he wraps both hands around my hips, sliding them under the soft shirt he gave me to wear. His hands glide over my waist, but he stops on my ribs, thumbs brushing against the sensitive undersides of my breasts.

He graces me with a lopsided grin and one sinfully quirked eyebrow as I brace myself against his chest.

"Do you like my reading glasses, love?"

"Hate them," I whisper as I lean in to press a kiss to his lips.

"Do you, now?"

"So much. I hate that they make me even wetter for you."

"Is that so?" He brings one hand down, sliding it over my sex, an approving groan rippling through his chest. "Too bad we have to go."

"No."

"Yes."

"Please, Carter . . . one more time."

He squeezes my core, pulling a moan right out of my throat as I throw my head back.

"Trust me, kitten." His lips press against my throat. "We

have to go."

I take in a slow breath, then pull back, rational thoughts finally drizzling through. "Did something happen?"

"Not yet, but I think it's coming to that. Martin Duval is dead."

"Wait." I recoil. "Did you guys kill him?"

He shakes his head. "Suspicious circumstances have been ruled out, and accidental overdose was cited."

Frowning, I sift through my brain for any indication in my previous research that this man ever did drugs. Or hard drugs, anyway.

"I don't remember finding any clue that he was any sort of addict."

"He wasn't," Carter answers with an amused expression. "I'm almost one hundred percent sure his father killed him and paid the right people off to rule it an overdose. This is revenge."

"Because of your attack on him, you think?"

"Well, he certainly found out there was a spy with nefarious intentions in his midst. He probably pieced together who it was all on his own."

I slide off of his lap, and he rises and walks over to his antique wood-carved wardrobe to dress. Such a shame to cover that tattooed ass and exquisite legs.

"He killed his own son . . ." I trail off, wondering what's to come now. If Duval is capable of that, he'll be capable of anything.

"We're going to Midnight. You and Morrigan, who's already there, will go with some of our security to meet Vincent's mother, Evelyn, and Maya. The guys and I will take our teams and get ready for Duval."

"No!" I rise to my knees at the edge of the bed, blood boiling at the idea. "Why are you separating us and sending me off with the women like I'm some chick who can't hold her own?"

He walks over, still towering over me as he stands at the edge of the bed. "You're not coming with us, Scarlet. That's out of the fucking question."

"But I can—"

His hand grips my throat, firm but careful. His other hand presses against my back, holding me close. "I know you're strong, but even I'm not sure what we'll be dealing with. I am not, under any circumstances, risking your goddamn safety, Scarlet."

His gaze bores into me, filled with raw sentiments I bet my ass he doesn't understand, but they fucking shine in his eyes.

"Do you understand me? You are important, Scarlet."

Those words echo through me, a rippling effect that caresses my soul, pulsing behind my ribs.

Eventually, I nod. How could I not when he speaks such things to me?

"Good. Now let's get your clothes from the dryer. We really need to go." He presses a final kiss to my lips and gives my throat a playful squeeze before he steps away.

Carter

FINNIGAN WALKS INTO THE SPEAKEASY only a couple of minutes after Scarlet and I arrive, bringing with him the last of the team leaders we're debriefing before we go into both defense and attack mode.

"Tina said there's no sign of the mercenaries." I waste no time revealing the tech team's findings. "There weren't a lot of them in the company, but the leftovers being MIA is not a good sign."

"Duval has also gone into hiding. He's not at home or any of his usual locations, and we can't track him down," Beau, one of our team leaders, says.

"Something's happening. It's too quiet." Finnigan runs a hand through his blond curls, worry etched deeply in his features.

"It's time to go. Beau, take your team and get Morrigan and Scarlet to safety. Maddox, I think—"

The rest of my sentence evaporates in deafening chaos.

The floor bucks under my feet. The walls tremble like they're ready to collapse. Heat slams an invisible fist into me as the air fills with smoke so thick it burns my throat.

"Scarlet!" I scream as I find her through the haze.

She stumbles, and I don't think—

I grab her waist and yank her behind me as wood splinters and plaster explodes above us. My pulse is a roar in my ears, but I force myself to focus, to think.

"The alarms!" someone screams over the commotion.

I scramble to pull out my phone.

"What are you doing?" Scarlet questions.

"The sprinklers aren't working. The alarm failed. I have to warn the others to evacuate!"

"What others?"

The front door crashes open, and figures pour in, dark silhouettes against the glow of rising flames. One of our men rushes forward, only to be met with the glint of a blade. Blood sprays.

"We own the whole building," I say. "Some of our army, our staff, they live above us."

"Warn them!" she shouts, quickly understanding.

"Stay low," I growl. I pick a name from my call list after she crouches down next to a table.

A man charges me, baton swinging. I sidestep, grabbing a shattered chair leg from the floor, and drive it into his ribs. The impact is solid, satisfying. He crumples, but there's no time to breathe. Another bastard rushes me as the heat of the flames licks my skin and the acrid smoke claws at my lungs.

I pull out my gun and point the barrel at a man charging Vincent from behind. The shattering pop aimed right at his torso is barely a whisper in the chaos around us.

Even Morrigan has a guy by the throat on the ground, punching his face in as Vincent attempts to pull her off.

"Get the fuck out!" Maddox thunders.

I swipe over a name on my phone and put the call on speaker as I look for the exit, but the smoke confuses me in what were once familiar surroundings.

Another explosion blasts out the back, and I swing to Scarlet, shielding her body with mine. A menacing creak ripples through the sound waves, and the ceiling trembles dangerously. Flames lick it, spreading further.

"Hello? Carter!"

"Code re—"

"Behind!" Scarlet bellows, and I swing without a second thought.

My gun hits muscle before I even aim it, and I fire, then shove the figure away, but he grabs my shirt collar and pulls me with him. I snarl as I pistol-whip him on the nose, then put a bullet in the middle of his forehead.

"Carter! What's happening?"

"Code fucking red! Evacuate! Now!" I shout into my phone before sticking it into my pocket without waiting for an answer.

Everyone fights around me, making a path of fallen bodies toward the exit. I don't know if anyone has gone out. I can't see through the bitter smoke. My pulse thrums in my ears as my Midnight crumbles around me, wood burning, leather melting, memories shattering.

"Scarlet!" I howl for her as I whip around.

She rises from between the two fallen tables she's hidden behind and moves for me.

"We have to get out!" I shout, and reach for her.

But the smoke behind her moves. A man in a gas mask walks through it, and I jump into a sprint just as he grabs her. He pulls her into the fumes as she flails and kicks to get him off, arms outstretched toward me. Her desperate gaze tears at something within me, and I finally get to her, clutching her hand in mine.

Her gaze widens in horror, mouth open in a scream I don't get to hear as a searing jolt erupts at the side of my head, and my world falls into darkness.

CHAPTER 38
Carter

Pain radiates against my cheek, ears ringing as the world floods my senses all at once. A loud crack sounds. My head whips violently to the side, neck straining as the same pain blooms against my other cheek.

Voices sound around me, senseless, muddled, as I open my eyes and fight through my blurred vision.

But one voice breaks through the haze.

"Scarlet . . ." I mutter.

"Leave him the fuck alone!"

"Just trying to wake him up for you, sweetheart."

I don't like the sound of that male voice. It's too condescending, laced with sleazy energy. As I blink through the haze, my surroundings finally come into focus. Old cobwebs dangle in the corners of the peeling wallpaper. Sparse, dusty furniture weathered by time stands against the crumbling wood-panelled walls, and a chandelier missing most of its bulbs lights up the room.

And there, among it all, is *Scarlet*.

She's tied to a chair barely ten feet away. Her gaze, brimming with hope that only makes me feel like a useless asshole, is locked on me.

Some guy stands in front of her, a menacing blade held tightly in his hand as he watches her. I go to rise, but I'm also tied to a fucking chair. Rope cinches my torso to the chair, my wrists at my back, and my ankles to the legs.

"Morning, princess."

My head snaps forward as the bald man stands before me, rubbing his fist in his palm like it's supposed to scare me. He steps aside, revealing a winged-back armchair, too new to belong in this place. And in it sits Duval himself.

"Kidnapping seems like the wrong kind of activity for someone who wants to portray himself as a stand-up politician," I taunt.

He sits on his *throne*, another of his leather-clad mercenaries standing next to him, betraying that persona he's working so hard to show to the public.

"It felt like the appropriate response, considering your blackmail attempt with all that information you delivered to me." Duval shrugs.

"That wasn't blackmail. It was a warning. Kidnapping me won't stop the wheels that have been put in motion unless you draw the line here, let us go, and back off."

"You must see that between us two, you're not the one in control here." He nods to the guy standing before Scarlet, and the breath sticks in my throat as he turns and backhands her across the cheek.

Her head whips to the side as she yelps, and my muscles seize.

"I'm going to have your fucking hand for that," I growl to the brute.

"We'll take the risk. Again," Duval orders.

I thrash against the rope, the chair creaking under the strain of my muscles. I lean forward, teeth bared like a feral dog as the bastard strikes her again. His knuckles collide with her face, accompanied by a sickening, stomach-coiling thud. Strands of walnut-colored hair stick to the blood trickling down her temple as her head snaps back.

Scarlet doesn't flinch. Doesn't cry out. But her silence eats at me.

Goddamn it, she's bleeding.

"Hit me!" I roar. "Whatever you want, do it to me, you fucking coward!"

Duval leans forward, a faint smirk tugging at his lips. "Ah, but that wouldn't hurt you, now would it, Carter? It wouldn't hurt them either." He extends his arm, pointing to the side of the room.

"What the . . . ?" I frown at the camera I notice in the far corner.

"I want the escort service. You better agree to it before she dies. And you better believe I'm serious. After all, I already left you without a bar and your precious Fightclub. I'm streaming this to your Sanctum so they know I'm serious too. Though, I'm not entirely sure who cares enough to watch. I sent them the link." He shrugs, amused.

"Why her? Why me?" I ask.

"Convenience. My preference was a couple, but I would have happily taken any two of you."

"And you think we'll still give you the fucking escort service if you kill her?" I say through gritted teeth.

"No, but at least we both lose something."

"Don't you fucking dare, Carter!" Scarlet screams, pulling

our attention to her, but she's staring straight at me. "I'll fucking hate you forever if you dare agree to this delusional motherfucker's offer. I'm not worth the life of all those people who'll be tortured at his sleazy hands." She turns to Duval. "I'd rather die than see you get what you want."

In the least feminine of ways, she spits toward the man. He flinches and pulls his foot away before it reaches him.

That's my fucking girl.

But she's asking me to sacrifice her for the escort service.

Duval shouts an order over my protest, and I grind my teeth so hard my jaw aches. But the brute by Scarlet just chuckles. My muscles coil as he circles her like a predator, savoring this, the sick fuck.

"Come on, sweetheart," the mercenary taunts, leaning in close, his hand brushing over her cheek like he's trying to be tender.

Scarlet jerks her head away, disgust flaring in her eyes.

"No need to be shy. It'll hurt less if you play nice."

I thunder, and the chair rattles beneath me as I lunge forward. "Touch her again, and I'll fucking kill you!"

The man laughs, low and ugly. "Touch her again? Sure thing." His fist flies into her stomach, hard enough to make her whole body jerk.

She doubles over as far as the ropes allow, the chair scraping against the floor.

"Stop it!" My voice rips from my throat, harsh and cracked, but it falls into the stale air like a plea instead of the threat I want it to be.

"Give me the escort service and I will stop," Duval offers.

I growl at the man as Scarlet screams her protest.

"Again," Duval orders, gesturing with two fingers like this is nothing more than another one of his political handshakes.

The mercenary obliges, landing a backhand across

Scarlet's cheek. Her head snaps to the side. Blood sprays from her mouth as her lips split open, and my chest tightens like a steel vise. My muscles scream against the ropes, but they don't fucking budge.

Scarlet lifts her head slowly, gaze unwavering. Even now, there's no fear in her. It gives me a unique, brutal glimpse into what she went through during her childhood . . . during the experiments.

She spits a wad of blood onto the floor at the guy's feet. "That all you've got?" she drawls.

His grin falters, and for a fleeting second, I see something close to doubt in his eyes. He doesn't understand her. Doesn't know her. But I do.

"Big talk for someone tied up," he snaps, grabbing her hair and yanking her head back to expose her throat.

Duval's voice filters through, asking for the goddamn escort service again, but I'm too focused on her. On the blood. On her unwavering expression that hides vulnerability.

"Don't you fucking dare—" I struggle harder. The ropes bite into my wrists, and the chair groans beneath my weight.

The brute laughs, dragging her face close to his. "We'll see how tough you are after this." His free hand curls into a fist, which he drives into her ribs.

Scarlet grits her teeth but doesn't make a sound.

The silence makes it worse.

"Keep going," Duval says, and I swear I see amusement flicker in his cold, dead eyes. "Break her."

That's when the blade appears in the brute's hand, glinting under the dim chandelier light. He slides it across her collarbone as Scarlet stares him down, unflinching. The bastard presses harder. Blood wells and drips, the menacing crimson spreading across her wheat-colored shirt. My stomach twists, cold and tight.

I can't fucking move.

The panic rises like bile, unfamiliar and clawing at my throat. My body shakes from the rage building inside me—an inferno, relentless and suffocating. She's mine. This isn't supposed to happen to her.

Scarlet locks eyes with me as the blade presses deeper. Her lips part, but she doesn't speak. Just stares. And in that moment, something inside me snaps.

It's not a calculated shift. That raging creature inside me that I've been protecting the world against rips through the mask. Primal. Uncontrollable.

Ropes dig into my ankles as I strain, my breath a low, guttural growl. The chair groans, wood splintering. With one last surge of strength, I lean forward, then slam back, shattering the chair beneath me.

The room freezes as pieces of wood fall around me. For a heartbeat, no one moves.

Then I lunge.

My shoulders slam into the asshole holding the blade embedded deep in Scarlet's chest. His weight topples under mine, but only he falls to the floor. My foot comes down hard, driving his head through the rotting wood, smashing against the concrete base beneath, and I stomp on his skull until it shatters like a fucking melon.

The others move, their boots scuffing against the floor.

Raging, I turn.

Another man charges me. Whipping around, fists still bound, I drive my head into his nose. Cartilage snaps. His blood sprays hot against my face. He stumbles and I knee him in the balls until he topples over. Grasping the moment, I side-kick him straight in the face. He drops like a stone, but I don't take any chances. I slam my foot onto his head until his skull cracks beneath my boot.

In the far distance, a commotion sounds, but I have no brain space for it.

Sharp pain blossoms in my side, but it's Scarlet who bellows in response to it. Grunting, I twist in time to see the last mercenary pulling his hand from my ribs. When I reach down, a blade sticks out of me. I pull it out and maneuver it so that I can slice the rope holding my wrists as the man charges me headfirst.

I'm not sure if I cut the rope, but the ligatures give in when I strain against them, and my hands are finally free. My teeth find his ear as he slams me against a creaking wall, and I bite down until I feel the crunch of cartilage. He screams, trying to pull back, but I hold him to me and drive the knife into his neck. Blood fountains, hot and thick, drenching me.

When I turn, Duval is on his feet. He scrambles backward, shouting orders, though I'm not sure to whom. Maybe more of his mercenaries litter this old house, but I couldn't give a shit about them right now.

Yet, there's a response to his call somewhere in this house. Gunfire erupts, startling my spine straight, but I have to get to Scarlet.

Reaching forward, I grab Duval by the collar and twist around, launching him to the floor where I can fucking see him.

"Stay there!" I command.

I turn to Scarlet. Her head hangs low, crimson trickles from her wounds, and her breathing is shallow.

The knife that could have plugged the hole in her chest lies on the floor, and too much blood flows out of the wound. I drop to my knees, pulling at the ropes binding her, my bloodied hands trembling as I cut through the restraints with the same knife that cut her.

"Scarlet," I whisper, my vulnerable tone unrecognizable even to me. "Kitten?"

Her eyes flutter open, and she gives me the faintest hint of a smile. But it falls once she looks down. "You're bleeding."

I know. I can feel myself weakening. That asshole must have hit something important. Pain rips through my lung but it's her state that concerns me more.

My answer lodges in my throat as Duval makes a desperate lunge. I grab the blade off the floor and catch him by the throat mid-charge, slamming his back against the wall.

"I don't care what you did to me, motherfucker. But her? My fucking Scarlet?" I rage, holding him by the hair.

I sink the knife into the base of his throat, then slice upward—a deliberate move that spills his life onto the ground. I plunge my hand into the gaping wound, grasping and ripping until I find his spine, and with a harsh yank, the bones snap. Duval crumples, lifeless at my feet.

The room falls silent, save for Scarlet's and my shallow breaths.

I collapse beside her and pull her into my lap, ignoring the pain radiating from my wound. Brushing the stray strands of hair off of her blood-stained face, I look into her coffee-colored eyes that hold so many emotions for me.

I failed her. And yet she looks at me like I hung her moon.

"Stay with me," I murmur, my voice shaking. "You're mine, Scarlet. Forever. You don't get to leave me."

Her hand twitches, weak but alive as it grips mine. And something burns within me, searing behind my ribs. It's not rage this time. It's something far more terrifying.

The door crashes open. A tall, wide figure fills the frame, and I tense. But when he rushes into the space, I swear the scarred beast looks like a veritable angel.

"Maddox, thank fuck."

"Are you okay?" He falls to his knees before us.

Sliding my arms under Scarlet's body, I try to lift her to

him, but agony slices through my body, and I fail to swallow the pained grunt as I look into his eyes. He blurs and darkness wobbles as the light above us flickers.

But I realize it's not the light at all . . . It's me.

"Save her," I beg into the darkness, but it swallows me before I'm sure the words reached out.

CHAPTER 39
Scarlet

I wake up with a start, blinking through the haze to bring the room into focus. But even with the faint moonlight streaming through the tall stained-glass window, I can't see much because it's still the middle of the night. I turn and reach next to me through the darkness, but all I feel is the barely warm, soft sheet.

The moody chords of a violin filter through, caressing my senses, calling to me.

I answer, throwing the sheet off of my body and climbing out of bed. Barefoot on the ancient stone floor, I walk out of the bedroom, toward the haunting melody.

It can't be Carter.

It's too slow. Too sad. Too . . . emotional.

But as I walk into the church's main nave, I find him lying back on the sofa, eyes closed as he holds the instrument under his jaw. He strokes the strings like he caresses each and every one, a delicate, tragic song spilling off of them like tears.

It's been a few weeks since we were both given a clean bill of health and released from the hospital. He woke up a couple of days before me, and Morrigan confessed he threatened every single nurse and doctor in that place, explaining in vivid detail everything he would do to them if I'm not well and whole. And he was still strapped to IVs at that point.

That story gives me hope that maybe he does care about me more than the others. I know "love" is off the table. I understand it's something I'll never have from him. But I think I've made peace with that.

He cares for me. He protected me. He fought for me.

And that's more than I could have asked for.

Now, if he would stop coddling me, that would be great.

Due to my CIP, the doctor advised me to take it *very* easy for at least another month, but the man took it like the only thing I'm allowed to do is rise from the bed to sit on a chair. The heaviest thing he'll allow me to lift is a fucking fork. I love the attention, but I'm fucking fine.

My family, on the other hand, seems to agree with him. Even if they're fucking furious at the man and may never forgive him for what happened to me. The fact that he almost died seemed to have buttered them up a bit, though.

But I'm fine . . . and I need him.

Stepping over the stones and soft rugs, I reach him just as he opens his eyes; he's slightly startled by my presence.

"Don't stop," I whisper as I ease my sleep shirt over my head and bend over him.

I slide against his body, situating myself under his bent arm as he maneuvers the bow over the strings. Straddling him gently, I keep my shoulders under his arms and try not to disrupt his song. The slow melody is too mesmerizing to ruin, the chords played with incredible passion, touching parts of me that ignite at the sounds.

One particular part especially, which has been begging for the man.

I reach between us, find the seam of his loose pajama bottoms, and tug it down until his cock breaks free. With my head against his chest, listening to his increasing heartbeats melting into the melody he creates with his precious violin, I stroke his length. He hardens beneath me, soft groans vibrating through his chest as precum coats his broad tip.

Carter's melody falters but doesn't break. With his dark eyes locked on me, he follows every shift of my body as I guide him where I want him.

The haunting notes wrap around us—a slow, melancholy tune that feels like it's being ripped right out of his chest. It vibrates through him, humming in the air. In my body. My strokes along his length match the tempo of his bow, slow and deliberate.

I don't rush, keeping the pace teasing, watching him fight to maintain control of the song. His fingers tremble slightly on the strings, and a raw edge creeps into the notes as I shift my hips, positioning my core above him.

The head of his cock presses against me, and I lower myself slowly, taking him inch by inch, piercing by piercing, a quiet gasp leaving my lips as he fills me. His bow drags across the strings, the sound vibrating sharply and aching in the air.

"You're cruel," he murmurs. But he doesn't stop playing.

"Not cruel," I whisper against his ear. My breath brushes the shell as I begin to move, rolling my hips in slow, deliberate circles. "Just making sure you remember I'm still alive. *We're still alive.*"

He groans softly, and the sound blends with the violin's mournful song. It swells, the notes trembling with each movement of my body, each time I rise and fall back around his length, taking him deeper. The rhythm of his bow adjusts to match the pace I set, slow and sensual. A wordless conversation between us.

His head tilts back slightly, exposing the strong line of his throat as he shifts the violin more over his shoulder. His jaw remains tight, as though he's barely holding himself together. I kiss the curve of his neck, tasting the faint salt of his skin.

"Scarlet," he rasps, my name rough on his tongue. A plea and a curse all at once.

"Keep playing," I urge softly, pressing my lips to his pulse.

Arching my back, I let his cock drive deeper, and the music breaks for a split second. A sharp, quivering note slips into the melody before he catches himself.

The violin cries in his hand as my fingers glide over his chest, feeling the hard planes of muscle, the rapid thrum of his heart beneath my palm.

The tension builds between us, the music like a thread weaving our movements together. Binding us closer with every aching note. His eyes are on me now, his gaze dark and burning, and it sends a shiver down my spine and straight inside my aching core.

When the melody reaches its crescendo, so do I. Raw pleasure tugs at my nerves as I shake against him. He tenses beneath me, muttering soft, dirty curses into the darkness as his cock twitches viciously inside me, filling me to the brim as I dig my nails into his skin and shake through my orgasm.

My breath catches as he sinks further into me, my lips brushing against his chest as his arms wrap around me, violin forgotten.

For a moment, there's nothing but the quiet hum of our breathing and the fading echo of the music in the air.

But my heart is too full to let this silence reign.

"I love you . . ." I whisper into the night, against his warm skin.

"Look at me." His words sound almost sharp.

Reluctantly, I lift my head and meet his gaze.

"Say that again, looking into my eyes this time."

But my lips tremble, that fear brimming against his intense gaze.

"What are you afraid of, Scarlet?" He tangles his hand in my hair, forcing my focus onto him when I try to look away. "Tell me."

"You," I blurt out. "I'm afraid I've ripped my heart out of my chest and stuck it in yours to take care of and keep safe when you can't do the same for me. When you'll never feel the same." The words spill once they start coming out. "I understand it's your nature, and for the most part, I made peace with that. But it's hard not to wonder if it will affect me eventually. And if, because of your lack of empathy, you'll fail to see it."

"You're caught up in semantics and societal standards. They blind you, Scarlet. Call it as it is. You think I'm incapable of loving you. I'm not sure what love looks like to you, and even after extensive research, I haven't fully understood what it means to others. All I know is that you are mine, heart, body, and soul. If you are hurt, I feel that pain for you. I bleed for you. And I will happily cull any soul that dares to hurt you. Even if that may just be one single tear falling over your cheek."

He pauses long enough for me to hear the mad rush of heartbeats behind my ribs.

"I may not know what love is, but it better not be less than this, because you deserve so much more. And I let you in, Scarlet, with a conscious decision that went against all my instincts. You saw me in moments I didn't want to see myself, and here you are, still . . . afraid I will never care for you as you care for me. I call you 'mine,' but all I've done so far is prove that I am yours."

By the time he finishes his speech, I'm somehow the breathless one.

"If this is love, Scarlet, then you have it. You have me. All of me. And now that you do, you'll never be rid of me. *Ever.*"

A tear slides down my cheek. I didn't realize I was crying. But here we are. A man seemingly without emotions, without empathy, stole my breath straight out of my lungs and replaced it with far too many sentiments.

"I love you," I whisper, my gaze firmly fixed on his.

I was wrong. He's shown me how he feels, and I've been caught in conventions. Carter is mine just as much as I am his.

"Good." A cocky grin pulls at his lips, making me want to smack him and kiss him all at once. "I thought my darkness was too devoid of stars for you when, in fact, it was just waiting for the brightest of them all to come along and claim the throne. My scarlet queen."

Heat fills my belly, vibrations resonating straight through my soul, caressing that darkness that exists within me as well.

"I think you love me too, Mr. Pierce."

"I think I might just."

EPILOGUE
Carter

Six months later

"So? What do you think?" Scarlet claps her hands, bouncing on her feet as glee sparkles in her coffee-colored eyes.

Arms crossed against my chest, I cock my head and take a step back. I inspect the giant triceratops skeleton sitting proudly in the middle of my church, as if I hadn't made up my mind months ago, long before the fossil stepped foot in here. I know now that I would agree to anything as long as it puts that mesmerizing glint in her eyes.

"You have to admit, it looks amazing! The stained-glass rainbow of colors bouncing off of it, the way it fills all this empty space perfectly, fitting in with everything old you have around here . . . Come ooon. Please like it." Her bratty moan stirs my cock beneath my trousers.

With a deep sigh pumping my chest, I step next to her, eyes trained on the dinosaur. "I think it—"

"You like it!"

"I didn't say that."

"I will not accept any negativity toward Tabitha, so I'll make up your mind for you."

She crosses her arms against her ribs, distracting me with the cleavage spilling from the deep V-neck of her dress.

"Is that so, kitten?" I step into her space, dropping my head as she cranes hers, meeting her defiant gaze.

"Yep. It's decided."

I tangle my fingers in her hair and hold her firmly as my lips meet hers. Swiping my tongue over their seam, I demand entrance. She moans softly into my mouth, arms unfolding as she grips my sides and aligns her body with mine.

I break the kiss with soft, peppered pecks and feed on the hum of satisfaction vibrating low in her throat.

"You do like it," she murmurs.

When I pull back, she's all smiles. Victorious, with a hint of lust woven through.

"I think it fits perfectly."

She bounces up and down like an excited little pixie, the strands of dark-green she dyed on the underside of her brown hair flowing around her pale skin.

"Shall we go?" I reach for her hand.

"Hell yeah! Are you excited?"

"Intrigued, I think."

"Intrigued?"

I nod as we head out, hand in hand. I'm not entirely sure what I feel about our new speakeasy. Maybe the memories of Midnight are holding me back. If I ever cared for an inanimate thing, that was it.

It's no longer burned to a crisp. The building has undergone consolidation work, and renovations are on the last stretch. But Midnight and The Fightclub are gone—officially, due to a gas leak. We're keeping the space for the apartments our people live in, and everything else will be training space.

"I bet you're a little happy that you're doing this in the building Duval snatched from you all those years ago," she says.

I lock the heavy wooden door and head to the dark SUV parked right up front. She climbs up when I open the door and offer her my hand, and then I walk around, mulling over those words.

"I am. Funny how things come around."

She snickers as we set off through the wrought iron gates and ease onto the streets of Queenscove.

That building put him on our radar. He was supposed to be a rising-star politician, all straight and rigid. But he was just another criminal in disguise.

Now that he's dead, with no heirs or wife, his estate went on sale and the old Duke's Lodge is ours. It's just off the main boulevard that cuts through the city, on a parallel street to Loreley's building, where she and Morrigan have Metamorphosis. Right behind them, actually; only a small alley separates our back gardens and parking lots.

The four-story building's intricate, period features and beautiful facade come into view. I pull around back, gaze flickering to Scarlet beside me.

She inches forward in her seat, leaning in, likely trying to understand what she's looking at.

"What is that?" She shifts forward fully, barely waiting for the car to park before she rips her seatbelt off and jumps out.

I chuckle as I climb out and follow, watching her circle her precious dark-green Mercedes.

"Carter, is this . . . ? It's the same number plate . . . Is this—"

"Your car, love," I confirm.

"I don't understand. It was totaled." As she walks over and wraps her arms around my neck, that addicting happiness in her gaze gleams.

"Almost. After I had it towed, I sent it to my garage and had them repair it for you. I know you missed it, and I hoped it would have been ready sooner, but I didn't realize it was a special, limited edition, and some parts required custom orders from the manufacturer."

"Oh my god! I knew you had it towed, but this . . . Carter, it's too much."

I shake my head, dropping a kiss to her parted lips. "It's not nearly enough. I know you like driving my cars now, so I hope this is still . . . umm . . . useful." I don't know what this sensation I've been feeling for the last few days is, but it seems to have bloomed now.

I kind of second-guessed my decision to do this for her when I realized she might not care about her old car anymore.

"Useful? Carter, I love it! Yes, I like your cars, but this baby is mine. I worked hard and greased a few hands to get it." She peppers my face with kisses, holding me to her like I might escape. "Thank you, thank you so much for this."

"Get a room, you two!"

We both flinch at the disruption and turn to find Finnigan and Evelyn pulling in, the man shouting out the window of his car with a stupid grin on his face.

I groan and Scarlet chuckles, but we untangle to join the two and walk into the building. The women are hand in hand, snickering to each other as we join the rest of our group inside. They've become close fairly fast, especially with their love for the more morbid side of art.

"It's beautiful!" Evelyn exclaims.

It looks great, yes, but not all that different from Midnight. Same old-world vibe, mismatched wooden chairs, and armchairs upholstered comfortably in leather or tweed. All tables have been sourced from antique shops, as I wanted all the wood to be beautifully carved and weathered. Mismatched lamps are dotted around the space to keep the atmosphere low and intimate, perfect for all the secrets that will be shared here.

The bar is my favorite piece in this space; its whole facade is carved in an Art Deco design. A thick, light-colored marble countertop weighs the whole thing down.

One thing survived Midnight—our metal starburst emblem within that golden circle that was fixed on the wall behind the bar. Only the realistic eye within it required replacing. We put that back in the same spot, behind the bar. Above it sits our new name in brushed gold lettering.

"It's going to be hard to get used to it." Maddox appears beside me, staring at the same spot. "But it's a good name. It fits."

I nod in agreement. I'll miss Midnight and what it represented, but a change was necessary, regardless of the fact that we were forced into it.

"*Dusk* is a good name—simple, short, and fitting," I say.

"New beginnings and all."

I turn to him, noticing the blonde woman standing by the bar. I've seen her with him before. "For some, newer than others."

He glances over his shoulder. "I'm trying out something."

This is not the direction I thought he would follow, but he does deserve to let loose. He's not one to indulge, definitely not publicly.

"Is she going to come to your first match in the new club?" I ask, knowing full well he's never brought a woman before.

"She will. It's opening night, after all," he answers, but his gaze narrows on me. "You look like you're about to ask me if I'm sure about this, and that's so not you, Pierce. Don't disappoint me."

"No, it's not, and I wasn't going to ask that. You're a grown man, Severin. You should already be aware when you're making mistakes."

His eyes bulge, but I don't wait for any reply or further reaction as I turn away to inspect the space.

Customers are already arriving at Dusk's opening night—a night that could decide our fate. We weren't sure how many of our old customers would believe the gas-leak story we fed the press. We suspected most would presume something more nefarious went on. Which is why we were curious if they would return, considering the danger they could be in. But, so far, things are looking good. Hopefully, I'll feel the same way a few hours from now.

* * *

"Gentlemen." Scarlet appears next to the table I've been sitting at for the last half an hour or so.

"Darling, don't you look ravishing. That dusty pink looks wonderful on you." Jonathan gives her an appreciative once over.

"Thank you!" she exclaims, twirling once so she can soak up all the admiration.

My sexy, mad pixie.

Even if he wasn't exclusively interested in men, I would still feel the same pride at that compliment. She looks good enough to eat in that pink, flowy dress that just about touches her knees. The fabric hugs her waist and breasts so damn nicely.

"I need to come over to your shop soon. I heard a rumor

that you brought some *interesting* pieces in." Scarlet wiggles her brows.

"Please do. I see you're enjoying decorating your new home."

She laughs, and that melodious sound strokes behind my ribs.

"I am! We installed Tabitha today," Scarlet says. "You must come see her."

"Tabitha?" Cillian asks from his seat next to Jonathan. These two are getting along surprisingly well since the business partnership we facilitated for them.

"My triceratops," she says with a wide grin.

Cillian frowns, lips parted as he shoots me a look like he wants to ask if she's being for real. I nod at him, quirking my lips.

"Scarlet, I must say, you're slowly becoming my favorite customer. You keep me on my toes with your *unique* tastes." Jonathan chuckles. "And yes, I would love to. I'll come by for coffee this weekend."

"It's a date!" She claps her hands, then turns to me. "Can I borrow you, please?"

"Gentlemen." I nod toward the table, then rise and follow the kitten.

"I wanted to wait until we got home," she tells me over her shoulder as she leads me toward our secure back rooms, "but I can't wait anymore."

"What is it, love?"

She grabs my hand and pulls me through the corridor, steps rushing as she heads toward the nearest door and tugs me inside. But I don't get to ask why I'm in here, because a door slams shut at the end of the corridor and Scarlet flinches.

"Don't you need to go back to your new girlfriend?"

We exchange curious looks and lean in to peek through

the cracked door.

"Are those Lulu and Madds?" she asks, noticing the tall, blonde woman.

"Mhm."

"Why do you have to be so damn stubborn?" Maddox mutters on a deep rumble.

"It's not your damn business, that's why!"

Maddox steps into her space, his intense, shadowed gaze boring into her.

"Is it just me, or do these two—?"

"Want to kill each other?"

"That's definitely not the direction I was going in."

"Then my new girlfriend is none of your goddamn business, either." He storms away, door slamming behind him as he leaves Loreley alone in the corridor.

Scarlet and I exchange looks once again.

"Fuck!" Loreley shouts before she leaves too.

"Well, that was . . . umm . . . interesting?"

"Why are we in the cleaning closet, Scarlet?"

"Because I wanted to show you something in private and couldn't wait. You're not the only one who had a surprise tonight." She fumbles for the light switch and flips it on.

"Right!" She jumps and reaches down to grip the hem of her dress. "So, I did something. I'm not sure how you're going to feel about it, but . . ."

I frown as she lifts the dress to her hips.

"On your knees, killer-boy," she whispers, smirking.

I cock an eyebrow, then drop to one knee, holding her gaze. But when I look down at that sweet spot on her upper thigh, I freeze.

Right there, following the triangle of her bikini line in delicate cursive letters, "Carter" is etched in red ink.

"What do you think?" A tinge of insecurity brushes her tone.

I'm stunned. She's almost untouched. Creamy, soft, bare skin, and the only thing marking her is . . . my name.

I dip in, pressing my lips around the tattoo, over and over, digging my fingers into the flesh of her thighs. I'm not sure how to express how this makes me feel. Words must exist, but I can't grasp them. I keep kissing her, dotting them all over her flesh, the apex between her thighs, her belly. Rising, I crowd her against the wall, her head firm in my hands as I crush my lips to hers, breathing in that lemon-rose scent that's just hers.

Leaning back enough to catch her magnificent eyes, I open my mouth, but no words come out. I wrap her in my arms, pulling her into my body until I'm sure neither of us can breathe right.

"I'm happy you love it," she whispers against my chest, circling her arms around my waist.

This is why she's forever mine. She can hear what I can't express.

"Come on, let's go join the others." She pulls away, a shy smile curling her lips, cheeks flushed.

I want to stop her. Words are stuck in my chest, my throat, caught on my tongue, and I can't speak any of them as she tugs me along through the corridor and out into the animated speakeasy.

Very few customers are left. Most of the patrons are us, our Sanctum, spread around the space, laughing and chatting over a good cocktail. It's such a calm atmosphere, bathed in the gold hues of the dim lamps, decadent scents, and a sultry, old song that fills the space.

Scarlet leads me toward the bar, but I stop, tugging at her hand.

"Carter, what are you—"

But when she turns around, I'm back on one knee, a green

velvet box in my hand. Her brows scrunch, her lips fall open, but I leave her no time to react.

"Scarlet Brasa, be mine forever." The right words finally spill off of my tongue.

For the first time, the kitten is speechless, lips parted, hand on her stomach as she looks between me and the contents of the little box.

"Yes! Oh fuck, yes!" she squeals, and throws herself into my arms as cheers burst out around us.

The next moments go by in slow motion. She can't stop kissing me, shock and happiness both taking up real estate in her gaze when she pulls away. I pluck the Art Deco style ring I spent a few months searching for out of the box and slide it onto her trembling finger.

She looks at the baguette crown cluster diamonds set in platinum and smiles from ear to ear. "It's so you. I love it! But why, Carter? You know I don't need a ring or marriage or anything. Just . . . just you. Always you."

"I wish I could give you a rational explanation, but I've got nothing. Only this searing feeling inside my chest that never existed before you. And it feels fucking exquisite, Scarlet. I want more. More of it, more of you, and this is the only way I knew how—by making you my wife."

Her smile brightens the room, and happiness fills every fiber of my being as everyone loses patience and crowds in to congratulate us.

"I can't wait to marry you," she squeals.

"You won't wait long, love. I want to call you my wife before the end of the year."

"And you . . . *my husband.*"

"All yours. Only yours."

* * *

**Thank you for reading Scarlet and Carter's story.
Mad Lullaby is up next. Maddox and Loreley's
happy ending awaits!**

ALSO BY THE AUTHOR

Series
The Sanctum Synidcate
#1 Dangerous Strokes, a Dark Mafia Romance
#2 Reckless Covenant, a Second Chance Mafia Romance
#3 Manacled Hearts, an Age Gap Mafia Romance
#4Carved Obsession, a Dark Mafia Romance
#5 Mad Lullaby, a Dark Mafia Romance

Standalones
My Kind of Monster, a Dark Contemporary Romance
Even in Death, a Romantic Horror Novella
Blissful Perdition, a Lesbian Romance Short Story

**Follow Lilith on Amazon and never miss out
on new books!**

ACKNOWLEDGEMENTS

My Sirens, thank you for patiently waiting for me to write a new book, for being part of my author journey, and for always being so excited about what's next. I'll forever be grateful to have you as my ARC readers.

My May, thank you for always giving my characters a chance and for being part of their story. Their happy endings wouldn't be the same without you.

Brooke, your magical editing fingers are miracle workers. Thank you not just for your skills but for the confidence you give me. And Michele, thank you not only for your proofreading expertise but for truly loving my characters.

To my lovely readers, whether you've been here since My Kind of Monster or you've only just discovered my words, I'm so incredibly grateful for each and every one of you.

And to my husband, none of this would be possible without your endless support. I love you more every day—even when I want to strangle you just a little bit. We're about to embark on an incredible journey, a new chapter in our lives that we never expected, and I'm so fucking excited to do this with you.

All my love,
Lilith

ABOUT THE AUTHOR

Lilith Roman is a romance author who writes stories laced with danger, intense passion, and dark themes—always ending in a happily ever after.

She's an introvert with an addiction to pretty hardbacks she'll never read, anything chocolate, and steamy books. But her love of horror movies and vampire villains has convinced her, without a shadow of a doubt, that even the monster under the bed needs a love story.

For exclusive insights, join her Newsletter, or
Lilith Roman's Corrupted Souls Facebook group.

scan the QR code